WINGS OF DAWN

LIGHT AND MIDNIGHT
BOOK 2

CORT CHANNON

To Casey, my life's companion, my soulmate, always and forever.

To St. Jinx, for demonstrating to me that spirituality, sexuality, and creativity can come hand in hand.

For Fi and Fa, for snuggles, love, and only occasionally walking across the keyboard when I was trying to lkjwejgl;

And for my father, who always believed in my writing but didn't live to see these books published. Not that I would have let him read them anyway, because they contain an awful lot of buttsex.

A NOTE FROM CORT

Thanks to Casey for constant love and support and for help in the proofreading process, and special thanks to Melissa, Brian, Leah, and Blaze for support and advice throughout the publishing process. Thanks to St. Jinx for the wonderful cover art and for being a friend and cheerleader as I finished bringing these characters to life. I couldn't have done it without you all.

A NOTE ABOUT CONTENT

The *Light and Midnight* books are about queer identity and self-actualization. Characters suffer adversity, but the tone of the book is intended to be empowering, sex-positive, hopeful, and liberating. Additionally, the books interrogate the relationship between sex, spirituality, and religion, and reframe some theological and spiritual concepts through a queer lens.

The author believes in happy endings in every sense of the term, and so these books contain a very high level of heat: there is a great deal of suggestive language, as well as very explicit descriptions of physical bodies and of consensual sex between male partners.

In *The Wings of Dawn*, there are some elements of the story that readers may find distressing, such as cases where characters suffer emotional abuse at the hands of their families, instances of religious aggression and discrimination, or cases in which power imbalances are misused. There is also a case in which one character speaks of sexual violence that happened to someone else in the distant past. Care has been taken to handle topics in as sensitive a way as possible to avoid gratuitously causing suffering to either characters or the reader.

CONTENTS

I

THE CALL

"Are you ready?" Cuan asked me, looking around cautiously.

"Yeah," I nodded, pausing to take a deep breath.

I really shouldn't have. The air *stank*. I stifled a sputtering cough.

"Stop that!" Bianca hissed on the other side of me. "Are you trying to get us caught?"

"Sorry," I gasped. "It just... smells really bad here."

"Don't be such a baby," Bianca replied condescendingly. "It's not that bad."

"Really?" I asked. "You don't smell that? Must be you, then."

Bianca flipped me off and turned her attention back toward keeping a keen lookout. I didn't know how she could make out anything in the dim light, but then, I hadn't been bitten by a vampire and inherited a number of their powers. I assumed that the ability to see in the dark, clearly, was one of them. Or maybe just echolocation? Probably echolocation.

The tunnel we stood in was dark and cold, the long, winding corridors looking very much like the long, winding corridors we had explored earlier that day. And the day before. And the day before that.

I had been an official member of the Midnight Hunters for three days now—though 'official' in this sense merely meant recognized as such by their (sorry, *our*) enigmatic, sunglasses-wearing leader Cedric, who organized and mobilized our ragtag group of supernatural misfits. I probably would have joined much earlier, but during their first attempt at recruitment we'd had a short... falling out of sorts. It probably had something to do with our fearless leader's firing a crossbow at me to test my powers.

While I had since—no thanks to Cedric—come to understand those powers slightly better, they were still largely a mystery. I had awoken a week or two ago in a foggy basement with no memory of what had happened or how I had gotten there (or of anything at all, really), but I soon discovered that I had an unusual power that involuntarily surfaced every time I was in immediate danger. I hadn't been able to get a handle on that power until I received a helping hand from the Angel of Death himself—who was actually a pretty decent guy once Cuan and I got to know him. But now, I had some modicum of control over my peculiar ability—and that is why I was here in this tunnel with a sociopathic Lucy Westenra reject and Cuan.

Cuan.

The tall, handsome, red-haired twenty-something was standing at attention, sniffing the air as he looked around with his piercing golden eyes. Cuan had been a member of the Midnight Hunters for pretty much his whole life: Cedric had found and rescued him after he had been abandoned as an infant, likely due to his ability to shift at will into the form of a sinewy, speedy, red-maned, grey-furred werewolf, who retained all his faculties but overlaid his sweet personality with an all-encompassing surge of fight-or-flight. In that form, Cuan was an unstoppable fighter, but he was no slouch in his human shape, either. And it was a very fine human shape indeed: one-hundred-percent fat-free muscle and flawless, moonlight-colored skin that was entirely smooth except for his head and a handsome tuft in... another place. He had an incredibly fantastic body to go with his incredibly fantastic heart, and it had been my privilege to enjoy both: Cuan was loyal and true and ridiculous in bed; he was there for me when I first lost myself in my powers and patiently supported me from afar when I left the Hunters and their trigger-happy leader to find sanctuary in, well, a literal sanctuary known as the Church of the Holy Guardian. There I enjoyed the company of a family of churchgoers forming a branch of a global religious order called the Order of Light. That hadn't gone well either, though, as the head-priest-cum-zealous-sociopath tried to murder Cuan and trap me into being their eternal slave so that the Order could keep my powers for itself.

Thankfully, that plan didn't quite pan out, and my powers—and my body—remained my own.

And now it was time to put those powers to use. Again.

Very cautiously this time, I took a second deep breath. I stared at the locked office door in front of me, the outline of which I could only just make out in the dark. Perhaps, since I couldn't see it well, this next part would be easier. In my mind, I held a clear image of my body, complete with everything I was wearing and the contents of my pockets. I strove to carefully, deliberately, delineate the limits of what was 'me' and what was the rest of the world. Then, I pictured that world becoming a bit... less solid. It was a world where things like walls and locked doors were just thick clouds of mist, blocking the light but not me. I held the image in my mind. And then I just... stepped into it.

Everything in the world started to leave afterimages in front of my eyes. The tiny breeze that passed through the tunnels wasn't blowing on my skin now; it was moving unhindered through me. My lungs had to work harder to pull and push air, but at the same time they didn't need to, as the air permeating me was already there for the taking. The ground held me up, but only by suggestion and convention. If I wanted, I could sink through it like it was newly fallen snow instead of dirt and tiling.

I turned my attention back to the door, the faint borders of which were even less well-defined to my senses. I reached my hand out, felt it reach the door, push through the door. With a step, my body followed.

Black. I paused for a moment, giving my eyes a few seconds to adjust. The tunnel we had just been in was dim, but here there was no light at all. Carefully, I pulled out my smartphone, which, as it had been in my pocket and I had identified it as 'me', had made the transition with me into incorporeality.

I wouldn't be able to use the phone to do something like make a call or send a message; that much I already knew. My incorporeal phone would be useless in picking up and transmitting cellular signals, and the built-in mic would likely have a great deal of trouble with sound, as well. One thing, however, was relatively unaffected by my body's incorporeality: Light. I tapped the screen on my phone, careful not to let go or drop it and thus have it become like the rest of the world and impossible for me to pick back up. The screen lit up, and I tapped the spot on the screen that turned on the flashlight.

Immediately the reverse side of my phone leapt to life. I blinked, disoriented by the flood of afterimages that accompanied the light and the multiplicity of moving shadows it cast.

I was looking at an empty, abandoned office. At least, that's what I thought at first.

"Holy shit," I breathed faintly into the air.

The room was abandoned, but clearly it had been in use until recently. Dust hung thickly in the air, but spots on the desk where something like a computer tower or a monitor had sat were clearly outlined rectangles standing in stark relief against the remainder of the dusty surface. A file cabinet stood empty and ransacked, without a single scrap of paper overlooked or left behind.

"Another miss," I managed after I'd stepped back out through the office door. "Something was there, but now it's not."

That had been the frustrating pattern we'd endured since I officially joined the Hunters' ranks. In the days preceding, monstrous ogre-like creatures had been emerging from underground in various places in the city, and the Hunters had been largely occupied with trying to contain them. That changed, however, when I recognized one: Marcus, a guy I'd been dating prior to losing my memory, and the first person to find me after the onset of my amnesia. Marcus and I were not meant to be, however, as he had a fairly substantial drug problem. It was only after he was enrolled in one of the city's public rehabilitation-programs-slash-homeless-shelters that he resurfaced as a seven-foot-tall hulking blue beast, recognizable only by my name tattooed on his ass.

Marcus was now kept sedated in our base, The Hunters' Home, as Lester—our resident mad doctor—worked to reverse his condition and that of the other captured humans-turned-ogres, whom he kept at his lab. Marcus's appearance did, however, provide us a much-needed clue as to where to look for evidence of what had happened to him, and so members of both the Midnight Hunters and the Order of Light took the investigation into the abandoned subway station under the square where the ogres had first emerged, which had once been a colony of homeless prior to the new mayor's election. It was there, in a small maintenance office, that I'd found a monitor full of information and a folder indicating that the entire operation was being overseen by the mayor's office and the local police department.

Unfortunately, that discovery was immediately succeeded by Cuan's aforementioned attempted murder and my spending three days trapped in a tiny box at the Church of the Holy Guardian before being rescued by Julia, a forward-thinking, no-nonsense, and all around badass (now probably ex-)Order of Light member who had finally managed to find her way into the room I was in.

After all that ordeal, however, I thankfully still had one critical piece of evidence about the city's undertaking: my smartphone with a photograph of the aforementioned folder, as well as of a monitor suggesting that the ogre program was a widespread and organized initiative.

Unfortunately, that was the only evidence we had been able to find. When I showed the other Midnight Hunters the photo after my recuperation, plans were quickly made to return to the underground and gather more information, but upon our arrival we found the place completely emptied. We had spent the days since on regular sorties into other parts of the abandoned subway network in hopes of finding any sign of where the program had been moved, but each attempt had turned out like today's: signs that a lot of stuff had been cleared out very quickly, if any signs were present at all. Even the security cameras that had been at the station entrances were gone.

On the bright side, however, with the disappearance of the evidence of the program also came a reprieve from the onslaught of ogre attacks, which had been increasing in intensity on a nightly basis. Unfortunately, we were also left with no understanding of why they had begun in the first place, no idea of why they had one day seemed fixated on the Church of the Holy Guardian, and no idea how widespread the program had been.

I took a breath. I'd become somewhat comfortable with the process of becoming incorporeal—which my undercover angelic tutor Az had referred to as 'fading', in spite of the fact that my body remained visible—but the transition back was still difficult. The challenge wasn't so much becoming solid again, but rather the rub was in what happened after that. It was oddly a two-step process: the first was letting the world solidify around me—or me solidify into the world, depending on your perspective—which sort of made all the afterimages coalesce and overlap. But that left me with fog, to say nothing of a body that was trying to deal with suddenly feeling temperature and air pressure and sound waves and everything else.

"I'm going to revert now," I said, and Cuan watched me with concern. I extended my hands and placed them slightly above his.

"Ok," he said. "Remember your name. Cole."

He began quietly and deliberately repeating my name to me as I stared into his bright, golden eyes, letting the whole world turn on his eyes, center on his eyes, solidify around his eyes. The afterimages slid together, and my lungs gasped at the sudden substantiality of the air. I let my hands fall and he caught them, still repeating my name.

At least, it should have been my name. But now, to me, Cuan was speaking a foreign language, so foreign that even the word that should have been my name was unfamiliar. Az had identified that in this state I hadn't lost all sense of language, but instead spoke and understood the Tongue of Souls, the ancient language spoken in what would later be known as the Tower of Babel. It was the universal language of the Divine, known only to human souls when they weren't busy living out their fleshy lives incarnate on Earth. But as to why I spoke it not when incorporeal but after returning, that remained a mystery —as did my complete loss of English comprehension. What seemed to bring me back, however, was my name: thus Cuan's repeating of it. I listened, straining to find familiarity in the unfamiliar syllable. Somewhere in that sound was my name. I just had to hear it.

".o..."

There was the vowel.

".ol.."

There was the consonant pulling it closed.

".ole."

That was it rounding to its finish. Now I just needed the sound that kicked it off, the source, the grounding from which it sprung. I strained. Then I recognized it.

"Cole."

And with that, the fog solidified, and Cuan was in front of me, squeezing my hands.

"That's my name," I said.

He grinned.

"Welcome back," he replied.

"Yes, yes, touching," Bianca said impatiently. "Now can we get the hell out of this hellhole?"

I nodded. The stale stink of an abandoned subway tunnel was bad enough any time, but when it hit a nose that had a moment ago been less than fully there? *That* was nasty. The city air was a very welcome change.

"They wouldn't just cancel an initiative like that at the first sign that it had been discovered," Cuan mused as we made our way back to The Hunters' Home. "It was too big for that."

"They've obviously moved somewhere," Bianca said. "It's stupid for us to keep looking in the subway."

That was what was most worrisome of all: we had no idea where the program had moved to or when the attacks would resume. It was that sense of uncertainty, more than anything else, that was stressful.

"We have the photo linking the program to the police and the government," I said. "Why can't we just turn them in?"

"Right," Bianca said sarcastically. "Because *so* many authorities have taken action over a single blurry photo suggesting official involvement in supernatural phenomena. Who would believe us? The press? Certainly not anything mainstream or reputable. And who else could we go to? We don't even know how far up this thing goes. But fine; you wanna go into City Hall waving your phone around and claiming conspiracy theory? Great; go do that, and then I can say 'I told you so' when you make your one phone call to us from Guantanamo."

I blinked at her. "What's Guantanamo?"

Did I mention I had amnesia?

Bianca pointedly rolled her eyes at me.

"Is it possible we missed something?" Cuan asked. "Is there something else in the photos you took on your phone, perhaps?"

"We've been over those photos again and again," I insisted, pulling my phone out of my pocket. "Lester has even run them through all kinds of software. I don't know what we could expect to see that we haven't already—oh."

"What?" Bianca asked.

I hadn't even made it to my photo reel. Instead, there on the lock screen of my phone were notifications that I had four missed messages, all sent in the time that I was in the tunnels, all sent by the same person.

"Professor Norton sent me messages," I said.

"Your professor from before you lost your memory?" Cuan asked.

"What does that guy want?" Bianca asked.

"He wants to meet me again," I said. "Look."

I held the phone up for them to see. Four messages had been sent in sequence:

7:22 PM: 'Cole, come meet me in religious studies immediately. bring any materials you had from your studies.'

7:35 PM: 'Where are you?'

7:38 PM: 'Oh right you made a big deal about my no longer asking you for things after hours. meet me tomorrow then.'

7:41 PM: 'but not in religious studies. How about the same coffee shop as last time. 1030am. still bring your old notes'

"Well he's a pushy old fucker, isn't he?" Bianca asked.

I sighed. "Apparently it's not unusual," I said. "According to Marcus, that accident that cost me my memory happened when I was en route to the university after the professor called me in at the middle of the night. Then when I finally met him after the accident, he was kind of self-centered. All he knew about me was that I had a really hands-off aunt and uncle. He didn't even seem all that invested in my own work."

"What *was* your own work?" Bianca asked.

"From what I could tell, I was in comparative religion, investigating queerness in ancient world religions and challenging anti-queer interpretations that emerged over the course of world history."

Cuan looked at me with an impressed expression.

"Finally, someone doing something useful with religious studies," Bianca said with a smirk.

"What's that supposed to mean?" I asked, slightly affronted.

"I mean, you're actually using your platform to challenge systemic oppression. It's refreshing to see someone interested in religion who isn't all about power or blindly following the orthodoxy or evangelizing people into tribalistic self-righteous factions of hate."

I blinked at her. Who was this person, and what had she done to Bianca?

"I mean," she continued, looking down the street ahead of us, "I'm more in favor of 'burn it all down; kill them all', but, whatever, your way's fine too, I guess."

Ok, phew.

"So... what's this about 'any materials you had'?" Cuan asked.

"I really don't know," I said. "I mean, I have some notes and things, but... I don't remember anything about them. I don't even know what year I am in my course of study. Professor Norton mentioned my being an undergraduate, but beyond that..."

"Well, maybe meeting him can tell you more," Cuan suggested. "Where are your notes?"

I sighed. "In my apartment."

My apartment. 48 Oak, Apartment 32. I had known it was mine because Marcus and I had hooked up at my place on at least one occasion, and he remembered the building. After some embarrassing searching, we had managed to find an apartment door that matched the keys I'd had in my pocket—one of the only things that had survived whatever accident caused my amnesia. The apartment had been my base of operations until the first run-in with the ogres, whereupon when I first involuntarily faded, my trousers were dragged into the square's underground with my keys and money still in the pockets. I had run across them again later, during our first investigation under the city, but was again incorporeal and fleeing at the time, and so couldn't reclaim them. When we had gone back for later searching, they were gone.

That said, now that I had some degree of mastery over my incorporeality, I did have the means to return inside those walls. Considering that my neighbors didn't seem like the most pleasant sorts, however, I didn't want to leave the place unlocked, which would mean that traveling to the apartment would involve transitioning back to solidity inside the walls and dealing with the inevitable sickness and disorientation, only to have to repeat the whole process in order to leave again. That idea did not hold much appeal. Furthermore, leaving the apartment with anything in hand would be a tall order—unless I had someone to go with me.

At the same time, I hadn't been back there in over a week. Perhaps it was time to visit home.

"If I'm going to go back to my apartment, I'll need help taking out anything I can find," I said. "Plus, it's easier to transition back from incorporeality if I'm not alone."

"I'll come with you," Cuan said. I smiled at him.

"Not me," Bianca said, face twisting in disgust. "I have better things to do than play scavenger hunt at some dirty college boy pad. You couldn't pay me enough to dig through piles of greasy old pizza boxes and dirty sweat socks."

"What am I, some drunken straight frat boy?" I asked, affronted. "You know me better than that."

"Fine," Bianca replied. "You couldn't pay me enough to dig through piles of greasy old dildos and dirty condoms," she sneered. "Better?"

"Much. Thank you," I said, and the corner of Bianca's mouth curved into a begrudging smirk of respect as Cuan burst out laughing.

We rounded the corner, and the familiar façade of the Hunter's Home came into view. It was a simple house with black shingling; it looked to be a tight two stories plus an attic but experience had taught me to be skeptical of what the building's exterior seemed to reveal. Inside, the architecture's tight, long halls allowed for comfortably sized rooms in a building that extended deep into its lot. Furthermore, the basement had been converted into a kind of exercise-slash-training-space plus a locked, private storage area that was Cedric's personal space. The upper floor was where Cuan, Bianca, Bran, and Lester had their rooms, each with its own small bathroom. It was modest but comfortable, though now that I shared a room with Cuan and Lester had converted his living space into a kind of hospital bed for Marcus, it was admittedly getting a little tight—not that Cuan and I minded sleeping on top of one another, mind you. Cedric's bedroom was elsewhere; I assumed it was in the attic or on the ground floor, along with whatever room Lester was sleeping in now that he had given his room over to Marcus.

Our communal time was spent in the kitchen, which was where we were headed now after passing through the small enclosed porch and the dark, narrow hallway beyond.

The kitchen was warm if simple, featuring a small bit of

counter space (which was shared by a small cathode-ray TV) and a small stove, along with a fridge and small pantry. Much of the room was given over to a long wooden dining room table. Most everyone sat around the table except for Bianca, who had created a corner of her own near the stairs to the basement, where she usually lounged in a plush cushioned chair, watching the rest of us with the imperious disdain of a spoiled but territorial cat. It was here that she proceeded immediately upon entering the room, after announcing our return with an abrupt "We're back."

"Welcome," said Cedric as we sat around the table. He was at his usual place at the stove, where he almost always seemed to be preparing food. He was wrapped in his usual brown cloak, which I almost never saw him without, and his eyes were obscured behind ever-present sunglasses, which he wore even in the dark. His usual wide-brimmed hat, however, hung on the side of his chair, and so I had a rare sight of his thick, slicked back hair, a deep brown that seemed to shine orange when the light from the incandescent bulb overhead hit it just right.

He turned, slipping some scrambled eggs off of a pan onto a set of waiting plates.

"Care for something to eat?" he asked.

"Didn't you cook us dinner before we left?" I asked.

"Nothing wrong with a little extra," he said hospitably. And as I *was* hungry—fading took a lot out of me—I gratefully accepted. Cuan chowed down as always, and Bianca likewise helped herself to a small bite.

"Thanks for the food," I said as I took a bite of eggs. Like all of Cedric's cooking, they were characteristically delicious.

"How did you fare?" Cedric asked. "Find anything of interest?"

"Absolutely nothing," Bianca replied.

Cedric frowned as he sat at the table with a plate of eggs in front of him. Behind him, the news came on the little TV on the counter.

We turned to watch at the mention of a statement by the mayor, Dennis Grafton. On the slightly blurry screen I could see a man in a blue blazer come to stand at the podium, tall and confident and oozing the kind of charisma that looked to essentially be well-packaged smarm.

"The city has seen a great number of accidents in recent days," the mayor said. "Pipes have burst, buildings have been damaged, and fires have broken out. These are the kinds of tragedies that result from my predecessor's poorly funded, poorly planned urban development initiative."

"Bullshit," Bianca spat as she ate her eggs. "Is that how they're trying to pass off all the ogres' destruction?"

"Thankfully, our analysts and hard workers at my new department of public works were able to identify these impending problems and evacuate affected areas before countless lives were lost. It is a tragedy, however, that we were not able to prevent the pipes from bursting when they did. While my predecessor's administration was responsible for putting this failed infrastructure in place, I nonetheless recognize that my team should have been able to prevent this damage from happening. This happened on our watch. We have to accept responsibility for that, no matter whose fault it is."

"And yet you continue to insist that it's not your fault at all," Cuan grumbled.

"He's a good politician; I have to give him that," Bianca said. "It's like he genuinely believes that the damage was caused by faulty pipes."

"Which raises the question," Cedric asked, "of whether he really knows what is happening in the city at all, or if someone else is deliberately keeping him in the dark?"

"This city is my home, my family's home," Mayor Grafton continued, ushering a scared-looking girl with blond pigtails and a pink party dress to stand next to him on the stage. "It's my daughter's home," he continued, and we all groaned. The mayor seemed very fond of parading his daughter in front of the press lately whenever he needed to justify taking some action on behalf of 'families' or 'children'. According to the others, while the mayor had admitted during the election cycle to having had an affair, the fact that the union had resulted in a child remained completely unknown until after Mayor Grafton was in office, when he suddenly began showing her off. I'd heard speculation that she was leveraged heavily to gain favor for the mayor's controversial plan to build shelters designed to funnel drug users and the homeless off of the streets and into paying jobs. It was this program, intended to help some of society's most lost and vulnerable, that someone had pre-empted and used for the sick human experimentation and weaponization system that we'd uncovered—a program that evidently enjoyed some level of municipal approval. The Midnight Hunters had been a cautious and secretive group before that discovery; now, we didn't know who to trust, and that made us even more insular.

That said, however, the Hunters had committed to helping me learn about my forgotten past. Part of that meant learning more about my connection to Professor Norton, and since he'd finally reached out, it was time to follow that particular trail of crumbs. After the news story concluded, therefore, I told Cedric about the text messages I'd received.

"I'm going back to my apartment to see what I can find there," I concluded; "I remember seeing some things that related to my studies."

"Be careful," said a voice behind me. Bran had walked into the kitchen during my explanation. He was tall, strongly built, and friendly, with bright eyes that stood out particularly sharply against his dark brown skin. He was wearing a red zippered jacket and blue jeans, looking for all the world like any other guy in his mid-to-late twenties, as though he'd come back from a brisk walk rather than some mission of importance. Even with his jacket and jeans his muscular frame was evident, though it had been my privilege to see him in his glory on a few occasions, as Bran was known to cross the upstairs halls completely naked after a shower. Apparently Cuan had hooked up with him several times in the past, and I understood why, though Bran shared the other Hunters' tendency to talk down to Cuan a bit, which I wasn't a fan of. That aside, Bran seemed amiable enough, though to be fair he was often away on solo excursions, and so he remained largely a mystery to me. He ran a hand through his feathered black hair, eternally styled back, before sliding into a chair at the table.

"You don't know the guy," Bran continued, fixing me with an intent gaze. "He may know you, but you don't know him. And you don't know what you have in your apartment that he wants. Maybe it's fine, and maybe he's just happy you're OK and he wants to stay in touch. But it's weird that he wants you to bring research material with the University closed."

This was a good point. University wasn't in session; it had been shuttered and, for the most part, evacuated after the 'pipe explosions' nearby. But from what little impression I had of Professor Norton, I suspected that no university edict was going to get him to quit working if he wanted to continue.

Cedric slid a pair of scrambled eggs onto a plate and held it toward Bran, the offer implicit.

"No thanks," Bran said, waving him off. "You know I don't eat bird."

"This is eggs," Bianca noted.

"Eggs is still bird," Bran insisted. "Anyway," he continued, turning back to me, "He clearly thinks you have something he needs, or he wouldn't be texting you out of the blue after saying nothing for a week after you first reunited with him. My advice is, before you go turning stuff over to him, find out what he wants, and then make sure you're OK with him having it."

I nodded. It was sound advice. "Still," I noted, "this is a good excuse to try getting back into my old apartment. I've asked Cuan to come with me; I'll need a solid pair of hands to carry out whatever I find, since I'll need to make sure the apartment stays locked from the inside."

"Fine," Cedric said. "It is about time you started looking into your past, anyway. Meanwhile, we need to try planning our next move. We keep coming up with dead ends."

"Maybe we're going about it wrong," Cuan mused.

"Do you have a different suggestion?" Cedric asked, raising an eyebrow.

"I dunno," he said. "Maybe? I mean, we know that the police are somehow involved. We know that the city is somehow involved. So why do we keep looking for information underground, when they seem to have cleared out?"

"Because, dipstick," Bianca said, "we need to find out where they've *gone*."

"Yeah," Cuan agreed, "but maybe we're looking in the wrong place."

"Well, *clearly*," Bianca replied impatiently. "Any other bright insights? Or should you maybe just be a good boy and eat your people food and let us strategize in peace?"

"No, I..." Cuan started, frustrated. "I just mean, maybe the police know something."

"We are not going to the police," Cedric insisted. "We cannot trust them; you know that."

"I know," Cuan said. "I'm not saying we *ask* them. I'm saying we go there. Look around, I dunno. Do... do you know what I'm trying to say?"

"Wait, maybe I understand," Bianca said, leaning forward. "What's that, boy?" she asked mockingly. "Timmy's stuck in the well?"

Cuan frowned and sat back in his chair.

"Is this the same well you climb out of when people play that old fuzzy VHS tape?" I asked her.

"Bite me," she said to me.

"No thanks; don't want vampirism," I said.

"Fuck you!" she spat emphatically.

"No thanks; don't want chlamydia," I replied. "Now can you stop being a bitch for like two seconds, or will that literally kill you?" I turned to Cuan. "What are you thinking?" I asked calmly. "Tell me."

Cuan glanced uncertainly at the others and then turned to me. "What I'm trying to say is... maybe instead of trying to find evidence in the tunnels or something, we check out the police headquarters or city hall. You know, infiltrate, look around, see what we can find."

"That... that's actually a really good idea," Bran said.

"Indeed it is," Cedric agreed. Cuan looked from one to the other of them in uncertain surprise before a genuine smile began to form on his face, his telltale dimple appearing alongside his lopsided grin.

"Well, so how are we going to infiltrate the police?" Bran asked.

"Bianca can go," I said. "She can go complain that her street corner was damaged in a recent explosion and now there's nowhere for her to stand and wave herself at passers-by all night long."

"Wow," Bianca responded. "Way to denigrate sex workers."

"No," I clarified, "now see, sex work is a much-maligned profession in need of recognition and legitimacy. But who said anything about sex work? For it to be work, someone has to be willing to pay you."

Bianca moved to rise from her chair in fury, but Cedric stayed her with a look. "OK, so we have an idea, though *clearly* not a workable approach. It is enough to serve as a start. We will keep planning while you to go to Cole's apartment. Maybe we will come up with something. And Cuan," he added, giving him a small smile. "Good work."

Cuan nearly beamed.

"I can practically see your tail wag," Bran murmured, but it wasn't enough to spoil Cuan's mood. He hummed contentedly to himself all the way to my apartment building.

II

BREAKING INTO HOME

MY OLD APARTMENT building held an odd feeling of vague familiarity—not because of any particular sense of attachment, but because it was the first place I had been told to identify as 'home' after awakening. I supposed it was how someone would feel about a college dorm room or an apartment just after moving in. It was the place you were staying, but without the sense of history to really be yours. Of course, that feeling wasn't helped by the fact that I'd been locked out of my apartment only a few days after first learning of it.

"OK," I said to Cuan as I looked up at the tall building. "I'll fade through the door and enter into the building, and once I'm solidly in my apartment I'll let you in."

"Sounds good to me," Cuan said with a nod.

I took a deep breath and focused on the apartment building, concentrating until the world seemed to lose its substantiality. Once the whole world was leaving afterimages in my vision, I stepped through the glass door and past the mailboxes, through a second door into the foyer. The doors to the actual apartments were illuminated by dingy incandescent lightbulbs. I walked to the stairwell and put my foot on the first step.

It passed right through.

Dammit. Climbing stairs wasn't something I'd had to tackle while incorporeal before. I supposed I could try to let the world solidify, climb up to my apartment, and fade again, but the process of coming back from incorporeality was so taxing that I didn't want to do it any more than I had to.

I concentrated on the step. I didn't want it to feel solid, as that would likely shunt me out of incorporeality, but nor did I want it to be insubstantial mist. I tried to remember the last time I had needed to use something in the solid world as leverage, back when we first explored the area under the subway and I'd had to hastily escape through the tunnel walls to above ground. That time, the experience was like swimming. This time, I wasn't immersing myself in the staircase; I was just using it to hoist myself up. The key, I realized, wasn't in imagining the stair as solid; it was in realizing I was not. My body was insubstantial in this state, and so the only reason I wasn't sinking into the ground was that I felt I should be standing on it. There was just enough difference in density between the ground and the air that I knew where to place myself. By that logic, there should be enough difference in density between the steps and the air that I should be able to climb them.

It was nothing but rationalization, and yet perhaps that was all I needed. I placed my foot on the step. When I felt the slight difference in solidity, I decided that I ought to be able to stand on it: even if it only felt like thick mist, it should still be more than enough for my insubstantial weight.

Success. Purchase. I stepped up, one single step. Then another.

It was a long climb to the third floor. Twice I nearly fell through the stairs, but I managed to catch myself. At one point as I was approaching the second landing a sweaty man with a hairy belly that protruded out from under his shirt climbed the stairs *through* me, after which he suddenly stopped and looked around in confusion. I felt somewhat violated and was about to shout at him, but then I decided that it probably would be better not to have some greasy out-of-shape man suffer a heart attack in the middle of the building I was trying to inconspicuously enter, and so I waited patiently for him to get his afterimaged self back into his apartment before continuing my stair-climbing slog.

Eventually I stood in front of the closed door to Apartment 32. I took a deep breath, which was somewhat difficult considering that I had incorporeal lungs, and stepped through.

I knew this room. It felt familiar; safe—not because I remembered spending a lot of time there, but because what little time I'd spent here was from a time when I wasn't surrounded by monsters walking the night or people secretly plotting to enslave me. Here I'd just been present, able to read my books and breathe and relax in an unfamiliar world.

I exhaled, slow and long, my desire to be present in the space making the transition back to corporeality a comparatively smooth one. The afterimages all overlapped, solidifying without coming into focus, and suddenly the floor was solid beneath my feet.

I looked around the dark studio apartment, trying to get my bearings in the fog as my senses struggled to process everything at its renewed intensity. The climb had been a long one, and the longer I spent faded at any given time, the harder it was to go back. I felt a shot of vertigo and steadied myself against the back of the door.

A slip of paper on the floor caught my eye; it had clearly slipped out of the book that lay on the table. I remembered finding that book on my shelf and leafing through it back when I had been in the apartment before, and I remembered the slip with the illegible insert that had fluttered out of it when I opened it. The cover of the book was unreadable to me now, but the gold text on the page was crystal clear. This was part of the strange shift in my language processing that happened during my return from incorporeality: not only could I no longer speak or hear English, I couldn't read it, either; instead, my unaccountable understanding of the Tongue of Souls extended to written script. Whoever had written the slip of aged vellum inserted here had known that language. On it was a simple warning:

"Death will come for those who straddle the veil."

Yeah, no shit. Az had wasted no time in making his handsome self known to me after my first bout with incorporeality.

That was neither here nor there, though: my first order of business was to buzz Cuan in. As I turned toward the callbox, however, I heard a tapping at the window near my bed.

Even through the fog, I could make out Cuan perched on the outer sill. Of course. This was how he'd first shown up outside my apartment, after all. I made my way over to the window and undid the latch, pushing it open as far as I could. I blinked at him, trying to make out the details of his face through the fog of my senses.

"You know, you could have just waited for me to buzz you in," I noted.

The half-smile returned, and he shook his head patiently. Then he spoke, but I couldn't understand a word.

Right. Shit.

He extended his hands, and in spite of the sudden jolt of fear I felt that he'd fall backwards out of the window without his hands to steady him (a stupid fear, considering that I'd seen him perch on lampposts with absolutely no difficulty), I took his hands in mine. His golden eyes met mine through the fog. He repeated that familiar word, my name, and this time it only took me three or four times to catch it. Cuan came into focus, and I now I was gazing at his shining eyes, his smile, his vest, his muscular, bare arms, his legs in his tight compression pants as he crouched with his knees well apart, his bulging crotch eye-level with my face...

He'd been wearing compression pants the first time he showed up at my window, too. I remembered being flustered by the sizeable package presented right in front of my eyes. Now I smirked, however. Those pants had been a little more padded in the front. In these, I was able to make out both of his round balls and his sizeable cock pressed against the stretched fabric.

"Those pants are very flattering," I said with a smirk; "especially from this angle."

His lopsided smile widened. "It's always nice to be appreciated," he said, as I gently tugged his hands toward me. He hopped neatly through the window, somehow entering the small opening feet first without needing to release my hands, and stepped into a hug.

"You did good," he said, releasing me. "I saw you fighting with the stairs in the lobby."

I blushed slightly at his having seen me struggle with something as simple as a staircase, but there was no hint of judgement in his voice.

"Well, um, welcome to my apartment," I said, stepping back as Cuan looked about. He had been to my windowsill before, but this was the first time he'd actually been inside the apartment proper. "Let me give you the tour. Bed, desk, bathroom, kitchen, sofa, bookshelf, closet," I said, gesturing about. It was a studio; there wasn't much to show off.

Cuan nodded approvingly. "Homey. Bookish. I like it," he said. "Now then... what are we looking for?"

"Material from religious studies," I said. "I'm assuming, of course, that Professor Norton wants stuff relating to *his* studies, not mine."

"OK... so... where should we look?" Cuan asked.

"Everywhere," I said.

"Really?" Cuan asked uncertainly. "I don't want to snoop."

"Snoop away," I replied. "If I was hiding anything, it's a secret to me, now, too, so whatever you can find will be news to us both. Honestly, I feel like I'm snooping, too, and it's my own stuff."

"Well OK then," Cuan said simply, and immediately walked to the bookshelves. "I'll start here."

I walked behind him and looked over his shoulder. Even though I had just told him to snoop away, I was slightly self-conscious. You can tell a lot about a person from the books on their shelves—it was, in fact, the most telling source of information I'd found about myself—and I was a little nervous to know what Cuan's reaction would be to my collection.

Cuan whistled as he ran his eyes over the shelves. "Nice choice in fiction," he said as he perused the top shelf. "Holmes," he said with a smile. "Classic stuff." Then he moved his eyes to the second shelf. He stared at the titles.

This shelf was all religion. Not just one religion, but a ton of them. Bibles next to Buddhist texts next to the Library of Apollodorus, with all manner of religions, mythologies, philosophies, and commentaries in between.

"Holy crap," Cuan muttered. "You're really thorough. You've read all these?"

I shrugged. "I have no idea," I said.

"Ah," Cuan responded apologetically. "Right." He turned back to the shelf. "Well, is any of this what Professor Norton would be interested in? You're not going to bring him the whole shelf, are you?"

"He's probably already read any book on that shelf that would be interesting to him," I said. But then I remembered. "Except one," I added, turning to the coffee table.

"Huh?" Cuan asked, turning to me.

There was one book that I remembered finding in my apartment that was different from the others. It was older, thicker. I would have sworn it was a library book except that it had no Dewey decimal code on the spine. I had set it on the table when I'd first found it, after two notes had fluttered out when I'd first opened it. One was the ancient vellum with the text about Death in the Tongue of Souls. The other was on normal paper, and had said simply "Show to Professor Norton." It was how I'd discovered his name in the first place.

I lifted up the book and turned to hand it to Cuan. As I turned, I spied something lying on the sofa cushions out of the corner of my eye.

"*The Encyclopaedia of Angels and Demons*," Cuan read as he opened the book. "This is... this is intense. Is this the kind of thing Professor Norton would want, d'you think? ...Cole?"

I didn't respond. I barely heard him. Instead, I was absorbed in what I'd picked up off of the sofa cushions.

A simple hoodie, big and soft, blue and white. It was large for me. But that's because it wasn't mine. It was Alexander's.

Alexander.

I'd been trying not to think about Alexander.

Marcus's ex-boyfriend, whom Marcus had turned to for help when he first found me. It was Alexander who helped me get back to my apartment, helped me deal with Marcus's frankly insensitive overtures shortly after I regained consciousness. It was Alexander who gave me a place to stay after I left the Midnight Hunters when Cedric's 'training' involved firing crossbow bolts at me.

But Alexander was also a big tight-ass.

The youngest son of Father Jacob Lucent, pastor of the Church of the Holy Guardian and head of the local division of the Order of Light, Alexander was always cowed by his father and his older brothers. He lived and breathed religion of a particularly insular and conservative kind, which, for any gay guy, can be kind of soul-destroying. Even so, Alexander did his best to protect his family, his Order, his church, and his friends. He clearly still had feelings for Marcus, since the two of them had decided to maybe sort of try to give things another go, though as they weren't sure how it was going to end up, they both decided they'd see other people as well. As it turns out, 'other people' was me.

Did I mention his big, tight ass?

Alexander's body was a thing of beauty: broad and muscular but with a softness to it, with a golden tan that covered literally everything. He oozed boy-next-door charm, with blue-green eyes and golden-blond hair on his head, and a dusting of nearly invisible golden fuzz everywhere else. Perhaps because of living in an environment that wanted to suppress his sexuality, when Alexander fucked, he *fucked*. And he was good at it. But even so, he was terrified of any kind of sexual or even romantic expression anywhere near his church. He never mentioned any of his family's knowing he was gay, though I'd since learned that his immediate older brother Thomas knew and certainly didn't judge.

The rest of his family, however, were a different story. Alexander's father, at least, made his position clear, and Alexander's father's opinion meant more than anything. That certainly was true regarding the Midnight Hunters, whom Jacob despised as faithless heretics at best or monstrous demons at worst. It also meant that, until me, Alexander had always kept the guys he knew socially at arm's length. Alexander had even hesitated to bring Marcus to church back when they dated, though that was perhaps justified considering the day Marcus marched up to the church, high out of his mind, and mooned us to show off our names tattooed on his ass. That was too much for Alexander, who took Marcus to one of the public rehab centers, not realizing that it was being used to source unwilling human subjects and turn them into giant hulking ogres to unleash on the city.

Once we'd made the harrowing discovery of Marcus the Blue Ogre, Alexander resolved to do some investigating, and accompanied Cuan and me on our first excursion underground. What we didn't know was that Jacob and his oldest son Levi seized the opportunity to orchestrate Cuan's attempted murder in order to lure me back to the church to be their spiritual guardian-slash-slave. And when Alexander discovered the trap, well... Daddy's will won out, and he left me to be trapped in a gilded box behind the church's altar for eternity. Alexander did at least manage to save Cuan's life using the vial of Seraphiel's Tears—what had brought me to the church that night in the first place—but, as Cuan later pointed out, it hadn't exactly been an either-or decision. The fact of the matter remained that Alexander had left me to be enslaved.

Something like that really should have killed all my feelings for him. But once you've fucked someone senseless under a waterfall with the sun on your back in a secluded clearing in the private wood of an abandoned estate where they sneak away to exercise naked... well, that's the kind of experience that stays with you.

I held the hoodie up to my nose, inhaling its familiar chestnut scent.

"That's Alexander's...?"

I felt a hand on my shoulder and turned to see Cuan looking at me. I nodded.

"How'd you know?"

He tapped his nose. "Smells like him," he said. "But you already know that, clearly." His half-smile was a little sad.

I nodded again. Cuan squeezed my shoulder.

"I'm sorry it turned out the way it did," he said gently. "I know he often looked out for you. I was starting to think he might even be kind of a good guy. But... but what he did to you... I can't forgive that."

I nodded. "I know," I said, sniffing back a tear. I turned into Cuan's chest. "But it's also because of him that you're here now."

"He shouldn't get credit for that," Cuan said, an edge of anger in his voice. "You would have been able to bring that tincture to me yourself, had he not left you captive."

I continued nodding. "You're right," I said. "He just... he was starting to assert himself, you know? He was starting to think through his faith on his own terms. When his father captured me, he looked so pained. I wish... I wish he could have at least seen that what his father was doing was terrible."

"Well, he's not dead," Cuan said. "So there's still a chance he could come around. Not that he deserves absolution even if he does, but... he always has the option of trying to make things right with you, if he wants to."

I nodded, emphatically this time. "You know what?" I said. "You're right. Alexander has a lot to explain and to answer for, but there's no sense wasting energy worrying about him right now." I balled up his hoodie and tossed it across the room, where it landed neatly in the laundry hamper. "Besides," I said with a smile, "he's not the only one who's lent me clothes in my hour of need." I gestured over to my bed, and the pair of pants that lay on the floor near them.

Cuan walked over, then crouched down and looked at them.

"These... these are mine," he said with surprise.

"Don't you remember?" I asked. "You leant me those after my first visit to The Hunters' Home, when soup spilled in my lap."

"That's right!" Cuan recalled, still squatting on the floor. "I remember that night; that was when you changed in my bedroom and forgot you were wearing sexy underwear." He grinned at me. "You made quite an impression."

"*I* made an impression?" I responded. "I'm not the one whose first appearance was playing 'Dances with Phantoms' in the middle of the town square."

"Yeah, well, you know me, always happy to play," he reached down and picked up the pair of Wushu pants, then turned, something catching his eye under the bed. "Hey," he said, "You have boxes under here."

"Oh, right," I said, suddenly remembering discovering one of those boxes on my first night back in the apartment, "about those. Those are—"

"Well hel-loooooo," Cuan remarked, eyes widening as he pulled a box out and looked inside its open top.

My face immediately reddened.

"Looks like I'm not the only one who's happy to play," he said gleefully, reaching into the box and pulling out a large jar of coconut oil, setting it on the bed as he reached down to rummage through the remainder of the box's contents. "You've got two... three different dildoes, condoms, lube, a Fleshlight, a vibrator, some racy photo books, some sexy tarot cards, some REALLY racy comics, and... how many books on gay sex?" He chuckled. "Guess religion isn't the only thing you were researching in this apartment."

"Yeah, well... I wouldn't know. I only discovered that box myself again that first night back."

"Must have been quite a discovery," he laughed. But then, at my embarrassment, he quieted and stood up. "Hey, I'm not saying it's a bad thing," he said, his reassuring half-grin making his dimple reappear. "It shows a healthy sexuality. Honestly, I'd keep these books up on the bookshelf next to the rest of your little library; they deserve just as much respect as your collection on religion." He walked up to me, eyes glittering. "Still, though," he said, "what did you do when you found that box?"

"Honestly?" I replied. "I... I used that stuff to learn more about myself. There," I added, pointing to the mirror on the wall. It was a tall, floor-length mirror, the one place in the apartment where I could see my entire reflection at once. As I continued to stare at myself, Cuan's expression changed from gleefully mischievous to gently concerned.

"What is it?" Cuan asked.

"It was weird, seeing my reflection after losing my memory," I said. I reached up and lightly touched my own cheek. The face that looked back at me was, I thought, handsome, if unremarkable. Caramel-brown eyes blinked back at me under a head of short brown hair. I ran a finger down my high cheekbones and over my full, pink lips as Cuan watched me, his attention shifting from me to the mirror and back again. I was getting used to seeing my reflection, but it still felt somehow foreign, something I had only known for a matter of days rather than twenty-one years.

"It was confusing," I added, studying the face that stared back at me. "Like… like looking at a ghost that matched my movements. I guess that's the best way I can describe it. I mean, I had seen pictures, but a reflection was different."

"Pictures?" Cuan asked. Then his eyes widened and a broad grin spread across his face. "Wait, are you talking about your dating profile?"

I blanched.

"Marcus showed me," I muttered, remembering the mortification of having the first-ever things I learned about my identity after getting amnesia be a bunch of shockingly personal information about my romantic interests and sexual preferences along with some extremely suggestive photographs.

"Ah, here we are," Cuan said as he flipped through his phone before holding it out triumphantly. "NerdyHunk21."

And there it was: a photo of me lying naked on the sofa in this very apartment, reading a book, with only an artfully placed sheet covering my groin.

"Why do you have that on your phone?" I asked.

"Oh, come on," Cuan said to me as if it were the most obvious thing in the world. "Of course the first thing that I did after I learned about that profile was go online and download all the pictures."

"Of course you did," I said, rolling my eyes good-naturedly before turning my gaze back to the me in the mirror. Cuan watched me for a moment, his expression returning to one of quiet sympathy.

"It must have been hard for you," he said softly, moving close behind me, "coming back here and trying to piece together your identity." He stood behind me, gently laying a hand on either side of my waist, his head leaning softly against the side of mine as he looked over my shoulder, meeting my reflection's eyes.

"It was," I admitted. "I didn't know what to make of myself the first time I saw me."

"Well, I did," he said quietly, his familiar, affectionate half-smile forming on his face. I loved that smile; it made his cheek dimple. "I'd been looking for you, remember. You'd puked all over the place where you first passed out, and I'd been looking for the unaccounted-for person who'd been near the first explosion in the square. I'd been following that scent."

"The scent of my vomit?" I said skeptically.

"Among other things," he said, his grin widening. "Of course, the actual you smells much better." He leaned forward and brushed my neck with his nose, inhaling softly as he did so. "Your whole apartment smells like you."

"What do I smell like?" I asked.

"You smell like *you*," he said. "Cole. Breezy, clean; with maybe the lightest hint of ocean air and hyacinth. And a little bit of a sandalwood-infused musk that is oh, so sexy."

"You're all musk," I murmured as his heady smell encircled me. It was animal, fresh and dark and sensual.

"Then I found you," he continued, "out in that square after

that phantom had shown up, and I knew I you were someone special." He nuzzled against me, and I leaned into him.

"I'm not so special," I said.

"You don't realize how special you are," Cuan said softly. "It's part of your charm. You're earnest and sincere, and you have a smartass mouth, which I find highly amusing."

"Shut up," I said with a chuckle.

"And you see good in other people, even when they don't deserve it. You treat me like a person."

"You *are* a person," I protested, looking at his face as he watched me in the mirror. "And you do deserve it. Everyone has treated you like a monster for so long that you actually believe them. You're not a monster, Cuan. You're beautiful, inside and out. You're a sweetheart, you're gentle, you're friendly and forthright. You're the best person I know."

"You have amnesia," Cuan said. "You hardly know anyone."

"Believe me, I've met my share of assholes in the last week or so," I stated. "And besides, they don't matter. I know you, Cuan. That's enough."

"You're wonderful. You don't realize how wonderful you are," he said affectionately, wrapping his arms around me and hugging me from behind. "And you're so handsome. Right away, I was hoping I'd get to see more of you. More of your personality..." he ran his hands down my sides, his voice getting husky. "...more of your skin..."

"Well, you sure got your wish," I said blithely. "That first time I went incorporeal I dropped my clothes right in front of you."

"That's not the same," Cuan said softly. "You were scared, disoriented. I was just worried you were all right."

"Plus, you'd just shifted in front of me," I recalled. "You were super nervous."

"Everyone treats me differently after seeing that," Cuan mused. "Everyone but you."

"And yet you were holding me naked in your arms. You got to see me right up close right away."

"There's a difference between just getting to see you," Cuan said, "and getting to take you all in."

"If I remember correctly," I said with a mischievous grin, "I was the one who took *you* in. Every hard, wet inch of you."

"That night," Cuan said softly. "Getting to touch you... feel you... breathe you.... Getting to explore you... have you really explored yourself, Cole?" he asked.

I nodded, breathing heavily. "That's... that's what I did that first night in front of this mirror. Tried to get to know myself."

"Sometimes that's easier with help," Cuan said with a sultry half-smile. "Shall we reprise?" He slid his fingers under the sides of my gray long-sleeved shirt, running them up my skin, carrying the fabric upward as he teased my sides with his fingertips.

I watched in the mirror as the skin of my cream-colored abdomen appeared, almost shockingly thin but also finely muscled, with just the hint of abs. My skin tingled tantalizingly under his touch.

"That feels good," I breathed appreciatively.

Cuan smiled and lifted my shirt further, hooking his hands under my armpits, until the bottoms of my pecs appeared, red nipples standing out against my skin. He reached his fingers forward and began to lightly tease them, pressing his body against me from behind.

I gasped sharply as the sensation of his fingers on my chest sent ripples of pleasure through me. As though they shared a direct line to my cock, I began to stiffen as I groaned with appreciation.

Encouraged, Cuan lifted his arms higher still, pulling my shirt over my head. He looked over my shoulder at my reflection. Even though Cuan had essentially no body fat, my bare, lean torso looked a little small in comparison to his muscular frame. Cuan kissed my neck, his hand running along my right arm, lifting it as he traced the muscles of my bicep, reaching in to brush the dusting of brown hair in my armpit.

I let out a shudder at his touch. I hadn't realized that could feel so good.

"You have a beautiful body," Cuan mused as he looked at me in the mirror.

"If we're talking about beautiful bodies," I said, "we need to take a look at yours. Take your shirt off."

"Not yet," Cuan said, his voice gentle yet firm. "This is about enjoying *your* body." He reached his hands down to my waist, nimble fingers undoing my belt.

"You're really enjoying this, aren't you?" I asked dryly.

"I really am," he admitted with a grin, pulling my belt out of the loops of my khakis with a flourish. I breathed with anticipation as he undid the button of my trousers and zipped them down, opening them over my hips and letting them slide down my legs.

I looked at the underwear I had on: a flattering indigo jockstrap of Cuan's. I had been wearing borrowed clothes since getting locked out of my apartment, and Cuan's underwear wardrobe consisted almost entirely of jockstraps—considering the nature of his transformation, it was important that his underwear accommodate the possibility of a tail. This particular pair was designed as much for fashion as for function, and it held my cock and balls slightly up and forward in a handsome bulge. The underwear was designed with a little extra space in its pouch, something I appreciated as I, like Cuan, had large testicles. These weren't yet visible, however—the fabric was slightly strained by my semihardness, but it still succeeded in covering what it was meant to cover. Just above the pouch, a brushing of curly hair was visible near the base of the neat V of my hips. Cuan ran his fingers along this ridge, then along the waistband toward my hip bones, my body tingling under his fingers.

He kicked his shoes off and then pulled at my socks and ankles with his toes, getting me to step out of one shoe, then the other. He turned me toward him as he kicked my shoes, socks, and khakis out from under me, and I looked up to see nothing but his intense gold eyes.

The smell of him was all-encompassing now, heady and musky and sensual, and my body nearly swooned as he gazed at me.

"Beautiful," he said, and kissed me deeply, the sweetness of his saliva pushing deep into my mouth as I let his tongue encircle mine. I kissed him again and again, my body pressing against his, until at last he pulled away, nodding back toward the mirror. I looked over my shoulder to see that I was angled away from it, the line of my back arching inward between the lean musculature as it extended toward my hips. Below the waistband, my butt stood out, round and pert and shapely in spite of my thinness, the cheeks accentuated even more than usual with the straps of the jock pulling them up to prominence.

"I do love your ass," Cuan said appreciatively, sliding his hands down my waist. "Beautiful, like the rest of you," he added as he squeezed my cheeks in his palms. I moaned with pleasure and turned back toward him as we kissed once more. Then he reached his hands back toward the jock and pulled it forward and down. I felt it slide off of me, my cock and balls slipping out of the pouch as it peeled away. He turned me again, kicking the jock away from my feet as he did so, and now I was looking at myself, completely naked in the mirror as he held me gently from behind.

My semihard cock was lengthening, the deep red head beginning to peek out from its fleshy hood. As it pushed forward, a long drop of precum began to drip down from my length toward the floor. Cuan caught it in his palm and brought it to his lips, sucking the pale liquid from his fingers, savoring my taste.

"As sweet as the one who made it," he said.

"Ok, you're gonna give me cavities," I said, rolling my eyes with a chuckle.

"Hey!" he protested good-naturedly, "I'm trying for a moment here!"

"Don't worry; you're doing fine," I said with a grin. My smile quickly turned into a gasp of pleasure, however, as Cuan's hand dusted the bottoms of my balls, hanging low and free of their fabric prison. Everything else faded into the background as my body was encompassed by the feeling of him fondling me, his fingers slipping over the round surfaces of each testicle and then teasing the hairless skin with his palm, my cock bouncing above them as he did so.

"Is that good?" He whispered sultrily in my ear.

I nodded, too enticed by the image of his hands on me in the mirror to speak.

He slid his other hand up and down the muscles of my abdomen as he slowly let his fingers wander upward from my balls, brushing the skin of my shaft. Each tiny point of contact was like an electric spark, the pleasure coursing around me as he continued, my balls twitching and reddening beneath. Slowly the fingers became a fist wrapped around my length, his thumb reaching up to tease my red cock head, now fully exposed from its sheath. The touch was like a bolt of lightning, and I shouted with pleasure as my whole body twitched. Cuan, encouraged, tightened his grip, his thumb stroking my tip quickly and deliberately.

I writhed with pleasure and sensation, my body twisting and shuddering. He reached his left arm across my chest to steady me, and he held me fast to him. His fingers found my right nipple, and he began to tease it above as he continued to tease me below.

I cried out at his tantalizing ministrations, the pleasure almost too much to bear. It was almost a relief when he shifted to outright pumping my cock with his right hand, the thoroughness now intense and focused enough to start speeding me to orgasm. I watched in the mirror as he quickened his pace, my abdomen heaving with every breath, my balls jumping and dancing enticingly as the strokes pulled my scrotum up and down, faster and faster. The skin reddened, my balls tightened, and my breath quickened. I felt myself getting closer, the wave starting to crest... Cuan standing behind me, stroking me...

Fully clothed.

"No. Uh-Uh," I said, wrestling myself free, turning to him with a panting grin. He looked at me with a combination of interest and surprise, and maybe a twinge of disappointment. "You've still got your clothes on. No good. When I cum tonight, I want to soak you, not the floor."

The twinge of disappointment in his face turned to gleeful anticipation as I pulled his vest off of him, pivoting around him to place him in front of the mirror now, where his bare torso, adorned only by the silver chain on his neck, was on full display. I ground my erection into the back of his compression pants as I looked at him in the mirror, my own body still heaving as I continued panting from the near-orgasm.

Cuan's torso was a thing of beauty: pale, perfect skin unbroken by hair, marked only by the odd freckle here or there. I ran my hands up his sides, feeling his body react as I did so, bringing my fingers up to his large, tight pecs, watching him gasp and shudder as I brushed my fingertips over his red erect nipples.

Where I am skinny, Cuan is lean, entirely muscle. I often

comment that Cuan has absolutely no body fat, but that's not completely true. While his body is completely devoid of excess, there's just enough distributed throughout him to give a touch of softness to the sharp lines of his muscles, making his perfectly trim figure look lean and fit instead of emaciated. I pulled his arms up, the action filling my nostrils with his musk and making me shift my gaze between his reflection and the body right before me. A particular consequence of Cuan's unusual werewolf ability was that most of his human shape was completely devoid of body hair: he had the hair on his head and an attractive puff of equally bold red crowning the base of his shaft—still covered by his compression pants, though not for long, if I had anything to do with it—but the rest of him was smooth skin. His underarms had nothing to obscure the way his arm muscles met the sides of his pecs and bottoms of his shoulders, and I leaned forward instinctively to give his skin a teasing lap with my tongue.

He gasped, letting out a sharp cry of pleasure as his body twitched. The taste of his musk egged me on further, and I slowly turned him toward me, continuing to hold his arm up as I made him writhe with my tongue. Then I moved my head downward, taking his left nipple between my lips as I teased his right between my thumb and forefinger.

Cuan's body shook as he moaned, his hands scrabbling on my arms and back as I continued to raise his ardor. Finally I glanced down and saw the front of his compression pants straining toward me. I grinned and straightened up, placing my hands against his hips and grinding my erection into the front of the fabric, kissing him deeply, feeling the need in his hot breath as he panted around the edges of our mouths. I twisted my thumbs inward at his waist and hooked the edge of his compression pants, and then pulled them down over his rear, releasing the kiss to admire his reflection over his shoulder. Where I had expected to see the waistband of a jock, I instead saw an unbroken line of skin from his back down over his exposed cheeks.

"You... you're not wearing underwear?" I asked.

Cuan turned slightly to look behind him at his reflection, ass winking at me as he did so. "Not today," he said matter-of-factly. "I mean, I wear it when I need to, for, y'know, safety and stuff, and there's something to be said for the aesthetics of a well-chosen pair, but these leggings are more comfortable when there's nothing extra in place."

I stared at his ass in the mirror. While Cuan was exceptionally lean, he had an ample backside, two impressive mounds of muscle standing starkly out from his waist. With his cheeks hanging over the edge of his compression shorts, his ass looked particularly kneadable, so that's exactly what I did.

Cuan groaned his approval as I took a handful of his behind in each palm and squeezed and pressed, massaging his crotch against me. I kissed his shoulder, my eyes still on his butt as the muscles stretched and compressed under my hands.

"I want... more," he whimpered, and I grinned acknowledgement at him, tracing the waistband of his compression pants around to the front. They bulged with urgency now, and I granted their contents freedom, stretching the band forward and down over his long cock and then kneeling, giving the exposed red head a spritely peck of a kiss as I peeled the pants off his legs and pulled them over his bare feet before tossing them aside.

This was a view I loved: a full-on, close-up eyeful of Cuan's endowment. The crown of red hair stood in stark contrast to the rest of his hairless body, like a mark on a map indicating one of Cuan's most treasured features. His balls hung before my eyes, pinkish and low and swollen with arousal, and I ran my fingers over the soft, smooth skin, Cuan gasping above me as I did so. His cock pointed at me, long and firm and handsome, the exposed glans red and glistening with precum, the sweet, salty taste of which still lingered on my tongue. His length stretched toward me, urgent and eager, and I was nearly overcome with the temptation to wrap him in the warm embrace of my lips. I knew he would cum if I sucked him off, however, and I had a different finish in mind.

I stood, looking at his earnest expression and at his tightly muscled back and legs and full, round ass in the mirror.

"This... now this is beauty," I said quietly, and his adorable dimple reappeared with his half-smile before he leaned forward to kiss me. We traced one another's bodies with our hands before finally wrapping our fingers around one another's erections, and we stroked each other with the same slow, deep sensuousness as our kissing.

Heat rose in my body as the sweet taste of Cuan's tongue mixed with the scent of his musk and our low, guttural moaning. Slowly, I walked him back toward the bed before gently pushing him down onto it, straddling him with my knees on the mattress.

"Lie back," I suggested.

He did so, positioning his body lengthwise on the bed, his head on my pillow.

"The whole bed smells like you," he mused appreciatively. I looked down at him. His whole body lay against the bed as though it would sink into its embrace—all but his cock, which stood straight at attention, as though reminding me of its presence.

As if I could forget.

I reached for the jar of coconut oil Cuan had set on the bed earlier. I unscrewed the lid and set it aside, then dipped my hand into the jar and took a liberal dollop in my fingers, which I gently massaged into Cuan's length as he moaned appreciatively. He breathed heavily as he watched me work.

"Are... are you going to ride me, Cole?" he asked.

I smiled at him. "Would you like me to ride you?"

He nodded vigorously, eyes full of anticipation.

"I should warn you, however," he added, "you'll find that I'm not a breakable mount."

"I'm counting on it," I grinned, spreading more coconut oil at my entrance. "I want you to buck me with all your might."

"I think you got a letter wrong," he responded slyly, the broad half-smile reappearing.

That dimple was more than I could resist. I lowered myself onto him, feeling him slide into me. Normally I would be fastidious about protection, but we had discovered that one of the side effects of both Cuan's and my supernatural conditions was that our bodies were untenable to almost all foreign substances. That included every imaginable sexually transmitted infection, so ours was probably the safest sex anyone could possibly have. And when it came to each other's cum, our bodies were *very* tenable.

Cuan moaned with pleasure as my tight ass gripped his penetrating length, and I breathed back at him, our eyes locked as he pushed further and further inside me. Finally, I felt my weight on his thighs, the little cushion of red fur crowning his shaft teasing my balls as they rested on him. I groaned happily as he twitched inside me, feeling the head of his cock pressing against my prostate.

Slowly, he lifted his hips into me, and I lifted my body slightly, just enough to give him room to move, gripping him inside me and pressing back. I could feel him against me as the pleasure began to roll through our bodies in low waves, his abs rolling like the ocean tide as he moved.

Gradually, steadily, our pace increased, and I watched Cuan's expression grow more intense as the slow rocking gave way to steady pumping, then piston-like pounding.

Cuan's mouth was open, his breathing as ragged as mine as he bucked against me, kneading my prostate with his rock-hard cock, which only seemed to be getting firmer and larger as we continued. Pleasure flooded me with each pound, each impact against my insides sending pure sensation splashing through my body, tossing me like a rowboat in an ocean storm.

With all the intensity of our motion, we still kept our eyes locked. Cuan's bucking was powerful without being violent, and we fucked with the kind of abandon that came from feeling one another fully rather than losing each other in the moment.

His thrusts continued to send pleasure crashing through me, and I knew the flood of sensation was about to be followed by a flood of his essence. I felt his body tighten, saw the lines of his chest and abs sharpen as his muscles tensed. My own balls tightened and rose, the wave growing inside of me about to crest.

And then Cuan cried out, low and guttural and ragged, eyes still locked on mine as he exploded into me, hot cum blasting against my prostate. At the exact same time, my ass clamped on him as the wave burst through the dam, semen spraying from me like a fountain. The force and the sensation and the feeling of him pulsing inside my ass immediately made me cum even harder, and as I squeezed him, his orgasm intensified to match as we continued to buck and spray. I felt his sticky essence pour out of me onto his waist as I blasted again and again, soaking his face, his chest, his abs, the sheets, my cum rich and white and thick. Cuan continued watching me, blinking his face once as a spray spattered across the bridge of his nose, and the sight of his soaked body only drove my own ecstasy to further heights.

We cried and moaned as our mutual orgasms fed one another, the electric torrents of pleasure coursing through us as liquid pleasure sprayed out from us. Even after the fountains ceased, our bodies continued to buck, riding the orgasm long and deep and hard.

Finally, at long last, the tempest of sex began to subside, and our bucking slowed, the tide gradually tapering away. My breathing eased, and I gasped once more as his cock gave one last powerful twitch against my prostate, and then, finally, the orgasm abated, leaving just the calm intimacy and affection that followed the storm.

"Holy cow..." Cuan breathed as I half-slid off of him, half-collapsed onto his sticky, cum-soaked chest. As he slid out of me, I felt his semen pour out of me like a bottle uncorked and I sighed against him as he beamed.

"Are we cow metaphors, now?" I asked breathlessly.

"We were talking about mounting," Cuan replied contentedly, coughing once as he caught his breath. "You never specified it was horses. I guess... in this scenario, are you a jockey or a cowboy?"

"I dunno," I grinned. "What's the term for when a guy barebacks a ridiculously fucking hot man?"

"I'm not sure," he said, "but that is a rodeo I would definitely watch."

"Well, you're in luck," I responded, "because there are about a hundred sites online that provide that kind of entertainment."

"Eh, I dunno," he replied. "I prefer active participation myself. Especially now that I have my partner of choice."

I looked at him dubiously. "Please don't say 'I choose you'," I joked. "And please don't say you're about to try to put me into a little red and white ball. This isn't Pokémon Go."

"How about Pokémon Cum?" he asked, and then he smiled that adorable half-smile of his, and all I could do was kiss him.

"We should probably clean up," he mused.

"Or, we could just lay here," I suggested.

He let out a contented sigh. "In that case, can we lay here all night?"

"You mean, until the morning?" I asked.

"That is generally what 'all night' means," he noted.

"I mean, not go back to The Hunters' Home tonight?" I clarified. "Smartass," I added with a grin.

Cuan looked wistfully at the ceiling. "We just... spend so much time in a cramped space with other people," he said. "I mean, we have privacy in my bedroom and bathroom, but there's always someone just down the hall, or always the danger that someone's going to want to come in with a question or a request." He sighed. "Wouldn't... wouldn't it be nice for it to just be the two of us, even for just one night?"

A grin spread across my face. "That, Cuan," I said, "would be absolutely divine."

I kissed him again, deeply, affectionately, and then nuzzled against him, and we slept there until dawn.

III

BED, BREAKFAST, AND COFFEE SHOPS

I SIGHED CONTENTEDLY as the long fingers of the dawn stretched across my face from between the blinds. There was something blissful about waking up in bed with Cuan in a quiet studio apartment. I slowly glanced up to his face.

He was snoozing contentedly, his eyes closed, his breathing easy. The silver chain around his neck rose and fell gently with his chest. His left arm was stretched up, bent at the elbow, his hand resting above his head on the pillow. He seemed more at peace than I'd ever seen him.

Peace. That was what I felt, all through me, as I nuzzled back into his chest. This was what every morning should be.

The next time I stirred and looked up, his hand had moved under the back of his head, propping it up slightly. He was watching me quietly with a soft smile on his face.

"Good morning," he said gently.

"Mornin'," I yawned sleepily. "How long have you been awake?"

"Only for a few minutes," he said. He reached over me with his right hand and held me against him, slowly stroking between my shoulders. "Your apartment's nice," he mused softly. "I like how it looks in the morning."

"Did you sleep well?" I asked.

"Like a rock, after what we did," he said, his emerging half-smile bringing his adorable dimple with it.

"Yeah," I chuckled. "That was very nice. Though I'll probably have to burn the sheets."

"Eh, nothing a good laundering can't fix," Cuan shrugged.

"Yeah, but if there are washing machines in this apartment building—which of course I assume there are—I can't get the sheets back and forth to them without keys, can I?"

"I could run the laundry, or I could watch the apartment while you run it," Cuan said. "I mean, don't get me wrong, if you absolutely *want* to have a sheet fire then knock yourself out, but I really don't think there's anything wrong with a little cum."

I laughed quietly. "Cuan," I said, "That wasn't a *little* cum."

"Fair enough," he grinned.

"Well, I suppose we ought to shower, huh?"

"Is it alright if I shower here?"

I gave him a flat look. "Do you really think I'd make you stay covered in dried cum all day?"

"Well," he shrugged, "I could always just shift and burn it off."

I smiled. "That reminds me of the first time we had sex." Slowly and somewhat reluctantly I peeled myself off of him, the dried cum that had been sticking us together stretching and cracking on my skin. I stood and stretched in the morning light.

"You mean when you were worried because we hadn't used a condom and you didn't know your sexual history?" He recalled.

"Yeah," I nodded. "And even though your body burns off pathogens and bacteria and stuff when you shift, I'm still glad I got tested later."

"You never told me all the details of that test," Cuan noted as he stood. "All I know is that your blood won't harbor disease and you don't really have a blood type, or something?"

"It was weird," I said. "The doctor who ran my test at the clinic, Doctor Peterson, said that the specialists and stuff found that my blood somehow dissolved or eliminated everything they put in it. Bacteria, viruses, everything. He said it's entirely red blood cells and plasma, nothing else."

"Wait, no white blood cells?" Cuan asked, incredulous. "And yet you're somehow disease-immune?"

"They wanted to study me," I said.

"And no *platelets*?" Cuan continued. "Does your blood clot?"

"Um.. yeah, I think so," I said. "I mean, when I got scrapes and stuff during all those ogre scuffles, they stopped bleeding."

"Well, then, you must have platelets, or something like that," Cuan mused. "And what about albumin? Lipoprotein?"

"How do you know so much about blood?" I asked.

Cuan shrugged. "I majored in biology," he responded.

"Wait, you have a degree?" I said.

"Yeah," he said. "I had just started my Masters in zoology when the university closed."

"You go to my college!?" I exclaimed, grabbing his shoulders. "Do the other Hunters know about this?"

"I assume so," Cuan said with a shrug. "I mean, they were at my graduation. And I might start working at Lester's lab at some point."

"But... I mean... you did college. You're working on an advanced degree... so why..."

"Why what?" Cuan asked as I hesitated.

"Why... does Bianca treat you like crap whenever you suggest something?" It was the only way I could think to put it.

Cuan shrugged again. "That's how they are. It's like I said before, Cole. You're kind of different from the rest of them. They see me as a wolf. You treat me like a person."

He said it matter-of-factly. So matter-of-factly, in fact, that something twisted in my heart.

"I don't really do well with people," he continued. "People who aren't you, anyway. That's pretty much why I chose zoology. I like animals better. People can kinda suck."

"Yes, I do agree," I said, hugging him. "But you're people," I said. "And I like you."

"You too," Cuan said with a grin. "Although I do like it when you suck. You're extremely good at it."

"Damn right," I smiled.

We took turns taking care of bathroom needs before I turned on the shower and invited him in with me. My apartment had a modest shower, but it was just big enough for two people to stand in comfortably, even though the water pressure left something to be desired. I soaped up a body sponge and slowly, gently, began to wash Cuan's chest, holding the sponge in my right hand and caressing his muscles with my left.

He smiled as I worked his body into a lather, inhaled slightly as I bent to work the soap around his balls and on his cock. He pulled back his foreskin and cleaned underneath before I turned him and worked on soaping up his back and his muscular ass.

After that, we switched places as Cuan returned the favor. It was a leisurely, intimate shower, erotic without being sexual, and there was something about just being close to Cuan, feeling his wet skin against my own, that put me at ease.

After we toweled off, I walked toward the kitchen. I didn't bother putting clothes on. It was nice to just walk around naked, to feel the air on my skin, to know that I was inviting Cuan's gaze on my body and that he was just as happy to have mine on his.

"I have... cereal, if you'd like," I said, opening a cabinet and looking in. "And maybe the milk is still good?"

Cuan's body was up behind me, his arms affectionately

around my torso, his chest pressed against my back as he looked over my shoulder. "Chocolate cereal?" he asked incredulously as he looked at the box.

"Hey, it's vitamin fortified," I said defensively.

"It'd have to be," he said, and I could feel him grinning. "I mean, look at the 'part of this complete breakfast' picture on the side. There's a glass of milk, and orange juice, and an egg, two slices of toast, an apple, and... is that a salad? Isn't this still a complete breakfast even without the cereal?"

"So, I take it you don't want any?" I said.

"The hell I don't," he replied. "Gimme a bowlful."

As we sat across from one another, crunching quietly on our cereal, that feeling of contentedness washed back over me. The morning sun was still filtering through the blinds, reflecting off the polished wood cupboards and the faded yellow faux-linoleum tiled floor, casting a warm light across the tiny kitchen area. Even Cuan's pale skin looked a touch cream-colored instead of its usual pink. The light danced off of his hair, the deep red bursting into bold, fiery highlights wherever the morning sun kissed it. As he took another spoonful of milk and cereal to his lips, he looked up from his bowl and met my gaze. His golden eyes glittered brightly in the light, and the edges crinkled slightly as he gave me a small, warm smile while he crunched away.

"This is nice," he said after swallowing.

"It is," I agreed. The kitchen in The Hunters' Home was generally hospitable, but it was always a bustle of activity, full of comings, goings, meetings, planning, cooking, and Bianca snarking away in the corner. And don't get me started on the mandatory daily brunches in the Church of the Holy Guardian, where the Order served their eggs with a hefty side of judgement and the condiments of choice were salt, scripture, and prejudice. Here, in the kitchen of my apartment, things were still and quiet, so much so that I could hear the occasional car pass by or a door open and shut from somewhere in the foyer. Cuan, with his superior senses, was probably hearing all this and more. But within these walls, it was just the joy of the morning and one another's company.

Cuan took a swig of orange juice (I had found a bottle in the refrigerator that was still good, along with the milk) and then gestured with his spoon to his bowl of cereal. "This is pretty nice, too," he said. "Who'd have thought chocolate marshmallow cereal could make for a nice morning?"

I raised an eyebrow incredulously. "Only every privileged six-year-old in the country," I said.

"And yet it's in your pantry," he replied mockingly.

"Maybe I'm just young at heart."

"Young at heart, mature in body," Cuan smirked. "No wonder you're so energetic in bed."

"You're not exactly a slouch, either," I replied.

"Hey, I never said I wasn't young at heart, too," he grinned. He finished his cereal, then stood up, sliding the empty bowl and glass along the table as he stepped toward me. Then, all of a sudden, he bent down and kissed me, sweetly and sincerely. His lips tasted like chocolate.

"What was that for?" I asked.

"To thank you," he said, dimple showing in his cheek. "Breakfast for me is always a whirlwind. It's nice to be able to really enjoy it for a change."

As I looked at his smile, at his perfect body bent slightly over me, my heart skipped a beat. I felt for a second like a schoolboy with a crush. But of course, in this case, the object of my feelings had already had sex with me several times and was now standing naked in my kitchen, so the metaphor only went so far, but that feeling of longing was still there.

Cuan straightened up and took his bowl and glass from the table, and then, unprompted, turned to the sink and began to wash them out with the dish soap that was there. I sat and watched him work, the defined muscles in his back moving as his shoulders and elbows scrubbed, the round muscles of his ass rising and falling provocatively as he shifted his weight from one foot to the other.

Finally he set the bowl and cup and spoon in the empty drying rack by the sink, then turned to me. "I'll take your bowl," he said.

"Uh-uh," I replied, standing with my empty bowl and glass. "I just got to watch your sexy ass at my sink; why should I have all the fun?"

"Ooh, I like this," he replied with a smile, backing away and leaning back on the table. I went to work washing the dishes, and as I was finishing, I felt a strong hand squeezing my right ass cheek.

"Sorry," came Cuan's low voice in my ear, "I couldn't resist."

"Less apologizing, more squeezing," I smiled.

His arms wrapped around me as he pressed himself against my back. I could feel his sizeable length against me. He was hard, and the feeling of him was quickly making me the same.

"I love this morning," Cuan hummed. "Just... being with you."

"I really thought I was going to lose you a few days ago," I said, feeling my body lean back into him as I held his arms to me. "Just being with you now is... it's like a dream come true." I turned in his arms to look him in the eyes, our groins now pressing together, the heat of the contact spurring me on. "So..." I added tentatively, the schoolboy crush in me making my heart patter, "are we, like, together?"

"Cole Hamilton," Cuan asked, "are you asking me to be your boyfriend?" The dimple returned in force. "Because nothing would make me happier."

Joy took me in force, and Cuan's face twisted slightly in concern.

"Are you OK?" he asked. "There's a high-pitched noise coming from the back of your throat."

"Yeah," I managed, nodding vigorously. "To both questions."

Cuan smiled widely and kissed me deeply, pulling my legs up around his torso and supporting my ass in his palms as he held me. Then he turned and carried me to the bed, where he dumped me back on the sheets next to the jar of coconut oil. He crawled above me, hooking my knees over his elbows, and then leaned forward, kissing me more passionately still. He reached over to the jar of coconut oil and twisted off the cap with one hand.

A multiple wet, passionate, mutual orgasm later, and we had to take another shower. And I *definitely* needed to burn those sheets.

We brushed our teeth after this shower, Cuan borrowing my toothbrush for his turn. He had toweled off and was now standing back in front of my bookshelf, buttocks still glistening with droplets of water and slightly flush from our recent exercise.

"Is this sheet music?" he asked, pulling out a book. "For clarinet?"

"Yeah," I said as I finished toweling off. "Apparently I play."

"That's so cool," Cuan smiled. "I love music. Haven't had much chance to practice, though."

"You play an instrument?" I asked.

"Kinda?" he said. "I can't really play at home; the Hunters aren't really big on the music appreciation. But when I was at college I'd sneak off to the music department and get some lessons. I tried a bunch of different things, but there were a few I was good enough to perform on at a recital or two. I like the lute. And the vibraphone.

"The lute?" I asked incredulously.

"Yeah," he said simply. "I like the sound quality better than the guitar."

I chuckled. "Maybe I should pick up the recorder, then."

He smiled, then looked at me with tentative expectation.

"Will my boyfriend play me something?" he asked.

I smiled in return, but then caught a glimpse of the clock on the nightstand.

"You probably should have asked that *before* we had another round of vigorous sex," I said. "Not that I'm complaining, mind you—but we gotta get dressed and leave soon."

"We haven't finished going through your notes," Cuan replied.

"Yeah," I responded, "but maybe that's OK. Like Bran said, let's not turn over everything right off the bat. Let's find out more first."

Cuan nodded in agreement.

"Now, then," I said, "I suppose there's the matter of clothes."

Cuan turned to my dresser and pulled open the bottom drawer to reveal some khakis, two pairs of blue jeans, and one pair of black. "I might need to be the one borrowing some clothes today," he said.

"What you had on yesterday is probably still good," I noted. "I mean, you weren't wearing it for that long once we got here."

"True, but they smell like a subway tunnel," Cuan responded, crinkling his nose. "Plus we want to make a kind of college impression, right?"

"Fair enough."

I pulled a pair of khakis out of the drawer, while Cuan pulled out the black jeans, holding them up in the mirror and appraising them.

"These look like a looser cut," he said. "They'd probably fit me."

We each selected a button down from the drawer above, and then I pulled open the top drawer. The left was lined with neat rows of trunks, some plain, some in slightly brighter colors. The right side was what looked like a stack of towels.

I remembered this drawer.

"Lift up the towel," I instructed.

Cuan complied, and his eyes widened as he uttered an appreciative "Well, hi there."

I clearly had a thing for sexy clothes. There were tight shirts, see-through pants with provocative pouches, mesh underwear, jockstraps, and all manner of other accoutrements.

"This. Definitely this," Cuan said, lifting out a leather jockstrap, the pouch of which was fastened to the strap by a pair of metal rings. I grinned at his selection, then stepped forward and pulled out a pair of red trunks.

"Not that I have anything against your jockstraps," I said, "because I rather like them, but I haven't worn trunks in forever."

"It must be nice," Cuan mused, "getting to wear familiar clothes for a change."

"They're not that familiar," I noted. "I don't remember them any better than anything else I wear. But at least I know they'll fit."

"Good point," Cuan agreed. Then he looked toward the bathroom. "Hey," he said, "I saw a comb by your sink. D'you mind if I use it?"

"Go nuts," I said, somewhat surprised by his request. Not once since I'd met him had Cuan ever styled his naturally shaggy hair. It never looked messy per se, but it always had a touch of natural wildness to it.

Cuan slipped into the bathroom with his bundle of selected clothing as I dressed in front of the mirror. The red trunks were flattering on my thin frame; they seemed designed to support me in the front and had a little bit of elastic around the back to boost my butt up and out a touch. The brown khakis and tan shirt were a plain choice, but they complemented each other well and were set off nicely by my skin tone. All in all, I looked ready for a college visit.

"You look good," came Cuan's approving voice as he exited the bathroom. "Just like when I first met you."

I stopped dead at the sight of him. He turned, checking himself carefully in the mirror, and I just continued staring as he fixed the buttons of his shirt.

Until now, the wardrobe I had seen Cuan in had consisted exclusively of Wushu pants or compression pants, topped with a sleeveless shirt or a vest that was occasionally adorned with a splash of ornamental faux fur at the shoulders. While the look was always eminently flattering, I knew that it was also selected for the practicality of potential combat, including the possibility that he would need to shift into his werewolf form. As such, the clothes usually had a hint of give, or were spacious, and were otherwise selected specifically for ease of movement and the possibility of a tail.

Now, however, Cuan was wearing a pair of black jeans that, given the difference in our heights, stopped at his ankles. These were intended to be loose-fitting jeans but over Cuan's muscular legs they were almost form-fitting, and particularly flattering in the butt, most of which was visible under his untucked button-down shirt.

The untucked look worked well on him, and that was probably for the best, since the shirt, like the jeans, was made for a slightly smaller body and so probably wouldn't have stayed tucked for long on his frame. The shirt was a deep red on the sides and sleeves, with a wide vertical section of dark violet in the center of the front and back. The shirt would have been a little big on me, because it buttoned neatly over Cuan's chest without restricting his movement, though the hem of the shirt did rise just above his waist as he raised his arms to adjust his collar.

And then there was his hair. Cuan had combed it neatly to

the side, the volume of his mane giving the style an attractive wave, with the sides combed neatly back so that his ears kept any errant hair in place. He looked every bit the preppy college boy ready for lecture.

"Well, fuck me," I stammered appreciatively.

"We just did that," he said, looking at me in the mirror, dimple forming over his half-smile and making my heart melt.

"You're the hottest fucking college boy I've ever seen," I said.

"Well, take a look at yourself in the mirror again," Cuan replied, turning to me. "You know," he added warmly, "it's a shame that your power seems to include going unnoticed. You're very easy on the eyes."

"Well, you always seem to notice me," I said.

"How could I not?" he grinned. "I mean, look at you."

I beamed and kissed him again.

As I stood back and looked at his grin, a pang of vague recognition shot through me. "Hey," I said thoughtfully. "Do you think it's possible I ever saw you on campus?"

"I suppose it's not out of the realm of possibility," Cuan mused. "I mean, Religious Studies does share a building with one of the bio labs. I was almost never in that particular lab, though. And believe me, Cole, whether you were mysteriously inconspicuous or not, I definitely would have remembered seeing you. Plus your scent would have seemed familiar when I came across it later." He inhaled deeply. "I love that it's on these clothes, you know... makes me feel like I'm being enfolded by you."

"Well, I would enfold you right now," I said with a mischievous grin, "but, again, time."

We selected socks—white for me, black for Cuan—and once we had our shoes on I hefted the encyclopedia and handed it to Cuan. "You think you'll be all right getting out of the window with this?" I asked.

Cuan nodded, but then turned to the window near the bed

and considered it for a moment. "So, I've been thinking..." he said, "How critical is it that this window remain latched?"

I considered his question. The window with the fire escape was on a different wall. Nothing was out that window but a little sill, and then a three-story drop.

"Um... not very, I guess," I mused. "But, I mean, you can get up here, so I suppose it's conceivable that somebody else could."

"Better safe than sorry, huh?" Cuan agreed. "Ok then. I was going to suggest you let me lock the door behind you and then I'd climb out the window, but in that case... I can just walk down the stairs to the lobby."

"Good point," I agreed. I held the door for him and he walked outside, then I locked the door behind him and concentrated for a moment before passing through the closed door to meet him on the landing. A few deep breaths and several repetitions of my name later, and I was back to my solid self, and we walked out to the street, side by side.

I wasn't sure how to get from my apartment to the little café where I had met Professor Norton before. The last time, Alexander had been with me, and we had headed there from the Church of the Holy Guardian.

Thankfully, however, when I described the shop to Cuan, he recognized the place and headed straight for it. We arrived at, according to my phone, 10:31AM.

"Hello, Professor Norton," I said as we walked into the shop, bell tinkling above the door. The professor was waiting at a table in the center of the nearly empty shop, his foot tapping impatiently. As soon as I announced myself, his eyes focused on me and he stood up.

"Where were you?" he said gruffly.

"Um... what? Hi?" I stammered.

"You're late," he said.

"Who am I, the white rabbit?" I responded. "I'm not late. You said to be here at 10:30."

"And you weren't," the professor said.

"OK, well then, goodbye," I responded, turning back toward the door.

"Get back here," the professor snapped.

"Oh, you want to start again?" I asked, turning back toward him. "Ok, let me start you off. 'Hi, Cole, thank you for taking the time to come meet me, even though the university is officially closed and nobody is supposed to be on campus.'"

"This isn't campus," he replied gruffly.

"Oh, sorry," I responded, "I didn't realize that the side of campus *closer* to one of the giant gaping holes in the sidewalk was somehow *preferable* to campus. Seriously, how is this place even open right now?"

"Perseverance," said an older man behind the counter.

"Amazing coffee," offered an elderly customer at a corner table.

"Gotta pay the rent," a somewhat-resigned-looking-but-really-cute-college-aged redheaded guy behind the pastry cabinet muttered.

"Entertaining floor show," a woman with short black hair at another table observed.

"OK, I like this place," I said, nodding approvingly. Behind me, Cuan smiled quietly.

Professor Norton scowled.

"You know," I said to Professor Norton, "you were a lot nicer the last time I met you."

"You weren't late," the professor said.

"This isn't class. I'm not turning in a paper. This isn't some hostage exchange. I am meeting you for coffee. One minute after the suggested time is well within the norms of acceptability."

Professor Norton sighed. "You were a lot more compliant before you had amnesia."

"Sorry," I said sarcastically, "I can't remember how to fuck and it's left me kind of bitchy."

The pastry boy burst out laughing. The elderly customer snorted coffee out his nose. I winced sympathetically. That had to hurt.

The professor gave me a flat look, then sighed. "Fine," he said. "I'm sorry. You're right. I've just been under a lot of stress the past few days." He managed a smile. "Sit down; let me apologize by buying you and your friend a drink." He turned and snapped his fingers at the counter. The man by the register looked to the pastry boy and nodded, and the pastry boy gave a resigned sigh and came over to us.

"Would you like to place an order?" he said, managing a smile. He had a tired expression, with green eyes, big ears, and lots of freckles. I recognized him from the last time we'd been here, and so I guessed that Professor Norton's peculiar personality was not new to him. I felt bad for the kid. It had to be stressful, working at a place like this while the world was collapsing around you.

Cuan, without missing a beat, launched into a complicated order that involved some kind of spiced apple cider concoction with a sprinkle of nutmeg and a stick of cinnamon. I didn't see it on the menu board, but the pastry boy nodded, his forced smile flashing genuine for a moment at Cuan's clear knowledge of what must be one of the shop's signature autumn beverages.

"Uh... make that two?" I asked, and the pastry boy nodded again.

"And another coffee," Professor Norton said before the boy turned around. "With three cubes of sugar; one cane, two refined. Not two cane and one refined, not one cane and one-and-a-half refined, but one cane, two refined.

The pastry boy gave a troubled nod as he cleared the

professor's saucer and empty cup and I suspected that there'd been some difficulty in procuring that first cup to his satisfaction.

As the boy left to prepare our drinks, Professor Norton turned his attention to Cuan, as though sizing him up. "You know this shop pretty well, huh?"

Cuan shrugged. "I've been here a few times."

Professor Norton looked at him a bit longer, then turned to me. "This isn't who came with you last time. Last time was that boy who put us back in touch. What was his name? Allen?"

"Alexander," I said. "Yeah, he didn't come with me today. He's—"

"Fine, fine," the Professor said impatiently, waving dismissively. His attention suddenly turned to on the heavy book Cuan had carried in, which we'd set on the table between us when we first sat down. "Is that all you brought?" he asked.

"Well, I have a ton of notes, and I wasn't sure what you could use..." I started.

"I asked you to bring everything."

"Well, I brought that." I pushed the heavy book along the table toward him. "Maybe there's something in it you'll find useful."

"I don't need *books*, I need *notes*," Professor Norton grumbled. "There's nothing in a book that I haven't already—holy hell." The professor stopped talking when the gold lettering on the cover caught the light and he could make out the book's title. Immediately he opened the cover and started to pore over the opening pages. Finally, he looked up.

"This... where did you get this?" he asked.

"I have absolutely no idea," I shrugged. "It was in my apartment, on the shelf. I'd written myself a note saying to show it to you."

"Well, you have good judgement, Cole," the professor said enthusiastically. His entire demeanor was suddenly different, as though I had passed some kind of trial and had moved from the outer ring of crusty asshole professor to an inner circle of appreciative asshole professor. "This isn't just any encyclopedia. This is old, somehow transcribed and printed and passed down from a version that existed before the church got its obfuscating hands on it."

"I thought you liked the church," I said.

"A bunch of stodgy fuckers," Professor Norton muttered, and Cuan snorted mirthfully. "Demonstrating the legitimacy of Christianity doesn't mean handing a pass to every church that has sought to monetize and weaponize Christianity for its own ends."

"Yeah, about that whole 'legitimizing Christianity' thing..." I started, but the professor was ignoring me now, instead reading aloud a passage from the foreword about the power of true names.

Cuan and I exchanged a look. Professor Norton's goal was to prove the existence of angels by invoking one of the heavenly beings and somehow getting irrefutable proof of having done so. His reasoning was that by doing so, he could demonstrate that Christian doctrine was correct and that it thereby was the supreme religion. I wasn't so sure of the logical soundness of the argument: after all, angels appeared in more than just Christian tradition. And furthermore, just because angels existed, why did that necessarily mean other religions' spiritual beings did not? When I discussed this with Cuan and Az, Az scoffed at Professor Norton's hypothesis, asserting that different religions the world over reflected different understandings of the Divine, and therefore all had claim to legitimacy—and all had supernatural manifestations, to boot. Speaking of Az, Cuan and I were in no hurry to divulge his true identity as Azrael, Angel of Death, especially not to a professor we barely knew. If the time was going to come for Professor Norton to meet an angel, that was going to be on the angel's terms, not ours.

Instead, we sat quietly as Professor Norton continued to read from the opening passage.

"And so," he read enthusiastically, "by proper application of the names contained herein, the only and true names of the angels, both those above and the fallen below, the aspirant may succeed in invoking their presence in real and tangible ways, and committing their cooperation in the aspirant's worldly pursuits. It is due to the power of these true and only names that those who would seek to control and manipulate man's faith have sought to obfuscate angels' identities, and thereby ensure their positions as sole intermediaries between man and the Holy Father. But I have sought to preserve man's ties to God and not sever them, so that he who knows the proper invocations and rituals may again feel the presence of God's faithful servants, and secure their help in re-attaining man's rightful place in Eden, which was Adam's home before Eve conspired with the serpent to take it from him."

Cuan and I exchanged a look again. We said nothing, but we didn't need to hear one another to understand exactly what that look meant:

What the fuck is this bullshit?

"Cole," Professor Norton said, smiling widely as he continued to stare at the pages, "this is *perfect.*"

"Do you know what rituals the book is referring to?" I asked.

"I'm still working on that," the professor replied, "but this will go a long way to helping my goal be realized."

The pastry boy returned with a tray of drinks. Two were tall glasses with pedestal-like bases, which were clearly the cider— if the warm apple smell wasn't tell-tale enough, the big sticks of cinnamon were a definite giveaway. The third cup was the coffee, which was on a saucer next to three cubes of sugar: one cane, two refined. They were perfect cubes; clearly a great deal of care had gone into their selection. The pastry boy set the cider in front of Cuan and me, and then lifted the saucer with the coffee on the tray and began to try to place it on the table, though most of the space in front of Professor Norton was now occupied by the open book.

"Here you are, sir—" the boy began.

"Get that away from here!" Professor Norton snapped. "Can't you see that this book is a valuable antique? What's the matter with you?"

"Sorry, sir," the boy said, his frown stretching his freckles. The saucer shook slightly in his hand as he started to place it down, and a splash of coffee spilled over the side of the cup onto the plate.

"Get it together, boy!" The Professor snapped, and the boy visibly winced.

"I'll take that," Cuan said gently, deftly lifting the saucer out of the boy's hand. "Thank you," he said as he set the saucer between us. "These ciders look amazing."

"Jesus," I muttered as the boy retreated to the pastry counter. "Calm the fuck down, Professor."

"You don't seem to understand how valuable this book is," the professor insisted. "Bringing coffee near it? Why would he do such a thing?"

"Because you ordered it?" I noted.

The professor scoffed. "No excuse for ineptitude. I cannot risk this book getting damaged. This is a critical step on the path to the success of my research. If something were to happen to it, I couldn't afford time looking for a replacement."

"Time?" Cuan and I asked in unison, looking up at the professor.

The professor looked up at us sharply. For an instant he said nothing, and just stared at us. "Yes, time," he said at last, his voice agitated and rapid. "I mean, look around you. The city is exploding around us. The university is shutting down. My office, all my research, my books, everything—I will only have access to it for so much longer."

"Don't you have stuff backed up on a computer or something?" Cuan asked.

The professor shot him a withering, disdainful look that could easily have given Bianca a run for her money. "You would disparage a text such as this one by converting it to ones and zeroes?" he spat.

"There's something to be said for the affordances of a well-crafted digital scholarly edition—" Cuan began.

"Sophomoric nonsense," the professor said dismissively. "Programmers don't know anything about proper responsible scholarship."

"The fuck we don't!" called the short-haired woman seated at another table.

"Oh, go read a book," the professor snapped back at her. "Or better yet, learn how to write longhand. Do you even know what a pencil is?"

"Yeah," the woman called back. "It's a stick you write with. Kind of like the one you have shoved up your ass, but smaller and it doesn't smell like *shit*."

I grinned at the woman from across the café. She smirked at me as the Professor, oblivious to our silent exchange, grumbled and turned his attention back to the book, leafing eagerly through its pages.

"So," I began, "what do you think you'll—"

The professor grunted and waved me to silence as he continued to flip through the pages, looking at each one intently before grumbling and turning to the next.

Cuan and I exchanged a shrug and lifted the glasses of warm cider.

"Cheers," Cuan said, tapping my glass lightly with his own before bringing it to his lips with a contented smile on his face.

I followed suit, bringing the glass toward me. I could feel its warmth even before the liquid touched my lips, my nostrils filling with the comforting scent of woody spice. As soon as I tasted it I felt it reach to all of my extremities, filling me with the sweet, soothing touch of autumn.

"Mmmm, that's good," I mused happily, ignoring the professor's irritated grunt.

Cuan and I sat together in peaceful, contented silence for several minutes, the incredible cider more than sufficient to draw our attention away from the agitated jackass and his vigorous page-flipping of the tome that took up half the table.

At one point, as we were about halfway done with our ciders, the pastry boy brought a slice of cherry pie on a plate to the short-haired woman at the far table.

"On the house," he said gratefully as he set it next to her, and she beamed at him.

We were nearly finished with our ciders when the professor heaved a sigh—of exasperation or satisfaction, I couldn't tell—and slammed the book shut with a loud thud.

"This'll do, perhaps," he said. "Thank you, Cole." He stood up as the pastry boy came to ask if we needed anything further, and tossed a crumpled dollar bill onto the table in front of him. "Learn how to get an order right and treat books with respect, and next time it'll be better," he said with a scowl. Then he turned to head to the register to settle the balance of our drinks, muttering "It's the only way these kids'll learn" as he tucked the book under his arm.

As the professor walked away, Cuan reached into the side of his shoe and pulled out a twenty, which he slipped, with an apologetic smile, into the pastry boy's palm. The boy's eyes widened and I think I saw a grateful tear form in the corner of one as he whispered genuine thanks.

At the register, the professor was reaching into his wallet when he looked up at the man behind the counter in shock.

"What do you mean, the ciders are \$14.75 each?" he demanded incredulously.

"Wait," Cuan asked quietly, turning to the freckled pastry boy as he took our glasses from us, which were now empty save for the sticks of cinnamon. "Aren't they only \$5.50?"

A smirk spread across the redheaded boy's face, and Cuan and I grinned at one another. The pastry boy's smirk turned back to a sullen frown again, however, as he gingerly retrieved the professor's untouched coffee, carefully selected sugar cubes and all.

"Well, thank you, Cole," the professor said from the doorway of the café, receipt in hand. He sighed, then smiled. "And I genuinely mean that. This book will be a huge help to my work. I hope if you find anything else among your notes that may be of interest, you bring it to my attention. Or better yet, share what you have even if you *don't* think it may be of interest; I may spy something that you've overlooked, or that you've forgotten the significance of. Don't forget, if I can successfully complete this research, it will change our human understanding of religion. We're doing important work, you and I—we're bringing mankind closer to God."

The bell above the door tinkled musically as he left.

"What a load of shit," I said, staring at the door after him.

"You're telling me," Cuan nodded. "You remember perfectly well how to fuck."

Behind us, the freckled pastry boy spilled coffee all over the floor.

IV

THE UNFORGIVEN

"It's good that you haven't told Professor Norton about me," Az said when Cuan and I arrived at his hotel room for my usual training. "The more you tell me of him, the more I dislike him. Yet another self-righteous, sanctimonious human who believes his own faith to the be one and only truth."

Az normally seemed eternally unruffled, but he had been in a particularly bad mood since my betrayal by the Order of Light, and today was no exception. He leaned back against the desk of his lavish hotel room with an irritated expression on his face.

While I suspected that Az's choice of lodging may have been partly for comfort, I knew it was also largely born of practicality. When Az joined the Midnight Hunters, The Hunters' Home was already largely fully occupied. With Marcus being treated at the home and my officially joining the ranks, the home had no free rooms for additional occupants. More likely, however, Az's priority was keeping his true identity as Azrael, the Angel of Death, as secret as he could. As far as we knew, Cuan and I were the only ones who had been entrusted with that information.

The room he'd chosen for himself was well-outfitted, with red velvet curtains, a large king-sized bed, a little kitchenette, and a separate room for the toilet. It must have been designed for romantic escapes, since the shower was not in the bathroom but was instead in a glass-enclosed corner opposite the bed, clearly visible to the rest of the room.

Az did not seem particularly romantically inclined, however, especially not at the moment. Instead, he was scowling, his perfect, flawless features sour with what almost looked like barely-contained rage.

"I'm sick of these misguided or, worse, blindly power-hungry humans who commit terrible acts and believe themselves to be following the Divine. It's like the leader of this local Order of Light. Trying to enslave you in the name of 'protecting the church?' That man sickens me."

"You seem to have taken what happened to me particularly hard," I observed.

"And why wouldn't I?" Az straightened his immaculate black suit before running a porcelain hand through his neat blond hair in exasperation, blue eyes sparking. "I swore an oath that I would protect you both while here on Earth. And then Cuan gets shot with wolf's-bane, and while I'm trying to keep him alive you simply... disappear. You and the entire Church of the Holy Guardian, gone from my sight. From my ability to even *sense*, were I standing directly in front of it." He scoffed. "How's that for irony? A church so obsessed with hiding itself from the eyes of demons, real or imagined, that it hides itself from the Heavens, as well."

"Wait," Cuan said, "you mean the Church hid itself from God?"

"No," Az clarified, "nothing hides from the Divine. But while angels are divine, we are not *the* Divine. But we each have our specialties. And for me to not be able to sense the souls in a place? Well, that's some very strong obfuscation."

"Which brings us back to the question…" I looked down at my hands. "What am I?"

Az screwed up his features. "Honestly, I'm not sure," he said. "What I do know is that I need you to master your power of transitioning to and from incorporeality."

"And just why is that, exactly?" I asked pointedly. "I know that you need me to help with finding a trapped soul, and you say you know where it is, but nothing beyond that. So… where is it?"

"I will tell you when you're ready to help," Az replied. "That's not yet. You've gotten very good at fading, but you have difficulty with the reversion. Why it's a two-step process for you, I don't know, but you need to be able to make that final step without outside help."

"I did that," I said, "…once."

I looked over at Cuan. He watched me silently as I recalled that one shift, a few days ago, after Julia let me out of my confinement and I raced to his side. He gave me a sad smile.

"Once isn't enough," Az said. "Not unless you can harness whatever you were feeling then and call upon it at will."

What I'd been feeling. I didn't like remembering that feeling. Fear; desperation. On the other hand, there was also a deep-seated *need* embedded in that feeling that never really went away. Was that what had made it possible for me to snap back on my own? Or… was it as simple as having a reason to return, someone to come home to?

I wasn't sure. But we practiced, just like we always practiced, with me fading into incorporeality, babbling to the Angel of Death in the Tongue of Souls on the return trip, and Cuan on hand to help me make that final step back. At least the process was becoming less and less exhausting: I was able to repeat it four times before Az decided I needed to stop.

"You're getting better," Cuan said with a smile as he and I walked back to The Hunters' Home.

"Yeah, but I'm still not there yet," I said.

"You'll get there," Cuan smiled at me. "I believe in you."

When we arrived back at The Hunters' Home, Bran and Bianca were on their way out.

"What's up?" I said as they passed. They both turned to me.

"Hi there," Bran said with a grin. "We're off to do recon. To see how viable Cuan's idea was."

"Oh, so you're gonna go find Bianca her street corner after all?" I asked.

Bianca simply flipped me off as they turned and went on their way.

Cedric was in his usual place in the kitchen, washing dishes.

"How did things go?" he asked when we walked in and said our hellos.

"Training, or meeting Professor Norton?" I asked.

"Both." He nodded to a pair of plates on the counter. "Saved you some salmon and rice."

"Thanks," I said, taking a plate. "But... are you ever not cooking? Is it even a mealtime?"

"I try to have things ready for when people get in," Cedric replied. "You are a little later than usual today."

"We delayed training a little to have time to meet Professor Norton," I said.

"Cole's doing better in training," Cuan offered between mouthfuls. "His stamina's improving."

"Good to hear," Cedric nodded. "And... what of your professor?"

"Well, for one, he's a dick," I said.

"That seems to be an opinion you hold about a lot of people," Cedric noted.

"No, seriously, he's a dick," Cuan affirmed. "You should have seen how he acted toward the other people at the café."

"Wait," Cedric stopped washing dishes and turned to stare

at us. At least, I think he was staring; it was hard to tell with his ever-present sunglasses. "You met him in public?"

Cuan nodded.

"What did you discuss? Did you mention anything about the Hunters?"

"He seemed remarkably uninterested in us beyond what we could bring him," Cuan noted. "And besides, I know better than to talk about the Hunters to just anyone."

"Oh, really?" Cedric responded, gesturing toward me with his chin.

"That's different," Cuan protested; "he literally saw me fighting off a phantom from less than ten yards away. A phantom that, mind you, was ignoring him. I think there was more than enough to that situation to justify bringing Cole to the Home."

Cedric said nothing, but tipped his head in a sort of shrug of acknowledgement. "Was your professor interested in anything you had?"

"An old encyclopedia of Angels and Demons," I said, taking a bite of the (very delicious) salmon and rice. "It purported to offer the one true name of every heavenly and infernal being."

Cedric was still for a second, though in shock or disbelief or something else entirely, I didn't know. Finally he scoffed.

"Stuff and nonsense," he said. "Is he trying to form a pact of some sort? He will need a lot of more than just a name to help him out. He is probably just another amateur enthusiast of the supernatural, or a religious zealot—albeit with a degree behind him. I do not think he is someone we need to worry about." He paused for a moment, then sat down at the table. "But, Cole, there is something I want to discuss with you."

This was an unusual change of pace. Normally Cedric didn't discuss *with*, he discussed *at*.

"What's up?" I asked.

"As I am sure you recall, back when you first agreed to aid

us, we promised to aid you in turn," Cedric said. "But, circumstances being what they are, the Hunters have been somewhat remiss in upholding our end of the bargain. And now you are not merely someone who has aided us, you are one of us. So now that things have quieted for a bit, I think it is as good a time as any for us to help you investigate your lost memories."

"I... what?" I stammered. I know it was something they had promised, but in the midst of everything else going on, it had kind of slipped to the back of my mind. "Really?"

"I think that's a great idea," Cuan nodded. "Tomorrow let's go back to where I first caught your scent."

"You mean where I puked all over the lawn in front of some building?" I said. "Fun times, that."

"I think it is a wise next step," Cedric agreed. "Or first step, as it were, since we have done little to help you thus far." He stood from the table and walked across the room to the door to the basement. "I am going down to train and work on a few things. Please do not come down while I am there; I need my space."

We nodded our assent, and Cedric started downstairs.

"Oh, and wash your plates after you finish, will you?" he added as the door shut behind him.

We were just toweling off the dishes when a loud, unfamiliar ding resounded through the room, making me jump. With one neat motion, Cuan dipped down and caught the dish I dropped before it shattered on the floor and deposited it neatly in the drying rack.

"That was a spectacular save," I said to him, but his attention was focused on the doorway to the hall.

"Who the hell is ringing our doorbell?" he asked, brows knit. "Nobody *ever* rings our doorbell."

Cuan walked out into the hallway, and I followed behind. He opened the door to the porch, and as the light poured around him, I saw his entire silhouette stiffen.

Panic shot through me. The last time Cuan suddenly stiffened like that, he had been shot with a dart full of wolf's-bane. I sprinted toward him, but then I heard him speak, and I stopped.

"What are you doing here?" he demanded of whoever was on the other side of the door.

"I... was just coming to check on you and Marcus, to see how you were recovering," came the voice.

A voice I knew.

Alexander's voice.

My body did exactly what Cuan's had a few seconds earlier. Every muscle tensed. Blood rang in my ears.

Cuan continued to stand in the doorway, saying nothing.

"You look different," Alexander said. "I don't think I've seen you in regular clothes before."

Cuan did not reply.

"Can... can I come in?" Alexander asked.

"You should leave," Cuan said coldly. His posture was threatening, as though he were ready to pounce.

"Cuan," Alexander persisted. "What's the matter? Why are you so upset?"

More stony silence. Finally, Cuan spoke, his voice icier than ever.

"Do you know where Cole is?" he asked.

No response.

"Because I do," Cuan added.

"Cuan, I..." Alexander's voice was barely audible: it was shaky and weak. "I... couldn't... I can't..." he trailed off.

I waited for another moment, but Alexander offered not another word. This had gone on long enough. I walked to the porch doorway behind Cuan. He continued to stand in the door, protectively guarding me, but I placed a hand on his shoulder and he assented to slide aside.

At the other end of the porch, Alexander was standing in

front of the screen, eyes downcast. He looked sullen, his features drawn, as though he hadn't slept in days.

I stepped around Cuan onto the porch, and walked across the short expanse of boards to the screen door. Lightly, I lifted the latch and pulled it open.

It was only then, as the opening door drew attention to myself, that Alexander looked up, pupils focusing on me. His eyes widened, his mouth gaped, and he stared.

"Hello, Alexander," I said.

Tears formed in Alexander's eyes. He threw himself at me, wrapping his arms around me, hugging me tightly to him.

I didn't hug him back.

"Oh, Cole," he said, face buried in my shirt, his voice breaking, "I'm so, so sorry."

"I didn't say you could come in," I replied coldly.

Alexander let go of me and stepped back, his face a mask of fear and remorse.

"I'm so sorry," he said again, his voice a whisper. "I didn't... I couldn't... I can't disobey the Order. My Father. I..."

"So you left me," I said. "You left me captive in that gilded box, without a form, without a body, to be a prisoner for all eternity in service of you and your family and your church."

My body started to shake, a combination of trauma and rage, and suddenly I felt Cuan's hand on my shoulder, his chest against my back, steadying me. "You left me to *oblivion*," I said hotly. "Endless oblivion. You denied me identity, freedom, the right to exist."

"It was my father—" he started.

"Bullshit," I cut him off. "Your father is a piece of shit, yes. But *you* made that choice. I'm sure it felt like an impossible situation, but you sacrificed me, in my *entirety*, for what? Your father's approval?"

"I did it to save Cuan—" he offered.

"Don't give me that shit excuse," I spat. "Yes, you did save

Cuan's life, and for that I am extremely, deeply thankful. But at no point were you making a decision to save me *or* him. You could have stopped your father, and we could have taken the tincture to Cuan together."

"Father never would have allowed that," Alexander insisted. "He would have shattered the vial of Seraphiel's Tears if I'd tried to stop him."

"Empty conjecture," Cuan said.

"Your father wasn't anywhere near the tears, and you know it," I said. "Otherwise he would have shattered the vial anyway."

Alexander was still for a second. "I..." was all he offered before trailing off.

"Stop trying to justify your actions," Cuan said coldly. "There is no rationalizing the unforgivable."

"It was bad enough that you let your father take me," I said, voice starting to shake as I struggled to keep hold of myself. "But even worse was that you *left* me there. For *days*. You could have come back."

"They wouldn't let me near the sanctuary! Don't you think I wanted to go back there?" Alexander cried.

"Did you?" I demanded. "Who was stopping you, really? What, did your father ground you, and so then magically you couldn't walk out the door to your room? You couldn't sneak out at night?"

"You don't know what it was like for me," Alexander protested.

"You're right, I don't," I said. "And, honestly, I don't think I care."

Alexander sniffed, casting his eyes back downward. "I was so confused," he said. "Father kept telling me it was better this way. He kept quoting scripture and referring to all kinds of theology. He said you were a ghost, and if you were doomed to haunt the world for eternity you might as well be a force for good. That way you couldn't hurt anyone, couldn't hurt yourself, you'd be in the protection of the Church, and maybe if you did God's work for long enough you'd earn your way to heaven. He said it was best for you, that as a ghost—"

"I. Am not. A FUCKING GHOST." I was nearly shouting, but I didn't care. "You have *known* me. I have a body. I have a life. I don't need to be summoned through a seance. I'm not wandering around with a sheet over my head. I'm not sliming you while you're in bed. I'm not out there hunting Pac-Man. I'm not fucking guiding your hands as you make pottery. I'm a person. I've talked with you. Ate with you. Fought alongside you. Slept next to you. I *came* in your *ass*."

I paused.

"OK, So maybe I *kind of* slimed you," I admitted.

"That kind of casts the end of *Ghostbusters* in a whole new light," Cuan mused off of my tangent. "'Marshmallow', my ass. Or marshmallow your ass, as the case may be."

I rounded on him. I may have interrupted my own tirade, but Cuan had now fully derailed it. "A, I have no idea what *Ghostbusters* is. And B, did you just make 'marshmallow' a verb? Because I think I approve. But C, not helping," I said. "And what's with the sudden pop-culture wit? Who are you? Me?"

"Maybe you're kind of rubbing off on me," he suggested.

"Well if you want me to *keep* rubbing off on you, let me finish," I retorted.

"I do like it when you finish," he smiled.

"OK," I half-smiled back in spite of myself. "I know I have this coming, but can we please do it later?"

"Cum later," Cuan nodded. "Got it."

"I am not a ghost," I said with finality, turning back to Alexander, "but even if I *were*, that still doesn't justify imprisoning and enslaving me. What do you think they were going to do with that box? Throw some stamps on it and ship it off to Heaven? You know as well as I do that if I were left in that box, I'd never get out."

Alexander was quiet for a moment. I think I made my point, even with Cuan's 'assistance'. Finally, Alexander looked up at me.

"So..." he asked weakly, "how *did* you get out?"

I stared at him silently. He watched my face searchingly, and suddenly realization dawned.

"Julia," he said. "It was Julia, wasn't it? ...So that explains it."

"Explains what?" I asked.

"Julia disappeared a few days ago," Alexander said. "Not a word to anyone, at least not to anyone willing to tell Father. She took her spear Gratia and a bunch of other equipment with her. Father is on the warpath. He says that Julia is a traitor and if she ever resurfaces, we are to strike her down on sight."

"Of course he would say that," I nodded. "Fucking asshole."

Alexander stared at us for a long time. Then, finally, he spoke again.

"I'm sorry," he said. "I mean it. I'm sorry. For everything. And you're right; there's no excuse for what I did. I understand if you hate me."

For a moment, I didn't respond. When I did, the words weren't what I expected.

"I don't hate you," I found myself saying. "I should, but I don't. I don't know why. Maybe it's because I know what your family is like, and I can imagine what growing up in that place did to you. Maybe it's because you saved Cuan's life. I don't know. All I know is, I don't hate you. But I don't forgive you, either. And I don't trust you."

Alexander sighed. "Well, I guess that's something." He paused again. He looked to Cuan. Cuan said nothing, but I could hear a low growl from deep in his throat. Alexander swallowed. "So..." he said at last, "I know there's no reason for you to let me in, but... I really want to see Marcus. Please... can I see him?"

Cuan did not move. A large part of me didn't want

Alexander in the Home. A tiny part of me didn't want to see him ever again, but most of me that didn't want him to come in simply felt that he didn't deserve to. But at the same time, I knew what it felt like to be separated from someone you care about. I reached down and squeezed Cuan's hand.

"I think we should let him in," I said quietly.

"Are you sure?" Cuan asked, turning to me.

I looked into his deep, golden eyes and immediately felt safe.

"Yeah," I said. "We should at least let him see Marcus."

Cuan ran upstairs and got Lester's OK, and then came back down and the three of us headed up to the room that Lester had turned into a makeshift hospital bed for Marcus.

When Marcus and I were dating, back when he found me, he was a thin, albeit fit, black-haired college boy with olive skin and a drug problem. When he'd shown up after having been enrolled in the city's 'rehab' program, he was a hulking blue monster recognizable only by the tattoos on his ass. Now, as Alexander, Cuan, and I stood in the side of the wire- and tube-strewn room where he slept, I noticed that while Marcus was still misshapen, he somehow seemed a little smaller in size, and his skin a little less blue. He was breathing peacefully in his sleep as Lester, unkempt gray hair—what he had, anyway—sticking out over the collar of his black coat, fretted about him.

"Thank you," Alexander said quietly after we had watched him in silence for a few minutes. "Thank you for helping him."

"You've been plenty of help yourself, boy," Lester said to Alexander as he continued to flit about. "Your knowledge of him was a huge help in figuring out not only that these beasts were actually humans who had been experimented on, but also in giving me ideas on how to potentially reverse the process."

"You can reverse the process?" Alexander asked.

"Not yet, but I'm working on it," Lester nodded. "For his sake, and for the sake of the others who I keep down at the lab."

"Well," Alexander said quietly," I'll help however I can."

"Good lad," Lester nodded. "I'll be sure to take you up on that."

We stood in silence for another minute or two before Cuan sighed deeply.

"Thank you," he said, staring across the room at the opposite wall.

"Hm?" Alexander asked, looking at him.

"I said 'thank you,'" Cuan growled, then sighed again. "You saved my life," he said. "So... thanks for that. I mean it. I would have died without Seraphiel's Tears. But... I also can't forgive you for what you did to Cole."

Alexander nodded. "I know," he said sadly. "I'm sorry."

He was quiet for another few seconds before he spoke again.

"Cuan... something my Father said has been bothering me."

Cuan said nothing, still staring at the opposite wall.

"Cuan?" Alexander asked at last. "Did you... did you kill my mother?"

"WHAT?" came an incredulous scoff. It was Lester. He roared with laughter. "Don't be ridiculous. When did your mother die?"

"Before I can remember," Alexander said.

"So you see?" Lester said. "Cuan would have been a tiny infant. The only way he could have killed a woman is if she died in childbirth."

Cuan and Alexander both blanched. They looked at one other.

"But..." Alexander stammered.

"Are you...?" Cuan asked.

"Don't be ridiculous," Lester said dismissively. "You're not related."

"And... how do you know that?" Cuan asked.

"Because your DNA doesn't match," Lester replied.

"And… how do you know *THAT*?" Alexander demanded.

"Well, I have DNA profiles of all the Hunters," Lester said simply. "And when you gave me blood to use as a transfusion for Marcus, I ran an analysis of yours as well."

"That's a massive HIPAA violation," Alexander said, affronted.

"Well, good thing this isn't a hospital," Lester replied with a shrug. "And really, you can't blame me. A chance to get a DNA profile of a member of the illustrious Lucent family, stewards of the local Order of Light? I definitely couldn't resist." Marcus stirred and grunted, and Lester turned his attention back to him, adjusting a few levels on a machine attached to multiple IVs. Alexander gawked at him as he worked. Then Marcus twitched again and he winced.

"Poor Marcus," he said. "I wish I knew who did this to you."

"Oh," I said. "About that…"

"Hm?" Alexander asked, turning to me.

I pulled out my phone and pulled up the photo I had taken in the maintenance office in the subway tunnels. I held it out to Alexander, and he squinted at the logos on the folder. Then he jerked his head back in surprise, nearly dropping my phone as he did so.

"*Holy fucking shit*," he gasped. "Holy. Fucking. Shit. The fucking police are in on this? Fucking *city hall*? What the actual *fuck*?" He looked from me to Cuan to Lester. He nearly dropped my phone again, so I took it from him and slipped it back into my pocket. "We… we have to do something. We have to investigate!"

"No," came a firm response from the door. We turned to see Cedric in the doorway, staring coldly at Alexander from behind his sunglasses. "*We* are investigating. *You* have to leave."

"I… I want to help," Alexander protested.

"We cannot trust you," Cedric said. "For a time I was beginning to think I could. But you have demonstrated to me once again that the Order of Light are not our allies. Cooperating with you nearly cost us Cuan *and* Cole. And for what? For the help of a boy with a glow-in-the-dark sword? Sorry, but the math does not work out on that one."

Alexander's face fell.

"However, you have been useful in helping us understand the ogres," Cedric continued, "and so you may continue to consult with Lester regarding the health of your friend and the others at the lab. It is for that reason alone that I am not forbidding you from setting foot in this house. You may come when invited, and stay while supervised, until you are told to leave. And now, I am telling you to leave."

Alexander hesitated. "Ok. Thank you. I'm sorry. I—"

"I said 'leave'."

Alexander nodded, defeated. "Bye Lester. Marcus, Cuan... Cole."

None of us said anything. We just stood and watched him as he turned, headed down the stairs, and left.

Cedric turned to me. "Are you all right?" he asked.

I nodded. "I think so," I said.

"Good," he said. "Bran and Bianca will be back soon. Let us start dinner."

V

WHERE IT ALL BEGAN

THE AUTUMN AIR was brisk and cool as we headed out into the city. Cedric, Bianca, Cuan, and I wound our way through the streets in the general direction of the square. Cuan led the way, expertly slipping between alleys and side streets, making a beeline for the first place he remembered catching my scent. The farther we went, the more unkempt the streets became; debris and wreckage were scattered across the road, and the fallen autumn leaves crunched underfoot as we walked. This part of the city was essentially abandoned, the businesses shuttered and boarded up, the citizens evacuated after the so-called pipe explosions began.

It was a strange dichotomy, seeming both post-apocalyptic and oddly peaceful and quiet.

Cuan suddenly jerked his head up, then pulled us into an alley and ducked behind a dumpster.

"What?" I asked, but he held up a hand to shush me. A second or two later I heard a quiet motor, and a patrol car drove slowly by, windows down, officers peering carefully down alleys and into windows.

"So the police are patrolling," Cedric grunted. "Of course they are."

"Well, if this whole project is a big secret, maybe they don't know what's really going on," I suggested. "Maybe they were just told to patrol and look for people who need help. Maybe if we talk to them, they'll—"

"OK Casper, I know your memory is basically a black hole," Bianca said, "so I'm going to give you the benefit of the doubt and assume that's the only reason you just said something so stupid. Listen to me. The cops are not your friends. You think the Order of Light is bad? Try doing your little ghost trick quickly enough to dodge bullets."

"She's right," Cuan said gravely. "We can't trust the police. Nobody's supposed to be out and about in this part of the city since it was evacuated. If we're spotted here, then as far as they're concerned, we're criminals."

"Surely they can't all be like that," I said. "I mean, they became cops to serve and protect, right? Some of them must be taking that to heart."

"Sure, there might be some who have their hearts in the right place," Cuan said. "But Cole, it's not that simple. Police are the product of the institution that creates them. And our city's institution is one that's treating the homeless and those struggling with drug problems as less than worthless, as human fodder for a weapons program. Think about that. Cops who've been trained through an institution that thinks like that aren't cops who you're gonna wanna trust. And if an officer *didn't* buy into that mindset? If they instead stood up to the system? Do you think the city is gonna assign cops like that to patrol an area that's basically a giant cover-up for a human trafficking program?"

"Listen to Talking Dog," Bianca insisted, and Cuan scowled at her. "If the po-po see us, it'll be 'shoot first, ask questions later'."

"What about 'innocent until proven guilty'?" I asked.

"That is for the courts," Cedric sighed. "The police here are trained to treat anyone they see as suspicious as a potential criminal."

"And we all seem suspicious, just by being here," I realized.

Cedric nodded. "Yes, though all to different degrees, in their eyes." He scowled. "Why do you think I elected not to ask Bran to accompany us on this particular outing?"

"Well, shit," I whispered. They were right; I knew they were right. I swallowed hard. Suddenly the stakes for our little city jaunt felt much higher.

The sound of the engine disappeared, and Cuan listened intently for another minute or so before he decided that it was safe to keep moving.

We slipped down another two or three streets before finally arriving at the edge of a small lawn.

"Here," Cuan said triumphantly. "This is where you puked. I can still smell it, a little."

"Charming," Bianca said flatly. She looked around. There were some buildings here and there, but nothing immediately next to the spot Cuan indicated. I felt a little exposed, now that we had no alleys immediately close at hand to duck into.

"So, where did you come from, that you wound up here?" Cedric asked.

"I... I haven't a clue," I said. "That whole night is a blur."

"Very helpful," Bianca said sarcastically. "Well, puke pile found, mystery solved, let's go home."

"No," Cuan said. "Give him a minute." He turned to me, voice gentle. "Cole, what do you remember? Even broad strokes. Tell me about that blur."

I struggled, trying to piece together anything about that first night, when I woke up in a basement of a building in a cloud of fog.

A basement.

"A basement," I said.

Cedric and Bianca both turned their attention from the surrounding streets to me, and they watched me closely along with Cuan.

"I... I had to go up to get out," I said, remembering. "Up stairs. The doors... the doors I went out had..." I made a pushing motion with both hands in front of me. "Push bars," I said.

"OK," Cedric said, "So likely an office or a public building or something like that."

"Anything else?" Cuan asked. "Anything else you remember? Anything from where you first woke up?"

"It was... foggy," I murmured, straining at my memory. "So, so foggy. But... something was scattered all over the floor. Rectangles...." I remembered suddenly the one that was open on the floor. "Books."

"A bookstore, maybe?" Bianca asked. "Isn't there a boutique bookstore on the other end of the lawn?"

"Not with a basement," Cedric said. "And the front door has a handle, not a push bar."

Cuan's eyes widened. "The campus library is less than a block from here." He looked from me to Cedric to Bianca. "It has a push door like that. And it has two basement levels, though they're just archives. Students aren't allowed into them without permission from the faculty."

"I was running an errand for Professor Norton when whatever accident happened," I pointed out. "Maybe he had asked me to retrieve something from the library basement?"

"That all adds up," Cedric nodded. "OK, Cuan, where is the library?"

Cuan led us back to the edge of the small park, then led us down a sidewalk along the street.

"I'm not sure how we'll be able to get in, though," Cuan mused as we walked. "The whole university's closed down; the library'll be shut tight. Even if Cole fades and opens the door from the inside, we'll probably have security alarms to contend with."

Cuan's concern turned out to be unfounded, however. The library was not in good shape. Clearly some of the 'pipe explosions' had occurred near the building, as two of its windows were blasted and one of the exterior walls looked scorched. Two buildings away, the sidewalk on the opposite side of the street ended in a large hole, similar to those we'd seen ogres clamber out of.

The front of the library was crisscrossed with police tape, but the leftmost of the three doors in front of the building was bent and ajar.

"That is our point of ingress," Cedric said.

"What about security?" Bianca asked. "Motion detectors, and such?"

"I think the power's out," Cuan said, squinting at the front windows. "I don't even see exit lighting on."

After checking to make sure the coast was clear, we slipped through the open door and into the dark lobby. Dust hung heavily in the air, glinting in the faint afternoon light that sifted in through the windows. The lobby looked like white marble, with a set of access gates—likely where students presented identification—standing empty and unattended. I didn't remember these—perhaps they had been standing open on the night of my accident? Beyond these, a set of three steps led up to doors leading to the stacks, with an emergency stairwell to the left and a main stair to the right.

Cuan neatly vaulted the gates and walked through the lobby, looking this way and that. I was squeezing between the gates behind him when he stopped suddenly, crouching down and sniffing something on the ground.

"Well, we're probably in the right place," he said as I caught up to him. He pointed at a splat of dried red on the floor. "That's your blood."

The memory hit me with such force that I staggered. Not with as much force as the floor had, though, I recalled. "I fell here," I said. I straightened and looked around. "I fell heading toward the entrance. There was a light above me when I came in here.... That one," I said, pointing toward a large rectangular "EXIT" sign that hung above the emergency staircase. It was illuminated in my memory, but here it was as dead as the rest of the lighting.

"Backup battery must have died," Cedric noted.

"Well, good," Bianca said, pointing at the top of the exit door frame, where a large metal rectangular bar was set against a metal plate on the door. "Electronic locks. Those usually go off when the power fails."

Sure enough, the door pulled easily open, and presently we found ourselves in a stairwell. Unlike the lobby, however, there were no windows here, and once the door shut behind us we were completely in the dark. Bianca continued down the stairs unperturbed, but even Cuan stopped walking.

"Hold on," he said; "let me get my phone light."

"No need," Cedric said. I looked in the direction of his voice. He was, like the rest of us, completely wreathed in the dark, and yet, I somehow could make out where his sunglasses were. It was almost as if, behind them, there was a tiny source of... light?

"Cedric?" I asked. "Are your eyes—"

"No," Cedric responded, and then he snapped his fingers. A sphere of red light illuminated over his hand, and suddenly the entire stairwell was bathed in dull crimson. Whatever illusion of brightness I had seen behind his sunglasses was either gone or subsumed by the light.

"Here's a landing," came Bianca's voice from below us. We heard the sound of a door being pushed open.

"Wait, Bianca," I said, hurrying down to the door, Cuan at my heels.

Bianca was standing at the open door, beyond which was complete blackness. It wasn't until Cedric descended to the landing, red sphere over his shoulder, that the interior of the space was filled with light, stretching long shadows across the floor.

Stacks of books. That's all we could see. Some of the shelves had been disturbed, and books lay strewn on the floor, but beyond that, we couldn't make out anything.

"Let's go in," Bianca said.

"No," I replied.

Bianca turned to glare at me. "Why the hell not?" she demanded. "Don't tell me you've come all this way just to get all scared. If you're a scaredy cat, doggo here will eat you."

"Don't be a bitch," Cuan said flatly.

"I'm not scared to go in there," I said. "I just don't see the point."

"And why the hell not?" Bianca demanded again.

"Because I remember coming up TWO floors. We've only gone down one," I said.

Bianca blinked. "Oh."

"Bitch," I added, and she smirked at me.

One more flight downward, and we were at the bottom of the stairwell.

"This is it," I said.

Cuan put a hand on my shoulder. "Are you ready?" he asked.

I swallowed hard, steeling myself. "Yeah," I said, pushing open the door.

As the red light spilled into the room, we all inhaled sharply.

"Ok, now *this* is interesting," Bianca said.

Where before we had been looking down a row of bookshelves, now we were looking into an open room. The book-shelves were still there, however; but many were overturned and others had been outright demolished. Books were scattered on the floor, some intact, many not.

Slowly, gingerly, we stepped through the doorway into the room, long, outstretched shadows slithering across the floor as Cedric's red globe of light followed him through the space.

We passed a long metal bookshelf that had survived some-what intact—due to being bolted to the ceiling and the floor—and all gasped.

"Holy shit," Bianca said quietly; "what happened to the wall?"

The opposite wall of the library basement was a gaping black hole. The building foundation was smashed through, leading to what was apparently a dried up and long-unused sewer.

That, however, was not what had captured my attention.

I stared, wide-eyed and gaping, at the opposite side of the room.

"Are those... cameras?" Cuan asked, looking in the same direction as I was.

That section of the room looked as though it had been the site of a bonfire. A bonfire that had exploded. And had been ransacked by wild animals. Not necessarily in that order. A circle had been drawn on the floor in chalk, or charcoal, or something of that nature. It looked red—but then, everything looked red in the current light. The circle was an intricate array of symbols, most of which were smudged out or scorched. Around it, like points on a compass, were the toppled and melted remains of tripods, three of which had cracked and smashed cameras still attached. The floor inside the circle was black, the center of a blast zone, with cracks running deep in the concrete. Up above, the ceiling was dark recessed lights crisscrossed with angry swaths of black.

My heart started pounding. This... this was familiar. Most familiar of all, however, was the center of the circle.

It had been there when I first woke up.

The blasted, charred remains of a wooden chair.

"What the hell happened here?" Cedric asked.

"These cameras have numbers on them," Bianca observed.

The voices around me grew more and more distant as I stared at that chair.

"Whatever happened, someone wanted to film it."

"This camera's melted to shit; there's no way we're getting the memory card out of this, if it's even still intact."

That chair. Something happened in that chair.

"Hey, this is camera number 1."

"This one over here is 3, but it's just as busted."

"4 is a lost cause."

"Where's 2?"

Something happened. To me.

"Cole, are you OK?"

"Perhaps whoever did this took 2 with them."

"Doubtful. The top of the tripod looks like it snapped off."

"Cole, hey, look at me."

The memory of fire pressed on my mind.

"Well then, if it snapped off, it must have flown... that way."

"Did the bookshelf fall on top of it?"

"Cole, say something."

Fire. Burning. Constraints.

"Nothing under here."

"What about this pile of books?"

"You're scaring me, Cole. C'mon, it's me, Cuan."

Then I saw it. On the one remaining intact arm of the chair, a fragment of rope.

"Wait, here; help me lift this metal desk; I see something."

"Cole, do you feel that? I'm squeezing your hand. Squeeze mine back, Cole."

Rope. A million images flashed through my mind, one after the other, none of them lasting long enough to catch, none of them making any sense. Just... burning. Struggling. The smell of sulfur. Fear.

"There, that's it; camera number 2."

"Can you reach it?"

"Cole, speak to me."

"Yeah, I got it. You can let go now."

"Come back to me, Cole."

"This one... the camera's busted, but the memory card's intact. Looks like the camera smashed but it was blown far enough away that it didn't melt."

"Cole."

I opened my mouth, my voice shaking, as images continued flashing through my head in a confused jumble. "I..."

"Cole."

I squeezed the hand in mine. "Cuan... I..."

"I'm here. It's OK; I'm with you."

Then a memory hit. Not an image, not a sound or a smell or anything tangible.

Just fear. Pure, abject terror. And with it, searing, unbearable pain.

And I screamed.

I screamed, a hollow, ringing, blood-curdling scream, rising up from somewhere deep inside me and tearing out through my entire being. My knees gave way, and I sunk, wide-eyed, still screaming, collapsing as I felt Cuan's arms wrap around me, holding me tightly and protectively, pressing the side of my head to his chest.

"I've got you; I'm here; you're safe," he kept repeating, quietly, intensely, as I screamed and screamed and screamed, screamed until I felt something crack in my throat and my voice went hoarse.

And the whole time, he held me.

Finally I stopped, shaking, still wide-eyed. I don't think I actually calmed down. I think I was just out of screams. I stared at the center of the circle, panting, clutching Cuan's arms around me in white-knuckled terror.

"Cole, what is it?" he asked urgently. "What happened?"

Static clouded my brain. I struggled, trying to grab onto a thought, failing. Finally I stretched out a shaking hand, still failing to catch my breath as I pointed at the ruined chair.

"I... there... that was... me."

I heard a thunk behind me as Bianca dropped a book she was holding and it thumped heavily to the ground. The red light wavered as Cedric's concentration faltered for a moment. Cuan's arms tightened around me.

"...Holy fucking shit," Bianca whispered.

"You... someone used you as the focus of a ritual?" Cedric asked, aghast. "What... what did they do?"

"I... I don't remember," I rasped.

"Well," Bianca said, "This explains everything and nothing at the same time."

"We need to get him out of here," Cuan said over my head. Then he looked down at me, and I felt his hand on my cheek. "It's OK, Cole," he said quietly. "We're gonna leave, OK? You don't have to—"

Suddenly he jerked his head up, alert, muscles tensing.

"What?" Cedric asked.

"We need to go," Cuan said firmly. "Now." He helped me struggle to my feet, his own urgency spurring me to action.

Then, we all heard it: a crash from somewhere down the sewer tunnel.

For a moment, we froze. The crashing grew louder. We had just turned to run when a piece of the concrete wall exploded inward, smashed by a giant iron ball on a chain. Dust, debris, wood splinters, and paper filled the air as we dove for cover. Cedric's light wavered but did not wink out as Cuan and I scrambled back to our feet behind an overturned bookshelf, trying to get our bearings.

"They're baaaack," I whispered in a sing-song voice.

"Well, someone seems to have recovered from their full-on meltdown," Cuan observed.

"Not as much as you'd think," I rasped, fighting back the static in my brain. "But yeah, being attacked by a giant spiked-ball-wielding monster does tend to bring some clarity."

"We need to get out of here," Cuan whispered urgently. He paused, listening intently for a moment, until the tell-tale sound of the chain retracting began. "That'll give us a few seconds," he said, standing up, "unless—"

He suddenly dodged backward as a leg from a tripod hurtled by in front of his face.

"—unless there are more of them," I finished for him.

The pattern of shadows on the floor began dancing across the room, telling me that our source of light—and thus Cedric—was on the move.

"Cuan!" came Cedric's voice. We turned to see him standing, cloak billowing around him, firing a bolt from his outstretched crossbow. "There are three of them. We cannot stay and fight down here; we are at a huge disadvantage in this tight space." He dodged quickly behind a pillar as part of a bookshelf flew into it and shattered.

"Did you have that crossbow with you the whole time?" I asked.

Cedric smirked from his cover. "I always have my crossbow with me."

"But where do you—" I started, then stopped short as a hulking creature came into view between us. It looked light-colored in the red light, so it must have been red or yellow itself. The ogre whirled and swung a heavy fist at Cedric, who ducked and rolled out of the way. The fist smashed into the pillar, splintering concrete everywhere.

"If we stay down here, they'll bring the library down on top of us," I realized.

Cuan nodded. "Plus, the entire place is like kindling ready to burn," he added.

"Which means most of my skill set would be just as dangerous to us as to them," Cedric added.

"Well, then, we'll need a different set of skills, won't we?"

Bianca was behind us, standing tall, a menacing expression on her face. She held a camera with a big '2' on it in one hand. She raised her free hand and black mist billowed about her, then suddenly coalesced into a cloud of smoky black bats. She flexed her fingers and the bats swarmed forward, screeching as they tore across the room toward the three ogres. I heard angry roars as the mist-formed creatures buffeted and harassed the hulking beasts, driving the yellow ogre backward and buying us a moment to catch our bearings.

"The stairwell is across the room on our left," Cuan noted.

"So that is where we will go," Cedric nodded. "We just have to get past these things."

"We shouldn't kill them," Bianca added. "They were human too, once."

"We do not have the leeway to subdue them," Cedric said. "We cannot fight well here."

"So can we run?" Cuan asked.

Bianca suddenly lowered her arm and dashed out of the way as the metal ball and chain flew across the room, blasting through the swarm of phantasmal bats and crashing into the far wall. Immediately it started to retract again.

"We can't get a clear run to the door," Bianca said. "There's too much debris in the way. The ogres won't let us near it."

I looked to the other end of the room, but to the right rather than the left. There were several rows of bookshelves, some intact, some not.

"Not without a distraction," I realized.

"Huh?" Bianca asked.

"Bianca, can you cover a run toward the door with that bat-mist of yours?" I asked.

"Sure, but the ogres can just toss things right through it, or fire that ball-thing," Bianca said.

"But only if that's where they're looking," I noted. "Cedric, can you send your little ball to dance in the other corner of the room, behind those bookshelves?"

"I suppose," Cedric said, "but the ogres will not pay it heed for very long if it is unaccompanied."

"Oh, it'll be accompanied," I said.

"Cole," Cuan looked at me with concern, "what are you thinking?"

"I'm thinking that it's about time I got noticed," I smirked.

"No way," Cuan said. "That's way too dangerous."

I grinned as Cuan's face, and the rest of the room, took on an afterimage quality. "Don't worry," I said, forcing the words through my lungs as I stepped backward through the book-shelf. "Whatever they throw at me will be... immaterial."

Cuan's alarmed visage disappeared as my head passed back through the shelf of books. I whirled around toward where the three ogres were in the middle of the room. The perhaps-yellow-perhaps-red one that had punched out the column was climbing back to its feet after apparently having tripped back-wards over an overturned bookshelf escaping the bats. The larger, hulking creature armed with the spiked-ball-and-chain had almost finished rewinding its arm-based weapon. The third ogre, which looked a darker hue in the red light, was not paying us much mind, though... instead it was hurriedly gath-ering up stacks of loose pages on the floor—to what end, I had no idea, but I wasn't about to wait around and find out.

Cedric's light began drifting toward the back right corner of the library. A moment later, there was a whoosh, and the left end of the library became a torrent of black mist. Predictably, the ogres turned their attention toward it. The large one raised its arm, but before it could fire, I shouted at the top of my lungs.

"Hey, Tweedle-dee, Tweedle-dum, and Tweedle-dipshit, it's time to COME. GET. SOME."

All three of the beasts turned toward me as I sprinted directly at them, at least as quickly as I could without being able to get purchase on the floor, doing my best to avoid passing directly through any furniture and give away the ruse. The benefit to being essentially weightless was that it allowed me to be quite acrobatic, and I vaulted a bookshelf and did a double somersault through the air as I spun toward the three creatures.

The large one and the yellow one predictably turned their attention to me, preparing to grab or swing or fire giant bone-crushing metal spheres. The darker ogre stepped away from me, greedily clutching its wad of pages to its chest. As I darted between the giant ogre and its yellow/red companion, Yellow lifted up another of the broken tripods off the ground and took a giant swing. I reached my hand down toward a bookshelf as I passed it and, just as I had done with the pavement back when I turned incorporeal after an ogre tossed me through a truck, I used the friction to alter my in-air trajectory, and my body slipped under the swing of the tripod. This not only preserved the illusion that I was a solid target, but there was the added unexpected benefit of the wild swing connecting with the large ogre's shoulder, which cracked loudly. The creature roared with fury as I touched off the ground and headed toward the right corner of the room, where Cedric's sphere of light was now dancing behind the bookshelves, casting complicated shifting shadows across the floor.

I leapt as the giant sphere crashed past me, blasting shelves apart and sending pages everywhere. Dust flew up in a giant cloud as I felt the unsettling feeling of chain and wood and paper pass through my body. I concentrated on the floor, using it to slow my momentum, then whirled around to peer at the three creatures from between the books on part of the shelf that remained.

"Missed me," I rasped in a mocking, sing-song voice. The tripod-wielding ogre roared with anger and started toward the stacks in mad bull-rush, and at the same time I heard the tell-tale click-clank as the metal spiked death sphere began retracting.

And I also heard a distant click as the emergency exit, obscured by the black mist, opened and shut.

Time to go.

Just as the yellow ogre crashed into the stacks, I leapt through a gap in the books in the shelf head-first, making a beeline for the corner of the room where I knew the exit was, behind the diminishing mist. The hulking creature looked at me in a moment's confusion, apparently unable to decide if I had truly just squeezed through a gap in the books or if I had actually passed through something solid. I vaulted like a human torpedo, continuing my head-first trajectory toward the exit. As the mist cleared I could see the door more clearly between the dancing shadows, and I reached down to use an overturned shelf as leverage to slightly course-correct. The action caused my body to rotate slightly, and as I blew past the darker ogre, which was still frantically gathering up pages, my eyes fell on a large piece of parchment in its hand.

The afterimages were still obscuring my vision, but one line of text at the top of the page was bold enough and dark enough that I could see it clearly as the light from the sphere shone across it for an instant.

'The Key of Solomon.'

Then the light from the sphere winked out, and I was in pitch darkness.

I continued my trajectory through the air for a moment, trusting that I had oriented myself correctly, and presently felt the unsettling sensation of solid metal and concrete as it passed through my body. An instant later, I was awash again in red light, this time of a new sphere, which illuminated the stairwell behind the closed emergency door. Cedric and Bianca were up on a higher landing already, but Cuan was waiting just outside the door. He gripped the beam of the banister at the base of the stairwell and reached his hand out to me. I reached for it immediately, desire to touch him causing the afterimages to overlap and coalesce. My hand clasped around his wrist as his closed on mine and he spun me, gripping me as I pivoted in the air, bracing my feet once on the opposite wall before getting purchase on the stairs. Cuan steadied me as I landed in a standing position and caught my balance two steps above him.

Without a word, I jerked my head upward, and we ran.

This was a familiar impression, escaping upward through the library while my head was in a fog. This time, however, I had direction and purpose. And a memory of the layout.

And I had to tell them what I'd seen. In words they could understand.

Desire to communicate, to be heard, combined with an awareness of place and the awareness that Cuan was with me. He was with me. And I had something to tell him. To tell all of them. I was the only one who could tell them.

Me.

Cole.

That's right, I realized; my name was Cole.

We sprinted up two flights and threw open the door to the lobby. By the time I was leaping down the three steps that I had previously faceplanted from, the world was crystal-clear. I vaulted over the opening gates alongside the others and we made for the slightly open door, then hurried down the steps and made the half-block run toward the park.

We stopped, panting, and Cuan turned to me, concern

written across his face. He reached out both of his hands. I took them.

"Hi, Cuan," I said.

His golden eyes widened as his jaw dropped.

"You... that's English," he said.

"That's right," I said.

"But... how...?"

"I have something you guys need to hear," I said, looking from Cedric to Bianca. Then I turned my attention back to Cuan. "And, I think, knowing that you're here to hear it is enough, now. You just being here is enough to bring me back."

Slowly, Cuan beamed.

"Pardon me whilst I vomit," Bianca said dryly, still clutching camera '2'.

I pointed to the spot in the park where Cuan had first identified my scent. "That's the designated puke point," I said. "Knock yourself out."

Bianca narrowed her eyes at me.

"What do you need to tell us, Cole?" Cedric asked.

"The Key of Solomon," I said.

They all looked at me. "What?" Cedric asked.

"That's what that third ogre was collecting," I said. "Scattered pages that read 'The Key of Solomon.'"

"Holy shit," Bianca muttered.

"So that is where the other half went to," Cedric said thoughtfully. "Of course. That makes perfect sense."

"Other half?" I asked.

"The Key of Solomon—the original version—exists in two parts that serve particular purposes: one for summoning, and one for binding. That must have been the summoning one."

"How do you know this?" I asked, but Cedric waved off my question.

"If the ogres are after the summoning half," Cedric continued, "then they must also be after the binding half... and that is at—"

"The Church of the Holy Guardian," I realized.

Cuan looked at me. "Do you think that's why the ogres were so fixated on the church before?"

"Most likely," Cedric nodded. "And if they tried once, they will probably try again."

"We need to go there," I said.

"Why?" Bianca asked. "The Order of Light are no friends of ours. They tried to *enslave* you. Those fuckers deserve whatever happens to them."

"Perhaps," Cedric said, "but the fact remains: if whoever is organizing those ogres is set on getting both halves of the Key of Solomon, then we must not let them succeed."

Cuan and I nodded in agreement.

"Bianca," Cedric said, turning to her. "Get that camera to The Hunters' Home. Once it is secure, you can come meet us." Then he turned to Cuan and me. "Boys," he said with a grim smile, "it is time for church."

VI

CAIN AND ABEL

CEDRIC, Cuan, and I hurried through the streets toward the Church of the Holy Guardian. It was too far to reach at an outright sprint, so instead we moved at a brisk walk. This suited Cedric well enough, as he was several strides ahead of us talking urgently into his phone, mobilizing Bran and Az.

As we hurried along, I noticed that Cuan was uncharacteristically silent.

"You OK?" I asked.

He shook his head. "Not really. I'm worried about you. You sure you're all right after all that happened in that library?"

"No," I admitted. The frayed memories that the sight of the destroyed chair had stirred still flickered like static in the back of my mind. "I'll need some time to process that. But right now, we've some obnoxious zealots to visit."

"Also...." Cuan stopped walking. I stopped too, a step ahead of him, and turned to look at him. He screwed up his face, like he was struggling to process his own thoughts. "It was hard for me to see you rush off alone to distract the ogres," he said at last. "I mean, I know you can handle yourself, but... I couldn't help worrying that something bad would happen, and I wouldn't be there to help you."

"I can understand that," I admitted with a sigh. "I mean, the last time we were apart for any length of time—"

"…you were enslaved into that box…"

"—and you'd been shot with wolf's-bane," I said, nodding. "Since then, I haven't really wanted to leave your side. I mean, being near you makes me feel safer and more confident, but part of me also worries about another terrible thing happening when you're next off fighting or patrolling. I've seen you fight off phantoms and ogres with ease, but when that shot of wolf's-bane came out of nowhere? I never want to feel that powerless to help you again. It's no surprise that you'd feel the same after what the church did to me."

Cuan stared at me for a moment. "I'm not used to having someone worry so much about my well-being," he said. He took a deep breath and looked wistfully toward the evening sky. "Part of me wants to keep you safely tucked away where nothing bad can happen to you. But then, I feel like that would just be enslaving you into a different kind of box. I don't want to do that to you."

"There's a difference between protecting someone as a partner and denying them their autonomy." I noted. "You've never once done the latter. I appreciate that. And I know everything that's happened has shaken us both. But Cuan…." I stepped forward and took both his hands in mine. He met my gaze, his golden eyes intense and clear. "If we're going to be with one another," I continued, "it should be because we *want* to be together, not because we're afraid to be apart."

"I want to be with you, Cole," he affirmed.

"I want to be with you, too," I said. "So let's be with one another." I leaned forward and kissed him deeply, and he returned my kiss with earnestness.

"And in those moments when we *do* have to be apart," I

added after we pulled away, "trust that feeling you had. Do you remember? What you told me when you were unconscious and I was trapped?"

Cuan nodded. "I still felt you," he said. He tapped his heart. "I felt you with me. A white flame, right here."

"So remember that," I said with a smile. "We're always together, even when we're not. OK?"

"OK," he smiled back, that adorable dimple forming in his cheek. "And for the record," he added, "what you did back there in the library? That was incredibly brave. It just proves once again that you're as much a Midnight Hunter as any of us. I'm proud of you, Cole."

I beamed at him.

Behind me, I heard a voice impatiently clearing its throat. I turned to see Cedric staring at us, arms crossed.

"Touching as this display of borderline co-dependency is," he said dryly, "we do have places to be."

We nodded, and then, still clasping hands, continued to hurry toward the church.

As we approached, it quickly became apparent that our instincts were correct: ogres were indeed swarming the church. The whole scenario felt distinctly familiar: it wasn't long ago that the Hunters had pursued ogres to the church on their first approach. At that time, Cuan and I had been making our first visit to Az's hotel room, and when we heard the news of the attack we didn't know what to expect or what their objective was. This time, we understood why they were so focused on the building. The Order, however, had no idea. In fact, I realized, they also likely had no idea I had escaped imprisonment.

They'd have expected that they were safe, protected by the shroud my enslavement provided. They'd have been completely unprepared.

The scene that greeted us on our arrival was one of disarray. There was no coordinated defense of the church's primary entrances, no clear stations covered by the members of the Order. Instead, there was a lot of running and shouting as ogres attacked the walls from every angle.

"I will take the front of the church," Cedric said hurriedly. "Cuan, you take care of those in front of us," he added, pointing to where a large blue ogre and its purple companion were confronting someone who barred their access to the churchyard wall. "Cole," Cedric added, turning to me, "act at your own discretion. Only be noticed if you wish to be."

I nodded. Cedric peeled off to the right. Ahead of us, a blue ogre and a violet ogre were attempting to make headway toward the church. Cuan rushed forward, and I followed as best I could. Cuan leapt up and, spinning in the air, kicked the blue ogre in the back of the head. It stumbled forward and to the left with a surprise grunt, giving me a clear view toward the churchyard wall. Any question I had as to who had been holding them off was immediately answered when I saw the flashing chain that whirled through the air and burst with flame.

Thomas.

Alexander's older brother by a year or two, Thomas was one of the few members of the Order of Light who had treated me not just with respect but with genuine kindness. While he usually wore a serious expression, his current one was a mask of determination, as he stood his ground in an odd combination of black button-down and white jeans, swinging his chain whip Prominence through the air in front of him. Whenever the chain approached the ogres it would erupt in a tongue of flame—thus its name—and the display was, at least for the moment, succeeding at keeping the ogres at whip's length.

Thomas's eyes lit up at the sight of Cuan knocking the blue ogre aside.

"Reinforcements!" he cried. "Thanks be to God. I know the Order and you Hunters aren't always on the best of terms, but you always come through when it counts." At his expression I felt, not for the first time, a pang of familiarity. I didn't have much time to contemplate that feeling, however, as the blue ogre was quickly recovering and the violet ogre charged at Thomas.

As usual, no one paid me any heed; Cuan was, I suspected, the only one who even realized I was there. He made no move to draw attention to me, however, and so I remained incognito. Cuan didn't say anything to Thomas, either, just looked coldly at him and continued to fight back against his blue assailant. Thomas, seeing Cuan's response, made no move to continue conversation, instead turning to the violet ogre. He did, however, offer one additional instruction.

"Try not to hurt them too badly," he said as he dodged a punch and swung Prominence over his head. "They're human, too, don't forget." He whipped Prominence forward and the chain sprung to fiery life, the violet ogre roaring as it hovered just out of the whip's range.

"I know that," Cuan said as he landed a kick in the blue ogre's solar plexus, sending it staggering back. "Let's just knock them out if we can."

"And then what?" Thomas asked.

"One of the Hunters is working on a cure," Cuan responded.

"And what, you guys are keeping the ogres you subdue somewhere safe while you're working on curing them?"

"Something like that."

Thomas whipped Prominence again as he considered this. "Well, don't tell Father," he said. "He'll think you're amassing an army." He paused. "You're not amassing an army, are you?"

"What do we need an army for?" Cuan asked, flexing his fingers. "I *am* an army."

"OK," Thomas nodded, "you get points for that. That was a pretty cool line."

The blue ogre lunged at Cuan and he vaulted upward over it, spinning in the air and thwacking the creature on the back of the head with his hand. The creature stumbled forward toward Thomas, who swung out with Prominence and lashed the ogre across the chest. The ogre recoiled and roared, but then regained its balance and rounded back on Cuan, charging him again.

Thomas continued swinging his whip overhead, turning his body as he prepared to lash at the violet ogre. The violet creature, however, sensed an opening and lunged. Thomas switched his footing and leapt backward, but his dodge was awkward due to Prominence's momentum, and the ogre managed to thwack Thomas's wrist. The impact loosed his grip on Prominence, which flew through the air carried by its own weight—directly at me.

"Crud!" Thomas cried, watching the whip flutter away from him.

I watched the whip's trajectory as it hurtled toward me. It was as good a time as any to let my presence be known, I supposed. I ducked sideways as the spiked ball topping the whip flew by me, then reached out and caught Prominence by the handle as it sailed past.

The instant my hand closed around the whip, I understood what Alexander had meant when he said that the Order's divine weapons had wills of their own. Because I felt it: I felt Prominence make a decision. The weapon seemed to gauge me, feeling me out from the inside. Alexander had said that the weapons bonded with their users, choosing them as much as being chosen.

I felt Prominence make its evaluation. It was committed to its bond with Thomas, and would not therefore bond with me (not that I wanted it to, anyway), but it recognized something in me that it seemed to acknowledge, and so consented to allow me to wield it. A white gleam ran down the chain as the whip granted me provisional permission to brandish it, and I immediately whirled it overhead. It sailed smoothly through the air, guiding me as much as I guided it, and I snapped my wrist forward, lashing out at the violet ogre's knee. The chain wrapped tightly around the creature's leg, singing with white light as it did so, and I pulled sideways just as the monster pivoted on its foot to see what had ensnared it. My yank caused its knee to buckle, sending it crashing to the pavement. It smacked its forehead on the ground with enough force that I winced, and then lay still, knocked unconscious.

Thomas looked wide-eyed as the creature fell in front of him, but his eyes widened even further as he followed the chain of Prominence from the ogre's leg to my hand. I flicked my wrist again and Prominence loosed from the creature, then pulled back and the whip neatly coiled in my hand. Thomas looked into my eyes, his own brown eyes shining under his brown hair, his expression one of shock as I walked up to him and held Prominence out.

"I think you dropped this," I said.

"Cole!" he exclaimed, his face suddenly breaking into an expression of pure joy. He leapt at me and, instead of taking Prominence, embraced me tightly. "Where have you been?" he asked. "I've been so worried."

Something compelled me to hug him back, and then I released him and looked searchingly into his face.

"You don't know?" Cuan asked from behind me, having disabled his blue-skinned assailant. His expression was suddenly a lot less cold.

Thomas shook his head, then looked back at me. "I haven't seen you since you went with my brother to investigate the underground. Nobody would tell me what happened to you."

I looked at him searchingly. His expression was so genuine that I had no doubt he was telling the truth.

"You... you really don't know," I realized.

"Alexander refused to speak on it, but he seemed... kind of broken, after that day. I thought maybe you'd been hurt, or kidnapped, or..." his voice trailed off.

I sighed. "You don't know the half of it," I said.

Just then, a crash reverberated down the street from around the corner of the church.

"Well, we don't have time for you to tell me about it now," Thomas said, looking in the direction of the sound as he took Prominence from my outstretched hand. "But Cole, I'm glad you're back," he added with a smile.

His smile.

It was a big, genuine smile. I had talked to Thomas on several occasions, but this was the first time I'd seen him smile so fully. It was a handsome smile, lopsided, and as it stretched across his face a dimple formed in his cheek.

Recognition hit. Hard. I knew that smile.

That smile was right next to me.

That was Cuan's smile.

I looked from one of them to the other, wide-eyed. Now, with them standing together, the resemblance was uncanny. Their eyes were different, but that mouth... that was Cuan's mouth.

"You... you look so much alike," I muttered, and Cuan and Thomas turned to one another in surprise.

The same instant, there was another crash, and suddenly Paul rocketed between us, propelled backward through the air, holding a large shield protectively in front of his tall body. He clamped his feet down onto the pavement and took several steps backward before he managed to stop himself.

"Phew," he said, shaking his head. "That was quite a blow." He looked to Cuan and Thomas, then back down the street where he had come from.

"Come on," he said; "I need your help!"

He ran, and we all ran with him.

"So… that's quite a shield," Cuan remarked as we ran.

"This is Conviction," he said as we sprinted, holding up the large, kite-shaped shield. White metal bordered a surface polished so finely that it looked like the face of a mirror. "It reflects and returns momentum. Basically, it is ill suited for offense, but as a defensive weapon it is fantastically useful. However, it clearly has limits as to how much it can absorb," he added, looking ahead of him to where a giant spiked sphere lay embedded in the side of a building and a red ogre was struggling to retract it from the wreckage. Clearly Paul had blocked the firing sphere, sending it careening across the street and into the distant building, while the impact had sent him flying down the street in the opposite direction.

That ogre seemed to be out of commission, what with its giant spiked sphere entangled in the twisted metal of the building. Two other ogres had stepped up to cover its position, however, one green and bristling with muscle, the other orange and brandishing what looked to be a street sign. They were attempting to clamber over the wall to the church when suddenly a black streak passed through the air in front of them, driving them back. The streak smacked into the stone wall, and I was able to make out a sword, blade glistening with black bile, embedded in the wall. A moment later, a suited figure alighted on the top of the wall, and the sword dissolved into a beam of black light before reforming in the figure's hand.

"Az!" I exclaimed, running toward him.

"Wait, Cole?" Paul remarked, looking at me in confusion.

"Yeah," Thomas cried. "He's OK; isn't that fantastic?"

Paul opened his mouth to say something, but there was a roar, and suddenly the orange ogre brandishing a street sign at him demanded most of his attention. He swiftly pivoted toward it, bringing the large shield in front to protect himself. The street sign collided with the shield face, and Conviction erupted with a flash of light. The sign jerked backward like a rubber ball, the sudden rebound wrenching the ogre's arm, which bent unnaturally at the elbow as the sign yanked it back. The beast howled in pain as it released the sign, the residual momentum carrying the metal pole a short distance through the air before it clattered to the pavement.

The green ogre, meanwhile, rushed Az, who leapt over its head, swiping at the beast's shoulder with his blade. The cut was just a graze, and I understood that it was intentional: Quietus was the blade of death, after all, and the black gall dripping from its blade was a powerful poison that could kill in even small quantities. A scratch like the one that Az inflicted would, at the very least, debilitate within minutes.

We heard a crash as another ogre arrived on the scene, this one also green and angry and roaring. Thomas and Cuan moved to intercept it, but as they did so, Thomas shouted and pointed. I looked in the direction he indicated to see the red ogre changing its position, its spiked ball loosening slightly from the wreckage of the building.

"On it," I said, sprinting between the angry green ogres toward the red hulking beast.

"Hey, Thunderbolt Ross, wanna play?" I shouted at the red beast. It turned toward me, roaring as its eyes focused on me. It flailed at me with both its arms, its chain unwinding in the process. I jumped backward, letting the world fade into after-images as I did so. The creature ran at me, and I ducked around a large concrete-reinforced steel lamppost as the creature followed me around it. I turned to face the beast, plugging my thumbs into my cheeks and giving it my best finger-wagging "nyah, nyah" as I backpedaled, feeling the taut chain pass through my legs as I moved.

The ogre followed me in single-minded rage. It took two steps before tumbling over its own chain, collapsing face-first into the pavement and knocking itself unconscious. The orange creature, seeing this occur, roared and followed me, still cradling its injured arm.

"Come on; it can't be this easy," I mocked, stepping in front of the fallen red ogre as the orange one ran at me. The creature reared up and swung its good arm at me, its fist passing clear through my body, the momentum carrying it forward as it tripped over its red brethren and the chain it lay on, collapsing on top of it. As I walked back toward the church, I saw a large purple beast with another ball-and-chain far down the street, heading toward the front door of the church.

The afterimages congealed into fog as the road grew solid beneath my feet. I concentrated on the message I had to convey, fighting back the nausea that pressed against my mind.

That's right; I told myself, the key isn't just having something to say: the key is having someone to say something *to*.

"Cuan," I called firmly, as the world came into crystal clear focus around me. "More ogres that way." I pointed in the direction the purple ogre was running. "We need to help."

One somersaulting leap and Cuan was at my side. "Right," he nodded. "Let's go."

One of the green beasts reared up at us, but Paul intercepted it, blocking a swinging fist with his shield.

"Thomas, go with them," he shouted. "This Az person and I can handle things here." He looked toward Az. "If that's all right with you, I mean."

Az nodded. He swiped his sword at another ogre, then he looked over at me.

"You seem to have a handle on your abilities," he said.

I nodded. "I'm getting there," I agreed. "Though... I don't think I'll be able to manage fading again tonight."

"Well then, I'll make sure you don't need to," Cuan said, taking my hand in both a gesture of reassurance and to hurry me along. "Let's go."

As we ran, we passed Bran and Rebecca, who were fending off another assault on the church's walls.

"Are you OK?" Thomas called to Rebecca as we ran.

"Yes, thanks to this visitor here," she said, nodding appreciatively to Bran. She was holding a long staff that glowed white at both ends. As an ogre ran toward her, she held the staff aloft, and a beam of light shot from of the top crystal and traced a shape on the ground, which then burst with bright light. The ogre skidded to a stop in front of it, roaring.

"Nice," Bran said appreciatively.

"It would be a lot easier if Julia were still here with us," Rebecca said to Thomas, "but we have things under control here. It's the front of the church that needs you."

Thomas nodded and we ran on. Rebecca wasn't wrong: the front of the church looked like a war zone.

As before, the front entrance was being defended by Levi and Alexander. However, in this case, they had the added support of Cedric and Bianca. There were five ogres assaulting the entrance, one of which had a single large spiked ball mounted on its right arm, and another of which had two large round spheres where its hands should be. These, too, fired on chains, which then retracted.

They weren't favorable odds, but nonetheless the group would likely have been having much less difficulty if Levi didn't seem as interested in targeting Cedric and Bianca as he did the ogres. He hefted his long-handled hammer Perdition in two large black gauntlets that looked like welding gloves. The handle of the hammer steamed and smoked slightly as he swung it, which he seemed to be doing with blind rage. Cedric was unable to level a shot at the ogres without interruption, though to his credit he also managed to refrain from turning around and shooting Levi in the leg. Or neck.

"We're here!" Thomas cried out as we approached, and Alexander looked up with a relieved expression on his face.

"Thank God, a friendly face!" he cried.

"Don't get too excited; we're not *that* friendly," Cuan growled as we followed behind Thomas. Alexander turned to see Cuan's face and his expression registered a hint of trepidation. Thomas glanced between them questioningly, but the roar of the large ogre with the two spheres drew their attention. Immediately the two spheres fired toward the front of the church, one after the other; Alexander leapt out of the way as one smashed into the side of the front gate, sending stone debris everywhere; the other sphere flew between Levi and Cedric and smashed into the front door of the sanctuary, causing wood to fly and splinter. An instant later and the spheres began to retract. Quickly.

Cedric levelled his crossbow at the ogre now that he had an opening, but again he had to duck out of the way of Levi's hammer swing and the bolt flew at an errant angle.

"What are you doing!?" he demanded of Levi. "I am trying to help you!"

"I will not abide your lies, heretic!" Levi roared, swinging wildly again.

Bianca and Alexander were each occupied with one of the smaller ogres, leaving one more for Thomas to intercept. Black misty bats and white flashes of Alexander's blade Candela were joined with flares from Prominence as the three deftly held back the assault on the church door.

"That leaves the big guys," Cuan said quietly to me.

"What's the plan?" I whispered back.

"Simple," Cuan said. "Two ogres; three balls on leashes. Time to get some wires crossed."

I nodded, understanding. "What can I do?" I asked.

"Find something that'll make a lot of noise when you throw it. Just be careful."

I nodded again. "I've faded a lot today. I don't think I can shift again without exhausting myself."

Cuan smiled that half-smile of his. "Thankfully," he said, "I can."

He threw his head back and howled, a deep, sonorous howl that saturated the air and reverberated through the streets. As he did so, his whole body became suffused with light, his muscles swelling and changing, his feet and face elongating, his body stretching his vest and filling his Wushu pants. Light poured out a sewn flap in the back of the pants and took the shape of a tail, and his hair lengthened into a fluffy mane. When the light faded, Cuan had taken on the form of a lithe, gray werewolf, red mane running between his ears and down the back of his neck. This was Cuan ready to fight: all of his senses were sharpened, his sympathetic nervous system in full control. There would be no sarcastic quips or wry flirting while Cuan was in this shape, even if he were able to form human words with his muzzle. Though he remained in full control of his faculties, until he reverted to his more familiar shape all of those faculties would be solely focused on a single goal: disabling all threats to the survival of himself and the others around him.

"Wh... what... *what*...."

I turned to see Thomas, wide-eyed and shaking, staring at Cuan with an open mouth. He looked on the verge of a full-on panic attack. I realized then that Thomas had never seen Cuan shift before.

"What is wrong with you? Pull yourself together!" Levi screamed at him.

The ogre that Thomas had been holding off took the opportunity to swing at him, but Alexander intercepted it, the blade of his shortsword Candela flashing white with such brilliance that the ogre, dazzled, lost its balance and stumbled forward. Thomas continued shaking, staring at Cuan, barely aware of what had just happened near him.

"Hey, Thomas, stay with me," Alexander said urgently, taking Thomas's arm. Thomas turned to him, stammering.

"But... Cuan... he..."

"I know," Alexander said. "But it's OK. He's here to help us, all right? Don't be afraid of him."

"But..."

"I need you to be my strong big brother," he said, turning back over his shoulder as two ogres began approaching. "There will be time to freak out later. But Cuan isn't the enemy—"

"The hell he isn't!" Levi shouted, taking another swing at Cedric.

"Cuan *isn't the enemy*," Alexander insisted. "The ogres are the enemy. And we have to stop them. Can you do that?"

Thomas nodded, taking a deep breath. I saw him swing his whip up over his head, but I couldn't afford to pay attention to him any longer. Cuan was darting in front of the two ogres that had massive metal firing mechanisms instead of hands, and was goading them into aiming at him instead of the church. I started looking for something that would make a lot of noise when thrown, and found a slightly bent license plate on the curb that had dislodged itself from a parked car.

Perfect. I picked up my find and waited.

The red-skinned ogre with the two smaller steel balls for fists took aim at Cuan and fired one, which Cuan neatly leapt over as it rocketed across the street and embedded itself in an already-shattered storefront window. Cuan pivoted and dashed toward the spiked-ball blue-skinned ogre, then suddenly changed direction as the huge spiked ball went careening past him and into a parked car at the side of the road, thankfully missing the fuel tank.

Another dodge and another leap, and the second steel ball fired, missing its mark.

The trajectories of the three spheres had caused their chains to cross one another, just as Cuan had planned. If the ogres weren't careful, they'd have a problem. So, then, the key was to make sure they weren't careful.

Cuan barked at me and jerked his muzzle toward the red-skinned ogre, and then immediately leapt at the blue creature as it started to retract its chain. The creature had a free hand and swung at Cuan, but Cuan nimbly ducked under the swing, slid between the creature's legs, and then stood behind it. The creature whirled around to face him, still retracting the chain behind it.

Meanwhile, I hurried around the edge of the street and hurled my license plate toward the red ogre like a bent Frisbee. It clattered to the ground behind the ogre, and the creature turned in alarm, starting to attract its own spheres at a frightening pace.

It took only seconds before the spheres all collided, the force and irregular shape of the larger spiked ball causing the smaller steel orbs to ricochet at strange angles, making them wrap themselves around the larger ball's taut chain. As the retraction continued, the chains pulled themselves into a tight knot, the sudden resistance causing the red ogre to stumble backward, its body being pulled slightly toward its blue-hued compatriot before all of the retracting ground to a halt. The creatures roared, turning their attention to one another and to the tangle that connected them. They were, for all intents and purposes, out of the fight.

The corner of Cuan's jowl curled upward as he shot me a little grin, but the celebration was short-lived. We heard a shout and turned back toward the church.

While Thomas, Bianca, and Alexander were occupied with their respective ogres, a fourth one, nimble and yellow-skinned, had appeared and charged right past them all, heading straight for the broken sanctuary doors.

"Stop the runner!" Alexander shouted.

Cuan and I sprinted toward the church, but I knew that even Cuan wouldn't be able to make it in time.

"I have him!" Cedric called, raising his crossbow at the ogre. Just as he was about to fire, however, Levi's hammer connected with the center of his back with a crack. Black smoke billowed out of Cedric's cloak as the impact knocked him through the air, his crossbow shot going wide and glancing off of the stonework as the ogre burst through the sanctuary doors.

"*CEDRIC!*" Bianca screamed.

"I'm fine," he croaked, standing up, the back of his cloak black and singed. He did, indeed, look perfectly fine. How the hammer hadn't broken every bone in his body, I had no idea. Apparently neither did Levi, who looked genuinely surprised at Cedric's recovery.

"What the fuck is wrong with you?" Bianca shouted, mist billowing around her, but the ogre in front of her swung out, again demanding her attention.

"You don't pack the punch you think you do," Cedric said with a dark grin. "Now stand down... we're trying to *help* you."

"You can't deceive me with your lies," Levi declared.

"That. Is. *Enough*," Cedric growled, striding toward Levi. Levi lifted his hammer again for a second mighty swing, but Cedric threw his hand out in front of him and snapped his fingers before Levi's face. There was a bright orange flash and Levi staggered backward, dropping the hammer, clutching at his face and screaming.

"MY EYES!!" he shrieked. "YOU'VE BLINDED ME!"

"It's just a flash of light," Cedric said impatiently. "Get over yourself." He turned to the rest of us and shouted, "We must stop that ogre; it is after the Key of Solomon."

"The Key of Solomon?" Thomas asked as he tried to put distance between himself and the ogre that was assailing him. His voice was laced with confusion. "What are you talking about?"

There were crashing noises from inside the sanctuary. One of the tall stained-glass windows shattered, shards of colored glass cascading down across the churchyard like glistening rain.

Cuan vaulted over the ogre that Bianca had been fighting and continued his run toward the broken sanctuary door, but just as he was approaching the door the ogre burst back through, a sheaf of papers clutched in its arms. It barreled forward like a huge ugly linebacker, and Cuan dodged out of the way to avoid being trampled. He pivoted on his foot and prepared to pursue the creature as Cedric levelled his crossbow, but before anyone could strike, the air was filled with the sounds of gunfire, and we all ducked for cover. Peering over the side of a parked car, I saw Father Jacob in the sanctuary's shattered doorway, firing what looked like a semiautomatic pistol again and again at the retreating ogre. Some shots ricocheted across the street, but several bullets embedded themselves in the ogre's back, who continued sprinting away without even being slowed. As I watched it flee, I remembered Julia's telling me once that the Order didn't bother with firearms because supernaturally effective bullets were inefficient and costly to prepare. These clearly hadn't been prepared.

Father Jacob roared with rage, continuing to click his emptied gun as the ogre vanished down the streets. As soon as it was out of sight, the other ogres disengaged and similarly retreated. Even the two monstrous creatures we had left tangled together headed solemnly away, dragging their chains between them like Jacob Marley after visiting Scrooge.

"Why are you shooting a gun?" Cedric demanded, whirling on the priest. "We would have stopped that creature if not for you and your son."

"Do not try to deceive me with lies, heretic," Jacob growled. "Look at what has happened to our church! This place *should* have been shrouded and safe. The only way these creatures could have found it is if you led them here."

"Are you hearing yourself?" Cedric growled back. "If your church were shrouded and secure, how would I have found it?"

"You must have the Adversary's own power," Jacob scowled.

"You're right, Father," Levi said, still blinking as his vision returned. "Even Perdition left barely a mark."

"Either you or that hammer seems to lack the conviction you assume," Cedric said to him. "And if either of you truly believe that I brought the ogres to your doorstep only to stay with my fellow Hunters and try to hold them off, then you are an even further divorced from reality than I thought."

"That was obviously a ploy to shroud your true intentions," Jacob said. "What other explanation could there possibly be for why these beasts are again assailing our doorstep?"

"I can think of one," I announced, stepping forward across the street next to Cuan, who, in a shroud of light, reverted to his familiar human form.

Levi blinked at me in shock, rubbing his eyes as though he couldn't trust what he was seeing. Jacob, meanwhile, looked fully taken aback.

"What are you doing here?" he shouted in fury. "How are you free?"

"Wait... free?" Thomas asked in confusion.

"Alexander," Jacob accused, ignoring Thomas. "Did you do this? Did you release him and doom us all?"

"How could I have?" Alexander protested. "You haven't let me anywhere near the back of the sanctuary since."

"Then who...?" Jacob began, then suddenly his face darkened. "Julia," he realized. "That explains her desertion. But... how did Julia know?"

"How did Julia know what?" Thomas asked, confusion giving way to agitation.

"That Father had ensnared Cole and was keeping him in the back of the sanctuary, leveraging his powers as a human magical shroud," Alexander said darkly.

"That boy is no human," Levi insisted.

"Says the one who conspired to trap him there by poisoning Cuan and using the antidote as bait," Alexander spat.

"Wait, you did *what* now?" Thomas asked, disbelief and anger flashing across his face. He whirled on his father. "You orchestrated this? And Julia knew about it?" he demanded.

"She shouldn't have had any idea," Jacob said. "We were careful. So," he added, turning to Alexander, "how did she know?"

"I told her," Alexander replied defiantly. "I was ashamed—*am* ashamed—that I stood aside and allowed you to do such a thing. So I told her. She is strong enough to do the things I can't, even when I should."

"And so she betrayed the Order, stole from us, and released our best hope at remaining safe and secure in a world increasingly in the grip of evil," Jacob declared. "Look at what your decision has wrought: the loss of security of our home, untold damage to the sanctuary we are sworn to protect, destruction of numerous relics, the theft of an important holy text. When you first brought Cole here and we learned of his abilities, I thought that perhaps you had finally brought us our salvation. But no: you have failed. You are a failure as a member of the Order of Light, as a member of the church, and as a member of this family. It was a mistake to raise you. You are undeserving of the name Lucent. I should have turned you out like any other wretch."

Alexander's face turned ashen.

"How can you say that about your own son?" Bianca asked, bristling with anger. "That's your flesh and blood."

"That disappointment is not my son," Jacob said. "And, mercifully, neither my flesh nor my blood."

Alexander stared, Candela clattering to the pavement. "But... I...." he stammered.

"You're not making any sense," Thomas protested. "I know I have a younger brother. You said Mother died when—"

"Indeed," Jacob said. He pointed with the empty gun toward Cuan. "Meet Cain Lucent, my seventh son, and the one responsible for your mother's death."

As soon as the words were out of his mouth, the world seemed to come undone. Cuan, Thomas, Alexander, Bianca, and I gaped in shock, staring from one of us to the other. I noticed, however, that this did not seem like news to the others present.

"I... me?" Cuan stammered. "How...?"

"The moment you were born and I saw that red hair and those yellow eyes of yours, I knew the curse was true," Jacob said, his voice dark and flat. "The seventh son of a seventh son, damned at birth to assume the shape of a wolf. I should have killed you right there and then, but your mother begged me to give you a chance at life. So I did, but I named you Cain because I knew from the beginning that you were a curse on this family. Sure enough, that very evening our church was assailed by a pair of phantoms we had been hunting. Reuben insisted that they had come to retrieve an emerald I had taken from their grave, but I knew they were summoned by the cursed child your mother had just brought into the world. My Rachel was still too weak to move, never mind fight, thanks to the difficult labor that you inflicted on her, Cain. We managed to distract one of the phantoms, but the other overpowered your mother and the two who had stayed to protect her, a young couple who had only recently become parents them-selves—parents a frail little blond boy. They were no match for the phantom, and when I returned to find my wife dead and the couple dying, they begged me to see that their child was looked after. Their one wish was that I keep their child's name; it was a family name." He looked at Alexander. "That was why you kept your pagan name of Alexander. I had wanted to change your name to Abel, because I saw in you a chance at having a redeemed son instead of the cursed progeny my wife had birthed. But I'm glad I didn't waste such a name on one who would turn out like you. I tried to raise you both together, but soon enough it became clear that the curse was indeed real, and Cain would sometimes take on that devilish animal form at night. So I eventually removed him from our church, and moved Alexander into his bed. I had instructed Clement to dispose of the monster, to bury him in the woods under a cross. I thought it a suitable test of his faith. I thought he had succeeded. Clearly he failed. I should have sent Levi."

We stared.

"So Cuan had nothing to do with your wife dying," Bianca insisted.

"Mother would have been able to defend herself if she hadn't just given birth," Levi insisted.

"And how is that Cuan's fault?" Bianca insisted.

"I... I was supposed to be buried?" Cuan stammered. He looked to Cedric. "But... how...?"

"A woman from an orphanage I was... associated with approached me one day," Cedric said. "She told me that a young church lad had brought an unusual child to her. She described the hair and the eyes and told me that the lad said he sometimes had fur. I knew what you were immediately. So I agreed to take you and raise you. But that name... Cain. What parent would choose that name for their child? So I renamed you Cuan. While I suspected at the time what family you had come from, I had no way of knowing for sure, so I likewise invented your surname, Ingolf."

Thomas stared at Cuan, slack-jawed.

"It was you," he said, and suddenly I knew what he was talking about. "All those years, the nightmares that there was a beast in the bed next to mine... the fears that Alexander was a monster..."

"Nope," Levi said, glaring at Cuan. "That's the monster."

I winced on Cuan's behalf, but Cuan glared back, standing tall.

"I'm not a monster," he stated.

"You're right; you're not," Thomas nodded. "You're my brother." He whirled on his father. "But you... You've told me all these years that I was out of my mind! That I imagined it all, that I was crazy, that I just had those nightmares because I wasn't strong enough!" He was almost shouting, the accusation pouring from his lips. "All these years... why did you tell me for all these years that I was weak?"

"Because it's true." Jacob's voice was cold as stone.

"Yeah, well, we'll see about that," he said, coiling Prominence in his hand. "If Clement could see you now..."

"Clement was weak too," Jacob said sternly.

"Clement was not weak," Thomas declared. "He was one of the only truly good brothers I ever had." He rounded on Alexander, fists clenched and shaking. "And I thought *you* were, too," he said. "But you... you were complicit in this? In basically enslaving Cole?"

"It was a mistake," Alexander said.

"I'll say it was," Thomas nodded angrily. "You cared about him. He trusted you. I mean, you two were..." he trailed off.

"Were what?" Levi asked.

"We were *fucking*," Alexander declared angrily. "Yeah. Right here in the Church. And I liked it. Because it was *good*. Yeah," he nodded, "it was really good. And I should know; I've had a lot of guys to compare him with. Cole is *good*."

"Preach," Cuan said, and I elbowed him in the ribs.

"But I threw all that away," Alexander added. "I tossed it away, all because I couldn't stand up to my father."

"All for Father," Thomas muttered. "I think I'm gonna be sick."

"Yeah, go be sick, then," Levi spat. "Sick and weak."

"Not weak," Thomas said, "disgusted. I can't look at any of you right now. I stayed because I believe in the Order of Light—the proper Order, that actually embraces the compassion of Christ—and its mission of protecting people. But we, here, haven't done that for a while. No," he clarified, shaking his head, "why I really stayed was because I thought Alexander needed me. Well, look at all the good this family did him." He turned and stormed away.

"Thomas, wait—" Alexander began.

"No," he said, rounding on him. "*No.*" He took a deep breath, and the look he gave Alexander was softer, but still filled with anger and disappointment. "Blood or not, you'll always be my family. But it's gonna be a while before I can call you my brother again." He stalked off, toward what I knew was another entrance to the church, close to his rooms.

"You see what your actions have wrought?" Jacob admonished angrily, glaring at Alexander. "Your decisions are tearing this family apart. First you threaten the safety of this house and drive Julia away, and now Thomas."

"No," Alexander said firmly. "No. *Fuck* that."

"Language!" Jacob declared.

"Language?" Alexander scoffed. "You want language? Well, how about this: you're a piece of shit father with a fucked up concept of God and religion. I can't believe I spent over two decades of my life seeking your approval. The only thing I've earned from you is poor self-esteem and first-hand knowledge of the fucking hypocritical morals that make up this cesspool of manipulation you call a church." He bent down and picked Candela back up. "The only good thing to come out of tonight is knowing that none of you are actually my family." His eyes widened. "So," he added. "Who *is* my family? Who were those people who were a part of the Order?"

Jacob scoffed. "Do you think I'd tell you something like that after the way you just spoke to me?"

I gasped. It all made sense. Pieces were suddenly falling into place. I remembered the estate Alexander had taken me to, how the church had asserted a claim to it after its owners died when Alexander was an infant.

"Alexander," I realized, "you're the missing heir."

"Be *silent!*" Jacob cried.

Alexander's eyes widened further. "Holy shit," he said. "It's true, isn't it? That's why you really raised me as your own, because you want the estate and everything my parents developed. You've been *keeping* that from me."

"No," Jacob said, "if you were a part of my family, and I controlled the estate, then you could still benefit from it."

"So it *is* true," Alexander glared. "You fucking piece of shit."

"You will not speak to your father that way," Levi said menacingly, hefting Perdition in his gauntleted hands.

"Good thing he's not my father, then," Alexander spat, holding Candela in front of him. Suddenly, the blade flashed white, and Levi staggered back, roaring again, dropping Perdition once more as he clutched at his eyes.

"Shit," Jacob muttered, scrabbling in his pockets.

But by the time Levi could see again, Alexander was gone, having run off toward the rear of the church.

"He will pay for that," Levi growled menacingly. "You all will."

"Oh, fuck off," Bianca shouted dismissively, giving Levi a withering look. "You've been less than useless this whole time. You blame Alexander for what happened tonight? You and your pathetic insistence on attacking us are the only reasons why anything was able to get by us in the first place. You're less than useless, a pathetic sack of shit, your asshole father's shill. Why don't you take that fetid rusty tool of yours and get out of here?"

Levi glared at her. "Don't speak about Perdition that way."

"I wasn't," Bianca snarled. "I was talking about your pathetic excuse for a dick."

Levi scoffed. "And how would you know? When have you seen my dick?"

"Well I assume it's hanging in front of your sickening ass," Bianca replied, then recoiled in mock surprise. "Oh, wait, I thought that was your ass, but it's just your face."

"I—"

"*ASS. FACE.*" Bianca snarled.

"I don't have to stand for this," Levi spat.

"You shouldn't. Normally one shits sitting down."

"That is *enough*," Jacob declared, and I heard a menacing click as another clip of ammunition locked into place in his handgun. "We are done here. You have five seconds to leave."

He wasn't going to give us five seconds. We all knew it. Bianca raised her arms and immediately a swarm of black, misty bats rose from the pavement, flying skyward in a wall of solid smoke. We dashed away, the sound of Jacob shooting into the solid mist fading into the distance behind us.

VII

THE FAMILY WE CHOOSE

THE WALK BACK TO THE HUNTERS' Home was an uncomfortably quiet one. Cedric and Bianca were visibly seething, and Cuan was sullen and withdrawn. Az had returned to his hotel after the ogre assault ended, and Cedric didn't seem in a hurry to catch him up on the evening's events. Bran, however, met us on the way back home and could tell immediately that something was up. When he asked what happened, however, he was met with stony silence.

As the city had become more and more abandoned, we had begun to see stars at night, but on this evening, dark clouds obscured the sky. Rain had just begun to fall as we reached The Hunters' Home. Inside, Cedric marched right into the kitchen and immediately started frying up some hamburgers alongside greasy bacon.

Comfort food.

We needed it.

Lester came down and joined us in the kitchen, casually asking how the day had been.

The four angry stares he received said more than any words could have.

"We do, at least, know what the ogres' objective was. Or at least one of their objectives," Cedric said at last, pressing a patty into a greasy pan and making it sizzle. "Unfortunately, we were completely unable to stop them from obtaining both halves of the Key of Solomon. To what end, we have no idea."

"Oh, and plus, apparently our local university library has a ritual torture floor," Bianca added.

"Wait, what now?" Bran asked.

"Also, it seems our local Order of Light has abandoned any pretense of piety," Cedric said.

"Fucking Levi," Bianca spat. "And what kind of priest is packing a handgun?"

"Um, can we circle back to the ritual torture floor thing?" Bran asked.

"It is where the first half of the Key of Solomon ended up, apparently," Cedric said. "And where Cole seems to have lost his memory."

I shuddered as the thought of the space overwhelmed me, and I fought not to lose myself in the deluge of confused half-recollections that flooded my mind. Thankfully, the topic changed almost immediately, giving me something else to focus on.

"Oh and it turns out we learned the pedigree of our pup here," Bianca added.

"Oh?" Lester asked with sudden, pointed interest.

Bianca and Cedric related the story, in turns, covering most everything that happened in front of the Church of the Holy Guardian. Cedric gruffly offered the general outline of events, while Bianca chimed in to fill in colorful and expletive-laden details. Cuan, sitting across from me at the table, said nothing, but chowed down on the two burgers that Cedric lay in front of him. To be fair, I did the same: incorporeality really took it out of me, and the solidity of the cow meat was surprisingly grounding.

"So, it turns out I do have a sample of Lucent blood," Lester mused. "Just not the one I thought I did."

"That's all you have to say?" Bianca asked.

"No, but it was the first thing that came to mind," Lester replied.

"Well, if you have nothing productive to contribute to the conversation, Uncle Fester, then stick a lightbulb in your mouth and at least give the room some light," Bianca said.

Lester gave her a sour look and left, greasy bun and burger in hand.

"Well, it's abundantly clear now that we are not going to build any kind of productive relationship with the Church of the Holy Guardian," Bran said. "Honestly, I'm surprised we even went to their defense tonight."

"We had to," Cedric said. "That was where the Key of Solomon was."

"And... what do we think the ogres want with it?" Bran asked.

"No idea," Cedric mused. "But clearly there is more to this picture than we realized. This whole operation of the city's is not creating mindless soldiers: the ogres are coordinated around certain goals, and that means that someone is dictating those goals to them."

"And if they're collecting information about summoning and controlling demons," Bran concluded, "then anyone who knows anything about those kinds of practices could be in danger."

"Oh, shit," I realized. "Professor Norton. I just gave him that book of angels and demons."

"He really shouldn't be anywhere near that university," Bran agreed.

I whipped out my phone and fired off a text.

"TEXT ME WHEN YOU GET THIS. UNIVERSITY IS NOT SAFE. THOSE WEREN'T PIPE EXPLOSIONS. I THINK

SOMEONE IS AFTER YOUR RESEARCH. GET OUT OF THE CITY SOMEWHERE SAFE."

"That should get his attention," I decided. "He seems like the type where if he thinks someone is threatening his work, he'll definitely take action."

"Do you think he will respond right away?" Cedric asked.

"No clue," I said. "He seems to keep weird hours. Maybe he'll look at his phone tonight; maybe it'll be a day or so. And who knows if he'll even bother texting back until he believes he's in a safe location? At least I notified him."

"In the meantime, we'll have to keep an eye on what's going on in the city," Bran said. "Here's what we know from our reconnaissance at the police station."

As he spoke in somewhat drawn-out detail about his and Bianca's infiltration of the police station, Cuan stood from the table and went to the counter, where he opened a drawer and pulled out a pair of spoons. Then he went to the freezer and pulled out an open half-gallon of chocolate ice cream. He brought the whole container with him back toward the table.

"No, no, chocolate is bad for dogs," Bianca teasingly admonished.

"I will kill you with this spoon," Cuan snarled, brandishing the silverware at her. She raised her hands in mock surrender and returned to her corner chair. Cuan plopped back down at the table and yanked the lid off the ice cream, then took a giant spoonful of chocolate and shoveled it into his mouth. After he did so, he jammed the second spoon into the container and slid it across the table to me. I understood the intent, and took a spoonful for myself. It was regular chocolate ice cream, smooth and rich and calming. I needed it. So did Cuan. As I savored my bite, I slid the container back across to him, and we continued passing the tub back and forth across the surface of the table, the cardboard rasping across the wood surface as we had our fill.

"And so while I filed the phony complaint with the police," Bran concluded, "Bianca managed to slip a USB stick that Lester prepared onto someone's desk. If they actually plug it in, it should run a worm he developed that will give us back-end access to the police database. We have no idea how long it'll last in the system before whatever security they have cleans it —provided it's not caught immediately—but Lester should be able to access it from a burner machine he has installed and routed through multiple proxy servers and two daisy-chained VPNs, and he can at least search the network for the name of the program that was on the folder Cole had a photo of, and we can see if anything comes up."

Cedric was thoughtful. "I dislike this plan," he said. "You put yourself at a lot of risk going into the police station. We do not know if the USB drive will even get plugged in, nor, if it does, whether we will even be able to find anything useful. We also cannot be certain we will not be traced if we do. That is a lot of uncertainty, and—will you two please stop playing ice-cream hockey across my table? That noise is driving me crazy."

Cedric glared at us behind his sunglasses, and Bran and Bianca both gave us looks that said essentially "Why are you still here," so Cuan plunked the rest of the ice cream into the freezer as I stood to go upstairs. I'd indulged in a bit of food, so my first goal was to brush my teeth. Cuan soon joined me in that endeavor as well, and we brushed in silence. He returned back to the room as I took care of some other evening needs in the bathroom, but when I walked back into our shared room he was sitting on the bed with a miserable expression on his face as the rain pounded on the bedroom window.

"Hey," I said softly, sitting next to him. "You can talk to me if you want to."

He looked into my eyes, his gold irises brimming with pain, both recent and longstanding. "I... I wondered my whole life what my parents must have been like," he said at last. "Cedric said... when I was young, he said it was natural that I was abandoned, that any family would have been afraid to have someone like me. So I thought... I guessed... well, maybe they were just normal people, you know? Like... gentle people, who didn't know what to do with... someone like me. Or maybe they wanted me, but the village was afraid, so they found someone to trust me with. Cedric... he never said anything about the orphanage stuff until today. He just said someone left me with him." His voice cracked. "I thought... maybe that was my parents. Maybe they knew they couldn't care for me, but they knew Cedric, trusted Cedric to do it instead of them. I thought maybe somebody loved me."

"Cuan..."

"But instead," he continued, the words still spilling out of him, "instead, my family is... what, religious zealots? Who wanted to be rid of me since the moment I was born? My father abandoned me. He asked his son to bury me in the woods."

"But he didn't," I said. "He cared."

"Yeah, and my father hated him for it." He shook his head. "And then... when they finally learned who I am... my own brother... my brother, and my father... they tried to kill me. Not even out of any particular malice; just because it was convenient as a means to an end. Because I might as well be an animal to them. Or not even an animal. A monster."

He was shaking, his eyes distant and haunted.

"Hey, no, Cuan..." I said softly, wrapping my arms around him. He leaned into my chest, so raw, so small, so vulnerable. "You're not a monster," I said. "You know that. The monsters are the ones who did this to you."

He opened his mouth to say something, but instead he collapsed into me, his body wracking with sobs.

I held him, my heart breaking as he clutched me, hot tears soaking the front of my shirt.

"It's OK," I said softly, stroking his hair. "I'm here. I've got you."

Cuan cried, twenty-three years' worth of tears borne from pain and abandonment and internalized self-loathing. He cried out his hopes and dreams for what his parentage might have been, the family he'd always imagined he'd had, out there somewhere. He cried as the rain cascaded down our window, and I held him, held him long after the tears ran dry, after the sobs stopped, when the intense sadness dulled into a still quiet.

Being close to him, being there for him, somehow quieted the torrent of confused half-memories that had been flooding my brain since the library. Even as his grip on me relaxed from white-knuckled anguish and he just rested his head against me, the calm that followed seemed to wash away the rest of the world. It was just us.

I held him like that for at least an hour. Finally, he looked up to my face. His eyes were still puffy from the tears, but his gold irises shone with need.

"Cole," he whispered. "Will you.... Can we... make love?"

It was a deliberate choice of words, and I knew it. I nodded, and leaned forward to kiss him, feeling his lips on mine, feeling him need me. I carefully drew down the hidden zipper on the front of his vest and it fell open over his pale chest. Sliding my hands up, I drew it off of his torso, then slid my hands gently down his sides, his body shuddering at my touch. I bent forward and closed my lips around his nipple, teasing it with my tongue as I sucked, and he gasped, fingers weaving their way through the hair on the back of my head as I pressed my lips against his skin. My other hand reached to the band of his Wushu pants, and he lifted his hips slightly to let me pull them down over his butt, drawing my palm over his skin as I did so, bringing the band to remain stretched only around his powerful seated thighs.

Slowly, I massaged the front of his jockstrap as I continued to lap at his chest, and he let out a low moan as he began to stiffen beneath the fabric. The knowledge that I was raising the ardor in him caused the blood to begin flowing to my own crotch, the feel of him, the smell of him awakening my arousal.

Cuan brought his hands to my face and drew me up from his chest to his lips, kissing me again, and then gently guided me backward to give him access to my torso. One by one, he slipped open the buttons on my shirt, pulling it off of me, running his hands over my skin, teasing my nipples with his thumbs as he passed them, making my body twitch in approval.

I kissed him again, deep and long, and as I did so I felt his fingers working at my fly, unbuttoning my trousers and drawing open the zipper. He reached under the fabric beneath and I felt his fingertips on my shaft, the light, dancing touch tingling across my length and awakening my body. His hand closed around me, and slowly he began stroking me to full attention, still kissing me deeply.

"I want... to be closer," he breathed into me. "I want to feel you embracing me, want to feel your insides tight around me."

I nodded, and slowly he lowered me back onto the bed. I reached down and drew off his pants and jockstrap as he removed my khakis and underwear, and I kicked off my shoes and socks as his own footwear thumped to the floor.

He was above me, eyes filled with need, length hard and pleading for contact. He lowered his body against mine and I wrapped my arms around his back as we kissed again, slowly frotting against each other, feeling his hotness and his slick precum eliciting tingling waves of desire that spread through my cock across my whole body.

"Enwrap me inside you," he said, the instruction a pleading question, and I nodded.

"I need you closer," I whispered. "Nothing between us." The words were the signal he had been waiting for, and his eyes glistened as he reached for the coconut butter he kept by the bed. He straightened, and I watched the muscles of his torso move provocatively under his skin as he coated his tall, handsome erection, the tip of his dark red head winking with anticipation.

Then, he lay back over me. I raised my legs and crossed them over his back as he moved his hips forward, slowly sliding into my body. I shuddered and gasped as my insides made way for him, inch by inch, and he breathed and shook as my tightness enveloped him, stimulating his entire length.

Finally he was fully inside me, and his eyes shone as he gazed into mine.

"This is where you belong," I whispered. "Welcome home."

Emotion flooded his face and he fell upon my lips, kissing me with renewed depth, our arms wrapped around one another as he slowly rocked his body against mine.

The feeling of him against my prostate wasn't the wild slamming of vigorous sex; instead it was a sensuous, rolling massage, each push of his hips releasing a slow stream of pleasure that coursed through my body. As he pushed into me I clung to him, rolling my interior walls of muscle against him, stroke after stroke of an internal embrace. His torso was tight against mine, my own cock and balls massaged by the kneading motion of his abs as he worked his hips.

We continued to kiss, our tongues wrapping around one another, our bodies striving to leave not a molecule of space between us, heat rising as the long, deep rolling of our hips intensified. The emotion, the heat, the sensations welled up inside us, my balls tightening as the passion building between us rose toward release.

When the orgasm came, it did not strike like lightning; instead it rolled forth like thunder, reverberating through our bodies, cascading through my fingers and the tips of my toes and back again. I felt the heat of Cuan releasing inside of me as hot semen poured forth from me, sealing our torsos together while they heaved and shuddered and rocked as we came. We moaned into our kiss as the rocking became deep thrusts, once, twice, three times, cum flooding into me, flowing between us, as we rode the thundering orgasm, until at last the storm subsided and we were again calm and close and quiet in one another's embrace.

He slid out of me as I lowered my legs back onto the comforter, and he continued to lie atop me as I held him close, still breathing one another, still kissing.

"You... you're... I..." he breathed after he finally released the kiss. He looked into my eyes. "I love you, Cole."

It was early for that, I knew. But at the same time, it was true. What we'd been through in the few weeks we'd known one another—what we'd come to *know* about each other in that short span—I couldn't imagine sharing that with anyone else. He had, from the very beginning, been there for me, helped me every step of the way, even when I turned my back on the Hunters, even when I was staying with the Order. And he... he was so genuine, so earnest, even though everyone else treated him like some sort of animal or monster. He wasn't a beast. He was Cuan. The mere thought of him filled me with warmth, with comfort, with desire. And I already knew I wanted to be with him. I already knew:

"I love you too, Cuan," I said, and tears formed in his eyes anew as he clutched me.

I had no desire to get up and clean off. I didn't want to move. I just wanted to stay there with him. He fell asleep on my chest, his breathing calm and slow, and I followed soon after.

The third buzz of my phone was what woke me up. I blinked sleepily at the sound, looking across Cuan, who was still asleep on my chest. I didn't want to move. But then, I thought, what if Professor Norton were finally returning my message? I reached over Cuan and sleepily took my phone off the dresser, blinking again at its lit screen.

2:14 AM, the time read.

Below that, notifications for three messages, in sequence:

"I'm outside"

"Please come down"

"please"

I blinked again.

"Oh," I muttered.

Cuan stirred sleepily, turning his body toward me.

"...mmpph?" he murmured. His eyes opened slowly, but then when he saw the expression on my face and the phone in my hand, sleep fell away from him.

"What?" he asked, sitting up.

I held my phone to him.

A few seconds later, I was pulling sweatpants over my naked, cum-caked hips and Cuan lugged on a pair of Wushu pants, and we descended the stairs of the quiet house, rain thumping outside against the windows. As we descended, the phone in my hand buzzed again, with yet another pleading message. We reached the front hall, Cuan and I gave each other a long look, and then I took a deep breath and opened the door to the porch.

Alexander was standing on the front steps in front of the screen door, drenched in the rain, Candela's wrappings getting soaked through as it hung from a strap over his shoulder. The hood of his hoodie was raised and he had an autumn coat on, but neither of those things made a lick of difference against the downpour. He didn't meet our eyes across the porch. Instead, he stared straight ahead from under his dripping hood, with the same lost, haunted expression that I had seen on Cuan a few hours earlier.

"My entire life was a lie." His voice was so small that I could barely hear it through the rain.

I stared at him, caught between sympathy and cold contempt.

"I've been wandering the city for hours. I didn't know where else to go," he continued, staring at the door. "My entire life was that church. Those people... I believed in them, I trusted them.... Thomas won't speak to me; he didn't even respond when I knocked on his bedroom door. Marcus is here. There's... nobody else I can go to."

He looked up, shattered, gazing past me. I stepped back from the door, toward Cuan, taking his hand firmly in mine, a gesture to show clearly where I stood.

"I... I know that I did something completely unforgiveable to you," he said meekly, shivering in the rain. "But... just for tonight... can we pretend I didn't?"

I stared at him silently, all my feelings of residual affection and amity battling with the memory of his betrayal, that he chose his parent's twisted approval over humanity.

And then, I heard a whisper next to me, barely audible over the rain outside.

"If you want to let him in, you can."

I looked at Cuan. He was staring at Alexander, clearly feeling conflicted emotions of his own.

"Cuan," I whispered back.

"I'm not saying you should," he continued. "You should do whatever you want to do. But I... I won't be upset if you let him in."

I said nothing, still unsure.

"Cole..." Cuan whispered again. "All I know is... these past seven hours... I can't imagine having had to spend them alone."

I looked back to the front steps, where Alexander continued to stare pleadingly through the rain. I walked across the porch and unlocked the screen door, then reached out my hand.

Alexander continued shivering and dripping as we brought him upstairs. He was soaked through to the bone and barely responsive, seeming instead lost somewhere inside himself.

We had to get him out of those clothes or he'd freeze to

death. Without a word, Cuan and I brought him into the bathroom and started to run a hot shower, and he stood silently as we peeled his soaked clothing from his shaking body. I unwrapped Candela, careful not to touch the blade or the hilt with my bare hands, and pressed a towel into it to absorb the rain so it wouldn't rust. Alexander let us undress him, moving only enough to raise his arms when we pulled off his hoodie and shirt and to raise his feet as we pried off his shoes and then again to step out of his trousers and underwear. We stepped into the shower with him, holding him as he shivered under the water, sharing our body heat as we pressed ourselves on either side of him. His skin was like ice.

There was a time when I would have thought that if I ever had Cuan and Alexander naked in a shower with me it would be because we were having wild, raucous sex. Or at least that I'd be caught gleefully in the middle while Cuan and Alexander vented their frustrations in a bout of angry sex. But while this shower was certainly intimate, it was not sexual—and not just because I'd just spent myself with Cuan. Even the kind of vigorous, cathartic fucking I'd given Alexander after he'd learned of Marcus's fate was out of the question: Alexander was too far gone for any of that. He stood dumbly as the water fell over him, his breath shaking, his lips purple and quivering. The shower wasn't enough.

I looked over his shoulder at Cuan, who was standing against him from behind, trying to help me warm him. Cuan met my gaze, seeming to know what I was thinking. He gave me a small nod.

I turned back to Alexander, and his glassy eyes focused on me as he continued shaking. His expression was still lost, haunted. Slowly, I leaned forward to his purple lips.

And I kissed him.

He didn't deserve it. I knew he didn't deserve it. And I hadn't forgiven him. Things weren't all right between us. But

Alexander needed an act of reassurance, needed to know that he had someone in his corner, even if only for the night. Alexander leaned into the kiss, drinking it in with desperation, and it seemed to give him a sort of grounding, even as his breathing was ragged around the edges of our mouths. His lips and tongue, like the rest of him, were like ice.

I released the kiss and straightened to see Cuan placing gentle, warm kisses on the back of Alexander's shoulder. Our hot water was going to run out. Alexander's body was a little warmer, but he was still shivering. Cuan and I washed ourselves—we were still coated with cum, after all—then washed Alexander. We turned off the water and took him out of the shower, toweling him and ourselves off.

Taking his hand, we brought him to the bed. Cuan pulled the soiled comforter off of it and dropped it to the floor as I tucked Alexander into the sheets. Cuan pulled a replacement comforter out of the closet and lay it over the bed, then climbed in next to us. His bed was a little small for two people; for three it was definitely inadequate, but that kept us close together.

Cuan and I held each other, enfolding Alexander between us, shielding him from the world. Naked under the comforter it was easier to share our body heat, and after about ten minutes, Alexander's skin didn't seem as cold. His shaking stopped, his breathing slowed, and soon, he was asleep. Cuan and I continued to hold each other, listening to the sounds of our breath and the driving rain on the window. Eventually we slept as well, and we stayed that way for the few remaining hours of night until morning.

VIII

BEHIND CLOSED DOORS

THE NEXT MORNING WAS—WELL, I wouldn't call it *awkward*, but nor was it exactly comfortable. Alexander was very aware that he was not a favored guest in The Hunters' Home, and was quite flustered and withdrawn from the moment he woke up. That was, however, a good bit later than Cuan and I, which was unsurprising since he had apparently been wandering the city half the night. I awoke when Cuan stirred, as he deftly slipped out of bed between Alexander and the wall. I slid out from under the sheets, easier because the floor was right next to me, and stood up to meet him as he stretched in the early light.

"Hey, you," I whispered with a grin, kissing him lightly on the lips. He smiled that dimpled half-smile at me and for a moment, all was right with the world. But then Alexander rustled the sheets in his sleep and we sighed, turning to look at him.

"I doubt the household will be particularly pleased when they find him here," Cuan whispered thoughtfully.

"Yeah... he's not my favorite person at the moment, but he's an outcast now, like the rest of us."

"True," Cuan admitted, "but he hasn't done much to earn

any actual goodwill. Cedric already said he couldn't stay here. And there's truth to that; we just don't have enough beds. And last night's arrangement is not something I want to do long-term. We need at least *some* space for ourselves. Besides," he said, looking appraisingly at Alexander, who lay with the comforter and sheets half off of his torso, "I mean, he's very hot, but eventually he's gonna open his mouth."

"Eh, his mouth isn't so bad," I responded with a shrug.

Cuan gave me a flat look. "It is when words start coming out of it."

"Fair point," I said, nodding. Alexander was still sleeping peacefully. "You know," I whispered, "part of me would have liked to see how he reacted when he woke up in bed between two naked men."

"You know," Cuan responded thoughtfully, "something tells me he'd just roll with it. And seeing as how I have no particular desire to roll around with him..."

I nodded in agreement. "So... what now?"

"Well, he's not going to have many friends when he gets downstairs. We'd be better off if we primed the rest of the Hunters with the idea that he's in the house."

"You mean, like you did when you first brought me home?" I asked.

"Something like that," Cuan nodded, "only with you, it was preparing them for someone they didn't know. With Alexander, it's preparing them for someone they don't *like*."

I looked back to Alexander where he slept peacefully. "...Do we?" I asked. "Like him, I mean?"

"Well, I mean, I don't *hate* him," Cuan said. "But..."

"But I can't really say I like him at the moment, either," I completed for both of us.

"Exactly," Cuan nodded.

"Still, he needs someone to be there for him now," I said.

"Right," Cuan agreed. "Well, it'd be smoothest if the others were ready for him. But I'm also not going to leave him alone up here. And I don't really want to be alone with him when he wakes up."

"Nor do I," I added.

"So I guess we wait," Cuan sighed, "and deal with the others when that time comes."

It was a quiet morning. We each had a turn in the bathroom and got dressed, then I carefully re-wrapped Candela in its now-dry wrappings. Alexander's clothes were still soaked and were caked with mud, so we set them aside to launder later and Cuan selected an outfit for Alexander from among what I imagined were his college outfits, and laid them out along with the most conservative jockstrap he could find.

"You think he'll like it?" Cuan wondered, looking at the undergarment.

"He won't really have much of a choice," I said.

"His butt will probably look fantastic in it, the fucker."

I stifled a laugh. Then we simply sat on the floor next to the bed. Cuan pulled out a small box from under the bed, and I fully expected to find it full of sex toys like the one in my own apartment, but instead it was full of books.

Academic books.

He pulled out a book about small mammals and began reading, handing me a book on marine mammals that was lavishly illustrated. I snuggled up next to him and we read in quiet for an hour or so until we heard stirring in the bed behind us.

"Good morning," I said without turning around, finishing a section on dolphins and porpoises.

"G'mornin?" came Alexander's sleepy voice. Then there was a long pause, until finally: "Thanks."

We both turned around, and he was laying on the edge of the bed, covers half off of him, propped up on one elbow and looking at us with his blue-green eyes. The scent of chestnut wafted from him as the very fine, almost invisible hairs on his golden pecs glinted in the light.

"This doesn't make everything all better," Cuan noted.

"I know that," Alexander replied.

"Still... we're here for you," I said, and Cuan nodded in agreement.

Alexander looked at us, and then over to the clothes laid out on the dresser, and Candela in its wrapping.

"You... got all that ready for me?"

We nodded in unison, and Alexander's eyes shone. Then he blinked, and cleared his throat, looking from us to the bathroom door.

"Um, I gotta..." he started. "Do... you mind?"

"Go ahead," Cuan said.

He hesitated.

"I think we're past the point of being self-conscious around one another regarding nudity," I noted. "I mean, you and I are *definitely* past that, and you did shower with Cuan last night. So... if you really don't want us to look at you naked, then fine, we respect that, but if you're worried about how we feel, well, don't go getting self-conscious for our sakes."

Alexander hesitated for another moment, then shrugged and tossed the covers aside, stepping out of the bed. As he passed, I noticed that he was ever so slightly hard. Cuan and I watched him as he walked to the bathroom door, the ample globes of his ass rising and falling as he walked. The door shut.

"God dammit," Cuan said, brow wrinkling in irritation. "Yup, his ass is going to look *fantastic* in that jockstrap."

As the three of us walked downstairs for breakfast, Cuan and I motioned to Alexander to hang back a bit, then walked into the kitchen ahead of him.

Cedric was in his usual place at the stove, while Bianca was lounging in her chair like a cat. Bran and, unusually, Lester were seated at the table, and all were enjoying plates of scrambled eggs and sausage, with a side of hash browns.

"About time you got up," Cedric said gruffly, cracking a pair of eggs into a pan.

"It was a long night," I said. "There was a lot to take in."

"I'll bet," Bianca said wryly. "Fido's not good for much, but I'll bet he's packing."

"That's not what I meant," I said flatly. "Though yes, for your information, Cuan is amazing in bed."

"Yeah, I'll second that," Bran said, raising his hand.

"See? Testimonials!" I exclaimed. "So there you go. Unlike *some* people," I added, "he actually *could* make a living as a sex worker."

"Fuck off," Bianca said. "If I wanted to go that route, I'd be so in demand that I'd have to hire staff."

"You mean to handle the complaints department?" I asked. "I suppose it could be helpful to have someone to handle refunds, since otherwise you wouldn't have any time left to disappoint additional customers."

"As entertaining as this is," Cedric interjected dryly, "I assume you were actually referring to having a lot to take in regarding Cuan's parentage?"

Cuan nodded. "Yeah, well... that, and..."

"And?" Cedric asked, turning to look at us expectantly.

"And... we had a visitor," I said.

Cuan stepped to the side and, meekly, Alexander stepped into the kitchen.

Everyone stopped. The air in the room stretched with tension. In the frying pan, the eggs started to burn.

"Um... hi," Alexander said. "I... didn't know where else to go. Cuan and Cole let me in."

The others regarded him coldly. Bran looked from him to Cuan and me. "You guys are OK with this?"

We shrugged in unison. "We couldn't just leave him outside," Cuan said.

"I'm sorry to intrude," Alexander said. "But you said you didn't ban me from the house. And... my world is kind of falling apart."

Cedric continued to stare. "Your father tried to shoot us," he said.

"He's not my father," Alexander replied.

"Oh, point for Alexander!" Bran interjected.

"Yeah, that's fair," Bianca noted. Then she turned to Cuan. "*Your* father tried to shoot us," she said.

"That man can eat shit and die," Cuan said hotly.

"Point for Cuan!" Bran exclaimed.

Cedric turned to me. "Cole, what do you think about this?"

"I think the eggs are burning," I observed.

Cedric cursed as he turned his attention to the frying pan. He dumped its ruined contents and then took out new eggs from the carton. This time, I noted, he cracked three eggs in the pan.

"Sit down," he said without turning around, and Alexander realized it was an indication that, for the moment at least, his presence would be permitted.

"Thank you," he said.

"Save it," Bianca responded.

Off in the hallway, we heard the front door open and shut. Everyone stiffened. We looked to one another, and then back toward the hall. The front door was left locked as a rule, and only the Midnight Hunters had keys. Everyone who lived at the house was present and accounted for. Though, of course, there was one other Midnight Hunter who didn't live at the house.

"Az?" Bianca called.

"In the kitchen, are you?" came Az's voice. "I should have known."

Az appeared in the doorway to the kitchen, dapper and

collected as always in his pressed black suit, and looked to each of us. I chirped hello and his eyes softened slightly as they fell on me, but then his gaze rested on Alexander.

"You," he hissed. "What are you doing here?"

"You're about five minutes too late for that conversation," Bran sighed.

"I'm done with the Order of Light," Alexander said with finality. He summarized the previous evening's events with bitterness, essentially outlining that Cuan was Jacob's son, and he was not.

"He lied to me. My entire life," Alexander concluded. "And he hadn't adopted me out of love. It was just because he thought I would be useful."

"That does not negate your treatment of Cole," Az responded.

"No, it does not," Cedric agreed. "But if Cole and Cuan can tolerate his presence here, so shall the rest of us." He turned to Alexander. "We still do not have a place for you to sleep," he noted. "And you are not one of the Hunters. But if you are going to be a guest here than I suppose we can treat you as one. You are welcome to spend time in the house as long as you are under supervision."

"I, for one, would appreciate the help," Lester added. "You know Marcus, and that could prove useful in his treatment."

"I'll do whatever I can," Alexander said.

"Good," Cedric replied, then turned to Lester. "And what about the tape?"

"Tape?" I asked.

"He means the SD card," Lester said. "From the library."

The library. The static pushed against my brain again, but comprehension remained still out of reach.

"Nothing yet, unfortunately," Lester said. "There's definitely something on there, but it's encrypted. Heavily. I've been working on it, but I'm not having any luck so far."

"Wait. From the video camera?" I asked.

"That's right," Lester said. "I don't know how it got encrypted while still in the camera. Maybe it was done remotely? However it was done, I can't find a key on the card itself, so right now I'm trying to brute force it."

"Well, keep at it," Cedric said with a nod. "I am going out for a short while with Bianca and Bran, just to check up on the street and make sure our location is still secure. You are welcome to stay and finish your eggs in the meantime. Az, I can fry up some for you, too, if—"

"No thank you," Az said amicably.

"I'll be upstairs," Lester said as Cedric left with the others. "Call up if you need anything."

Once it was just the four of us. Alexander looked distinctly uncomfortable, but that likely had a lot to do with Az silently staring daggers at him. Cuan and I finished our eggs and stood up to wash our plates.

"So, Az," Cuan said as he scrubbed, "mind telling us why you're here?"

"Hm?" Az asked, looking to us.

"You haven't exactly been one to just show up at The Hunters' Home to spend time and socialize," Cuan pointed out.

"That's a good point," I said, toweling off our dishes as Cuan handed them to me. "What brings you here today?"

"I noticed that you seem to have become more comfortable with the process of reverting from your incorporeal state," Az said.

"Yes, I think so," I said. "Is that what you wanted to talk about?"

Az looked back to Alexander with some hesitation, then sighed. "I suppose this is the closest we'll get to not having people around here," he decided, "and I'm not sure how large a window we have as it is. I'm here because I think you're ready."

"Ready?" I asked. "You mean... to help you release the trapped soul?"

"Wait," Alexander asked, as he took the last bite of eggs and Cuan took his plate; "trapped soul? What are you talking about?"

"Az... knows that someone is trapped somewhere?" I said, deliberately being as vague as possible. "And he apparently needs my help to free them."

"I wanted to be sure you understood the workings of your ability, first," Az said, "just in case you need to transition quickly."

"And you want us to do this now?" I asked. "When the ogres have the full Key of Solomon and are going to do who knows what with it?"

"When you were trapped," Azrael said pointedly, "if there were someone who was able to release you from that situation, would you have wanted them to put it off until it was convenient for them?"

"No," I realized, glaring at Alexander, "I wouldn't."

Alexander averted his eyes.

"Great," Cuan nodded, "but... couldn't you just tell him all this at training in your hotel room? Why come here?"

"Because," Az said gravely, "this is where the soul is."

The dish Cuan was washing clattered to the bottom of the sink. "Here?" he asked, picking it up again and re-washing it. "Wait, do you mean Marcus? But... Marcus wasn't even here when you first showed up."

"I do not mean Marcus," Az responded.

"But, then, that doesn't make any sense," Cuan frowned. "I've lived here my whole life. Where would a soul be trapped here? I mean, I've been in every room in the house."

"Maybe not *every* room," I realized.

The basement of The Hunters' Home was fairly spartan; it had been finished and repurposed into a training space. I hadn't come down here since Cedric's first attempt to train me, when I discovered that his brutal method of getting me to fade was to fire a crossbow at my chest. That, needless to say, did not go over well with me, and I had avoided the basement ever since. Cuan had suggested to me that his own training was similarly uncomfortable, though he'd never spoken of it in detail, and I figured he'd discuss it when he was ready. The particular half of the training room that we were in now was simple in design, with padded vinyl mats styled after bamboo tatami lining the floor and a few support columns wrapped in rope to cushion any impact. There was a second training room that apparently had more equipment, but I'd never ventured in there. There was one another door in the basement, however; one that should by all rights have been on an exterior wall of the foundation. This was a heavier metal door that Cedric claimed led to his private office and some of his own equipment. We were asked—well, instructed—to never enter, though Cedric assured us that this was not to inspire temptation but merely to respect his privacy. As an extra measure of security he kept the office securely locked. It was to this locked door that Az now extended a finger.

"There?" Cuan asked. "But… we're not allowed in there."

"I'm guessing there's a reason for that," Az said. "That's where the soul is."

"How do you know this?" Alexander asked.

"I can… sense it," he said.

"That's helpful," Alexander responded skeptically. He turned to me. "I don't think you should believe this guy."

"I believe him," I said. Cuan nodded silently in agreement. "You should, too."

"And why is that?" Alexander demanded.

"You don't deserve to know that right now," Az responded with finality.

I looked back to the door. "So... if that's where the soul is," I asked, "then why don't you go in and rescue it?"

"Because," Az sighed, "I cannot. The room is warded."

"Warded?" Cuan asked. "With what kind of ward?"

"The kind of ward that keeps someone like me out. It denies entrance to all who are... not earthly."

Alexander looked at him with interest. "Who the hell are you, then?" he asked, but Az dismissed the question with a wave of his hand.

"What matters now," he said, "is that you, Cole, can simply walk through the door and open it from the inside."

"I... I don't like this," Cuan said.

"But you'd rather leave a soul trapped in there?" Az asked.

"I didn't say we shouldn't do it," Cuan responded. "I just... don't like it. Why don't we just ask Cedric about it?"

"But Cedric never mentioned it to you before, right?" Alexander pointed out. "All he wants is for you to stay out of that room. I doubt he'd respond honestly even if you confronted him about it."

"You don't really get an opinion," Cuan glared.

"And yet, he has a point," I admitted. "We know that Cedric's methods can be kind of... severe. If he thinks it's better for everyone that he keeps some locked up soul a secret, then that's likely what he'll do. But we can't just leave someone captive, no matter the reason."

"Az..." Cuan said with hesitation, "you'd better be right about this."

"Here I go," I said. I breathed in, and breathed out. As I exhaled, I focused on the world, the door, becoming simply less solid. I stepped toward the door and extended my hand toward it.

It wasn't solid, but nor was it easy to pass through. It felt like I was trying to push two identical magnetic poles together. The room simply wanted to keep me out. But I persevered, and eventually found myself in a pitch black room.

I couldn't see anything at all. I fumbled behind me at the door and my hand passed through a heavy lock with a latch, but I couldn't move it in my current state. I breathed out, felt the world solidify.

There was a noise from somewhere further into the room. A rattling, and a faint glow of light passed toward me through the fog of my senses. I heard a weak voice say something I couldn't understand.

I was not alone. Urgency gripped me. Not only was I in the room with someone, but I also couldn't communicate with them with the fog pressing against my senses. I needed to focus. I reached behind me to the latch and pulled. It was heavy, but I managed to yank it open. As I did so, I felt a sense of pressure leave my body, and the feeling of the space trying to repel me abated.

The light of the room was almost blinding. As my eyes adjusted, I focused on Cuan, knowing I had to communicate something. His concerned face slid into focus, his eyes widening.

"There's someone in here," I said.

"What the fuck..." Alexander muttered, looking over my shoulder.

I turned. Now, in the light, I could make out the interior of the room. It was mostly packed by a desk and shelves cluttered with equipment, just as Cedric said. However, the opposite end of the small room was free of shelving.

Instead, it featured a giant, ornate cross, the top of which scraped the ceiling.

And bound to the base of that cross with glowing chains, his expression drawn and anguished, was a person. His eyes were closed and his face pale, his muscular arms bound tightly to his side, chains winding up and down his body. He was dressed in a long shirt with laces at the collar and what looked like hempen trousers that extended just below his knees.

"What... what is this?" Cuan asked in horror.

"A hot guy chained to a cross and trapped in a closet...," I said. "This must be Alexander's room."

"Shut up," Alexander replied.

I saw a rush of black light out of the corner of my eye as Quietus formed in Az's hand. He stepped forward, expression hard.

"I will grant you release," he said.

"Wait, what are you going to do?" I asked.

"When I sense a soul, it is because it is a soul that should have been granted death, but was denied it," Az explained. "It is time that I fulfill that obligation to this one."

"Hold up, you're going to kill him?" Cuan asked, aghast. He grabbed for Az's arm, and Az stared daggers at him.

"He should have died already," Az said.

"But he didn't," I insisted. "Let's at least figure out what's going on before we do anything."

"And what *is* going on?" came a voice from the stairs. We turned to see Cedric's feet descending toward the basement, Bianca and Bran behind him. As soon as Cedric's face passed into view, he took one look at the open door and froze. "Get away from there!" he shouted. "Do you know what you have done?"

"Ooh, you went in the forbidden chamber?" Bianca asked with interest, as Cedric reached his hand out in front of her to stop her descent down the stairs. "How 'Beauty and the Beast'."

"Bian...ca?" came a weak voice from inside the office.

Bianca blanched at the sound. Cedric reached down to grab at her but she pushed past him, running toward the door.

"Leo?" she cried, desperation in her voice. She looked inside the office, eyes wide, the color draining from her face. "Holy shit, Leo, is that really you?" She ran to him.

"Stop her!" Cedric ordered, but Bianca was already pulling the chains off of him.

The instant the man was free, he moved like a pouncing cat, grabbing Bianca roughly and immediately sinking his teeth into her neck. We all shouted in alarm as he took one deep, long pull and then dropped her to the ground, where she landed on her hands and knees, dazed and panting. Blood dripped from a pair of fresh puncture marks on her throat, and the man—the vampire—drew the back of his hand across his bloody lips. Then he smiled, white fangs glistening in the light.

"Ah," he said, "that's so much better. Now, then—"

Immediately Az wrested his arm from Cuan and lunged forward, sword outstretched. The vampire changed stance immediately and dashed towards him, but just before the sword found home, the vampire burst into billows of mist, blowing past us and reforming in the training room.

Cuan spun around, flexing his fingers and preparing to lunge. Cedric already had his crossbow at the ready and fired a bolt, but the vampire dodged nimbly, then looked sharply toward the stairwell. He seemed to be calculating a means of escape.

"Not so fast," Alexander said, stretching his hand in front of him. "*Murum Lux*," he declared, his voice resonant, and suddenly a wall of bright light sprang up in front of him like a shield. "*Rupti Sunt*," he added, turning his hand, and the wall suddenly exploded forward in multiple beams of light.

The vampire cursed, somersaulting away, then grunted as a beam seared into his shoulder. He pivoted in the air, his balance lost, and fell to the ground. As he stood, Bran planted himself between the vampire and the stairs. Cedric took aim again with his crossbow and Az charged forth from the office once again, sword in hand.

"NO!" Came a shout from the office, and suddenly the room was filled with a billowing cloud of black bats. They swarmed out from where Bianca stood in front of the cross in the sealed room, tumbling through the chamber, buffeting and harrying everyone in the basement. Cuan and I pressed ourselves against the wall by the door as the bats swarmed past us, and Alexander threw his hands over his head and crouched on the floor, yelling as bats smacked into him and burst into puffs of black mist. Az angrily swiped the air with his sword and Bran backpedaled into the corner.

Cedric raised his hand, and suddenly there was a burst of a bright orange sphere in front of his palm that caused most of the bats to dissipate. Those that remained fluttered up the stairs and out of sight.

We blinked at the empty room. The vampire was gone.

Cedric turned to us, his face contorted with rage. "What have you done?" he demanded. "That was the one room—the *one room*—that I instructed you not to go into. I kept it locked. I told you it was just my personal office. I did everything I could not to make it a temptation. And still you disobeyed this one request. You disobeyed *me*, after I took you in."

"No," Cuan said suddenly and firmly. "No, no, nope. You don't get to take some moral high ground with this one. You were keeping someone locked up in there, bound in chains so they couldn't move!"

"Wait, he what?" Bran asked.

"You would not have even known if you had not opened that door," Cedric asserted.

"Yes they would have," Az said calmly, "because *I* knew. Why else do you think they opened it in the first place? Idle curiosity? No, it was because we knew you had someone trapped in there."

"And how did you know that?" Cedric demanded. "Who told you? This should have remained a secret, and then everything would have been fine."

"Fine?" Cuan scoffed. "You had a captive in there! And to chain him up like that… that's inhuman!"

"You may have noticed," Cedric said, "but he is *not* human."

"Really?" I asked. "After everything that Jacob and Levi said and did, you're going to start making distinctions based on what you perceive as humanity?"

"He needed to stay bound," Cedric asserted.

"This is unbelievable," Alexander muttered. "All the indignation and outrage directed toward the Order of Light—which we deserved, mind you—because of my father's attempt to keep Cole captive in the church, and here you were doing exactly the same thing."

"It is not the same at all," Cedric replied.

"How is it any different?" Cuan demanded.

"Because Cole is not dangerous!" Cedric shouted. "You are comparing him to a vampire! A vampire who, now that he is free, will return to stalking the living and drinking their blood, and potentially siring even more vampires!"

"So your solution was to keep him prisoner?" I asked. "Bound like that? Tied to a cross? That wasn't even imprisonment. That was torture."

"You would have preferred I executed him?" Cedric asked. "Death penalty over imprisonment, is that it?"

"And yet, you've never had any qualms about slaying vampires before," Bran observed. "Why is this one so different?"

"Because," came Bianca's voice, shaky as she held onto the office door frame for balance, "this one is my brother."

We turned and stared at her.

"What's all the racket down—" Lester had come down the stairs, but he stopped short when he saw the open office door. "Oh," he added. No one paid him any notice—we were all focused on Bianca.

"Wait," Cuan said to her, "you mean *that* was your brother? The brother who bit you?"

"Um, we just saw her get bitten, Cuan," Alexander said.

"I mean before that," Cuan said. "The first time. It's why she came here in the first place."

"Right," Bianca said. "Because my brother was turned into a vampire, and I was the first person he bit. I came here; Cedric promised to help me find him. I had no idea he'd succeeded." She rounded on Cedric menacingly. "So tell me, you sorry Van Helsing knockoff, why did you kept it a secret that you'd succeeded in finding my brother?"

"Because when you're bitten, the vampire's will is nearly impossible to resist," Cedric explained coolly. "If I told you, would you or would you not have immediately come down here and done exactly what you just did?"

Bianca was still for a moment. "...You're right, I would have," she admitted. "Or at least I would have been tempted to. But that's still no excuse for keeping him a secret from me!" Her ire rose again. "And you told me that once you found him, you and Lester would be able to work on a cure."

"A cure?" Az scoffed. "For vampirism?"

"It's a theoretical possibility," Lester asserted.

Bianca turned to Lester. "And you! Why aren't you more angry about this? You could have been working on a cure this whole time!"

Lester said nothing.

"Oh my God," she blanched. "You've known all along."

"Of course," Lester admitted. "How else would we have been able to keep him alive?"

"How—holy shit," Cuan muttered, eyes widening.

"The samples," Bianca realized. "The blood samples you take from me every week, to check up on how the vampiric curse is affecting my body... you've been feeding them to him."

"That... that's sick," Bran gasped.

"I always thought you took an awful lot for mere samples," Bianca said. "Are you even working on a cure? Have you really even needed my blood at all?"

"Of course I did," Lester insisted. "It was important for me to keep track of your health. And I *am* planning on researching a cure, when time allows. But this way, the blood didn't go to waste. It was a win-win."

"Come here, Uncle Fester," Bianca said menacingly, advancing on him. "I'm gonna shove a light bulb so far down your throat that Cedric will be able to use your asshole as a reading lamp."

Lester retreated back up the stairs. Cedric moved to bar Bianca's path.

"Stop this," he said. "You can see why we kept him a secret. You would have been unable to resist his thrall, had you known. It was for your own good."

"For my own good?" Bianca hissed. "Is that what you tell yourself? Or... do you even believe that?" her eyes widened as she realized something. "No," she said. "You were doing this intentionally; feeding him my blood to keep the blood bond alive and well, to keep me in my powers."

"And why is that a problem?" Cedric asked. "You use your abilities often; you seem to have adapted well to being Bitten. Don't you like it?"

"Don't I like it?" Bianca responded incredulously. "No, I don't like it. Yeah, being able to conjure misty bats is fun and all, but my *blood itches*. Do you have any idea what that's like? It feels like I'm crawling out of my skin every fucking minute of every fucking day."

"Well, that explains why you're such a bitch all the time," I mused.

"Yes, it does," she rounded on me. "What's your excuse?"

"Amnesia," I shrugged.

"Fair enough," she admitted.

"But what there *isn't* an excuse for," I added, "is this."

"You are right," Cedric said. "There is no excuse. Because of your actions, a vampire is now loose in the city."

"That's not what he meant, and you know it," Bianca hissed.

"Do I?" Cedric asked. "I did what was best for all involved."

"No," Cuan growled. "You did what was best for *you*. You're mad at us for going into that room, but we did it to rescue someone. All we knew was there was a captive in there, because you never told us anything different. Keeping Bianca's brother a secret from all of us, tied up here, feeding him her blood, all the while promising her that he was still out there and you were looking for him—it was all to keep her close, make her trust you, and keep her semi-vampiric powers strong so that they'd be useful to you!"

"I did what had to be done," Cedric said, "to keep the city safe."

"And what about *us*?" Bianca demanded. "You... you've been like family to me. And yet you lied to me, manipulated me, all for some big-picture plan that you didn't let any of us in on? You talk about humanity as being self-absorbed and cruel. You decry the Order of Light as a corrupt organization that follows a leader with a twisted sense of right and wrong. But tell me: how are you any better? I always kind of thought Cole was just being a whiny little bitch when he complained that you shot at him in order to get him to go incorporeal—"

"Hey," I protested.

"—but now I know better," Bianca continued. "You'd shoot any one of us through the heart if you thought it would serve your 'big picture.' And here I thought we actually meant something to you."

"I..." Cedric started, but for once he actually seemed speechless. He stood, face drawn, silent on the stairs.

"Nothing to add?" Bianca asked sarcastically. "No pithy response? Well, I've one for you, to all of this shit: I'm out."

She marched past him up the stairs. Cedric made no move to stop her, or any of us, as we all walked up through the kitchen. Bran stopped there, hesitating on the landing.

"Where are you gonna go?" he asked Bianca.

"I dunno," she replied. "Not here. For now, my brother is out there somewhere, and what matters is finding him."

"That's right," Az replied coolly. "That is a soul that needs to be released."

"Don't you fucking dare," Bianca replied. "That is my *brother*, and I haven't seen him in years, so I am at least going to talk to him before you do anything, do you understand? If there's some other solution, we're going to find it."

"I have a duty to perform," Az said simply. "That's all there is to it."

"And what about your pledge to aid us?" I demanded.

"I pledged to keep you from harm," Az clarified. "Eliminating the vampire will also achieve that."

"And what if I say I'll kick their asses to hell and back again if you get the vampire first?" Bianca asked.

"Why is it that everyone threatens violence as a bargaining chip?" Cuan protested.

"You're not going to kick our asses," I said to Bianca, "because we're going to help you. You want to find your brother? Then we'll help you find your brother. *You*, not Az."

"Very well," Az said; "you have fulfilled my request of you. I won't interfere with your search. Now that the vampire is not so strictly bound, I cannot locate him with nearly as much precision. I shall not interfere with your search, but nor will I stop my own. And if I find him, I am duty-bound to complete my task. I have free will in some things, but that only extends so far. And," he added, turning to me, "if it looks like you or Cuan are in danger, I am bound by my oath to protect you."

"If it comes to that, then we'll welcome your intervention, I'm sure," I said.

"In that case, I shall take my leave," Az nodded, heading to the door. "Good luck in your search," he added.

"Forgive me for not wishing you the same," I said, and Az smiled sadly at us.

Bianca, Alexander, Cuan and I headed into the street. Az was already gone.

"Well, what now?" I asked.

"I... I can feel him," Bianca said. "Somewhat, anyway. He's in hiding. He's exhausted, but free, so he's regrouping. He's not feeding," she added, fingers wandering to the dried blood on her neck; "he's had what he needs for the moment. Tonight he'll probably just get his bearings and look for a more secure place to spend the next day. We don't have to worry about him for now."

"So... where should we go, then?" Cuan asked.

"About that," Alexander said, "perhaps I have a suggestion." He reached down into his pocket. "I found some stuff back when we were all investigating under the city. I brought it with me, and transferred it from my soaked trousers this morning. From the description you gave me of the day you first went incorporeal, I thought it might be yours."

He reached his hand up and held two things out to me. One was a wad of damp cash.

The other was the key to my apartment.

IX

FOUR'S COMPANY

I stared at Alexander.

"That's the key to my apartment," I said.

"I figured as much," he nodded. "When we were under the city and running from those cops, after I lost them and was finding my way out from the abandoned subway, I found a pair of khakis with a chain wrapped around the leg. It reminded me of what you'd told me about the night you first went incorporeal, and I found these in the pockets."

"I... can't believe you found these," I said, gratefully taking the key and the wad of money. "This'll make getting in and out of the apartment easier, huh?"

"I still prefer the window," Cuan smirked.

"Well," I sighed, "at least now we'll have a roof over our heads." I beckoned to Alexander and Bianca, and we walked through the streets toward my home.

As we walked, Cuan watched Bianca with concern.

"Is your neck OK?" he asked her.

"Yeah," she nodded, "it's fine. It'll heal. It makes my blood itch even more than usual, though. He only took a mouthful, but my head still feels kinda fuzzy. My awareness of him had kind of dulled, though now it's a lot sharper."

"How does that work?" I asked. "So... you know what your brother is thinking now?"

"No. It's... feelings," she said.

"So you're feeling your brother?" I said. "That's kind of frowned upon in most places, you know."

She gave me a dry look.

"Seriously, though, so it's just like... he bit you, and now you have misty bats and know what he's feeling?"

"It's not that simple," Cuan explained. "When a vampire bites you, it creates a kind of bond. A bloodbond, a spiritual and magical connection that lasts for the rest of the vampire's existence."

"It only forms when the vampire actually bites her victim," Bianca added. "That creates a kind of energetic link. After that, if the bitten dies while the vampire still lives, then the bitten becomes a vampire in turn, beholden to the one who created her."

"If the vampire dies before the bitten, then the bloodbond is broken and the bitten goes on to live a normal life," Cuan continued.

"So... why don't you just want to kill the vampire?" Alexander asked.

"Because he's my fucking brother!" Bianca hissed.

"But... you're cursed," Alexander said. "I mean, if you die while the vampire still walks the earth, then..."

"That's why Cedric and Lester told me they were researching a cure," Bianca said. "I'd been asking everyone I could think of for help, and after I asked enough questions to enough people, someone told me rumors about a hunter in the city. That eventually led me to Cedric."

"That all had something to do with that vampire that moved into the city a few years back, right?" Cuan asked. "You never explained all the things that led you to become bitten in the first place, though."

"That's because it was none of your fucking business," Bianca responded.

We had reached my apartment building. I put the key in the lock at the front of the building and turned.

"Well, considering how I just unwittingly unleashed your brother on the city," I said as I pulled open the door, "I think I would appreciate knowing at least *some* of the background."

"Fine," Bianca said as we mounted the stairs. "So, like Cuan said, some vampire moved into the city in search of new territory. He wasn't well-connected; he'd probably only been changed for a few years. Dunno if the vampire who made him was or is still around. But this new vampire was in the neighborhood, anyway. One night I was at a party and some guys were being massive dicks and things were getting nasty, and so I texted Leo—my brother—to come and get me. He told me he was on his way but he never showed up. So finally I called him, and he told me he'd been attacked in the park on the way over."

"The vampire," Alexander concluded.

"Very good," Bianca said, as though she were talking to a toddler who'd just managed to use the big boy potty. "But yeah. He seemed fine, but he was shaken up and he had some marks on his neck. We didn't think anything of it, but..."

"But the bloodbond," Cuan said.

Bianca nodded. "It wasn't hard for the vampire to find him again. Two days later he disappeared. There was a search. We didn't find him. But three days after that, he found me: he was at my window, wild-eyed and pale. It was that bloodlust that a new vampire has before they've had blood. I don't think he even knew what he was doing, he just..."

"New vampires usually crave familiar blood... someone close to them," Cuan said.

Bianca nodded again. "After he bit me, he panicked and

fled. I never saw him after that, but I could feel him, at least for a while."

"And once you found Cedric, he led us in a hunt for the vampires," Cuan continued. "We found the one who made your brother, and Cedric staked him—I saw it happen—but I didn't think he'd ever found Leo."

"Except that, clearly, he did," Bianca said darkly.

We were in front of my apartment door now. "Well, we're here," I said as I put the key in the lock and turned. "It's a small studio, so sorry about that, but there's probably space enough for you to sleep."

I opened the door and we walked inside. I flicked on the lights. The place was just as Cuan and I had left it.

"Ugh," Bianca grimaced, wrinkling her nose. "It smells like a porn studio in here."

"Yeah, about that..." I said. "You might not want to sleep in the bed. Or on the sofa. Or on the floor in front of the mirror."

"Jesus Christ," Bianca said. "I feel like I'm gonna get pregnant just by breathing in there."

"I'd have thought you had an inhospitable womb," I said.

"Fuck off," she replied.

"Yeah... there's probably been enough fucking in here for the time being," Alexander said thoughtfully.

"You don't really get room to talk," I said wryly, "since you're the reason she shouldn't sit on the couch."

"Oh, ew," Bianca said, then turned to me with a curious expression. "Okay, so if that happened before he betrayed you to his daddy, then I'm going to lose what little respect I have for him, but if it happened afterward, I'm going to lose all respect for *you*."

"Before," Cuan, Alexander, and I said in unison, Alexander somewhat reluctantly.

"Altar boy it is, then," Bianca responded as she walked straight to the closet by the door and threw it open. She looked around and then saw above my row of hanging jackets a shelf of clean sheets, which she began pulling down and scattering over the floor by the closet door.

"Um, make yourself at home," I remarked sarcastically as she continued to pull things out of my closet.

"I am," she remarked simply. "This is my corner."

"Um, no, it's still my apartment," I said. "But if you want me to get you some sheets so you can sleep over there, then—"

"No, this is fine," she responded.

I relented with a sigh. I didn't have the energy to fight right now. Instead, I pointed to the couch.

"You can take the sofa, then, Alexander," I said.

"Yeah, I guess that's OK," Alexander responded, slightly sullenly.

There wasn't much in the apartment in terms of food, only what Marcus had bought me way back after I first woke up, and what had been in the place before then that wasn't perishable. Thankfully, there was a modest stash of frozen Weight Watchers meals in the freezer. The milk was still hanging on, though there wasn't enough left for four glasses, so Cuan and I had water. Add to that an unopened bag of trail mix and we had at least the bare makings of a meal. It was nothing like what we had come to expect at The Hunters' Home, but it was the best we could manage for now. We'd have to do a grocery run before dark.

My little kitchenette table only had two chairs, but Cuan decided to lean against the counter and Bianca sat on the floor in the corner of the room with a slight pout as though she thought I ought somehow to have had the foresight of providing her with an easy chair, leaving Alexander and I to share the table.

"So, I've been wondering about something," I said to Bianca as she took a large bite of a pizza pocket. "You said something about the bloodbond that forms between a vampire and the bitten only happening when there's an actual physical bite, but you were accusing Lester of feeding Leo your blood to keep that bond strong."

"That's right," Bianca said, a bit of tomato staining her lower lip. "The physical bite is only necessary to first establish the bloodbond. After that, there's a kind of magical link between the vampire and the blood of the bitten."

"Bonds like that transcend physical space," Cuan explained, "though proximity does admittedly sometimes make their effects stronger. It's why Bianca can sense her brother even though he's far away, and, actually, why Bianca can be... um... *persuaded* by Leo's thoughts and desires, especially if he's recently had her blood."

"Persuaded?" I asked.

"Shut up," Bianca said, then continued with her initial explanation. "The bloodbond wanes over time, though people are split over whether it ever goes away entirely on its own."

"There was a report once of a woman who died in her nineties after being bitten by a vampire when she was thirteen," Cuan explained. "That woman still turned. But whether that was an exceptional case or not, we don't know."

"It's not like there are people out there doing controlled studies, after all," Bianca said.

"I can only imagine what that consent form would look like," I mused, and Cuan smirked.

"I did hear about a vampire once who was trying to do some sick experiment like that on his own," Bianca added, "but he was slain before any of his bitten died, and that kind of fucked up his results."

"I bet Elsevier would still publish it," Cuan offered, though I had no idea what he was talking about.

"Anyway, the point is," Bianca continued, "the bloodbond fades with time. But, if the vampire drinks the bitten's blood again, it makes the bond stronger. It doesn't have to come straight from the body after the first time."

"The bite is just the catalyst," Cuan summarized. "After that, the bond is the blood."

"Thus, bloodbond," Alexander nodded. "I get it."

"And if the bloodbond is strong, Leo can… influence you?" I asked.

"If I'm close enough, he's… hard to resist," Bianca nodded.

"If he possesses his faculties, that is," Cuan added. "That's probably why Cedric had him wrapped in the spirit chains and tied to that cross, and who knows what else. The less coherent his thoughts, the less he can actually influence Bianca, even though the bloodbond would keep her in her powers." His face darkened. "It's… kind of terrible, really."

"Does the cross really affect vampires like that?" I asked.

"Of course it does," Alexander said. "Vampires are evil, and—"

"And you're a douche," Bianca interrupted. "Really, it depends on the vampire," she explained. "And the cross. Some vampires get turned willingly and revel in hunting and drinking blood. If someone is truly 'evil'," she added finger quotes for emphasis, "then anything sufficiently holy—cross or no—will have an effect on them."

"It's like how Perdition punishes the wicked," Alexander explained.

"But not all vampires are like that. Some are turned against their will. Some drink blood only because they have to in order to survive. Some fight even that with every fiber of their being. Vampires like that… well, they won't be so affected by crosses and shit. Leo… I know Leo. He's gentle. Kind. He'd never have ever hurt someone on purpose. I think Cedric chose a cross just in case. I think it was more psychological warfare than spiritual warfare."

"But vampires are still undead," Cuan added. "Some of

what we would call 'holy' artifacts or forces are ones that preserve the wheel of life. Those don't judge—if something is interfering with the cycle, then they take action. Forces like that won't care if Leo is 'good' or 'bad' or whatever. If he's undead, they'll try to get him to move on, to keep the cycle moving."

Cuan wasn't saying it outright, but I knew he was referring specifically to Az. Of course the Angel of Death would want to have someone who ought to be dead move on to the next world. But that made me wonder… if I did turn out to be some kind of spirit trapped here… what would he do to me? I decided to worry about that later. For the time being, I still had more questions.

"You mentioned that a vampire could control another vampire that was born when a bitten with a bloodbond died, something like that?" I asked.

"Right," Bianca nodded. "That influence I mentioned before? Once a bitten dies and becomes an undead vampire, that influence becomes absolute."

"There are colonies of vampires formed around that principle," Cuan said, "one ruling vampire and a collection of obedient followers the vampire sired."

"Like a colony of ants with a queen," I observed.

"No, not really," Cuan said; "scientists have found that ants display a profound amount of independence and free will."

"Thank you, Animal Planet," Bianca said, rolling her eyes.

"The point is," Cuan continued, "vampires don't have a great deal of free will when it comes to their sires. An instruction from the sire is tantamount to a compulsion. And it doesn't have to be a spoken instruction, either; the bloodbond works off of thoughts and feelings, don't forget."

"But the vampire who sired Leo is dead," Bianca added, "so we don't have to worry about that."

"Well, of course they're dead," I said; "aren't all vampires dead?"

"I mean destroyed, then, smartass," Bianca replied.

"OK," I conceded, "But what about the sire's sire? If the vampire who made the one who turned your brother is still around, couldn't that one control your brother?"

"If the chain were unbroken, maybe," Bianca said, "because that one would control the one who made my brother, and so could compel them to compel Leo in turn. But with the one in the middle gone, that link is broken. I've heard some vampires feel that they deserve obedience from everyone down the line like some culty family tree, but there's no bloodbond at that point, nothing to enforce that on a spiritual level."

"I see," I said.

"Now then," Bianca said, finishing her meal and standing up from her corner, brushing crumbs off of her lap, "do you mind if I go out for a bit? I didn't exactly bring any clothes here with me, and I figure you probably don't have a fresh supply of bras kicking about."

"Can't say that I do, no," I nodded.

"Well, fine. I'm going to catch the bus to the mall. Bras are uncomfortable as fuck, but I like my boobs to have perk." She buoyed her bosoms in her hands.

"Um, I'm eating, here," I said, and she sneered at me good-naturedly.

"Are you sure it's a good idea to be out and about?" Cuan asked. "I mean, the bloodbond just got kind of reinforced, and you've lost a bit of blood…"

"I'll be fine," she said defensively. "I told you; Leo's holed up somewhere."

"I'll go, too," Alexander nodded. "I mean, I don't exactly have clothes here, either; I could stand to have one or two things. And I'll call right away if anything goes wrong."

"There you go, see? All good," Bianca said. "But… do you mind if I borrow a scarf?"

"It's not cold out," Alexander said.

"That's not what I'm talking about," she said, her fingers going to the pair of angry red puncture marks on her throat.

"Yeah, if I have a scarf, you're welcome to it," I said, standing up and going to the closet. A little digging later and I found one.

Her neck now suitably wrapped up, she and Alexander went out to hit the stores. Cuan took the empty plates off of the table (and from Bianca's corner in the floor) and began to wash them in the sink.

"You know," I said, walking up behind him and wrapping my arms around his waist, "I much prefer it when you wash dishes without your clothes on."

He grinned at me. "I shudder to think of what Bianca would do if she came home and the place smelled even *more* like sex," he said, handing me a towel. "Though I don't disagree with you," he added, as I took the towel and he handed me a plate to dry.

He was silent for a moment as we continued doing the dishes, his brow knit.

"Hey…," he said at last, voice a little quieter and laced with concern. "So… are you all right?"

"What do you mean?" I asked.

"We… haven't really had a chance to talk about it," he said. "And… I was kind of too caught up last night in discovering that I had six brothers and a fucking asshole father to give it the thought it deserved, but… the library. That place really spun you out. Are you OK?"

I sighed as I toweled off a dish. "I don't know," was my honest answer.

"You don't have to talk about it if you don't want to," Cuan said.

"No, it's not that," I replied. "I just… I haven't been able to make sense of it."

"That's understandable, I think," Cuan responded. "Was

that..." he paused, almost afraid to finish the sentence. "Was that chair... in that circle... was that what happened to you?"

"I think so," I nodded. "I recognized it, on some level. It's like... it's like I'm on the cusp of remembering something," I said, shuddering involuntarily. Cuan turned off the water and dried his hands before placing them reassuringly on my shoulders. "Since we were down there, there's been... something... pressing against the back of my mind, all static and rapid images, but I can't makes sense of any of it."

Cuan said nothing, just looked at me with concern.

"I feel like I need to remember something," I said. "I feel like... like whatever happened down there happened to *me*. But I can't recall anything more than that."

"It's OK," Cuan said, placing a reassuring hand on my back. "You don't have to push anything. It'll come when it's ready."

"That's what *he* said," I muttered.

"That's my boy," Cuan grinned, dimple forming in his cheek.

I smiled back, even though I was still a little nervous. Cuan was right; I shouldn't try to force things. I didn't want my brain to start fabricating artificial memories or anything, after all. I wanted to be sure that, when the time came, what I recalled would be an accurate recollection of what happened at the library.

The library. The university. Suddenly I remembered the text I'd sent the previous night. I pulled out my phone and looked at it. Sure enough, I'd missed a text message during the debacle with Leo. Cuan looked concernedly over my shoulder as I pulled it up. It was from Professor Norton. As expected, my mentioning a threat to his research had gotten his attention.

"whos after my research?" the text demanded.

"I don't know," I texted back. "Someone from the city, maybe?"

The response was swift this time.

"What do u mean"

"I'm not sure," I replied, choosing my next words with care. I decided to be evasive, but still get the point across. "I overheard two cops talking about something called the Key of Solomon. They said it could control spirits or something. They mentioned the university. Sounded close enough to your work to make me worried. Do you know why the police would know about your work?"

"fucking cops", came the response. Then a few seconds later, "I keep my research a secret. If theyre talking about spirits that makes me nervous. But do u think the pipe explosions are faked? are they covering up something?"

"I don't know," I texted back again, "But you might not be safe at the university."

"im not there now", he responded, and I breathed a sigh of relief. "but i have 2 go back in 2 days. if you hear something else let me know"

There was another pause, and then,

"stay safe"

"You too", I texted back.

"Do you trust him?" Cuan asked as I put my phone away.

"If I trusted him, I wouldn't have been so evasive," I said. "But I don't want him in danger, either."

"That's because you're a sweetheart," he said, leaning over and kissing me.

We had some time while Alexander and Bianca were out, so we decided to do a few things to make the apartment more livable. The apartment basement had a pair of washer-dryers, and as they were both free, we washed the sheets from the bed and did a load of laundry—and I made sure that Cuan's Wushu pants and Alexander's hoodie that I'd borrowed way back when were included.

While the laundry ran, we went out to a local market Cuan knew to restock the pantry. Thankfully, it was an area of the city that hadn't seen any ogre activity, so the market was still functioning as normal, and we were able to shop for food. If I knew anything of cooking, I'd forgotten it, but Cuan assured me he knew a dish or two, though mostly we got nonperishables and frozen meals.

It was nice, just being out together running errands. It felt comfortably domestic. It felt normal. Or, rather, I assumed it was normal. I didn't really have any memory of what 'normal' was, but I nonetheless enjoyed our grocery run, and our subsequent run to the drugstore to get some toothbrushes and other things that we thought might be of use with extra people in the apartment. I also made a copy of my key for Cuan, and another for inside the apartment—I didn't want to risk losing mine and getting locked out again. Even if Cuan lost his, if one was kept in the apartment I could always walk back through the walls and pick it up again.

Cuan grinned when I handed him his key, his smile a mix of boyish shyness and simple elation.

"Well, now I'll always be sure to wear that armband with the phone pocket," he said. "It has a key pouch, too."

When we got back, we put the laundry in the dryer and the groceries away. We also had to hand-wash a few things from the laundry that wouldn't have done well in the washing machine, like some of the less conventional underwear I had. This took a while, as Cuan kept getting turned on by the different articles of clothing (and sometimes I did, too; particularly when they were ones I didn't recognize) and we had to stop and remind one another that Bianca and Alexander could be back at any moment. We did all right, though we did need to stop to make out and grind a bit at one point after Cuan discovered what was essentially a G-string with a built-in cock ring. After that was done, Cuan stayed in the kitchen to figure out my stove while I put the clothes on a discreet drying rack in the corner and re-made the bed with a set of sheets that had somehow escaped Bianca's closet rampage, and we both let our blue balls subside. Shortly afterward we got a text from Bianca that they were headed back, and Cuan put the wok we'd bought on the stovetop and started to show me how to make a stir-fry with some vegetables and meat. He was a patient teacher, though I could only watch for a little while before I had to collect the clothes from the basement dryer. I had just finished folding them when the callbox sounded, and I buzzed our houseguests back into the building. A moment later, there was a knock on the apartment door.

Alexander and Bianca were arguing as I let them in.

"I can't believe that's where you went to get clothes!" he was saying as he dumped a pair of shopping bags on the floor. "You said you were going to the mall!"

"I did go to the mall, didn't I?" Bianca protested.

"Yeah, for like two things; then you dragged me to that other place for most of your wardrobe. I mean, who goes somewhere like that to buy an outfit?"

"You're such a baby," Bianca responded. "It's like you've never been in a sex shop before."

"I *have* never been in a sex shop before!" he protested.

"Well, it was long overdue, then," Bianca said, setting a pair of smaller black bags in the corner she'd claimed for herself. "Honestly, I think some of the stuff in there would really help you out."

"That stuff is scary!" Alexander protested. "I mean, I finally found one section that I thought was just normal tools and stuff, but after I went to the staff and was like, 'um, this flashlight doesn't turn on,' the staff took the cap off, and..." he trailed off, face bright red as Cuan and I busted out laughing.

"Well, I think the decor in this place is moving in that direction," Bianca remarked, looking at the drying rack in the corner with admiration.

"That!" Alexander exclaimed, pointing agitatedly at the red G-string. "They had that exact thing at the shop we were at!"

"Hm," I mused, "Perhaps I'll have to acquaint myself with that place. Or re-acquaint myself, more likely."

"Atta boy," Bianca said with a wry smile. Then she inhaled deeply through her nose. "What smells so good?"

"I made stir-fry," Cuan said.

"Ooo, I love your stir fry," Bianca said, making for the kitchenette. "Trust me, you two," she said to Alexander and me, "he may not be at Cedric's level, but this dog can still cook."

By the time I walked into the kitchen, Bianca was already seated in the corner with a heaping plate of stir fry in front of her.

She was right. Cuan's stir-fry was excellent. I leaned against the counter this time around, plate and fork in hand, while Cuan and Alexander shared the table. We ate in silence for a while, enjoying the rich flavor. When Bianca finished her helping, she stared quietly down at the empty plate for a moment. When she spoke, her voice was uncharacteristically quiet.

"Thanks," she said.

"Glad you liked it," Cuan smiled.

"Not that," Bianca retorted, then off of Cuan's frown, "well, not *just* that. I mean Cole. Thanks for... for giving me a place to stay. When I left The Hunters' Home, I just wanted to get out of there. I didn't think at all about where I'd go. You didn't have to take me in. I'm thankful that you did."

"I'm glad I could help, but don't get too comfortable," I said; "this isn't going to work as a long-term arrangement."

"No shit," she replied. "I mean, you have me sleeping on the floor!" Then, suddenly, surprisingly, she offered a small, genuine smile. "Still," she said, "Thanks."

"Welcome to the Isle of Misfit Toys," I responded with a sardonic smile.

"Isn't that from *The Perks of Being a Wallflower*?" Cuan asked.

"No, it's from a *Rudolph the Red Nosed Reindeer* movie," Alexander said.

"I don't know what either of those things are," I responded, and all three of them stared despairingly at me. Bianca stood up, plate in hand, and walked over to me. Then she did something that surprised me even more than thanking me. She took my empty plate along with hers, and, placing them both in the sink, started to wash them.

"Um, Bianca?" Cuan asked. "Are you feeling OK?"

"Fuck you," she replied.

"Yeah, she's feeling OK," Cuan concluded with a nod.

After we all finished dinner, Bianca and Alexander returned to settle into their respective spots in the room.

"Is it OK if I take a shower?" Bianca asked, looking into the bathroom.

"Sure," I said; "go ahead. I'll get you a fresh towel."

"Hang it on the doorknob," Bianca said. "I don't want anybody walking in on me while I'm showering."

"Ew," I said with a shudder. "Don't worry about that. Lady parts: Ew."

"And what makes you so sure about that, Mr. Amnesia?" Bianca challenged. "How do you know you don't like lady parts if you have no memory?"

I rolled my eyes. "Do you understand how insulting that question is?" I asked. "Sexuality and desire aren't dependent upon experience. That's like if I asked, how come you know you're straight if you haven't ever been with a girl?"

"I'm not straight," Bianca said matter-of-factly, "I'm bi."

"Oh," I said. "Sorry, I shouldn't have assumed—"

"Yeah, yeah," she said, waving me off. "You shouldn't have. But I shouldn't have said what I said, either. I mean, I didn't have to sleep with a girl to know that I wanted to lick a clitoris."

"Oh *God*," Alexander said, stifling a gag.

"Ugh," Bianca groaned. "What is it with gay guys being so

horrified at female sexuality? I guess I shouldn't finger myself in the corner tonight, then?"

"Um, no," I said, "there will be no public fingering if you want to keep staying here."

"Really?" she asked indignantly. "Says the guy who has apparently cum on every surface of the apartment?"

"I don't do that when guests are here!" I protested. "Well, at least not ones who aren't participating. Or who haven't asked to watch."

"Well, you're all welcome to—"

"Let's not," I said, rubbing my temples.

"Ugh, gay guys are no fun," she groaned. "But to each their own, I guess." She shrugged. "Still, I'll never understand how you don't see the appeal of breasts. I mean, when you have a pair that are big and swollen and round, the way they feel when you fondle them in your hands... that's just..." she shuddered with delight.

"You know, that's exactly how I feel about balls," Cuan chimed in.

"Amen," I agreed.

"Okay, what the fuck?" Alexander burst out, exasperation clear on his face. "Is this what it's like at your Hunter headquarters, where you just go on about anything? I mean, how are you *this* comfortable talking about sex?"

"Aww, was your little Church of the Moldy Cardigan too straitlaced for sexual liberation?" Bianca cooed.

Alexander glared at her.

"That might have just been Alexander," I said. "It certainly wasn't universal. I mean, Thomas didn't have a problem. How was it he described you to me again? 'Alexander's ass sees so much traffic that it should get state highway funding', something like that?"

Alexander blanched as Cuan and Bianca burst into hysterics.

"*Thomas* said that about me?" he asked incredulously.

"If it makes you feel any better, he didn't say it with disapproval," I noted.

"So... they knew I was...?" he paused.

"Thomas certainly did," I pointed out. "I mean, that's the whole reason he was playing the organ that night... to cover how loud you were."

Alexander fidgeted as the other two stared at him.

"Yeah," Cuan nodded, looking at Alexander appraisingly, "I could see how he'd be a screamer."

"You know," Alexander said hesitantly, "that... that *was* a really hot night. If Bianca weren't here, maybe the three of us would..."

He trailed off as all of us glared at him in stony silence. His audacity had not landed well.

He looked at me uncomfortably. "No?" he asked.

"You really think that'd happen?" I asked back. "I mean, I have no philosophical objection to the idea of threesomes, but I can't be with someone I still kinda want to beat the tar out of."

"I dunno, that sounds pretty sexual to me," Bianca pointed out.

"Go take your shower," I said, and Bianca grinned as she shut the bathroom door behind her. I sighed and turned back to Alexander.

"Look," I said, "I know we let you in yesterday, and we're having you stay with us today. But that doesn't mean things are back to business as usual. I..." I ran my hand through my hair in frustration as I tried to organize my feelings into something coherent. "I'm thankful for the key to my apartment. And I'm thankful that you saved Cuan last week. And I'm... glad that you've come to realize that maybe that particular church isn't the best moral point of reference, even if it does suck how it came about. But Alexander, what you did to me was really fucked up. When you just... walked away, leaving me chained and at the mercy of your father, that... that broke something between us. It's not something that a couple days is gonna make all better. I don't know if it can ever really get all better. Maybe... maybe we can eventually build a kind of friendship, I dunno, but... but I don't know that we'll ever share that kind of intimacy again."

Alexander was silent for a moment as my words sunk in. His eyes wandered to Cuan.

"Don't look at me," Cuan said. "I'm grateful to you for saving my life, and you're hot as balls and sex with you would probably be really fun under normal circumstances. But I *love* Cole. He's more important to me than anything. And ever since you did what you did to him, I... well, I sorta wanna rip your heart out and throw it up against the wall."

"Jesus..." Alexander gasped.

"Yeah, Jesus is probably mad at you, too," I said.

Alexander frowned and returned his attention to arranging the sofa. Perhaps I was being harsh, but the bluntness was clearly what he needed. The simple fact was that yeah, while Alexander was hot and enjoyable in bed, he seemed unable to fully appreciate the enormity of what he'd done to me. That, as much as the betrayal itself, was keeping me from feeling any kind of genuine sexual desire for him.

We remained in silence until Bianca emerged from the shower, towel wrapped around her, and picked up one of the small black bags from the corner of the room, then returned to the bathroom. When she appeared again, she was clad in a very scanty set of black lace underwear that prominently high-lighted her breasts, pelvis, and behind.

"I don't care if the effect is completely wasted on the three of you," she announced as she strode across the room; "I feel sexy."

"You do you, Bianca," I said with a nod.

The rest of the night consisted of quiet reading. Apparently there was enough on my shelf to satisfy everyone. Alexander curled up with the Gnostic Gospels, Bianca selected a book on queer spirituality, and Cuan and I shared a large book of Sherlock Holmes stories, reproduced directly from the original *Strand* magazine.

Once again, I felt an odd sense of domestic comfort, curled up with him in the bed. When it was finally time to sleep, we set the book aside and slid under the sheets together.

I really disliked sleeping clothed, but given the circumstances I decided it was best, and had changed into a pair of loose lounge pants in the bathroom when I'd brushed my teeth. Cuan, too, kept on his Wushu pants like a pair of pajama bottoms, though he discreetly slipped off his jockstrap under the sheets. I pressed myself into him, feeling him close to me.

"Goodnight," I whispered.

"Sleep well," he whispered back as he nuzzled into my neck.

X

IN THE BLOOD

Unfortunately, I did not sleep well.

In my dreams, I saw myself in the basement library. I was tied to the wooden chair in the middle of a glowing circle. I couldn't get my bearings, however; the scene kept shifting around me. But someone was there, just outside the circle, knowing, waiting.

Everything flashed away and suddenly I was surrounded by flames, screaming as they grew and reached toward me, red and orange and hot and hungry, joined moments later by flashes of white...

And then I was wrapped in Cuan's arms, in a bed in a dark apartment, still screaming and shaking as he clutched me to his chest.

"It's OK," he was saying over and over. "I'm here; I've got you."

"Is he all right?" The voice was Alexander's, though I could barely make it out over the screaming. My screaming.

"I'm here," Cuan continued. Stroking my hair. "I'm here; you're awake now; you're OK."

I breathed, still shaking. "Awake?" I croaked.

"Awake," Cuan nodded.

I looked around my apartment. Alexander and Bianca were staring at me in quiet alarm. I turned back to Cuan, his golden eyes filled with concern and compassion.

"I... was in the library," I managed. "I can't remember anything more than that. Except... there was fire."

"That place really fucked you up, huh?" Bianca said. Her voice was... gentle?

"What place?" Alexander asked, confused.

"We think we found where Cole lost his memory," Bianca explained. "We just... don't know how. But we saw the aftermath."

"Holy shit," Alexander said. "And it was the library?"

Just then we were interrupted by a furious pounding on our door. We all started; my violent shaking continued as Cuan clutched me protectively.

Silence.

Then the pounding came again, loud and fierce, and I flinched against it. This time it was followed by a loud male bellow.

"What the fuck is the matter with you?" The voice roared. "Shut the fuck up so people can sleep!"

"Oh, *hell* no," Bianca said quietly, standing up, the bedsheets falling off of her until she was clad only in her extremely sexy black lace lingerie. She quickly rummaged through the closet next to the bed and emerged with a metal-tipped black umbrella, appraising it approvingly. "This'll do," she said, and then swung open the door.

In the light of the hall I caught a glimpse of a greasy, out-of-shape middle aged man in poorly-fitting clothes with a missing tooth. I think I'd passed him once or twice on the stairs, but I only got the fleetingest glimpse as he looked Bianca up and down with a look of surprise tainted with predatory lasciviousness before Bianca advanced on him.

"Well, hello—" he started, then stopped short with a whimper as Bianca pressed the metal-tipped umbrella into his neck.

"Do you fucking mind?" she hissed as the man backpedaled into the foyer railing. "I am *working* here. So you'd better have five grand to make up for the business you're about to lose me because otherwise, I'm going to take this umbrella and—"

The door shut behind her, muffling her continued sinister threats. The three of us remained in statuesque, stunned silence, staring at the shadows shifting beneath the closed door. We remained that way for about two minutes until Bianca raised her voice and finished with "—while belting out *Singing in the Rain!*" This was punctuated by the abrupt *foomp* of the umbrella opening, followed immediately by a combination shriek-slash-whimper and then the sound of the man retreating down the steps at speed.

The door opened again and Bianca entered triumphantly, closed umbrella resting comfortably over her shoulder. She swung it down lightly and used it to push the door shut, then tossed it neatly back into the closet.

"I take it all back," I said appreciatively. "You'd make a *killing* as a sex worker."

She bowed with a flourish. "Thank you; that's all I wanted to hear," she said with a grin.

Alexander just gaped at her.

Sleep did not come easily after all that. When it did come, however, it was heavy and long and deep. It was late into the morning when I awoke, still in Cuan's reassuring embrace. Alexander was quietly reading a book on the sofa, and Bianca was still lying on her back in her corner, though her eyes were open and she was studying the ceiling.

"Hey," Cuan said, and I turned to see his warm smile.

"Hey," I said back, greeting him with a light kiss.

It was still a bit of a crowded apartment in the morning.

With Bianca having showered the night before, Alexander was first into the shower now. In the meantime, Cuan set about scrambling some eggs and cooking some toast. Bianca stayed mostly in her corner, getting herself into a rather formidable-looking leather getup comprised of a number of pieces connected with laces. The bottoms were composed of thigh-high boots and a leather skirt. The top was a black leather bodice with white lace accents that contrasted well with her black lace undergarments. I thought the overall effect was a bit much, but then I wasn't exactly the target audience, so who was I to judge?

I made sure that Alexander's borrowed hoodie was set out on the sofa before he emerged from the bathroom, already clad in newly-purchased shirt and trousers. He regarded the familiar hoodie with appreciation and slipped it on, remarking as he did so that it was one of his favorites and so he was glad to have it back again.

Breakfast was a simple enough affair, and after cleaning up it was Cuan's and my turn to shower.

"How're you doing?" Cuan asked me once we were alone and he was holding me close under the hot, cascading water.

"A little sleepy," I said; "and the apartment's crowded."

"Yeah," Cuan said as he took a step back and began to soap up my torso. "But I mean, how are you after last night?"

"The nightmare," I nodded. "I'm... about the same, really," I said, trying to weigh the feeling in my head against the day before. "All the flashes and the incomprehensible images are still there, pressing against the back of my mind, but nothing makes any more or less sense than it did yesterday. It's easier to not let them overwhelm me when I'm relaxed. Or when I'm focused on something pleasant. Like being close to you."

"Yeah?" Cuan smiled.

"Yeah," I said, smiling back. "I'm glad you were holding me last night. It's easier when I can feel your touch on—

mmm," I purred as Cuan's hand moved to washing my cock and balls. He fondled them a little more than he needed to, and I leaned into his hand appreciatively. "And that," I added; "that's best of all." I reached a hand over to him, too, feeling his length in my palm, playing with his scrotum between my fingers.

It wouldn't do to make a mess in the shower while we had guests staying, so we didn't indulge in any more than that, but the few seconds of playful contact was nonetheless welcome. We had, thankfully, brought the day's clothes into the bathroom with us, so I didn't have to worry about walking out of the bathroom with an erection tenting my towel.

The daytime passed somewhat tensely. Bianca sat in her corner, still and alert like a cat, focusing on what she could feel of her brother. Beyond waiting, there wasn't much to do, but I remained uncomfortable.

"So, what is the plan, anyway?" I asked. "Do we even have one?"

"We're going to find my brother so I can talk to him," Bianca said impatiently.

"Yes, sure, but then what?" I asked. "Is it just going to be 'Hey, Leo; how's tricks?' and everything will be fine? I mean, what if he's in more of a...biting mood?"

"Then we'll deal with that when it happens," Bianca said. "Look," she added quietly, "I know that talking to him is a long shot. I know that I might not be able to make anything change. But... Cedric denied me the chance to talk to him. I just want that much. He's my brother. Apart from the few seconds in the basement yesterday, the last time I saw him was the first time he bit me."

"And then he bit you again," Alexander pointed out.

"Yes, which is why I'll be able to find him at all."

"But..." I added, choosing my words carefully, "you said the bloodbond is stronger the closer you are to him, right? If you're in his presence, what about the influence that a vampire can wield over the bitten?"

"You should give me more credit," Bianca said.

"Forgive me for doubting the vampire's thrall," Alexander added abruptly. "Worst case scenario, he kills you, and then we've let *two* vampires loose on the city. Or he kills all of us, and then, well, I don't even want to think about that. Best case, what, you talk to him and then we drive a stake through his heart? Or he decides to play nice vampire and stops drinking blood and starves to death?"

We glared at him.

"Alexander, stop it," I said.

"No," Alexander insisted. "Get mad at me if you want, fine, but these are things we have to consider. Lord knows I hate saying it, but I don't see an upside to what we're doing."

"That's heartless," Cuan muttered.

"Oh?" Alexander challenged. "Then, what do you see as the benefit here?"

"At the very least, it gives Bianca closure," Cuan said, and Bianca nodded slightly. "And you talk about vampires like they're some crazed monsters. They're not. They're every bit as intelligent and rational as they were in life. Hunting is hard on vampires, especially unwilling ones. There's always the possibility that we can parley some kind of understanding. I know that it wouldn't kill me to donate a half-pint or so every so often."

"Cuan..." I looked at him in alarm.

"I don't mean letting him bite me," he explained. "But if he has some sources of human blood that don't require him to bite or kill, that might be enough for him."

"What the fuck kind of Faustian bargain is that?" Alexander asked.

"A good one," Bianca said.

"It's a plan, anyway," I nodded. "But is he just going to stand there and listen to us? I mean, he wasn't exactly in a talking mood the last time."

"He was hungry," Bianca said. "Plus he'd just been unchained; he was desperate to escape and to fulfill basic needs. Think about it: when you were just released, did you feel like standing around and talking?"

"No, I didn't," I admitted, looking to Cuan. "I had... more important needs."

"Right," Bianca nodded. "See? It's basically the same thing, just the need was different. Leo needed a mouthful of blood. You needed... I'm guessing an ass-full of cum?"

I gave her a withering look. What I had needed upon release, urgently, was to be near Cuan. But considering what we did when I found him, I really couldn't tell her she was wrong.

Cuan smirked as I met his eyes, the shared memory one we both savored. Then he turned back to Alexander. "We're not going into this blind," he said, "or unprepared. If things go wrong, we'll be right there to help."

"But... we don't have a stake," Alexander said.

"A stake in what?" I asked.

All three of them looked at me despairingly.

"I'm choosing to believe this is you being a dick rather than you having amnesia," Alexander said, and I shrugged in response. "A wooden stake," he clarified. "To kill a vampire."

"You're even more of an idiot than Cole," Bianca said to him.

"We don't need a stake," Cuan explained, as Alexander looked at Bianca in offense. "All that stuff about it being the only way to kill a vampire is a myth. You have Candela, don't you? Plus those light shows of yours. I'm guessing both of those would be very disruptive to undead like a vampire, even if Leo isn't the type to earn the ire of holy artifacts."

"If that's the case, then how did the myth about stakes being effective come about in the first place?" I asked.

"Oh, that's not a myth," Cuan explained; "just the idea that they're the only thing that's effective is. Stakes are just the most convenient and efficient method for most people who don't have supernatural abilities or access to powerful holy artifacts. Vampires and other undead aren't 'alive' in the traditional sense, so their bodies are very resistant to physical harm. It's generally something more spiritual or magical that's keeping them alive, so that's the most effective way to hit them."

"And stakes do that?" I asked.

"Yeah," Cuan nodded. "Plants are particularly strong expressions of nature, so they have lots of magical and spiritual properties. And vampires' power comes from the blood, so therefore piercing their heart with a stake made from wood with strong curative or spiritual properties like oak or holly will kill them almost instantly."

"Well, then, wouldn't it be better if we did have a stake?" I asked.

"Sure," Bianca said sarcastically. "If you happen to have an oak branch lying around and know how to whittle, be my guest."

"Really, though, we shouldn't need it," Cuan said. "Alexander ought to be able to take care of himself, and Leo shouldn't even notice you. Plus you can fade if you need to get out of there. Just in case, though, I do have something handy." He turned to the bag of groceries left on the counter from yesterday. I'd thought it was empty, but apparently there was one thing left inside, because Cuan pulled out a large bag of garlic bulbs.

"Garlic," he explained triumphantly. "Potent purifying plant. Powerful effect on the blood, so much so that vampires don't like even being near the stuff."

"Ugh, keep that away from me," Bianca grimaced.

"Even the bitten find it repulsive," Cuan added.

"Wait, it keeps Bianca away?" I asked. "Gimme, gimme," I added, reaching with a grin as Bianca flipped me off.

"So that's not a myth?" Alexander asked.

"Nope," Cuan said. "You should take some too, just to be safe."

"Speaking of safe," I asked, "what about you, Cuan? Alexander has Candela and I fade into the background, but will you be okay?"

"I should be all right," Cuan nodded. "You know that long-standing cultural concept about werewolves and vampires being mortal enemies?"

"Um, amnesia," I responded.

Cuan rolled his eyes. "Well, fine. Anyway, there's this trope in the popular consciousness about how vampires and werewolves hate each other. It's bullshit, of course, but stuff like that comes from a grain of truth somewhere."

"Is that why you and Bianca don't get along?" I asked.

"What?" Bianca asked. "No, of course not. I don't hate Cuan. He's just annoying. Like you. 'Cept that you're also feisty."

"Hey, I'm feisty," Cuan protested.

"No, you're *flirty*, which is different," Bianca said. "And since you have no interest of that sort in me, because you're gay, or have no taste, or whatever, that doesn't count for anything."

"I like it," I said.

"Yeah, because he's boning you," Bianca responded.

"I liked it before he was boning me."

"Because you *wanted* him to bone you," Bianca clarified.

"Well, I find him kind of annoying," Alexander offered.

"You don't count," Bianca replied; "you're bitter that they won't fuck you; of course you'd be annoyed."

"Um, can we get back on topic?" Cuan asked impatiently. "I'm kind of in the middle of an explanation here."

"See?" Bianca said. "Annoying."

"*Anyway*," Cuan continued with a glare in Bianca's direction, "the point is, that whole concept of vampires and werewolves hating each other apparently stems from the fact that a werewolf's transition—at least the transition of a werewolf like me—supposedly disrupts the bloodbond. Just like how when I transition it burns disease out of my blood, apparently it does the same to vampirism."

"So a werewolf can't become a vampire?" I asked.

"I suppose if a werewolf were bitten and then died before they transformed, they could become a vampire," Cuan mused. "But if I was bitten and then shifted into my wolf form, it would be like I was never bitten at all, apart from the physical blood loss. That's what Cedric told me, anyway; although I've never been in much of a hurry to test that, particularly now that we know Cedric has a habit of just saying things that suit his purposes. Thus, the precautions," he added, pointing to the bag of garlic bulbs.

Cuan's explanation left me feeling a little better: we weren't going in as blindly as I'd feared.

We returned to tense waiting, and it was just as the sun was beginning to go down that Bianca suddenly threw her head up from the book she was reading.

"Leo's on the move," she said. She looked slightly fearful. "He's hungry."

"Shit," Alexander replied. "Where is he?"

"I don't know exactly," Bianca admitted, "but I do know roughly where he's headed: the university."

"Fuck," Alexander said. "Why is he headed there?"

"Good hunting grounds, probably," Bianca said. "Lots of healthy young people, walking alone at night... It's a prime place for good blood, if you don't mind most of it being 50 proof."

"But the university is closed and evacuated," I said.

"He wouldn't know that, would he?" Bianca responded. "He might just be scoping it out. But even so, this is a good chance for us to get to him without other people around."

"Just potentially a bunch of ogres," I pointed out.

Bianca blanched. "Oh no," she said.

"Yeah, I *really* don't want to find out what one of those things is like with vampirism," Cuan said. "Let's move."

While we only had a vague idea of where Leo was when we left the apartment, Bianca was increasingly able to pinpoint his location as we approached the University.

"He's this way," Bianca said, pointing toward a quadrangle. "He's... frustrated."

"I don't doubt it," Cuan nodded. "Finding this place empty when he's on the hunt? That has to suck."

"Well, let's hope he's not doing any sucking," I said.

"Fair enough," Cuan admitted.

We walked around the side of a landscaping shed, and we saw him. He was standing on a path in the center of the quadrangle, away from the flickering lamplight, his white shirt and trousers nonetheless making him easy to spot. Bianca took a step toward him, but Cuan suddenly pulled her back into the shadows of the shed.

"What?" she hissed at him, voice a whisper. "He's gonna know I'm here regardless."

Cuan pointed, and we turned to see a patrol car pulling up to the edge of the quadrangle. Two cops got out, one very fit and one a little heavy. Both of them had stern expressions, and both had their hands on their holsters. They had Leo's full attention even before they spoke; Bianca and the rest of us had, for the moment, gone unnoticed.

"Hey, you, what're you doing here?" the heavy cop demanded.

"I'm just out for a walk," Leo explained nonchalantly.

"Snooping around?" the heavy cop asked.

"This is a restricted area," the fit cop said. "You can't be here."

"I'm sorry," Leo said, raising his hands in a display of surrender. "I had no idea."

"Bullshit," the heavy cop said, drawing his weapon and pointing it menacingly at Leo. "There's no way you haven't heard about this," the fit cop stated. "It's on all the news; we've had bulletins; the university shut down the dorms. You telling us you've been living under a rock?"

"No, but I've been tied up in my sister's basement for the past few years."

"Oh, funny guy, huh?" the heavy cop spat. "You're probably the one who's been poking around the subway, sticking your nose where it shouldn't be."

"Subway?" Leo asked. "What's in the subway?"

The fit cop drew his weapon now, too. "You don't get to be the one asking questions, shithead," he said menacingly. "Now get on the ground."

"Hey, I'm not looking for any trouble," Leo said, taking a step back. "I'm—"

We all jumped. Not because Leo took a step, but because at the very moment he moved his legs, both cops opened fire.

I don't know if any bullets hit Leo. They might not have even had a chance to. Instantaneously, his expression contorted with rage, and he flew forward in a billow of dark mist. The mist solidified in front of the fit cop as Leo transferred all his momentum into a slam punch into the cop's solar plexus, sending him flying back into the side of the squad car, denting the door on impact. The heavy cop tried to turn but before he could move Leo landed a massive roundhouse to his head, sending him sailing back into the car as well. Both cops slumped to the ground, unconscious.

Leo advanced on them, kneeling in front of the fit cop's

slumped body. He grabbed the cop's hair roughly, causing his head to loll back, exposing his neck. Then he opened his mouth wide, bearing a pair of sharp, glistening fangs.

"Really?" Bianca called. "You're gonna drink pig blood? I thought you had better taste than that."

Leo looked up sharply as Bianca stepped into the light of a nearby lamp.

"Sister?" Leo asked in genuine surprise, releasing the cop's hair and standing up.

"Of course, I really should know better than to ask whether you have taste," Bianca continued. "I mean, look at what you're wearing."

Leo stared defiantly at her, the top of his muscular chest visible through the open laced collar of his white shirt, his strong calves bare under the hem of his hemp trousers, which stopped just below his knees. He stared at her, eyes a piercing green under his mop of fine brown hair.

"Who are you to talk?" he challenged. "What are you wearing? Did you actually pick that out?"

"Yeah, no-one's gonna win that exchange," I whispered to Cuan. "Bianca might as well be a character from Karen Walker's dominatrix film, while her brother looks like the gym bunny version of Thackery Binks."

"Shh," Cuan admonished, snorting back a laugh. "You don't want him to notice you."

"Yeah, I chose this," Bianca was saying, "and it *slays*."

"Oh, please," Leo retorted. "All it's missing is a hood with rabbit ears. Also, bad choice of words, sister."

"Fair enough," Bianca said. "But still, did you pick *that* out?" She mocked. "You look like you should be doing colonial period porn. 'Oh, excuse me, you look like you could use some help churning your butter.'"

"I had limited options," Leo explained. The one who turned

me was a very old vampire. This was the best I could find in the wardrobe he provided."

"And you never thought you could do any better?" Bianca asked.

"Sorry," Leo replied bitterly, "I was a little busy being chained up in a supply closet."

Bianca was quiet for a moment. "You have to know I didn't know anything about that," she said.

"I know, sister," Leo replied, with a gentleness I didn't expect. "You would never have stood for that. And considering what transpired, I'm guessing the ones who found me didn't know either. Are they here?"

"I am," Cuan said, stepping forward into the lamplight. I appreciated how he answered the question while still preserving the thin incognito veil that kept me from being noticed unless attention was specifically directed at me.

"Your voice..." Leo concentrated for a moment. "You're one of the ones who liberated me."

"I'm Cuan. I'm... glad to speak to you under somewhat better circumstances."

"Yet not entirely amicable ones," Leo observed. "Is that garlic at your waist and around your neck?"

"Considering that you are standing over two cops whom you just sent careening into their squad car, I hope you'll forgive me the precaution," Cuan responded. "But I'm just here so Bianca can talk with you."

"She needs a bodyguard for that?" Leo asked.

"Considering how your last two interactions involved you sucking her blood, you can't blame us." Alexander glowered, stepping into the light as well.

"Alexander, dial it back," Bianca whispered pointedly.

"I needed to feed," Leo said defensively. "The first time, I'd just been turned. I was out of my mind. The second time, I'd been starved, fed drips of her blood to keep me alive for years."

"And that excuses blood-sucking?" Alexander challenged.

"Humans have done worse things to survive," Leo explained. "I need blood to live."

"So you took your sister's?" Alexander asked.

"You think I'm happy about that?" Leo protested. "Happy that I inflicted this curse on someone I love?" He turned to Bianca. "You have to know that I didn't wish this for you."

"I know," Bianca said quietly. "But it's done. Now we have to figure out what to do next."

"Well, I know the first thing I'll do," Leo said, turning his attention back to the fallen police officers. "I'm going to have a nice meal."

"Nice meal?" Bianca scoffed. "That's like thirty percent doughnut, sixty percent bacon, and twenty percent corruption."

"That's 110%," Leo replied.

"The point is, do you really want to put that in your mouth?" Bianca asked. "We'll get you some better blood."

"Sure, it might not be the best vintage, but it'll be warm and fresh," Leo said. "You can't get that from a vial. I... I *crave* that."

This wasn't going well. It wasn't a disaster, either, but we needed a plan B, just in case. I started to sneak around, quietly, making for the far side of the squad car. I saw Cuan's and Bianca's eyes flicker to me as I moved. They seemed to have a vague idea of what I had in mind. Bianca continued keeping her brother talking.

"And what about them?" she pointed at the two officers. "You're just going to drain the blood of unwilling victims? And do you really want a bloodbond with corrupt cops?" Bianca asked.

"Corrupt?" Leo responded, slightly surprised. "They just seemed like regular cops to me."

"This area... it's not safe," Cuan explained. "If they're patrolling here, they're likely at least complicit in what's going on."

"Now that you mention it," Leo asked, "what *is* going on? Why is the university so quiet?"

"You don't need to know that," Alexander spat.

"No, I think he does," Bianca responded.

"The last thing we need is to give a vampire ideas," Alexander retorted.

"So what, I'm just some monster to you?" Leo asked. His eyes narrowed. "Yeah, I remember you," he said. "You're the one who attacked me when I was released. You put on quite a light show."

"You haven't seen anything yet," Alexander replied, removing Candela from its wrappings. "You wanna push your luck?"

"Alexander, *stop it*," Cuan hissed. "You're making things worse."

"Leo, listen to me," Bianca said. "Don't bite the cops. We don't want to make Bitten out of the police, they're enough trouble as it is."

"Well, if they're Bitten, maybe I can convince them to be better public servants. They tried to *kill* me, Bianca. Just opened fire for no reason."

"Well, you're about to give *me* a reason," Alexander challenged.

"You just try it," Leo said. "Think you're fast enough?"

"To stop you from biting two cops? Yeah, I think the speed of light can cut it."

I had managed to get around to the other side of the squad car. Thankfully, the driver's side window was rolled down. I reached inside, waiting in case I needed to take action.

"Well, maybe I'll just pick one, then," he said, appraising the unconscious officers. "How about this one?" he decided with a grin, lifting the fit policeman by the hair again. "He's kind of a hottie. Maybe we could learn to like each other? 'Yeah, sure I sucked your blood, but you tried to kill me. Maybe we can just call it even after I've sucked your—'"

"*Lux,*" Alexander declared as a sphere of light formed in his palm.

Leo sneered and opened his mouth, baring his fangs above the cop's neck.

That was my cue.

I slammed my palm on the squad car's horn with all my might. The car blared out a shriek, and Leo, with the reflexes of a startled cat, burst into mist, dropping the officer and darting from the side of the car and reforming some distance away. He stared at the car, wide-eyed and panting.

"What the fuck?" he gasped. I had ducked back behind the car and out of sight, and so escaped notice as I retreated back into the quad.

The horn had also startled Alexander, and with his concentration disrupted the sphere of light in his palm fizzled out. He took a breath, however, and then repeated, "*Lux.*"

"Don't you dare!" Bianca shouted as Alexander pointed his palm at her brother. She lunged at him, and Alexander, surprised, spun around to dodge her, then faced her and raised his palm, sphere still glowing before it.

"*Murus,*" he declared as Bianca conjured forth a swarm of dark, misty bats. The sphere of light expanded into a sheet, the angry swarm buffeting against it and bursting into mist as they did so.

"Leave my sister alone!" Leo cried, rushing forward.

"Leo, don't!" Cuan shouted, dashing to intercept him. The vampire turned to strike him, and Cuan expertly parried his series of blows, not trying to land any strikes of his own, but nonetheless keeping the vampire occupied. Leo finally swiped at him and Cuan leapt back several meters to clear the assault.

"So, you wanna play," Leo asked, turning his attention to Cuan and preparing to dash at him. Just before he leapt however, there was a crack, and a beam of light shot down from above, crashing into the ground and sending dirt flying. When the beam dissipated, a spear was left plunged into the grass of the quad. A second later, a woman alighted next to it. She was tall, slender yet shapely, voluminous tight curls of black hair cascading over her shoulders. The gleaming white spear contrasted sharply with her dark skin. I recognized her immediately.

"Julia?" Alexander gasped, as he and Bianca stopped and stared.

Julia. The woman who was effusive with hugs and greetings from the very first time Alexander brought me to his church. The warrior and strategist in charge of ordinance and equipment at his branch of the Order of Light. The person who never seemed to take any of Father Jacob's shit. The one who rescued me after Father Jacob used the Key of Solomon to trap me in a little gilded box, and then quit the Order in disgust. I hadn't seen her since that day. Nor, to my knowledge, had anyone else. But here she was, and she looked ready to kick some ass.

Her combat outfit had always seemed a little edgy for Order of Light standards, but now that she had struck out on her own, she had gone all-out with her own style. Thigh-high black leather boots laced up the sides met a pair of tight trousers that continued the lacing pattern. Her heavy leather jacket hung open over a low-cut top designed mostly for support, but also perhaps to show off a little cleavage. The effect was not lost on Bianca, who let out a low whistle of appreciation. Julia shot her a quick smile.

"Sorry to cut in like this," Julia said, "but I've been keeping an eye on the area. I didn't expect to come across a scene like this." She looked to Leo, who hesitated, still sizing her up.

"You're here to take me down, too?" he asked.

"That depends," she responded.

"I just want to feed," Leo said, his expression momentarily

almost a plea. Then he added angrily, "Are you here to defend these cops, too?"

"Oh, I don't care a whit about those assholes," Julia scoffed. "Though I'd question whether you're really sure you want a bloodbond with one. But no, I'm talking about the rest of the crew here. I'm not keen on the idea of you hurting friends of mine." She looked around, offering Cuan a nod. "Cuan," she added. "I'm glad you've wound up OK. If you're here, then does that mean—?"

She looked around, searchingly, and her eyes fell on mine. I gave a silent smile and a wave, and she gave me the slightest flicker of a smile of acknowledgement. Then she continued looking about, an action that I realized was to cover that she'd seen me, to keep Leo from noticing as well.

"—you've made a full recovery," she finished, still addressing Cuan. "I'm glad. I was worried about you."

"Recovery?" Leo asked.

"The Church tried to kill me," Cuan explained in the simplest possible terms.

"Fuckers," Leo muttered.

"Julia…" Alexander said, his voice small and a little wounded, "where have you been?"

"Sorry for leaving without a word, Alexander," Julia said, "But I just couldn't stay in the Order for another minute after all that happened."

"Yeah…" Alexander said. "I've… kind of left, too."

"So I've heard," Julia said. "I'm sorry all that happened the way it did."

"You heard?" Alexander asked, confused. "From who?"

"From me."

We turned in the direction of the voice, and there was Thomas, Prominence coiled in his hand. He still was clad in his tight white jeans, though he'd traded his black button-down for an old-style high-collared black quilted jacket that hugged his chest tightly and was clasped with a series buckles from the right shoulder down to the middle of his waist. He wore a pair of long leather gloves and boots to match. The overall effect was both a little anachronistic and shockingly sexy.

"Thomas?" Alexander gasped.

"Hello, little brother," Thomas said, and Alexander smiled slightly at the deliberate choice of words. "And other little brother," he added with a nod to Cuan, and Alexander frowned.

"I'd left Thomas a way to get in touch with me in an emergency," Julia explained. "His deciding to leave the Order and becoming effectively homeless in the process constituted that. Now he's staying with me."

"Congratulations; I'm so happy for you," Leo said dryly. "But if you don't mind putting off your happy little reunion, I am *hungry*. So unless one of you has a better idea than—"

"Look out!" Cuan shouted suddenly, pointing.

We all turned. The fit cop had regained consciousness, and had his gun raised. He was looking around from person to person in a panic, and finally settled on a target.

"Drop the weapon!" he shouted at Julia. Then, immediately, he opened fire.

Julia barely managed to get out "*Lux Clypeus!*" before the bullets hit. A sheet of light appeared on her forearm in the shape of a shield, bullets ricocheting off of it and pinging into trees and the side of a nearby building.

"ENOUGH!" Leo shouted with fury as he dashed toward the cop. The policeman turned to aim his gun at his assailant, but Leo was too quick. He ducked down and uppercutted the cop in the chest with such force that he left the ground. He sailed several feet through the air, crashing down on the roof of the squad car before bouncing off of it onto the pavement. From where I stood, I could see a trickle of blood down the side of the cop's forehead.

Leo's nostrils flared. "Blood," he said, his voice deep and jagged.

"Shit," Thomas muttered. He uncoiled Prominence and cracked it in the air in front of him as Leo leapt onto the squad car. A tongue of flame leapt from Prominence and cut the air between Leo and the fit cop, making Leo rear back in alarm. The pause bought Thomas and Julia just enough time to position themselves between Leo and his target.

"I don't want to burn you, hot stuff," Thomas said, brandishing Prominence in front of him. "Let's find another solution."

"*BLOOD*," Leo growled, leaping forward. Julia swung her spear Gratia like a bat, catching him with its side and sending him spinning backward with a spark.

"It's blood rage," Julia said. "He's very hungry, and we've already interrupted his attempts to feed. Now that he sees and smells blood, it's all he wants. We have to shut him down."

"No!" Bianca yelled, raising her hands and conjuring forth another swarm of misty bats.

"Stop!" Alexander yelled behind her, grabbing her roughly from behind and holding Candela in front of her face. The blade flashed brightly and Bianca shrieked, the bats spiraling wildly off course and crashing through the window of a university building.

"Oh no," Cuan gasped, and I understood his fear. That building was next to the Library.

Bianca whirled furiously on Alexander. "Let him FEED!" she shrieked. She seemed as wildly angry as her brother, and I realized that their bloodbond was probably making her feel the effects of the blood rage as well. She lashed out at Alexander, and the two of them fell back to fighting each other.

Leo had landed on his feet, tumbling backward to break his own fall and then climbing back into a standing position. "Give me *BLOOD!*" he roared at Thomas and Julia. He lunged into a sprint.

"No you don't," Cuan said, darting in front of Leo. I'd half expected Leo to burst into mist again, but Cuan was too quick, and he caught the vampire by surprise. "I'm sorry," he said sincerely as he slammed his palm into Leo's chest. Leo staggered backward but recovered with remarkable alacrity, and immediately swiped at Cuan's face.

Cuan dodged out of the way, but just not quite quickly enough. Leo's nail grazed Cuan's cheek, slicing the surface like a razor, drawing a thin trickle of blood.

Leo's nostrils flared with satisfaction as Cuan's face betrayed a tiny flicker of fear. "You smell even better," the vampire grinned, licking his lips. "You'll do."

Julia raised her spear as Leo focused his full attention on Cuan, but whatever she was planning to do was interrupted by the sound of something storming up from inside the building by the library. A second later a green ogre burst through the shattered window, charging directly at Thomas and Julia.

"Oh, for fuck's sake," Julia groaned as she and Thomas turned their attention to the approaching creature, interrupting its charge before it could trample the unconscious cop.

Cuan continued to parry Leo's strikes, though the vampire was proving difficult to fend off. Leo clearly was somewhat troubled by the garlic—he was taking pains to avoid touching it and reared back somewhat each time a bulb got too close to his face—but nonetheless he was still a challenging opponent for Cuan.

I found myself wondering why Cuan hadn't shifted. He'd be more than a match for the vampire in his werewolf form. Then I realized that not shifting was part of Cuan's strategy. It was a precaution: if the vampire did succeed in biting him, he could shift immediately and theoretically put an end to the bloodbond before it started. If he shifted now, he might not have the energy for a transformation if one proved to be necessary.

As I watched them, Julia and Thomas's fight with the ogre became more heated. The ogre managed to lift the entire squad car and hurled it at them.

The car bounced over the pavement, crashing and rolling, thankfully missing both unconscious cops. Julia and Thomas dodged out of the way, but the car was rolling straight at me. I leapt to the side as the car smashed into a tree, shattering what was left of the windows and sending glass everywhere.

It was only an instant, the smallest glance to see if I was all right. Even so, Cuan's shift in focus gave Leo an opening. He lashed out with a side kick and caught Cuan in the chest. It was the kind of kick that probably would have shattered a regular person's ribs, but in Cuan's case it just sent him soaring back into the landscaping shed. He crashed through the door, which came off of its rusted hinges, and disappeared inside amidst the sound of clattering equipment.

"CUAN!" I yelled in alarm.

At the sound of my voice, Leo whirled around like an alert animal, eyes focusing on me. I froze.

"I thought I smelled more garlic," Leo said, for the moment seeming slightly calmed. "How did I not notice you before?"

"I'm easy to overlook," I said.

"That's a shame, since you're so easy on the eyes," Leo said, mouth curling up into a not-entirely-friendly smirk. "I remember you. You're the one who found me." He sniffed the air, and suddenly his eyes widened in interest. "That... what ARE you?" he asked.

I was confused at first until I felt a wet trickle on my left cheek. I reached up and realized that some flying glass from the crashing squad car had sliced my skin, and now a little drip of red flowed down.

"I've never smelled blood like that," Leo said. "Even with the taint of garlic in the air, that blood smells... perfect."

"I'd prefer it if you didn't drink my blood," I said.

"I'm not sure I can resist," Leo said, eyes wild as he advanced on me.

I looked around, fear creeping up my spine. Julia and Thomas were fully occupied with the ogre. Alexander and Bianca were still going at one another. There was no sign of Cuan after he'd landed in the shed. It was just me and the vampire.

"I don't know what you did to stay so incognito," Leo said as he approached, step by step, "but if it makes you feel any better, as soon as I smelled blood like that, I'd have noticed you even if you hadn't drawn attention to yourself."

He looked ready to lunge. I concentrated, hastily, on myself, on the idea that the world wasn't as solid as everyone seemed to think it was. Just as Leo leapt at me, afterimages followed behind as the world slid out of place. I had been hasty in fading, and in the process had completely failed to remain conscious of the fact that I had one bulb of garlic on a string around my neck and another at my waist. As a result, they did not make the transition into incorporeality with me, and fell impotently to the ground.

I felt Leo's hands pass through me. I saw a brief expression of surprise, then a smirk as his face evaporated before my eyes. It was another second before I realized what had happened: he had become mist. I felt him now, around me, enveloping me, infusing the space that should have been inhabited by my incorporeal form.

"Nice trick," came Leo's voice, hauntingly, from all around me, right at my ear. "But you won't be rid of me that easily. Thanks for dropping the garlic, though; I really hate that stuff."

I backpedaled, but he clung to me like smoke.

"You can't shake me," Leo continued. "Even if you drop

right through the ground, I'll just follow you through the cracks in the soil and be there, ready, for when you firm up again. Something tells me I can sustain this state longer than you—shall we see which one of us breaks first?"

Terror filled me—not the angry panic that I'd felt when Father Jacob captured me in spirit chains or the blind terror that the nebulous memories from the library instilled, but a cold dread that seemed to sap my very will. I hovered, unable to act. "Please don't drink my blood," I whispered.

"You must know there's something special about you," Leo's voice came again, "to have blood like that. It smells so pure, yet so potent."

"I don't want a bloodbond," I responded. "I don't want to be a vampire. Bianca said to us over and over that you're better than that. She said you're a good person. And you seem like one, even if you are dressed like a Renaissance Fair fan who gave up halfway through making his costume."

"Maybe we can work something out, then?" Leo's voice purred. "Perhaps draw some into a vial? Though I must admit, I can't help but wonder how amazing blood like that would taste, hot and fresh, straight from the source. You sure you wouldn't be game for a hickey?"

"Sorry," I responded dryly, "I have a boyfriend."

"Is that so?" Leo's voice responded. "Not the one with the whip I hope, he's rather cute."

"No," Cuan's voice said from next to us. He was dragging something dark along the lawn as he staggered from the landscaping shed. "It's me. And while I love visiting the park on a foggy night with my boy as much as the next guy, you know what I think of this particular mist?" He hefted up the large object in his hands: an industrial-strength leaf blower. "I think it blows," he growled, flipping the switch.

There was a roar, and Leo cried out angrily as I felt the air blast through my incorporeal form, the tendrils of mist spiraling away from me into the night.

The switch flipped off, the blaring stopped, and Cuan stepped toward me. The world solidified as I staggered into his arms, and at his touch, his kiss, everything came back into focus.

"Thank you," I said.

"I know vampires are enthralling," he grinned, dimple in his cheek, "but don't fall for the smoke and mirrors, OK?"

I snorted. "What's with all the wit lately?" I asked. "I must be bringing it out in you."

"You bring a lot of stuff out of me," he smiled, but then looked over my shoulder, his expression turning serious again.

"You'll pay for that," came Leo's voice.

"I didn't think you'd be gone for long," Cuan growled.

"One way or another, I'm getting blood tonight," Leo sneered. "I'd like his," he added, pointing to me, "but if I have to go through you first, then so be it."

"You want blood?" came another voice. "Because I'll happily spill some."

We turned. It was Az, alighting in the center of the park, Quietus in hand. He wore his usual tuxedo pants, but only a white shirt above them.

"Oh, come on!" Leo groaned. "And who are you now, another *deus ex machina*?"

"No," Az replied, standing up straight, ripping his shirt open at the chest in a somewhat overdramatic flourish. The fabric fell off of his shoulders, and as it did so, a pair of impressive white wings sprung from the back of his porcelain torso, spreading wide and proud. "*I am Death.*"

"Holy fucking shit," Alexander gaped as he and Bianca stopped and stared at the angel now standing in glory in the center of the park. Thomas and Julia, too, turned from the ogre they had just managed to knock unconscious and watched Az —Azrael—in stunned silence.

"They had their chance to find you," Azrael stated, voice echoing through the night with supernatural strength. "I gave more leeway than I perhaps even should have. But I cannot ignore this any longer. So here I am."

Leo stared at Azrael, stunned like an animal in headlights, as the angel raised Quietus in his left hand.

"Az, don't!" Bianca cried.

And then, much to my surprise, Azrael whipped the blade around, slashing his right forearm. Bright red luminous blood splashed forth, pouring down his white skin. Az flicked his left hand and Quietus evaporated in black light, only to be replaced with a silver goblet. Az held it under his forearm, catching his blood as it poured into the vessel.

"You want blood?" Azrael asked. "You won't find a better vintage than this. Come and get it."

Leo's eyes were wild, his nostrils flaring as he stared at the bright crimson liquid. Even I could smell it, sharp copper with sweet notes unlike any I had ever imagined. For Leo, it had to be irresistible.

Sure enough, Leo rushed forward like a fish on a lure.

"NO!" Bianca screamed. "He'll stab you!"

"Az," I pleaded, but Azrael paid me no heed. He simply stood as the vampire closed the distance between them like a flash. Just before Leo could clamp his mouth on his arm, Az darted aside, grabbing the hair on the back of Leo's head in his fist.

Then, to all of our surprise, he lifted the goblet to Leo's lips.

Leo drank, eagerly, desperately, the full contents of the goblet. No sooner had he finished swallowing the blood, however, then he clutched at his neck and began coughing violently. He gasped, falling to his hands and knees, sputtering, eyes tightly shut. Then he jerked his head back in what looked like a silent scream, eyes opening wide—except in that instant, they didn't look like eyes; they were two pools of white light.

"Brother!" Bianca cried, taking one step toward him before falling to the ground convulsing. Her body seemed to shimmer just below the skin, as Leo's positively glowed. Then Leo was still.

Azrael ran two fingers down the length of the gash on his forearm and the wound sealed completely, leaving not a single trace of injury. Then he stood and looked at Leo's still form.

"Az," I asked, looking at the shirtless angel as he stood tall in the quadrangle, "what have you done?"

"Freed him," Az said, and I swallowed hard as we all looked on in shocked silence at the scene before us. "...in a manner of speaking," he added, and Leo suddenly coughed violently again as he moved once more, climbing back to his hands and knees.

"Leo!" Bianca exclaimed, pulling herself up and running to him. She threw her arms around him, nearly knocking him to the ground once more, and he placed his hands on her arms and smiled, a warm, sincere smile. Then he looked to Azrael in confusion.

"What did you do to me?" he asked.

"I gave you my blood," Az responded. "You needed blood, didn't you?"

"I did," Leo replied, an awed expression on his face. "Desperately."

Thomas approached, cautiously. "But now... you don't?" he asked.

"No, he still does," Az explained, then turned back to Leo. "Angel blood is very potent. It's basically pure holy spiritual energy given liquid form. Most undead would find it toxic, but since vampires subsist on blood, it has an unusual effect. It... has fundamentally changed the magical and spiritual state of your existence. It will take some getting used to, and there will be a lot to learn about how you have been affected, but for now suffice it to say that while you are still a vampire and need blood to survive—though perhaps less than you did previously —you will no longer crave it in a way that threatens your sanity. You never again need fear falling into a blood rage, and you can no longer transmit the curse of vampirism."

Bianca blinked. "That's... that's why... my blood, it doesn't itch anymore," she said. "Am I cured?"

"You are still Bitten," Az explained, "as the one who took your blood still walks the earth. You will retain the abilities that status confers. However, you otherwise no longer are bound by any bloodbond, and furthermore you no longer carry vampirism; when your life ends, it will end like that of any normal human being."

"I... I feel so different," Leo said in awe.

"I expect you do," Az nodded. "Your abilities will behave differently as well. It is... a very fundamental transformation. And an unorthodox one. Given the circumstances, I could not exactly ask for your consent, but I can ask you now: you can continue this new existence, or I can do what I would otherwise have done already and grant you a swift death, freeing you from this unlife."

"You call it unlife," Leo said, running a hand through the mop of brown hair on his head. "but this feels like living to me. Our parents cut ties with us years ago. Not long after that, I was turned, then a slave to the one who turned me, and after that chained alone in a dark basement for I don't know how many years. I want to give existence a shot."

Azrael sighed. It seemed almost a sigh of resignation, as though he had been struggling with something and had finally decided to let it be, even if he were not entirely comfortable with the outcome. "Then so it shall be," he said. "You are free to carry on this new existence. Know however that your power is now not only one of blood, but also one of spirit. I would advise you to refrain from taking blood directly from a body until you fully comprehend the implications such an act now carries."

"Wow, cryptic much?" Leo frowned.

"Trust me, this is better than when he's blunt," I muttered.

"You will be ready for more, in time," Azrael said. "But for now, I bid you farewell." And with a great flap of his wings, he was gone.

We watched him leave.

"Well..." Alexander muttered, "now what?"

"Now my brother and I have some catching up to do," Bianca said, arms still affectionately around Leo's neck.

"Sounds good to me," Leo grinned, turning to face his sister. "I found a cozy spot last night; shall we go there and you can fill me in on the past few years?" he turned to the rest of us. "I'm sure you're all very nice people, and I'll be happy to get to know you under circumstances in which we're not trying to beat the stuffing out of one another, if that's something you're amenable to."

"I really don't blame you for tonight," I said honestly, as Cuan and Thomas nodded in agreement—Thomas somewhat vigorously.

"You're not the first vampire I've dealt with," Julia said with a smile. "Though I will say, you handled your blood rage better than most. I'm sure you're a stand-up guy."

"And you're a bad-ass bitch," Bianca said to Julia. "Which, by the way, I mean as a compliment."

"I took it as one," Julia smirked back at her.

"Well then, great," Leo said. "But I'm just going to spend time with my sister tonight. I'll speak to you all later."

"Don't wait up," Bianca said to us as she and Leo walked away from the quad. "Don't expect me back until sometime tomorrow. If I need to get into the apartment or something before then, I'll call."

"Well, isn't that all fucking neat and tidy?" Alexander spat as they left. "Meanwhile, what are we gonna do about two unconscious cops, a smashed squad car, and a knocked-out ogre?"

"Um... the ogre's not that knocked out," Thomas said, pointing. Sure enough, the ogre was stirring, clambering to its feet. We all braced ourselves. The ogre, however, took a look at the five of us and seemed to decide that those were not odds it appreciated, because it turned tail and made for the building it emerged from.

"O...kay," Alexander said, raising an eyebrow. "Well, that leaves officer ham and officer bacon."

"I don't give a fuck about these dirty cops," Julia glowered. "Let them wake up and deal with their squad car wrapped sideways around a tree. "I say we just get out of here."

"Sounds good to me," Thomas nodded.

Julia turned to Alexander. "Where are you staying, now that you've left? If you want to catch up a bit, why not crash at my place tonight?"

"You have a place?" Alexander said.

"I have a lot of things Father Jacob doesn't know about," she said with a sly smile.

"Well, okay then," Alexander shrugged. "I guess I'll see you two later," he said, turning to Cuan and me. "I'll touch base tomorrow?"

We nodded. I was grateful that he wouldn't be around tonight: I was more than a little irritated at him for basically just sparring with Bianca all evening.

"Thanks for, well, swooping in to our rescue," Cuan said to Julia and Thomas.

"Don't thank us," Thomas said. "You two did most of the heavy lifting tonight."

"You make a good team," Julia said, and Cuan beamed.

The three former Order of Light members left the quad, and Cuan and I hurried away as well—we had no desire to be there when the cops woke up. Once we were back on a quiet street, Cuan sighed.

"Holy crap, what a night," he said. "You all right?"

"Yeah," I nodded. "You?"

"I am. But tired. Should we go back to the apartment, or—"

"—or check up on Az?" I asked, finishing the thought we both had. Cuan looked at me and nodded.

"I can't believe what he did tonight," Cuan said.

"He seemed unsure about it," I noted. "For some reason, I feel like we should see how he is."

And with that, rather than go home and collapse together in bed, we made for Az's hotel.

XI

SACRED ACTS

GIVEN Azrael's sudden departure from the quad, as well as the possibility that he'd completed the task that had warranted this particular Earthly visit, we had no realistic expectation of finding Az back in his hotel room. It was, therefore, with some small surprise that I got an answer when I knocked on the door to his suite and called his name.

"Just push it open," came the voice.

I pushed. Sure enough, the door swung open, and Cuan and I walked into Az's spacious hotel room. Az was seated at the desk in the far end of the room, still shirtless, his back to us. His chair was turned sideways to accommodate the large wings folded behind him, taller even than his torso.

"After all that, you come to see *me*?" he said, still not turning around. "You really are full of surprises."

"We wanted to see how you were," Cuan said. "Talk about being full of surprises... what you did wasn't at all what we expected."

"Nor was it what I had originally planned to do," Az responded. His shoulders rose and fell as he sighed heavily, his wings rustling softly at the movement. "I've never deviated from my task so thoroughly before."

"Your task was to free a trapped soul, wasn't it?" I said. "Leo seems pretty free now."

"And yet he remains undead," Az responded. "I am the Angel of Death. My role is to handle those difficult cases in which the transition from life to death is not happening smoothly. I am supposed to keep the cycle moving, to keep the wheel turning. But in this case, I've stopped it entirely. It is the direct antithesis of what I was meant to have done."

"But perhaps it was best for Leo?" Cuan asked. "He was a vampire, locked in a basement. You've given him back some of his humanity."

"Ugh," Azrael turned to look at us. His expression was one of light disgust, but his platinum eyes betrayed deeper doubt and pain. "Worded like that, I feel even more like I've made the wrong decision. Humanity is horrific."

"I don't entirely disagree with you," Cuan said, "but why, exactly, do you say that?"

"Every time I visit the earth, I see humanity concerned with nothing but power and control. Not agency over oneself, but control over others, consolidation of power. Wanton destruction of nature, amassing vast amounts of wealth, manipulating and twisting the concepts of the Divine for its own ends."

"Where's all this coming from?" I asked.

"That young man was chained up in a basement," Az replied. "Cedric can give all the excuses he wants for it, but the simple fact is that he did it because it was useful. It let him keep Bianca close at hand, where he could leverage her trust to employ her as a weapon."

"It was really shitty," Cuan nodded. But that's why you came, to set that right."

"But then the Church of the Holy Guardian did the same thing to you, Cole," Az continued, standing up in his exasperation. I couldn't help but let my eyes trace over the muscles of his torso, smooth and hard as though they had been carved out of white marble. "All because Jacob convinced himself it would protect his church from demons." He scoffed. "They've lied to themselves for so long, they think it's truth."

"You mean there aren't demons?" I asked.

"Oh, there are demons, all right," Az said. "But demons aren't some cosmic force that has been at war with the Divine for millennia. Why would the Divine create some massive enemy? To perpetrate some huge war in which all of humanity will be tested? That's such a typically narcissistic human outlook." Az glowered. "No. Humans created 'demons' themselves, by literally willing them into existence. Demons of ancient times were created to serve different aspects of the Divine for different purposes, just as angels were. Even in the Torah, they often appear in service to the Divine. But humans are so hell-bent on creating scapegoats, things to blame their own self-destructive behavior on, that they manifested the very things that they fear. They hung that mantle on demons and then ascribe to various so-called 'adversaries' powers rivalling those of the Divine itself. Do you know how disrespectful that is, to the Divine, to all of us?" He shook his head vigorously, a mix of despair and anger. "All those people in Churches mewling about how the Enemy is stalking them, the Devil is on their tails and they must be vigilant against him; it's excuses and scapegoating and mind control."

"Like the seven deadly sins," Cuan nodded. "Or the excuse that 'The devil made me do it.'"

"Or the witch hunts," Az noted, "using accusations of possession or some devilish architect as a motivator for hate. And for what? Some promise of eternal life? Humans treat Death like it's the worst thing imaginable, and yet they thrive by killing everything around them until it suits them perfectly. And then they call me the Grim Reaper and paint me as some Hell-sent demon. And poor Lucifer... his job was to challenge humanity, to encourage personal and spiritual growth, and yet humans hate being challenged so deeply that they recast him as the worst demon of all, reviling him so much that he can't even show his face to humans anymore. All these monsters crawling up from the depths and prowling the streets at night, humanity brought them upon itself. They cry about people who murdered the Son of God and then they turn around and do the same to one another because they look different or speak a different language or love the wrong person or worship a different aspect of the Divine. They're so determined to control one another that they've perverted the world they call home. You humans want to play God? Well congratulations, you've created your own destruction. Again."

"You really do have a dim view of humanity, huh?" I asked. "Not that I blame you," I added, "but still."

"Don't you?" Az asked, staring at me. "The head of a church, a church supposed to uphold the concepts of goodness and righteousness, supposed to represent one of the faiths representing an aspect of the Divine that gave rise to my specific existence, locked someone away to leverage their power for his own ends. And I couldn't find you. I couldn't even *sense* you. Whatever he did to you, for that time that he held you captive, he reduced you to the pure ability to go unnoticed. Not a person: a *concept*. One so distilled that it hid his church from the very forces he was supposed to serve."

"He hid the church from God?" Cuan asked, aghast.

"Nothing escapes the Divine," Az said. "But I'm not the Divine. All those holy forces like me, all the angels and spiritual energies the Order likes to evoke; all of us were lost to that Church for as long as you were captive. I had pledged to protect you. I swore an oath, and yet..."

A tear—a hot, angry tear—ran down Azrael's face. I'd felt a

lot of different emotions toward the angel in the time that I'd known him. I hadn't expected sympathy to be one of them.

"It's OK," I said. "That wasn't your fault."

"I'm just sick of seeing 'holiness' and 'God' used as an excuse to perpetrate all kinds of hatred and heinous acts," Az continued. "Oh, and then, to add insult to injury, the same excuses are used to control and vilify some of the most holy acts a person can perform."

"Wait," Cuan said. "Are you talking about sex?"

"Among other things, yes," Az nodded. "But humanity's treatment of sex infuriates me the most." His platinum eyes darkened with rage.

I feared for just a moment that Az would start ranting about humanity being too free with sex, but to my surprise, his stance was nearly the opposite.

"Humanity has leveraged sex for millennia as a means of domination and control," he stated. "It's withheld or leveraged as a weapon to assert dominance, control women, control pleasure, control spirituality. That whole 'sex just for copulation' bullshit? More control. Sex, when all involved really desire it, is one of the most intimate, spiritual acts that can be performed. By oneself, with two people, with more people, between any combination of genders, all of it is sacred, generative, and spiritual. It is a literal act of worship of the Divine that is Love, and it honors and perpetuates the Wheel of Life just as much as my own task, perhaps even more so."

"Well, that is very gratifying to hear," Cuan said, glancing at me with a mischievous grin, his sexy little dimple forming in his cheek. I couldn't help but smile, though Az continued unabated.

"This whole religious opposition to any kind of sex that serves any purpose other than procreation is just nonsense. It's an attempt to block any form of spiritual fulfillment or divine understanding that doesn't depend on the church as an intermediary. Suddenly pleasure is demonic, like it's another divine test? How sadistic do humans think the Divine is? And all that degradation has really only served to make same-sex sexuality an even greater divine act, as it is an active affirmation of the spirit against oppression. And yet humans say it's unnatural? It's so natural that nature is designed specifically for it."

"Like dolphins," Cuan observed.

"Like dolphins," Az nodded.

"Excuse me, what?" I asked.

"Bottlenose dolphins," Cuan explained. "The males have what is essentially a pocket their junk is tucked into, and it works great for gay dolphin sex."

"You're kidding," I said.

"I'm not," Cuan said. "Plus there's tons of same-sex behavior with birds, as well as bats, lions, elephants, giraffes, sheep, dragonflies... there are even some species of lizard that reproduce asexually after lesbian sex."

"Then there's humans," Az said. "Women are far better at pleasuring other women than men are. And do you think it's a coincidence that the prostate produces soul-rocking orgasms but is placed penis-deep in the anus?"

"You know an awful lot about sex," I pointed out.

"I find the Church's proscription against sex between men personally offensive," Az responded.

"Wait, you mean—" Cuan started. "So... do angels have sex?"

"We have sex organs, right?"

"How should we know?" I said to the shirtless angel. "You're the only angel we've seen, and this is the least clothed we've ever seen you."

"Well, we do. Plus, thanks to our coming into being as a result of the need for Divine understanding in a strongly patriarchal society, the host of angels is overwhelmingly male," Az stated. "The whole host of angels is basically devoted to worshipping the Divine when we're not assigned to a particular task, and well... I've already told you that sex is one of the most sacred acts anyone can perform."

"Heaven suddenly sounds a whole lot more appealing," I said.

"I mean, not all angels have that particular interest, just like not all humans do, though since we don't share humanity's ludicrous need to control sex, a majority of angels identify as openly bisexual, or sometimes pansexual."

"And you?" Cuan asked. "If you don't mind me asking, that is."

"I have no interest in females," Azrael responded. "Plus, as the Angel of Death, procreation kind of goes against my nature. That's why I find the claim that sex is solely for procreation personally offensive."

"Hold up a moment," Cuan said. "If you're an expression of the Divine specifically to connect with the group that needed you... shouldn't you, I dunno, look more like them? 'Humanity made in God's image,' and all that? I mean, your skin is like ivory."

"Angels represent the full spectrum of humanity," Az said. "But even so, I often wondered why I looked the way I did. And then as history unfolded I realized that I looked like the race responsible for the single greatest amount of death in human history. So don't ever tell me the Divine doesn't have a sense of humor. Twisted though it might be sometimes," he scoffed. "After all, how's this for irony? The Church of the Holy Guardian has tried to kill you both, seen you as somehow less than human, and yet here you are, a hound of God and an enigma, showing more of the best parts of humanity than almost anyone else in this accursed city."

"Hound of God?" Cuan asked, raising an eyebrow.

"It's a term a werewolf in Livonia used to refer to himself once back in the 17th Century," Az said, a small smile finally breaking across his face. "I took a liking to it." The smile faded. "Perhaps I've been taking a liking to too much. I'm incarnate here almost all the time now on some task or another. But today, instead of shuffling an undead off into the next stage of the Cycle, I've stuck him more firmly in place. And why?" he asked. "Because I care, suddenly. Because the two of you and Bianca would have been upset to lose him. In the grand scheme of things, the cycle would have just kept on turning, and yet instead I lost sight of the forest for the trees."

"You saved a life today," Cuan said. "Perhaps more than one. That's something to celebrate, isn't it? You gave Leo a chance to live. A chance to reunite with his sister, a chance to exist free from the curse in his blood. That's compassion."

"And what do I have to show for it?" Az looked angry, lost. "I deviated from my set task, my sole objective."

"That's what free will is for, isn't it?" I asked. "To make decisions that might be better than a fixed general rule? To perform an act of love? You want to know what you have to show for what you did. How about gratitude? Gratitude not just for helping Leo, but for helping me to understand my powers, gratitude for your part in saving Cuan's life when he was poisoned."

Az looked at me, platinum eyes searching.

"You really are thankful, aren't you?" he realized. "Both of you."

"We are," Cuan said, voice soft, stepping close to Az, breath hot at his side. "You're so used to humanity fearing you," he added, "when was the last time you've been loved?"

"Apart from death cults?" he asked.

"We don't mean death cults," I said, screwing my face up. "We mean *love*." I leaned forward, staring into his eyes. "You're down here a lot, aren't you? Is there anyone... angel or no, who's shared that divine love you mentioned with you?"

"Not... not for a very, very long time," Az said. He swallowed.

"Then, perhaps your spirit could use some affirmation," Cuan said. His eyes flickered to mine, and I knew his thoughts immediately. I shifted my gaze back to Az, his face centimeters from mine, his expression hesitant. To see the confident angel flustered made me smile inwardly. He was... cute.

"You... you want to...?" he stammered.

"We want to give you something to show for what you did," I whispered. "The Divine is Love, right? So how about a sacred act?"

He breathed for a moment. His breath was sweet, like honey.

"A sacred act," he whispered.

And then I kissed him.

His eyes opened wide at the touch of my lips, but then they closed again as he kissed me back, hungrily, his right arm moving to the small of my back. His kissing was slightly awkward, inexpert, and I got the feeling that even though he was an ancient existence, kissing was not something he had much experience with—at least not recently.

I smelled Cuan's musky scent as he sidled around Azrael, kissing up the angel's left shoulder to his neck, and Az reached around with his other arm as he released my mouth and kissed Cuan.

I slid my hands up Azrael's abdomen and back, feeling my palm slide over his skin. Cuan's skin was smooth, but it was also had a silky softness to it; the angel's skin was like a warm statue, hard and perfect, as though it were completely devoid of pores. I slid a finger up to Az's pale nipple and brushed over its surface, and as I did so he gasped sharply, then moaned into Cuan's mouth.

"You like that?" I asked.

"Uh-huh," Azrael managed to nod. And then, breathlessly, "I... I want to see your bodies."

"You first," I said with a grin.

Azrael brought his hands back to his waist and slipped open the clasp of his tuxedo pants, letting them fall to the floor. He wore no underwear.

Cuan had no body hair other than the poof above his cock, but Az had none whatsoever. His cock was still soft, hooded and nestled between a pair of loose-hanging balls. Both cock and balls were pale as the rest of him and modestly sized, though the lack of hair made them stand out against the rest of his body. I ran my palm down his abdomen as it extended smoothly to the base of his shaft, then cradled cock and balls gently in my hand, feeling their softness beneath the solid skin.

Az took a breath of pleasure, his balls rising and falling in my palm. I felt him begin to stiffen slightly before moving his hand to my collar.

"Your turn," he said.

Cuan and I smiled, maneuvering him to the edge of the bed, ducking under his wings as we turned him around and had him sit. His wings had to spread a bit across the bed as they were too large to remain folded, and so the overall effect was like a blanket of feathers fanning out from his back and over the tops of his shoulders. He stared up at us, platinum eyes glittering with anticipation, and kicked off his socks as Cuan and I turned our attention to one another.

Cuan's Wushu pants were already tenting a bit, and I could tell he was as excited as I was as I kissed him passionately. It was a different experience from making out when it was just the two of us, when the entire world would melt away and Cuan was my entire existence. Now, we were sharing that intimacy with Az, and while it was therefore less focused, seeing him naked on the bed, feeling his eyes on us, hearing him breathe with anticipation, was a completely different kind of exciting.

I slid Cuan's vest off of his chest and he helped me out of my shirt, and we kissed again, running our hands over one another.

I felt his fingers brush my nipple and I grinned into the kiss as a spark of pleasure coursed through me; I traced the line of his silver chain down from his neck to his pecs, feeling their heft as they moved beneath his skin. As he undid the button of my trousers, I reached down and slid his Wushu pants over his buttocks, revealing his fancy (but eminently supportive) red-and-purple jockstrap. The fabric was a bit strained at the moment, and I knew that the added tension was making his butt pop even more than usual. I reached around and took a handful of each cheek with a grin. Cuan grunted appreciatively as his dimple reappeared.

I stepped out of my shoes and socks once my own trousers dropped to my ankles, kicking them all away. I pulled Cuan against me, grinding our crotches together, kissing him once more before hooking my thumbs into the waistband of his jock. In unison, we slid one another's underwear off, and then, a hand at each other's waists, turned to give Az an unobstructed view.

The angel stared at us, unashamedly tracing the contours of our bodies with his icy platinum eyes. His wings rustled as his shoulders moved, and his neat blond hair glinted in the light of the hotel lamp as he continued to look us over.

"You're... in very good shape," he said.

"Says the angel," Cuan smirked, and he had a point. Az had a defined torso and long, muscular arms and legs. He didn't have a hint of body fat, but then again, neither did Cuan. Az was starting to show his arousal: he was beginning to stiffen, though Cuan and I were by now pretty much fully hard. Az's nipples were also beginning to stand out, and were a little pinker against his pale skin. Absently, my tongue went to my lips.

"It's been a long time since someone looked at me that way," Az said, his semihard cock twitching slightly.

"We're gonna do more than look," I said. I put one knee up

on the bed alongside him, then leant forward to his chest. Cuan did the same on my left, and we closed our lips over Az's nipples. They were stiff and firm, giving me plenty to tongue and lap and otherwise play with. Az cried out in pleasure, and I felt his arms move. The way we were positioned gave Az access to our bodies, and a moment later his fingers wrapped along my erection. He began to stroke, and from the noise of sliding and Cuan's low moan I knew that he was doing the same to Cuan with his other hand.

Azrael was an inexpert kisser but he had no such difficulties jacking me off. His fingers rose and fell, his thumb slipping over the tip of my wet cock head at the top of each stroke, and at the bottom of each stroke he ran his thumb down under my cock head where my foreskin was attached. Jolts of sensation ran through me as his hand moved and I squirmed against Az's chest, the added movement only adding to the stimulation I was providing to his nipples and egging him on further. Cuan continued to moan and writhe next to me, and the knowledge that Azrael was pleasuring both my boyfriend and me at the same time was almost enough to push me over the edge then and there.

"More," Az cried, and Cuan and I stepped away for a moment, pulling ourselves free of Az's grip as we admired our handiwork. Both he and I were flushed now, rock-hard and dripping precum. Az, meanwhile, had a full-on erection, standing up an urgent six or so inches and twitching with antic-ipation as he breathed. His shaft and balls had gone pinkish, but his cock head and nipples were now a deep, beet red that stood out starkly against his pale skin.

"You want more?" Cuan asked with a mischievous smirk. "C'mon, then." He rolled himself onto his back on the bed, head near Az's lap, looking up at him with a gleam in his eye. The invitation was obvious. Az swallowed hard, then turned on the bed, positioning himself over Cuan, wings falling forward slightly as they did so, covering Cuan like a canopy of feathers. Cuan looked up at me from between Az's legs and shot me a quick playful wink, which quickly turned into a deep moan of pleasure as Azrael took his length in his mouth. Cuan focused his gaze on the angels crotch, and parted his lips to take him in his mouth until Az's balls rested on the bridge of his nose. They began to sixty-nine, moaning together, as Az's ass bobbed in front of me.

Azrael was lean, but he was also muscular, and his ass in particular was meaty and solid. I reached forward and planted my hands on the firm globes of his ass, squeezing it and steadying it in front of me. Cuan, without missing a beat, began to bob his head with greater motion, continuing to suck up and down Az's length.

I spread the angel's cheeks with my palms. Even here, the skin was smooth and hairless and, I noted, perfectly clean. His asshole, marble-white as the rest of him, puckered slightly as Cuan continued to suck him off. I leaned in and buried my face in his ass, lapping at his winking hole. Az let out a muffled gasp around Cuan's cock as I vigorously rimmed him, the taste of fresh, smooth skin on my tongue. Emboldened by the angel's reaction and the clean taste, I forged ahead with greater intensity, until Azrael was writhing so much from my ministrations that he popped out of Cuan's mouth.

"Well, someone's liking that," Cuan grinned, as Azrael, blowjob completely forgotten, titled his head back and cried out.

"Inside," he pleaded. "I want it... now."

"Go for it, Cole," Cuan urged.

That was all the invitation I needed. I knelt on the bed, positioning my erection at his entrance. Then, slowly, I pushed forward, his slick hole swallowing me eagerly. He was warm, and though he wasn't terribly tight, he gripped me firmly. I pushed into him again and again as he cried his approval, feeling the pleasure wash over me with each pump, as Cuan lay below us, stroking the angel off in front of his face.

"More," Az whimpered. "Harder. I...I like it rough."

Cuan stopped jacking Az off. "How rough?" he asked.

"Really rough," Az replied.

"Well then," Cuan grinned broadly. "Cole, hold up a bit. I have an idea."

Cuan's suggestion took a bit of repositioning, but eventually I was lying on the bed, my body overlapped by Cuan's, who was lying with his feet pointed toward my head. Both our cocks stood up together as Az squatted above us, facing me.

"You ready?" I asked.

Az nodded. He lowered himself down over my erection, and my tip slid back inside him. Cuan reached to his crotch and repositioned himself.

"When you're ready," he said, and Az shifted his body as Cuan held himself in place.

I felt Cuan ease into Azrael alongside me, and the angel's platinum irises widened as he gasped in what I realized was intense, tight pleasure. Cuan's hands found their way from behind him to Az's pecs, where his dark red nipples stood out starkly against his porcelain skin. As Cuan began to roughly pinch them, I wrapped my own fist around Az's length and began stroking, the red tip of his cock slick with precum and Cuan's saliva.

Together, we pumped him up and down as he gasped, his wings rustling loudly as the bed creaked with the motion. He watched me as we pounded into him, his mouth open, cock slick and throbbing in my grip. The motion, the tightness, and the feeling of Cuan's hot, pulsing length rubbing against my own was too much, and I soon felt the pressure welling up inside. I let out a cry as I fired into Az, filling the blond angel's already full ass, feeling my thick, creamy cum squirt out over my and Cuan's balls. I shot again and again, as Cuan, stamina as strong as ever, continued thrusting and pumping, and Azrael continued to groan and moan over us. Finally, I was spent, and I felt myself slipping out. I pulled out of the Angel, feeling my juice seep out of his ass as it tightened around Cuan's still-thrusting member, and switched my position, bringing my head down to the angel's bouncing erection. Opening my mouth, I took it inside. It was slick with precum, tasting of salty nectar and Cuan's saliva, an intoxicating combination. I let my head move into a rhythm that complemented Cuan's, maximizing the motion on Azrael's cock, letting my tongue run over and around his cock head each time it slid back to the top of my mouth, then relaxing my throat with each thrust as it pushed deep down inside me.

"Aa. AAH!" Azrael began to cry, and I could feel his head snap back in ecstasy even with my head so low. Cuan let out a groan, his breathing rough and ragged, and then:

"I'm... gonna..." Cuan growled before I sensed him fire, mixing his cum with mine inside Azrael's ass. After Cuan's second orgasmic thrust, Azrael let out a deep cry of his own, and I felt him explode inside my mouth.

There is a saying, one that I've always thought was a spectacularly colorful, crass way of describing something fantastically delicious: "It's like angels cumming in your mouth."

The saying is deserved. Azrael's semen was unlike anything else I have ever tasted. I don't think the English language quite has words to describe it. It was a little salt. It was a lot of sugar. It was entirely SEX.

I swallowed the first mouthful, and as I did so I felt something surge through me, a tingling down the entire length of my body that then focused in on my cock, balls, and prostate. As the wave shot through me, I suddenly felt as aroused and urgently horny as I had before I'd cum. My balls swelled, renewed and dangerously near overflowing, and immediately my cock throbbed back to full-on erection, so swollen and so insistent that I thought I would explode in another orgasm right then and there. Instead, Azrael's continued burst of semen was so strong that I could no longer contain him in my mouth. I pulled my head back with a cough as a second (or was it third?) blast hit my cheek, reaching down with my hand to continue stroking the angel as Cuan continued to pump his own seed into him. The next shot hit me in the forehead, followed by another square in the chest. The next three poured out over my arm, soaking me, as Cuan, his own orgasm subsiding, pulled out of Azrael, followed by a generous flow of his and my cocktail of sperm onto the sheets. Cuan slid his body out from under Azrael, who collapsed on the center of the bed, wings spread out on either side of him, arms spread out over them.

Cuan turned to me, eyebrows raising as he stared at my heaving body and full-on, urgent erection.

"Cole, what... how—" he started, confused and slightly impressed.

"Az's semen," I managed through my full mouth. "Want some?"

He nodded, and immediately I grabbed him, kissing him deeply, letting the mouthful of Az's cum I'd been holding between my lips flow into his own.

Cuan's eyes shot open and I felt the muscles in his throat move as he swallowed. Immediately I felt the muscles in his body twitch as his still-dripping cock rose back into a rock-hard, purple erection.

"Holy fuck," he gasped. "I need to cum again."

"Take me," I urged, and Cuan grabbed me by the shoulders and kissed me with all his might, then, with just the right amount of roughness, pushed me down onto the bed so that I was on my hands and knees over Az's reclining body.

Az watched me, aroused, as Cuan grabbed either side of my waist and pushed into my waiting ass. The insertion caused nothing but pleasure, what with his rock-hard erection's being so thoroughly lubricated with his and my cum and my own overwhelming, urgent arousal. He pressed up against my full prostate and I felt that pleasure pour throughout my body as he hit against it again and again, my whole body tingling, my cock about to explode.

Beneath us, Az began to stroke himself, his own cock sticking up below my balls. His expression was one of urgent need.

"Soak me," he begged, and it was all I needed.

"More, Cuan," I said as I gripped him with my insides, and he grunted as we hit the breaking point. We came at the same time, loudly and with abandon. Cuan grunted again and again as he shot into me with more force than I had ever felt before, while my own balls fired forth what felt like twice as much cum as they could ever hold, spraying the angel below me across the face and chest, spattering his feathery wings with sticky white semen. Azrael's body heaved as he, too, climaxed again, hot cum spattering against my balls, my taint, Cuan's balls, Cuan's pumping cock. The wet heat on my balls only made my orgasm intensify, and we continued like that for what felt like five full minutes before at last I collapsed, soaked and satisfied and panting, onto Az's chest, Cuan following likewise onto my back.

"Wow," Azrael panted as we breathed, our bodies a sticky mess.

"What... what was that?" Cuan asked.

"Angel semen," Az said with a tired smile. "We're spiritual creatures. Just like angel blood, the rest of our bodily fluids are essentially concentrated spiritual energy. My blood is one kind of vitality, thus its effect on Leo. My semen is another; the pure energy of life and sex."

"That explains a lot," I breathed.

"Although," Cuan mused, "your blood permanently affected Leo. Will your spunk do the same to us?"

"If you were impotent or suffered some kind of sexual

dysfunction, maybe," Az said. "Leo had a curse of the blood; the blood lifted the curse. You two... seem to be functioning perfectly well, so I don't think you'll see any long-term effect."

"Can't argue with the short-term one, though," I breathed.

"That was a hell of an orgasm," Cuan nodded as he rested his cheek against my shoulder. "Or *orgasms* plural, I should say. Messy, too."

"Was that spiritually fulfilling enough for you, Az?" I asked.

Az grinned. "And then some," he responded, his platinum eyes dancing. "You know what they say; every time a guy gets drenched in cum, an angel gets his wings."

I honestly couldn't tell if he was joking or not.

"You feel better, then?" Cuan asked.

Az nodded. Then his face turned serious. "Thank you," he said. "Both of you. I... I admit I did not approach you two in the most kindest manner, when I first solicited your help. I was thinking only about what I needed from you. But you've shown me compassion, affection, more so than I expected or probably deserved. Normally, I would depart the Earth as soon as my stated purpose was fulfilled, but... I'd like to stay and help you, if that's all right. I want to help Leo acclimate to his new existence, and to help you to understand your past, and to address whatever is going on beneath this city. If you'll accept my help, that is."

"We'd love it," Cuan said, and I nodded.

"You've already helped us," I said. "A lot. Anything further would just be above and beyond."

"Speaking of beyond," Az continued, "I'd like to extend my oath."

"Your oath?" Cuan asked.

"To protect you both," Az continued. "I swore to see that neither of you came to harm during this earthly sojourn. I can only extend it informally, given that I don't know where each task will take me, but I would like to continue to protect and assist you on future visits as well, when circumstances allow. Not merely as abstract guardianship, but in person. I'm here often, so... I would see you frequently."

"I'd like that," I said.

"And can we continue to... erm... nurture our spirits like this once in a while?" Cuan asked.

Az chuckled. "I'd say 'that would give me great pleasure', but I think that goes without saying at this point." He smiled at us, a warm, sincere smile. "I've interacted with humanity for millennia," he said, "Many people have felt many things toward me. But... I don't think I've ever been the object of someone's *affection* like this. The love you share runs deep, perhaps deeper even than you two yet realize. For you to share some of that with me, it... it means more than I can say. Thank you."

"We're happy to know you like this," I said. "You matter, Azrael."

"Or... you're a spiritual being, so maybe you're energy," Cuan added with a sly grin.

Az shrugged. "It's relative," he responded with a smirk.

We slept, nuzzled together in that big bed, Azrael on his back and Cuan and I on either side of him, facing each other, arms interlocked over his chest. The angel's wings cradled us, making a downy and soft cocoon, and I slept peacefully and soundly.

The next morning, Cuan and I snuggled on the bed, watching as Az showered in the glass-walled enclosure in the corner of the room.

"So... Death is our guardian angel," I mused as Cuan twirled my hair lightly in his fingers. "I gotta say, I can't complain."

"You know," Cuan added, "I've heard a lot of people say 'fuck Death', but I don't think anyone really expected it to be a literal possibility."

"Their loss," I grinned.

"And... that was OK for you? Last night?" Cuan asked. "I mean, you definitely seemed to enjoy it at the time, but I just wanted to check."

"It was," I nodded. "You?"

"Yeah," Cuan agreed. "It was great, but particularly because I did it with you, you know? It was a different way to explore being with you... and I think it was exactly what Az needed. Plus, sex with a hot angel?" he added. "Yes, please."

"My sentiments exactly," I said, rolling over to face him. "All of it," I added as I kissed him.

When it was Cuan's and my turn in the shower, we went in together. Az sat on the edge of the bed, watching us quietly, hand gently massaging his semihardness between his legs. As we were quickly coming to realize, Cuan and I both have a bit of an exhibitionist streak, so having an aroused audience quickly had its effect on us. Before long, I was hard as a rock, and Cuan was teasing my backside with his erection. Eventually Az joined us in the shower—which made for an intimate fit, what with three people and two large wings—and Cuan took me from behind while I braced myself against the glass wall, while Az knelt in front of me, wrapped his lips around my length, and took my load in his mouth.

I was just glad the hotel had plenty of hot water, because we probably used a good portion of it.

We were toweling off when Cuan's phone dinged. He casually picked it up, but his eyes widened when he saw the message on the screen.

"Um, it's Lester," he said.

"Oh," I responded, somewhat lukewarmly. "Do we care what he has to say?"

"In this case, I think we do," Cuan said. He held the phone out to me. On the screen was a little speech bubble with three words.

"Marcus woke up."

XII

WHAT THE OGRE SAW

"I got a reply from Bianca," Cuan said as we lugged on our clothes. "She'll head straight there."

"Sounds good," I said, fastening my khakis. "I've texted Alexander."

Az had selected a clean pair of tuxedo pants and now removed a new white button-down from the drawer of his dresser. He swung the shirt over his shoulders, and his wings vanished behind the fabric.

"That's some trick with the shirt," I commented.

"It's special angel garb," Az explained, "suppressing our wings for when we need to blend in, or for interacting with humans without reducing them to quivering puddles of fear and awe. Being unable to use my wings is somewhat inconvenient, but I've learned to adapt."

"It doesn't seem to slow you down much," Cuan noted.

"Not really," he nodded. "And it makes it easier to navigate the tight corridors and small doorways that humanity seems to be so proud of. Also Michael hates having to wear stuff like this, which I find highly amusing," he added with a smirk.

"Michael the archangel?" I asked.

"He's a bit of a self-righteous hothead," Azrael said. "As self-righteous as one who is *actually* righteous can be said to be, that is. But he's earnest, which makes him more endearing than irritating. Plus he's sexy. You humans would label his physical appearance... Latino, probably."

"Is he gay, too?" Cuan asked.

"I never thought to ask," Az responded. "Bisexual or pansexual, most likely, since angels like me who are solely interested in a single sex are rare. But he might be, since I've only ever seen him having sex with males. Including me, a handful of times."

Cuan dropped the shoe he was trying to put on, then stared at Az. "I am so turned on right now," he muttered.

"You're not alone," I said. "But, Marcus."

"Right," Cuan nodded, slipping his shoes back on.

My phone dinged.

"Alexander?" Cuan asked.

"Yup," I nodded. "'o-m-g, w-t-f, o-m-w,'" I read. "Is that supposed to mean something?"

"It means he's coming," Cuan said.

I looked back at my phone with a raised eyebrow. "Alexander makes lots of noises when he cums, but not sounds like these," I remarked.

"You know what I mean," Cuan smirked, giving me a light punch in the shoulder. I grinned at him.

"How about you, Az?" I asked. "You coming to see Marcus, too?"

Az shook his head. "I don't think that would be a good idea just now, considering my last visit," he said. "Plus, I need to see Leo, to help him understand a bit more of how my blood affected him."

"You know where he is?" I asked.

"I do, now that he's had my blood," Az said. "I made sure that he didn't drink directly from my body, but I nonetheless can sense my own blood while it is still in his system. I will go to him directly."

"Sounds like a plan," I nodded. "I guess we'll be off then."

"Before you go," Az said, "May I have that phone of yours? And yours, Cuan."

Curious, I handed the angel my phone, and Cuan unlocked his and did the same. Azrael tapped on the screens a few times, then handed the phones back. I looked down at the screen in surprise.

"Is this... your contact details?" I gasped. "You have a phone?"

"Some angelic smartphone?" Cuan added.

"No, a perfectly mundane one," Azrael said. "Cedric and Lester insisted I have one when I joined the Midnight Hunters, so they could contact me. It's essentially a burner phone; it won't be coming with me when this earthly visit is over. Nonetheless, while I can sense the whereabouts of the two of you thanks to my oath to keep you safe, neither of you have had a better way of reaching me than to drop by the hotel and hope I was here. I figure this will be a more reliable means of contact."

"It is," Cuan grinned. "Thank you."

Az smiled back. "Now, go."

"Catch you later, Joe Black," I called as we headed toward the door. When there was no response, we turned around. Azrael was staring at us, wide-eyed, mouth slightly gaping.

"What?" Cuan asked.

"I always hated that movie," Az muttered. He looked down at his hands. "I thought it a weak and insulting portrayal and a ridiculous premise. But look at me now. Now, I *am* him."

"Hey," I said as we crossed the room back to his side. "I'm sorry; I was kidding."

"I even look like him," he added, looking down at his black suit.

"Don't be ridiculous," Cuan replied. "you're way hotter. If anything, he looks like *you*."

"And you have a better butt," I added.

"And probably a nicer cock, too," Cuan noted.

"Also you're gay, which is an immediate plus," I said.

"And you're probably way better in bed," Cuan added.

"And you have a far better understanding of humanity," I noted.

"Plus you're a kickass warrior," Cuan grinned. "With a badass sword."

"And pretty wings."

"And magic cum."

Cuan's last observation finally made Azrael break out into mirthful laughter. I was almost taken aback at the sound, as well as the transformation of the angel's face into one of pure joy. An angel laughing, and an angel cumming: those might be two of the most wondrous sights a human can behold.

"See?" I grinned, "You're nothing alike."

"Death in that movie is socially awkward, worried entirely about his own needs, and is flabbergasted by emotion," Cuan noted. "You're none of those things. Just because you changed plans after empathizing with a group of humans, and just because we had sex—astonishingly amazing sex, by the way— that doesn't mean you're anything like that film."

"You're not some forlorn, out-of-place spirit struggling to understand humanity," I said. "You're the fucking Angel of Death. And yes, I chose that adjective deliberately."

"So go be badass," Cuan added, "and teach that Leo a thing or two."

Az beamed at us.

"Thank you," he said.

We each kissed him in turn, and then hurried out the door. As we were heading to the elevator to the lobby, I turned to Cuan.

"Who's Joe Black?" I asked, and he buried his face in his palm.

The morning air was cool and crisp, and the streets were characteristically empty.

"You sure you're OK with this?" I asked Cuan as we hastened toward the Hunter's Home.

"With the occasional angelic threesome?" he responded. "Fuck yes."

"Not that," I said. "Though, I also say 'fuck yes' to that, for the record. But I mean with going back to The Hunters' Home. We haven't really... talked about how you've been feeling after everything that happened with Leo."

Cuan was quiet for a moment. "I really feel betrayed," he said at last. "But looking back... I think I overlooked a lot of really questionable stuff Cedric has done. I always wanted to believe he had some really good reason for it all, you know?" He frowned. "But in the end, I think a lot of what he did was just for his own benefit, even if he convinced himself it served some grander purpose. Even so, I never thought he'd do anything so deplorable as keeping someone captive like that. I can't go back to just living there and calling myself a Midnight Hunter. But at the same time, he raised me. I... I never questioned being loyal to him. I still want his approval. He... he made me the person I am now."

"He did nothing of the sort," I replied. "The person who made you who you are—that's all you, Cuan. Someone like Cedric could never be responsible for such a sweet, generous, friendly, warm person like you. If anything, you're that amazing person in spite of him, not because of him."

Cuan sniffed back a tear. "God, I love you so much," he said.

"And I love you," I said. "Because of *you*, not Cedric. Now, listen: just because we're going back there, it doesn't mean you have to do anything, or be anyone, except for yourself. You don't have to obey him, or listen to him at all if you don't want to. I'm not saying you have to hate him; I'm not even saying you shouldn't rebuild some kind of relationship with him if you want. But things don't have to be the way they were. And I'm here, no matter what. OK?"

"Yeah," Cuan nodded. "Okay. Thank you."

"Always," I said.

Cuan's phone beeped. He took it out and glanced at it, then turned back to me.

"Bianca's on her way; she's just passing the sushi restaurant we like," he said. "That's about a block over." He tapped off a reply, and Bianca met us at the next intersection.

"How's Leo?" Cuan asked.

"Still a little shell-shocked," Bianca admitted. "I'm actually a little worried about him."

"He'll have help," I said.

Bianca looked at us suspiciously. "Why are you coming from this direction, anyway? Your apartment isn't that way."

"We were with Az," Cuan said. "He's heading to go see Leo, help him adjust."

"Oh," Bianca responded. She sighed. "What he did... for Leo and me... I didn't expect that. Someone really ought to thank him."

"Don't worry, we did," I responded.

She looked at me, then at Cuan, at the self-satisfied grins on our faces, and then down at our clothes—yesterday's clothes.

"Oh my God," she said; "you had sex with him, didn't you?"

"A lot," Cuan replied, grinning even more widely.

"This is insane," she cried, throwing her hands up in exasperation. "How is it that Casper and Rin Tin Tin are getting more play than me?"

"Touchy this morning, are we?" I asked.

"No, there's no touching, that's the problem!" Bianca cried. "You're off getting touched by an angel; I'm just getting touched by my electric toothbrush."

"At least you won't get cavities," I responded.

"I already have a cavity," Bianca replied, "and I need it filled. That's the point. Speaking of which, did you see Julia's outfit last night? I swear, all night, when I wasn't talking to Leo, I just had her in my head." She turned to me. "Is she single, do you know?"

"Um..." I began.

As we rounded the corner, Cuan turned his head sharply, alert. I followed his gaze, and saw Alexander heading down the block in our direction. I waved to get his attention, and he hurried to catch up with us.

"Hey," he said when he'd fallen into stride beside us. "Thanks for the text."

"Is Julia single?" Bianca blurted at him.

"Um... excuse me?" Alexander stammered.

"Don't worry about her; she's horny," I said.

"You have an okay night?" Cuan asked.

"Yeah," Alexander nodded. "Turns out that Julia has an apartment at the edge of downtown; she's made it a new base of operations. She and Thomas are staying there."

"Oh," Bianca frowned. "So she and Thomas are—"

"In separate rooms," Alexander clarified.

"Good to hear," Bianca responded, and Alexander rolled his eyes.

He turned to us. "So, do you think Marcus will be—OW!"

Before he could get another word out, Bianca whacked him hard in the arm. He turned to her with an affronted expression on his face, but she kept punching him.

"OW!" he cried. "What the f—OW! Stop it!"

"What the fuck were you thinking last night, you little bitch?" Bianca cried as she continued to strike him.

"Me?" Alexander protested. "You're the one who kept attacking me!"

"Because you kept going for my brother!" Bianca cried. "We

were trying to talk to him, and you kept escalating the situation!"

"You were really aggressive," I agreed. "Is that how it is with you? Just because someone's not human, you have it out for them?"

"He was a *vampire*," Alexander exclaimed. "He was literally trying to drink people's blood when we found him. And you want to talk about someone escalating the situation, what about those cops that kept trying to shoot us?"

"They can go to hell," Bianca spat, "but they're not entirely to blame."

"You kept brandishing your sword at him," Cuan pointed out. "That wasn't helpful."

Alexander groaned in frustration. "Thomas and Julia said the same thing last night. But he was on the verge of killing people! I don't understand why you all wanted to keep giving him the benefit of the doubt."

Bianca was silent for a moment. "What about Marcus?" she said at last.

"Huh?" Alexander asked.

"When he showed up, he was a big blue monster. He looked less human than Pound Puppy here."

"Hey!" Cuan protested, but she ignored him.

"Nonetheless, when you recognized him, we tried to help," Bianca continued. "But what if we didn't? By your logic, it would have been perfectly reasonable for us to decide that he was a lost cause. We had no reason to expect that what had happened to him could be in any way reversed. What if, instead of taking him in, we'd just slashed his throat when he was unconscious in the road and been done with it? You wouldn't be on your way to greet him now, that's for sure."

Alexander stopped walking.

"That would have been terrible," he said. "But... I know Marcus. I've known him for a long time."

"And I've known Leo," Bianca said. "Hell, I've known him my whole life, except for when he was tied up in the fucking basement. But as soon as you stood in front of him in that park yesterday, none of that mattered, did it? All you saw was a monster you needed to kill."

Alexander swallowed. "I... you're right, Bianca. You saw your brother, but all I saw was a vampire. But that's how vampires work, isn't it? Preying upon desire and familiarity, luring people into a false sense of security, enthralling them?"

"Do I look like some kind of fucking shrinking violet to you?" Bianca cried. "If he tried something like that with me, I'd have kicked his ass into next week."

"He did bite you twice," Alexander pointed out.

Bianca roared with frustration and resumed whacking Alexander. Alexander threw his arms in front of his face, crouching and cowering before her.

"Um... should we do something?" Cuan asked me quietly.

"Nah, they're fine," I said.

"OW! Hey, OW!" Alexander shouted. "Stop it! I'm sorry, OK? You're right; you're right."

Bianca relented, and Alexander straightened and looked at her apologetically.

"You're right," he said again, sincerity evident in his voice. "Had you guys not given Marcus a chance, he'd be dead. It's thanks to you that he's not. I didn't see Marcus as a monster because I knew him. I shouldn't have treated Leo the way I did. I made it worse for all of us; I could have ruined everything." He sighed. "I have a hard time getting over all that I've been taught about certain people just being inherently evil. That's no excuse, though; it just means I have to work harder to do better. I think about how excited I am to see Marcus now and how if I had just blindly believed everything I'd been told, that wouldn't be happening. So, I'm sorry. I really am. To you, to Cole, to Cuan... at some time or another I've treated all three of you with less compassion than you deserve. I will work to do better."

Bianca blinked. An openhanded apology was clearly not what she had expected. "Th… thank you," she managed. Cuan and I each offered Alexander a nod of acknowledgement. It was a start.

We started walking again, the air feeling a little clearer. But I knew that Alexander wasn't the biggest object of Bianca's ire.

"I'll be glad to see Marcus," I said, "But are you OK going back to The Hunters' Home, Bianca?"

Bianca shrugged. "It'll be good to see Bran," she said. "Lester, I dunno. It's great that he saved Marcus, but he was also secretly feeding my blood to my captive brother in the basement, so you know what? He can go to hell. And Cedric can fuck right off."

"So, this'll be a nice visit, then," I said drolly as at long last we approached the house.

It was the same building it had always been, the same steps and the same porch and the same windows. But somehow it felt less welcoming now that I knew it'd been used to keep someone captive against their will.

I went to ring the doorbell, but Bianca stepped past me and turned her key in the lock in the porch door, then strode across the porch and opened the front door.

Cedric was just inside; he'd clearly noticed us coming and had been on his way to let us in. He wore his usual broad hat and sunglasses, and regarded us with a stony expression.

"Welcome back," He said gruffly.

"Eat shit and die, Ray-Bans," Bianca spat as she pushed past him. We all followed, heading up the stairs.

"Excuse me," Cedric responded, an edge of irritation in his voice, "but I would like to have a word."

"Aren't you supposed to be eating shit?" Cuan called over

his shoulder as we continued to the second floor hallway. I flipped Cedric a quick bird before he was out of sight.

"Lester?" Bianca called as she headed down the hallway.

"In here," came Lester's voice from the room that had been given over to Marcus.

Inside, Lester was hunched over a machine, writing down a long list of vitals and comparing them to a set of notes. But we paid him barely any heed.

Instead, all eyes were focused on Marcus.

Many of the tubes and wires that had once clogged the room had been cleared away, and now Marcus sat up on the edge of the bed. He had an IV in his arm and a blood oxygen monitor on his finger, but was otherwise completely, unabashedly naked. He hadn't a trace of the blue that had once saturated his skin, having been restored to his more familiar olive tan. He was recognizably the Marcus I had known, just... a little bigger. Where he had previously been lean and a little ragged, now he was robust and muscular, with a barrel chest with big red nipples, defined abs, and pronounced muscles on his arms and legs. His face was his own, but perhaps a little taller. The only things that didn't seem large on him were his cock and balls, which hung in his lap below his black pubes, and I wondered if some aspect of the transformation procedure (or Lester's recovery process) had involved large doses of steroids.

"Hi there," Marcus said, his voice a touch deeper and more resonant than I remembered.

Before any of us could say anything, Alexander rushed forward, wrapping his arms around Marcus, tackling him to the bed. Marcus laughed as he fell backward, hugging Alexander back as best as he could.

"Well, hello to you, too," Marcus grinned. "Though if you're gonna climb on top of me, I'd rather you weren't wearing so many clothes."

"Careful!" Lester snapped; "you'll yank out his IV."

"I just can't believe you're really OK," Alexander choked, face buried in Marcus's shoulder.

"Apparently, I have this guy to thank for it?" Marcus said, pointing to Lester. "Oh, and all of you for not killing me," he added.

Alexander released Marcus and climbed back off of the table as Marcus returned to a sitting position. "So... you know you were a giant blue beast, then?" he asked.

"Sort of?" Marcus responded. "I mean, I kind of remember some things, but it's all really fuzzy. I've been getting filled in here by..." he turned to Lester. "I'm sorry, what's your name?"

"Fuckface," Bianca said, and Lester frowned at her.

"Do I detect a bit of tension?" Marcus asked. "Not on the best of terms?"

"He fed my blood to my brother while keeping him tied up in the basement," Bianca said.

Marcus gaped at Lester. "That's kind of fucked up," he said.

"I was keeping him alive while I worked on finding a cure for his condition," Lester protested. "Or I would have gotten around to it eventually, anyway. Granted, it probably would have been better had Bianca known about it, but I was under strict instructions from Cedric. This way, I got to continue my research."

"Thank you, Wernher von Braun," I scowled.

"Oh, is that your name?" Marcus asked. "Well, fucked-up side projects aside, you did basically save my life, so, thanks, I guess, Mr. von Braun." He extended his hand toward him, blood monitor still on his finger.

"It's Lester," Lester responded, plucking the monitor off rather than taking his hand.

"I thought Cole said it was Wernher?" Marcus asked.

"I am not Wernher von Braun!" he cried, exasperated.

"No, he's Fuckface Fester," Bianca said.

Lester threw his hands up in exasperation and turned back to the monitors.

"So... I know you, and you," Marcus said, pointing to me and Alexander. "But... who are you two?"

"I'm Bianca," Bianca said.

"And I'm Cuan," Cuan added.

"Weren't you two there on that church day?" He asked. "You guys are kinda badass."

"So you do remember that day?" Cuan asked.

"Sort of?" Marcus said. "It's kind of coming back to me. I had this sort of... compulsion to get into the church and find something. But I remember recognizing you," he said, pointing to me and Alexander. "Sort of, anyway. Something in the back of my mind made me not want to hurt you."

"Do you remember anything else?" I asked.

"I don't know," Marcus said, shaking his head. "I mean, most everything from when I was big and blue is gone. But, kind of like how some of this meat stuck with me," he said, cupping a large pec, "bits of the memories are still there. They just don't feel all that real."

"Believe me, I know what you're going through," I said.

Marcus gave me a long look. "Yeah, I guess you do," he said. "And I was kind of a dick to you about it. I'm really sorry. I've only lost a few weeks; you've lost basically your whole life. That really does have to suck. And not in the fun way."

"Thank you," I said, somewhat surprised by his genuine apology. Most of my interactions with Marcus since losing my memory had been while he was drugged out. This was more like the sobered up Marcus who'd thoughtfully gotten me groceries one day and asked about rekindling our relationship. He really was an entirely different person when he wasn't shooting up.

"So... you remember before you were transformed, then?" Alexander asked.

"Yeah," Marcus nodded. "I mean... at least the parts that aren't fuzzy from all the drugs." He blinked at Alexander. "Did... did you take me to a rehab center?"

Alexander was quiet. "Yeah," he said. "That's... that's how they got you. I'm sorry; I didn't know."

"Don't apologize," Marcus said. "I needed it. I mean, under any normal circumstances what you did would have been exactly right. You had no way of knowing that people were basically running some kind of sick Frankenstein ring out of there. Plus, look on the bright side," he said, looking down at his body. "It took a while, but I think I've been detoxed all right."

"Yeah, that's thanks to me, not them," Lester grumbled. "Plus being unconscious on a table for weeks will do wonders for an addiction. Still, once an addict—"

"—always an addict," Marcus nodded. "I know. But believe me, after all this, I don't think I'll be wanting to give up self-control anytime soon." He laughed softly to himself. "I mean, I was a wreck. Before you took me to rehab, did I show up at the church with ass tattoos?"

He twisted, trying to get a look at his backside, which was difficult from his seated position. He hopped off of the edge of the table, presumably to get a better look, and immediately his legs buckled underneath him.

Like a flash, Cuan was there at his side, steadying him. Alexander was there a second later, pulling Marcus's arm over his shoulder, holding him up.

"Thanks," Marcus said.

"You've been in that bed for weeks," Lester admonished. "You've got big muscles now, but that doesn't mean they're accustomed to being used. You'll have to take it slow."

"Gotcha," Marcus nodded. Then he twisted his body, turning his hips toward us and looking down over his shoulder.

We stared as Marcus tilted his ass toward us. It had always been a bit of a bubble butt, but now it was basically two solid mounds of meaty muscle. There on each tan cheek was the unmistakable tattoo of a name in elaborate script: "Alexander" on the left, and "Cole" on the right.

"Yup, looks like the welcome mat's still out," he said with a chuckle.

"It doesn't bother you?" Alexander asked.

"Naw; I think it's hilarious," Marcus grinned. "It's like a walking cautionary tale. Of course, I wouldn't be mad if either of you wanted to lay claim to this particular mountain range. It's got your name on it, after all." Then he looked between Alexander and me. "Though considering how long I've been out of the picture, I'm guessing the two of you are basically an item now?"

"Um, not exactly," Alexander said.

"That... didn't work out," I nodded.

"Why not?" Marcus asked. "You two seemed well-matched."

"It's a long story," I said.

"So... you're single?" he asked hopefully.

"No," I shook my head. "I'm with Cuan."

Marcus looked Cuan up and down with an approving expression. "Lucky you," he said to him with a wry smile. "Cole gives the *best* head."

"No argument here," Cuan grinned, giving me a playful squeeze.

"OK, I like you," Marcus nodded. Then his face twisted in brief discomfort.

"You OK?" I asked.

"Yeah," Marcus nodded. "It's just... now that I have all the tubes and the catheter out, I... kinda gotta pee."

"I'll help you to the bathroom," Alexander said, holding Marcus's arm as it hung over his shoulder. "Lean on me."

"Thanks," Marcus nodded. As they walked out of the bathroom, he added, "So what *did* happen between you two?"

"I'll fill you in," Alexander said. "Though I warn you, I don't come off looking particularly good."

"I was a drugged-out junkie who tried to sleep with Cole just after he basically woke up from a coma, then got transformed into a giant monster who was sent to attack your church. I'd be pretty shocked if you could top that."

"Well, prepare to be surprised," Alexander said as they walked out of the room.

Once they were gone, Bianca turned to Lester, her voice full of menace. "So, what's the plan here, Uncle Fuckface?" she growled. "Figure out what makes Marcus tick so you can make your own ogre army?"

"No," Lester said. "Maybe I legitimately wanted to help? Did you consider that possibility?"

"And yet...?" Bianca began.

Lester sighed. "I'll admit that the idea of reverse-engineering a serum did occur to me, but more out of scientific curiosity than any real desire to put it to use. But considering how widespread the ogre issue is becoming, it really was more important to find a way to reverse the process. Imagine how many people have probably been affected by this?"

"And... you think you can cure them all?" I asked.

"I'll have to test my cure on the others in my lab," Lester said. "It'll be a little rough as this was developed specifically to Marcus's physiology, so it might not work quite as smoothly on other people. But Marcus had also basically completed the transformation process. If we can find where they've moved their labs to and administer treatment to people who haven't yet been turned wholly into ogres, we might be able to completely revert the process."

"What about those who have implants?" came a voice from the door. We turned to see Bran stepping into the room. "Hey you all," he said to us with a smile, and Bianca gave him an uncharacteristic hug.

"Implants?" Lester asked.

"You know, like giant metal balls instead of hands; that sort of thing."

Lester thought for a moment. "Well, we can't regrow missing limbs, if that's what you're asking," he said. "We'll have to figure out some other solution to that. I think we have a few in the lab who've been subject to procedures like that, so I suppose that will give us an opportunity to see how deeply integrated the prosthetics are with their physiologies and whether we'll be able to safely remove them or replace them with useful substitutes."

"Well, it's a start at least," Cuan nodded.

"Glad you're not a total piece of shit," Bianca said.

"If he was, I wouldn't have stuck around," Bran said. "What they did to your brother was shitty, pure and simple."

"Well, glad you agree," she replied.

Footsteps approached from the hall.

"That's pretty fucked up," Marcus's voice came as he and Alexander reappeared in the doorway. "And Cole still talks to you after all that?"

"He's a good guy," Alexander said.

"No shit," Marcus said, glancing to me with a kind of awe. "Still, though, does this mean you're finally done with that crazy cultish shit from your particular church?"

"Basically, yeah," Alexander said.

"It's about fucking time," Marcus responded.

"Preach," I said.

"Oh, and Cuan, sorry your real dad's a trash fire," he added.

"Eh, I never had to live with him," Cuan shrugged.

"Well, you sure clean up nicely," Bran said, looking Marcus up and down approvingly.

"Oh, Bran, I didn't see you there," Alexander said, his face turning a bit red.

"Just passing by," he said. "I hope I'll see you later."

"Sure," Alexander responded as Bran walked out of the room.

As soon as he was gone, Marcus turned to Alexander with a mischievous smirk on his face. "Ooooo," he said in a sing-song voice, "someone's got a cruuuush!"

"So?" Alexander said. "He's friendly and ridiculously hot. Can you blame me?"

"No," Cuan, Bianca, and I said in unison.

"Right, well, if you're finished drooling," Lester said with a shot of irritation, "Do you mind helping Marcus back onto the table? I need to check his blood."

"Got another starving vampire in the basement, have you?" Bianca asked.

"Will you please drop that?" Lester groaned.

"No," Bianca replied. "And you *really* don't get to decide how long it is reasonable for me to be angry at you for stealing my blood and feeding it to my captive brother."

"Fine," Lester grumbled. "But I'm trying to do something right, here. Let me have it later, OK?"

"Sure," Bianca said. "I was going to do that anyway."

"You are all certainly taking your time up here."

We turned at the sound of the voice in the doorway. Cedric was standing there, wearing the same stoic expression.

"Sorry; I gave at the office," Bianca said. She moved to slam the door in his face, but he braced it open with his hand.

"We need to discuss Leo," he said.

"What's to discuss?" Bianca asked. "You lied to me and betrayed my trust, and I hope your death is slow and painful. That about sum it up?"

"I thought what I was doing was best," he said.

"Clearly," Cuan said coldly.

"Regardless," Cedric continued, "the fact of the matter remains that you have unleashed a hungry vampire on the city. We need to address that."

"Wait, vampire?" Marcus asked in alarm.

"Oh, that's all taken care of," Bianca said nonchalantly. "Leo's all better."

"What?" Cedric asked in disbelief. "How?"

"Angel blood," Bianca said simply.

"Wait, angels?" Marcus said.

"How on earth did you get angel blood?" Cedric asked incredulously. "Are you even sure it is real?"

"Believe me; it's real," I said.

"So Leo is no longer a threat to the populace, and Bianca is still Bitten but no longer carries vampirism," Cuan explained. It was an oversimplification, but it was enough.

"What the hell has been happening while I've been unconscious?" Marcus asked.

"Oh, much of this predates your even being committed to rehab," Alexander responded offhandedly. "More to fill you in on later."

Cedric continued to look between us all in disbelief as Cuan, Alexander, Bianca, and I stared coldly at him. Finally he sighed.

"Well, in that case, I am glad," he said. "You managed to accomplish something I could not."

"Did you even try?" Bianca challenged.

Cedric frowned. "I reasoned that you were too valuable an asset to risk depriving you of your powers," he said finally. "You are right that it was... perhaps not my finest decision. Nonetheless, if Leo is now alive and well and... 'better', as you say, then, while it may not justify my actions, I am nonetheless glad that I did not slay Leo directly when we first captured him."

Bianca scowled. "That's, like, the bare minimum of goodness," she said. "'Oh, someone found a cure for his disease; glad I just imprisoned and tortured him instead of murdering him outright'."

Cedric was silent for a moment. "Very well," he said at last, "your point is made. But I am pleased that he is well."

Bianca narrowed her eyes at him. "Fine," she said.

"Now then," Cedric continued, turning to Marcus. "I have some questions for you, now that you have regained consciousness."

Marcus blinked at him. "And who are you?" he asked.

"I am Cedric. I am the leader of the Midnight Hunters. We have been trying to learn more about the threat of the ogres in the city."

"Ogres?" Marcus asked.

"That's what we call the creatures like what you were," Bianca explained.

Marcus looked at us. "And you're all Midnight Hunters?" he asked.

"Not anymore," Bianca, Cuan, and I said in unison, while Alexander vigorously shook his head.

Cedric sighed in exasperation. "Even so, our goals remain aligned. You were there; there at a place where experiments were being done on people. Anything you remember?"

Marcus frowned. "I don't know," he said; "it's all kind of fuzzy. Maybe you'd have luck if you went back to the rehab center that Alexander had taken me to?"

"We did," Alexander replied. "It's been cleaned out."

"Dammit," Marcus said. He sat on the edge of the table and closed his eyes, concentrating. "I... I feel like some of the memories are there, but they're sort of mixed up," he said. "I kind of remember storming the church, but you were there, so that's not much help. I remember feeling a compulsion... we had to get something. Some kind of paper? A key?"

"The Key of Solomon," Cedric said.

"Yeah, that's right," Marcus replied. "Does that help at all?"

"Not really," Bianca replied. "Another group of ogres already succeeded at that."

"Shit," Marcus responded. He concentrated further. "There's... one other thing, I think," he said at last. "They were putting me under, back when they still claimed it was all rehab."

"They?" Alexander asked.

"The technicians at the rehab place," Marcus said. "They were talking to each other. I remember... they said the mayor and the police commissioner were coming to visit, to see how everything was progressing."

We stared. "Holy shit," Lester said.

"So the mayor likely does directly know what is going on, after all," Cedric growled. "This does extend all the way to the top."

"This fucking city," Bianca spat. "How did they even develop this fucking ogre thing? What kind of researcher is like, 'Oh, let's build an army of mutant hulks; that'll keep the peace'?"

"Research," Marcus said suddenly, looking up. "That's right; the technicians said something about some professor whose research the mayor was really interested in learning more about. Some guy named... Hortense? Horton?"

"Norton?" I asked.

"That's it!" Marcus exclaimed.

Everyone was silent for an instant.

"Holy fucking shit," I said.

"You know him?" Marcus asked.

"Yeah," I said. I turned to Cuan. "So they *are* after his research. That, or he's involved somehow."

"Either way, we gotta check it out," Cuan nodded.

"He said he'd be back on campus today, remember?" I asked.

Cuan nodded. "Looks like it's time for a class trip."

"I'll come too," Alexander said, pulling out his phone. "When he first e-mailed me, his signature had his office number on it. Maybe we can find it." He turned to Marcus. "Will you be OK here for a bit?"

Marcus nodded. "I've been OK so far," he said.

"I need to run another few tests to make certain Marcus has fully responded to the treatment before I try it in the lab," Lester said. "I'll take care of him."

"You'd better," Bianca said, "or, I don't care if I'm a vampire or not, I'll drain every drop of blood from your body and paint the goddamn walls Fuckface Red." She turned to us. "I'm gonna pack a bag or two of things from my room," she added, "so I'll keep an eye on things here and make sure everything's all right. Then I might check on Leo."

"Bianca, I—" Cedric began.

"Nope; you still don't get to talk," she interrupted.

Cedric bristled. "Do not—"

"Don't get to talk!" She insisted. "You wanna make yourself useful, go to the kitchen and make me a fucking sandwich."

"I—"

"*SANDWICH!*" she shouted, and Cedric finally relented and disappeared from view.

"I'll see if Professor Norton is around," I said, pulling my phone out. "Maybe make an excuse like I've found a new book he could use?"

Cuan put his hand over my phone, staying me. "If you do that, he might want to go to that café again," he said. "So this time, let's not let him know we're coming."

I nodded.

"Found the office on the campus map," Alexander said, holding up his phone triumphantly. "Let's get moving."

And with that, we headed back towards the University.

XIII

ETHICS APPROVAL MUST
HAVE BEEN A BITCH

"So, it looks like Professor Norton's office is in the auxiliary building now," Alexander said, consulting the university map on his phone as we snuck onto campus. "His profile on the university webpage had him in the main religious studies building, but his e-mail signature said that he'd moved recently."

"Isn't the auxiliary building the one that's shared with the bio labs?" Cuan asked.

"Maybe?" Alexander replied. "I'm not terribly familiar with that side of campus."

"Well, don't look at me," I said.

"We know," Cuan and Alexander responded in unison.

"Are we even going to be able to get in any buildings?" Alexander asked. "I mean, campus is closed. We could get in a lot of trouble just being here. The news on my phone says the police have upped patrols after 'rioting and looting' in the university quad last night."

"Rioting and looting?" Cuan asked. "That's what they're calling it? Is that what the officers on the scene are calling it?"

"No," Alexander said, "the police statement is that the officers who were on the scene are being treated for trauma and are having trouble remembering the event."

"I wonder how much of that is bullshit," I mused.

"Regardless," Cuan said, "we'll need to be careful as we approach the bio labs. Thankfully, I know a side entrance."

"Won't it be locked?" Alexander asked.

"Don't worry," Cuan responded. He led us down a side street that looked like a service driveway to the labs, and from there ducked down an alley between the buildings. The alleyway was narrow, maybe only seven feet wide. One building's wall was a solid brick face, flat and featureless. The other had a few windows about two or so stories up, as well as a fire escape with a raised ladder, but on ground level there was nothing save for a solitary metal door.

"I take it this is the entrance to the lab?" Alexander asked.

"Yup," Cuan replied, looking up at the windows above.

Alexander pulled on the door handle. It didn't budge.

"Um… it's locked," he said.

"Don't worry," Cuan responded again. He stepped back a few paces and then set off down the alley at a run. He leapt up, planting a foot on the lab wall, and used it to bound across to the opposite building, gaining some height in the process. He did the same with the featureless brick wall on the opposite side of the alley, and then reached up with both hands and caught the bottom of the fire escape. With the agility of a gymnast, he nimbly turned around, then pulled his body up, bending at the waist like a hinge and wrapping his legs through the fire escape railing. After using his powerful thighs to pull his body up and getting purchase on the railing with his hands, he slipped over it to stand neatly on the fire escape. I thought for a moment he was going to gain access to the building from the window there, but instead he leapt up, sprung off of the railing, and landed on a thin windowsill two stories above the door.

"Holy shit," Alexander gaped, and I no longer wondered how Cuan had kept showing up at the window outside my apartment.

"This window looks onto the postgrad work room," Cuan explained, sliding the window open. "The latch is busted, so it's never locked."

"Gone in that way often, have you?" Alexander asked.

"Nope, first time," Cuan replied before slipping through the narrow window and disappearing. A few seconds later, the door to the alley opened, and Cuan popped his head out. "C'mon in," he said.

"Those were some very impressive acrobatics," I said as we entered the dark building.

"Eh, it was nothing," Cuan replied with a shrug.

"I didn't realize you could bend at the waist like that," I added. "I can think of some fun ways to put that skill to use."

Cuan smirked at me as we walked down the empty hall. The walls were painted a clinical white; with the lights off they looked oppressively forbidding.

"OK," Alexander said after he'd finished rolling his eyes, his voice a hushed whisper. "We need to get to the religious studies offices."

"They're this way, I think," Cuan said, leading us through a pair of fire doors. A sign in the dim hallway read "Religious Studies" with an arrow pointing to the right, so that's the way we went. Presently we found ourselves looking at rooms with numbers like 'RS Aux 101'.

"We need RS Aux 203," Alexander said, consulting his phone. "Must be upstairs."

It didn't take us long to find a door to a stairwell, and once on the second floor, Professor Norton's office was easy to spot: light flooded from behind the slightly ajar door. We walked to the door and pushed it open.

"Professor Norton?" I asked.

The door swung open to reveal a small office, where Professor Norton was hunched over his desk. At the sound of his name, he jumped violently, spinning around in his chair to glare at us.

"Cole?" He asked. "What are you doing here?"

"I was in the neighborhood," I said, lying effortlessly. "I remember you said you'd be on campus today, and I wanted to make sure you were all right."

"Well, I was until you almost gave me a heart attack," Professor Norton groused.

"Also, I was curious how you were getting on with the book I loaned you," I said.

"Loaned?" the professor asked, raising an eyebrow. Then he waved his hand at his desk, indicating where the encyclopedia of angels and demons lay. "Yes, yes, there it is," he said dismissively. "You can have it back. It was very helpful, but I have all I need from it."

As I walked over to his desk to pick up the book, I glanced over Professor Norton's shoulder at the computer monitor that he'd been sitting in front of. A window was open in the file explorer, showing a progress bar and a large number of files, with the heading 'encrypting...'. In the USB port of the computer tower next to the monitor, a little USB key was sticking out, on which was affixed a handwritten label reading 'keys'.

"So, I assume that you came here because you're worried about me?" Professor Norton asked as I hefted the book in my arms. "I do appreciate your concern, truly, but I am perfectly fine." He looked between the three of us, suspicion flashing across his features. "The rest of the campus is evacuated. How did you get in here, anyway? The building is supposed to be locked."

"Through the bio labs," Cuan said simply.

"This is why departments shouldn't share buildings,"

Professor Norton muttered. "Anyway, you mentioned in your text a few days ago that you heard the police saying something about demons? Is that right?"

"Roughly, yes," I said.

"Well, you needn't concern yourselves," he said. "I'm very careful with my research. They won't have heard of me."

"Someone mentioned you by name," Alexander said.

Professor Norton blinked at us. "Who have you been talking to?" he demanded.

"Why does City Hall know about your work?" I responded. It was both evasive and direct; I didn't trust him enough to tell him what we knew outright, but I wanted to see if he was already aware.

"Who did you talk to at City Hall?" Professor Norton challenged. "Who's talking about my research?"

"You want me to remember the names of everyone I speak to?" I countered. "But why do they know about your research anyway? You've made such a point of saying how you keep everything a secret. What's really going on?"

Professor Norton narrowed his eyes at me. "People are jealous of my work," he said. "I'm sure someone is trying to sabotage my project, someone who wants to deny true divine understanding to the world."

"Do you hear yourself?" Alexander said. "That sounds like paranoid ranting to me."

"It also doesn't add up," I said. "Your research is all about proving the existence of angels, correct? Well, tell me then, what does that have to do with the city's security projects?"

"Security...?" Professor Norton responded. "I haven't any idea what you're going on about."

"Oh, really?" Cuan asked, looking past the Professor to his desk. "Then tell me, why do you have a folder with the city seal and the police emblem on it?"

I followed Cuan's gaze, and sure enough, sticking out from

the bottom of a pile of papers on his desk was a very familiar-looking folder. The text on the front was obscured by the pile, but the two seals were clear enough. The folder looked remarkably like the one I had taken a snapshot of in the maintenance office under the subway, when we'd first discovered some of the transformation labs. Cuan, with his keen vision, had spotted this similar folder from clear across the room.

Professor Norton blanched. He hesitated. "What do you know?" he asked.

"I know that humans are being used as test subjects for some project," was the most I was willing to divulge. "It certainly doesn't seem consensual."

"I'm guessing you know more than that," the professor said, "but believe me, I'm not interested in any of that. But here," he said, pulling open a drawer of his desk and reaching in, "if you want to know more, I have something that can help you."

Suddenly, the professor whirled around, brandishing a handgun that he'd pulled out of his desk. We all froze.

"Move away from the door," he said to Alexander and Cuan, gesturing slightly with little twitches of the gun. "Go over near Cole."

Cuan's eyes darted around the room, and I could tell he was strategizing. Cuan was fast, but he wasn't speeding-bullet fast. And there were three of us. Even if Cuan kicked his hand or something and the gun just went off, the room was small enough and we were close enough to the weapon that one of us would probably get hit.

"Just do what he says, guys," I urged. Cuan glanced at me questioningly, but then he nodded and inched around toward me. I, meanwhile, concentrated on the room, my body, the book I was holding, the contents of my pockets, the clothes I was wearing....

"You're going to ruin everything," the professor hissed. "I don't know what you know, or what you think you know, but I am not helping the mayor or the police. They may think I am, but I think what they're doing is appalling. I'm going to put a stop to it, but they have powerful support—more powerful than you know, I'm sure. And if you come in here and start asking questions and pushing for answers, you're going to ruin everything." He pointed the gun at us as he stepped back out the doorway. "I won't let you get in the way. Sometimes, sacrifices have to be made for the greater good."

He wasn't going to let us leave, then. He was going to shoot us. At least one of us, anyway, before the other two tackled him. I wasn't about to let Cuan or Alexander take a bullet. So I rushed him.

The gun fired. I grabbed my chest and crumpled to the floor as the bullet passed through me. Alexander and Cuan screamed my name, and as I fell I heard Professor Norton's footsteps retreating down the hall. Good. He'd panicked and fled. Exactly what I'd wanted.

"Cole!!" Alexander was screaming. "Oh my God, Cole!!"

Cuan simply stood, looking at me with a half-terrified, half-exasperated expression on his face.

"For Christ's sake, Cole, warn me the next time you're going to do that," he said.

"Sorry," I replied, looking up at their faces, watching them leave afterimages as they moved. "Couldn't tip my hand, now, could I?"

Alexander gaped at me. "Oh, for fuck's sake," he said at last. "I thought you'd been shot."

I pointed to the hole in the wall where the bullet had embedded itself after passing through my incorporeal form. "So does Professor Norton, hopefully," I said. "Now, help me up."

I let the afterimages overlap into fog as the world solidified beneath me, and Cuan's hand closed around my own outstretched palm, my other hand still clutching the heavy hardcover.

He pulled me into a standing position, then said something that I couldn't understand. I focused on his face, let the desire to hear him and be heard push the world back into clarity.

"Come again?" I asked as Cuan's face came into focus.

"I said, 'Now what do we do?'"

Suddenly, the building was filled by a deafening siren.

"The fire alarm?" Alexander cried.

"We get out of here; that's what we do," I said. I pointed to the folder on the desk. "Grab that."

Something flashed on the computer screen, catching my attention. A new dialogue window had opened. It read: 'REMOTE COMMAND RECEIVED. FORMATTING ALL DRIVES.' Quickly, I reached over to the tower and yanked out the USB stick with the handwritten label. "Let's go," I said.

In the hallway, it was already clear that the fire alarm wasn't as simple as Professor Norton yanking a switch: smoke was quickly filling the halls. There was a boom from somewhere down the hallway and suddenly flames came pouring through a door at the end of the hall. Along with them came a hulking green ogre, enraged and roaring. Some of its skin was blistering and red, but that wasn't stopping it from rushing us.

"Look out!" I cried. We couldn't afford to tangle with the ogre: In a few seconds, the smoke would make it impossible to breathe.

"Which way?" Alexander shouted over the din.

"This way!" came a voice from behind us. We turned to see Az at the end of the hall.

"Az?" I asked. "What are you doing here?"

"I sensed you were in danger," Az said simply. "Clearly, I was right."

"Wait, you sensed that *now*?" Alexander demanded. "Where were you when Cole was getting shot?"

"He's fine, isn't he?" Az said. "But you won't be for long if you stay here. Go down this stairwell and turn right at the first landing; there's a fire door leading to an emergency exit." He stepped past us in the hallway. "This green one's burns are severe, and we won't be able to get it treatment in time to save it. But I can at least make sure its death is swift."

He reached his hand out, and in a flash of black light, Quietus appeared.

"But... the smoke!" Cuan said.

"That won't bother me," Az said. "Now, go!"

We ran as Az faced off against the ogre, hurrying down the stairs and through the fire doors. Just as Az said, there was an exit, and soon we were out on the street. Sirens were already wailing as fire engines and police cars raced to the scene, so we quickly ducked out of sight down another alleyway Cuan knew.

"What..." Alexander panted. "What the fuck was that?"

"Well, that answers most of our questions about Professor Norton," I said.

"And any others we have, we might learn from this," Cuan said, holding up the folder.

"Or this," I added, holding the USB key. "I pulled it before it was erased. I have no idea if there will be anything useful on it, but we'll find out."

"You all OK?"

We turned to see Az walking toward us.

"Yeah. You too, clearly," I said. "All good with the smoke and fire, then?"

"I fed the ogre a drop of black bile from Quietus," Az said solemnly. "At least it is at peace." He turned to the building with a concerned expression on his face. "What worries me is... those are the labs, right?"

"Yeah," Cuan said.

"I wonder if they were in use," he said. "The ogre must have come from somewhere. I hope there weren't more down below."

Alexander frowned. "Rescue crews would freak out," he said. "Even so, what will they say when they see a dead ogre in the middle of the corridor?"

"I didn't leave a body," Az said quietly.

"Ah," Alexander responded.

Everyone was silent for a moment.

"So... where to now?" Cuan asked. "We'll need to look through what we've found."

"Well, we can look at the folder anywhere," I said, "but I can't get into my computer, so I don't have to way to check on the USB stick."

"Let's check back on Marcus," Alexander suggested. "Maybe between him and the folder, we can figure something out."

"I'm not particularly keen to keep returning to The Hunters' Home," I said, "but I suppose that's as good an idea as any."

As we walked through the streets, keeping to the shadows to keep from being seen by authorities, Cuan kept glancing at me with a concerned look on his face.

"You OK there?" he asked.

"Huh?"

"I mean... your professor just shot you."

"I'm... a little shaken up, to be honest," I said.

Cuan squeezed my hand as we continued down the streets.

Before long, we were approaching The Hunters' Home. Bran was in the street in front of the building, talking to two people. As we got closer, I realized they were Leo and Bianca.

"Hey," I called. "What are you two doing here?"

"Well," Bianca said with an irritated expression, "we were with Az, and then suddenly he jerked his head up, muttered something about how you were in trouble, and then literally leapt out the window."

"I half-expected him to rip off his suit and have brightly-colored tights on underneath," Leo said.

"SuperDeath," I nodded. "I like it."

"You are not giving me some comic book name," Az grimaced.

"You know that makes you Lois Lane, right?" Bianca said.

"Who's that?" I asked.

"Damsel in distress, essentially" Alexander said.

"No, that doesn't sound right," I said.

"He's more like Nightwing," Cuan said. "Trainee-turned-hero; smart and sneaky; *amazing* ass."

"Now *that* sounds like me," I nodded.

"Except Nightwing's basically been shoved into the closet since some moral panic over queer coding in comics in the '50s," Leo added.

"And that sounds like Alexander," I said.

"Har har," Alexander responded.

"Wait, you read comics?" Cuan asked Leo.

"Yeah, but I'm basically a Marvel guy." Leo said. "You?"

"I read mostly indie stuff, but Marvel is my favorite of the mainstream," Cuan replied. "If you like their stuff... well, you have a *lot* to catch up on," he added with a grin.

"I have no idea what any of you are talking about," I said.

"Shocker," Bianca said flatly. She turned to Leo. "That reminds me, though; I have a ton of trade paperbacks you can read."

"I love comics talk as much as the next guy," Bran said, "but, to quote Hulkling: 'Do you smell smoke?'"

"Yeah, about that," Cuan said. "University's on fire."

"WHAT?" Bianca and Bran exclaimed in unison.

"Perhaps we should discuss this inside?" I suggested.

Leo hesitated. "I'm... not particularly keen to go back in there," he said.

"Understandable," Bran responded. "But if Cedric tries to

do anything to you, you can bet you have six people here who will kick his ass into next week."

"That is... comforting," Leo said.

"Besides, I need some help packing up my room," Bianca said.

"You're... really leaving, huh?" Bran asked.

"You really don't expect me to stay here after Cedric had my brother tied up in the basement, do you?" Bianca hissed. "Honestly, I'm kind of surprised you're sticking around."

"I didn't say I was," Bran said as he opened the door to the porch. "I'm just... still deciding."

"By the way, Leo," Alexander asked, "How are you outside right now? It's daylight. Shouldn't you be burning up, or at least sparkling?"

"Do *not* fucking suggest that I should be sparkling," Leo said darkly.

"Not all vampires are averse to sunlight," Cuan said.

"Right," Leo nodded. "We're generally nocturnal, but the whole 'burst into flame when exposed to sun' is pretty much a myth."

"Only a select few vampires suffer in the sun," Az nodded. "Like a lot of other things, it is dependent on the circumstances of the vampire's creation."

"Plus, I'm sure the angel blood helps," Leo added.

"I'm sure it does," Az nodded with a small smile.

"Is that you, Bran?" Cedric called from the kitchen as Bran opened the front door. "Get the hell in here, now."

Cedric's face registered no small amount of surprise when six people crowded into the kitchen alongside Bran. He scowled at Az and frowned at Leo, but otherwise didn't say anything.

Breaking news was playing on the small television on the counter, covering the fire at the university. The official word was arson, blamed on the same mystery terrorists who attacked a police car the previous night. The authorities claimed that there were no casualties, though the basement lab was completely destroyed and a great amount of work was lost. Firefighters found a tunnel in the lab that connected to the library basement and then continued on, but police had advised them to pull back from exploring the tunnels, saying that they would take over the investigation once the building was declared safe. The suggestion on the news was that looters had entered from the tunnels, stolen what they could, and then torched the place.

"Professor Norton must have run out that way," Cuan said.

"As did probably anyone who was still in the lab," Az noted. "Probably the others who were experimented on were removed that way too, except for the hapless one who was sent after you two."

The news cut to an impromptu press conference by the mayor, who vowed to leave no stone unturned as the city and the police worked to ensure the safety of the city's inhabitants. Again he blamed the current situation on shoddy work by the previous administration, and again he paraded his poor, frightened daughter in front of the cameras in her pink party dress like some smoke-and-mirrors show, declaring that he would stop at nothing to make the city safe for children everywhere.

Bianca blew raspberries at the TV throughout the report.

Cedric turned to us after the report finished.

"What on earth happened there?" he demanded.

We filled him in fully as we were able. I set the heavy book down on the table and mentioned how Professor Norton had been eager to read it.

"Do you think he wants to summon an angel by name?" I speculated.

Az's eyes narrowed at the book, and he flipped open the cover.

"Perhaps," he said. "It's not good for much else. All this

about true names is stuff and nonsense, though. A name, chosen or assigned, has no power in and of itself, except by the meaning it carries for whomever it's attached to. But the idea of one true name for anything? Preposterous. An assigned name is like an assigned gender: it says nothing about the core individual it's attached to beyond conveying the expectations of the one who assigned it."

"I don't know what his research entailed, but Professor Norton also was doing something on his computer," I said. "He deleted everything after shot me, but—"

"He shot you?" Bran asked, alarmed.

"I hadn't gotten to that part yet," I nodded, "but yeah. But when he was deleting everything from his PC, I did manage to grab this." I held up the USB stick.

"Ah, that's my department," came Lester's voice from the door. "Guess I have good timing coming down," he added as he walked over. "May I?" He asked, and after I nodded he plucked the USB stick from my fingers. "'Keys', huh?" he said, looking it over. "Give me a minute with this. I'll be right back."

With that, he was gone. We continued our story about how Professor Norton was being very evasive but clearly seemed to know something.

"But he shot you?" Bran asked.

"Bullet went right through me," I said. "Thankfully, I knew it was coming when he drew the gun on us."

"And why did your professor draw a gun on you?"

"Because we found this in his office," Cuan said, holding the folder aloft. Cedric's eyes widened at the sight of it.

"Is that..."

"Sure seems to be," Cuan said. "We haven't had a chance to look it over yet."

"Well, give it here," Cedric said, holding his hands out.

"Oh, not so fast," Cuan said. He set the folder on the table in front of us. "This is something for us to look at together."

With the folder on the table under the incandescent light, Cuan flipped it open and spread out its contents. It was, as expected, a dossier about the ogre program, here called the 'augmented defense initiative', but seeing it in stark black and white was nonetheless jarring: it outlined the city's plan to create what was labeled as a 'civil defense force', composed of 'an obedient militia' intended to 'limit the city's reliance on state and national security forces in the event of civil unrest."

"This is really fucked up," Leo said.

"I know there have been a lot of protests in recent years," Alexander muttered, "But I didn't expect a city to take these sorts of measures."

"Really?" Bianca responded. "Because I've seen a lot of local governments doing shit that's about this level of messed up."

"Look at half the country during election season," Bran nodded.

The first part of the dossier detailed a Stage One, and it outlined much of what we'd already experienced, filling in some of the missing details. Everything on the development of the 'augmentation' program, including the process itself and who was responsible, was redacted, and the readable section of the dossier started with the establishment of city-wide shelters and rehab centers to clean up the streets and improve the current administration's approval rating by directly addressing the homelessness issue. This 'homeless repurposement' project would simultaneously reduce crime and contribute to urban beautification, the dossier claimed, as well as providing an influx of 'research subjects' who had no established community ties and thus wouldn't be reported as missing.

"That's the most fucked up thing I've ever read," Leo gasped.

The city's extensive abandoned subway system was selected as an ideal location for the establishment of 'R&D labs', the dossier continued, with the added benefit that the inhabitants of the tent cities who were currently squatting there would not have to be relocated far.

The dossier also included a number of stipulations about contingencies, including how to pass off various accidents in ways palpable to the public (numerous mentions of 'pipe explosions' here) and also guidelines for preventing information leaks, with clear instructions on preventing the fire department and public health services in particular from discovering the program. There were also strict instructions that if the secrecy of the program were somehow suspected to be compromised, the labs were to be abandoned and moved to a 'location beta', indicating a set of undisclosed established labs that could be accessed due to the secured cooperation of a redacted affiliate.

"That must be the bio labs," Cuan said. "Perhaps that's where your professor comes in."

"It makes no sense, though," I said. "I mean, what does that program have to do with proving the existence of angels?"

"Perhaps it's a side interest?" Alexander suggested.

"That's doubtful," I said. "I mean, he seems pretty single-minded."

"Well, that question will have to wait for another time, then," Cuan said, and I nodded.

"There's something else here," Bianca said, flipping pages on the table. There was one more set of documents, clipped together, that read "Stage Two."

"Holy hell," Alexander gasped after we turned the page.

Stage Two was a facility. A massive, large-scale facility, capable of processing up to six hundred 'subjects' at a time. It was a roughly circular structure, consisting of a central lab with multiple branches of 'processing units' and a complicated internal system for distributing formulae, venting gases, eliminating waste, and conveying essential 'processing solutions in liquid suspension'.

"This is nightmarish," I said.

"And look," Cuan noted, pointing to the specifications at the top of the page. "According to this, Stage Two should be starting tomorrow."

"But... where?" Cedric asked. "All location information is redacted."

"Well, we'd better find out soon," Bran said.

"So... I found something," came Lester's voice as he re-entered the kitchen, carrying a laptop.

We all looked over at him. "So did we," Cedric said. "And it probably demands more immediate attention than whatever you have."

"I'm not so sure about that," Lester responded.

"Does it have anything to do with the ogres?" Bran asked.

"Not that I know of," Lester admitted.

"Well then, why are you bothering us with it?" Cedric challenged.

"Because it's kind of a big deal," Marcus said as he entered the kitchen behind Lester. He was still completely naked except for a cane that he was using to help him walk.

"You're recovering quickly," Alexander noticed.

"He has plenty of muscle mass," Lester noted; "his body just needs to get used to using it. He should be walking fine by midday tomorrow."

"Is that your news?" Cedric demanded.

"No," Lester said, setting the laptop down on the table. "This is. You know that USB key you took from Norton's office? Well, it turns out it was an index of encryption keys. And two of them were a pair of one-time pads used to run multiple layers of encryption on the video files on the camera in the basement."

"And?" Cedric asked impatiently.

Marcus cleared his throat uncomfortably. "And... Cole, you really need to see this," he said.

Lester tapped a key on his laptop, and a video came to life.

It was a still camera, set atop a tripod at the edge of a circle.

The library basement.

Only in this video, the library basement wasn't destroyed. Space had been cleared away for a circle in dark red paint—at least, I hoped it was paint—lined with unlit candles. The circle itself was intricately detailed, lined with myriad symbols and designs.

"What... what is this?" Az breathed.

I stared. I knew this circle. And not just because I saw it in the destroyed basement.

There was some shuffling behind the camera. At the opposite end of the circle was another camera, red light already lit. But that wasn't what the camera was focused on. It was focused on a wooden chair, firmly in the center of the room, attached to the floor with what looked like screws into the concrete, leather straps bolted to legs and arms. It was, currently, empty.

Off-camera, the sound of a door opening.

Then I heard it. My voice.

"Professor Norton?" the voice said. "You really have to stop texting me for errands in the middle of the night."

Footsteps.

This. This scene.

I remembered this.

Coming around the corner of the bookshelves in the dark library, walking toward the spot of light...

"This is too much," I murmured in unison with the voice on the video. Everyone in the kitchen looked at me in surprise, but I paid them no heed; all I could do was stare at the screen. "I was out. It's the weekend," I continued in time with the me from the computer speakers. "This is the last time you give me an errand like this."

Then the footsteps stopped. The sound of a bunch of papers being dropped to the floor. I had seen the circle.

"What the hell...?" the me in the video gasped, and then there was a loud thump, followed by the sound of a body falling.

"You're right," came Professor Norton's voice. "This is your final task."

No response.

In the kitchen, I was hyperventilating. I felt Cuan's arms around me, his hands taking mine, holding me to him. His chest was warm against my back, his cheek soft against mine as he leaned over my shoulder.

"I'm here," he whispered. "I've got you."

I nodded. But all I could do was stare at the video. Cuan did the same.

Professor Norton appeared onscreen, dragging my limp body, carefully maneuvering me into the circle so as to not disturb the red outline. He muttered to himself about the difficulty of finding good help and how much easier it would have been if he hadn't had to drag me over as he hefted my body into the chair and strapped me into place, then slowly began lighting the candles. Finally he moved out of the circle, out of the frame of the video. There was rustling.

So it was me in the chair, after all. All the confused memories that had been flashing through my mind since we revisited the library basement slid into place, like pages of a book falling into order.

I felt some of the others in the kitchen close in on me, not in a threatening way, but rather a comforting one. A hand on my back, on my shoulder, in my hair, support and reassurance, a far different kind of touch than the tight leather straps on the chair. Everyone in the kitchen was standing with me as we discovered this video. Except for one key difference:

They were watching the events. I was living them.

I opened my eyes, groggy and confused. The back of my head ached for some reason. I tried to move my arm up to feel it, but it wouldn't budge. Something was holding it in place. I tried my other arm. No luck. Looking down, I saw the chair, the straps holding me in place. It was then that fear hit, and I began to yank and pull against the bonds. The wooden chair was a lot sturdier than it looked. I was held fast—not that it stopped me from struggling.

"That won't do you any good," came a voice. I stopped and looked up, finally aware of the edge of the circle. Lit candles with bright, reaching flames surrounded me. The overhead light that had been on before, luring me in like a moth to a flame, was extinguished, and so the only sources of light were now the flickering flames and a few tiny pinpricks of red that indicated the cameras recording from the perimeter of the circle.

The voice had come from Professor Norton. He was now clad in a long red robe, standing in front of a podium that he'd placed like a lectern at the edge of the circle. This, too, was enclosed in a smaller circle of what looked like chalk rather than the what-I-hoped-was-paint that surrounded me. Professor Norton was only somewhat visible in the candle flames, lit from below like some sort of camp counselor preparing to tell a ghost story.

"What the fuck is going on?" I asked.

"I've been waiting for you to wake up," Professor Norton responded, his gravelly voice taking on a sinister edge. "But you can't get loose, so don't waste your energy."

"You know, there are better ways to get people to come to your office hours," I glared at him.

"Impudent as ever," Professor Norton groaned. "You are fortunate I have consistently chosen to overlook that particular character flaw on your evaluations."

"Yeah, well, this is *definitely* going on your faculty feedback form to the department," I said.

"No need to be brusque," Professor Norton said. "You are here for a very important reason. I need you, Cole."

"What is this, *Riverdale*?" I asked. "I'm more than just a piece of meat, teach."

The professor scowled at me. "You flatter yourself," he said gruffly. "Right now, you're exactly a piece of meat. Though I must thank you; you've been extraordinarily helpful as a research assistant for the past year. I must thank you also for staying in town over the summer to continue to help me with my work."

"Like I had anywhere else to go," I said.

"Ah, yes. Your aunt and uncle traveled without you again, correct? Well, in any event, it meant that you were available, which has served my needs wonderfully. It was thanks to your diligent research that I was able to track down this ritual here in the archives." He held up a sheaf of worn, yellowed papers triumphantly, before dropping them back on the lectern. "To think, something so valuable right under our noses! What a surprise!"

"Surprise, indeed," I said. "Weren't rumors about angelic rituals the very reason you got yourself transferred to this university?"

"Yes," the professor grinned, "but that's not exactly what I found here, is it?"

"How the hell should I know?" I retorted. "How about you get me out of these straps and I come take a look for you?"

"No, no, that won't do at all," the professor said. "I need you right where you are. You're the guest of honor, after all. I can't think of any better way to show my gratitude for all your hard work than to give you the privilege of being the sacrifice."

"Sacrifice?" I glared. "What the hell kind of angel wants a sacrifice?"

"None of them," Professor Norton admitted, face falling slightly. "That's part of what makes them so difficult to pin down; it's hard to find something they'd want. But demons, on the other hand... demons are much easier. Dangle a piece of meat in front of an open door and some demon or other will be salivating there in no time."

"You can't be serious," I said. "Why do you want to summon a demon?"

"It's the next best thing to an angel," Professor Norton shrugged. "If I cannot demonstrate the existence of an angel directly, at least by demonstrating the existence of demons, angels can be logically inferred. Plus, it would still prove the validity of Christianity."

"I... don't think that reasoning holds," I said.

"Well, fortunately, you are in no position to debate with me," the professor replied blithely. "Still, you should be honored."

"I'd be more honored if you *didn't* decide to use me as a sacrifice," I said.

"Don't be ridiculous," he responded. "Still, it's a shame to be losing such a valuable assistant," the professor added with a sigh.

"You're insane. You're fucking insane!" I shouted.

"Well, now it's less of a shame," he frowned. "Anyway, enough talk. Let's begin."

"What demon are you trying to summon anyway?" I asked.

"I don't care," Professor Norton said. "The *who* is immaterial. All I need is for any demon to appear in the circle, where they'll be contained until I have sufficiently captured them on film and dismissed them. But enough talk—let me start working. You just sit tight." He paused for a moment, then chuckled to himself. "See? I can be funny too," he added.

Before I could respond to anything further, he threw his head back and started reading some incantation at the top of his lungs. It was a bizarre mix of English, Latin, and some other language that I couldn't place, though even so, it was obvious to me that he was butchering the pronunciation. But he didn't seem to mind; he just barreled on, and as for me, I wasn't particularly focused on the words in the first place.

I was far more concerned with the fact that the candle flames were rising, and the red circle had started to glow.

Until that point, part of me had just expected that the professor was out of his gourd. I thought that maybe it was some elaborate prank, or that at worst the professor would start all his chanting and nothing would come of it. A tiny part of me had worried that maybe he would try to slit my throat or something and spill my blood in the circle, but I'd figured that if he'd tried to come near me at least I'd have been able to headbutt him and attempt an escape. But now there was no question that the ritual was very real. The professor's voice rose louder and louder until it became a fevered wailing. Wind began to brush my face, dust started to stir in the circle, though the tall candle flames did not waver in the slightest.

I could feel it: energy, something almost crackling in the space, like the air in the middle of an electrical storm. The air was getting hot, and my chest was tightening into a small knot of fear. A moment later, that knot exploded into full-blown panic as the entire circle burst into red flames.

The heat was unbearable; I could feel it clawing at me, as though my flesh would bubble up and peel off at any moment. I tried to shut my eyes, but I couldn't. The professor's chanting was drowned out by another noise, a deafening noise: it was a moment before I realized that it was my own screaming.

I screamed and screamed; it was all I could do. Amidst the red conflagration, white flames licked up here and there, streaking across the circle and around the glowing circumference. Wherever they flew, the inferno died back a tiny bit like oil before water, before closing back in in their wake.

The me in the kitchen felt a flash of recognition; I'd seen those flames once or twice since, such as when they flickered along the spirit chains when I was bound in the church. Here in the circle, though, they were tiny licks, overpowered by the raging fire around them. But a moment later, there was another flash as a burst of white flame traced the circle, then leapt to the adjoining circle that professor Norton was in. In a burst, his podium exploded, sending papers scattering everywhere, the professor careening backward into a bookcase and slumping unconscious to the ground as books piled atop him.

"What just happened?" came Bianca's voice from the kitchen.

"I don't know; it was off camera," Alexander's voice responded.

The flames in the circle didn't stop. They didn't even slow. On the contrary, the red fires swirled, faster and faster, until the entire floor was a disk of red. And then, something seemed to rise from it. Even right in front of me, I could barely make it out through the wall of flames. The screen in the kitchen, too, showed just a silhouette. But it was hulking, muscle and sinew evident in its vaguely humanoid outline. The head turned, and two glowing embers stared at me, into me.

I continued to scream, the edges of my vision turning white. White flames licked along the outline of the demon, and it screeched with anger, writhing and roaring.

Perhaps whatever incantation Professor Norton had been planning was left incomplete, and the demon was having difficulty materializing. Or perhaps something else was inhibiting its arrival. Whatever the reason, the creature was growing mad with rage, flailing its limbs about as it wailed. Finally, it twisted its head at me, focusing on me once more with its eyes, and reached toward me. From between the flames a clawed, sinewy hand emerged, wicked and sharp, and reached to me, closer, closer... Then, its nail touched the center of my chest.

On the screen, there was a quick flash, a burst up from my back, white fire in the shape of flaming wings billowing out from my shoulders. At the same instant, a white shockwave burst forth from the center of the circle—whether from me, the demon, or the point of contact, I had no idea—and the candles and cameras flew backward, the paint-that-was-probably-really-blood circle blasting apart. There was a crack, some static, and then darkness as the camera that was filming slid under the shelf to the corner where we would later find it.

My memory, too, ended there.

Silence prevailed in the kitchen as the video continued to play back silent static recorded by the camera, its mic and lens broken from the impact with the floor or a leg of the shelf.

Everyone stared at me. Cuan gripped me tightly.

"What... the... hell?" Bianca gasped, breaking the silence. "What was that? What happened to you, Cole? And, don't take this the wrong way, but... how the hell are you still alive?"

I felt Az's hand move from the hair on the back of my head as he leaned forward, eyes still wide in disbelief.

"Well fuck me sideways and call me David," he gasped.

"What?" Bran asked.

"Oh, sorry," Az responded, slightly self-consciously. "It's a saying we've had for ages. Gabriel used to say that seeing Moses part the Red Sea was nothing compared to seeing Jonathan part—"

"I KNEW IT!" I shouted triumphantly, and everyone jumped.

"Knew what?" Leo asked.

"What Az said," I responded.

"Oh," Alexander said. "OH. Well, Holy shit."

"Ugh, I hate that term," Az responded with distaste. "What does it mean, anyway?"

"Maybe when the Pope takes a dump?" I asked.

"Popes aren't always that holy," Az pointed out.

"Well, what about angels?" Cuan asked.

"Angels don't defecate," Az said with finality.

"Oh. Well, that explains why your ass was so clean," I said, and Cuan nodded in agreement.

"Wait, *WHAT*?" Alexander exclaimed.

"Hold up. Az is an angel?" Bran asked.

"Shut up, shut up," Marcus said, waving his hands agitatedly. "Cole, how are you not a complete mess?"

"I... I'm probably about to be," I admitted. "I'm... I'm still processing. It's just... I remember that." I pointed to the camera.

"You do?" Cuan said.

"Yeah," I responded. "In fact... I remember that whole night. I remember the professor getting knocked unconscious, and then the demon reaching out to me..." I shuddered slightly.

"Holy shi—I mean, oh my God," Alexander gasped.

"I... I think I'm in shock," I said. "Like, my brain can't deal with it all at once, so it's just kind of like, 'fuck it'."

"Well, since you're already in shock..." Az started.

"What?" I asked.

"That... those flames. The white flames. Coming from *you*," he said.

"So they *were* coming from me," I breathed. "What... what about them?"

"There is no mistaking those wings of flame," Cedric said gravely.

Az nodded. "I don't know why I couldn't see it before. Someone must have really wanted to hide you away."

"What?" I asked.

"Cole," Cedric said grimly, "that was angelfire."

"Angelfire?" I asked.

"Heavenly flames wielded only by some of the angels," Az said. "And their children."

"Children?" I asked.

"Children like you," Az said. "Nephilim."

XIV

HIDDEN TRUTHS

"Wait, Nephilim?" I asked, unable to process what I was hearing. "The children of angels and humans?"

"That's correct," Az said.

"But... I... but... what?" I stammered.

Bran shifted uncomfortably. I realized he'd had a reassuring hand on my shoulder as he removed it. "Yeah, so... it's a little crowded in here," he said. "Bianca, Leo, lemme take you out to lunch, huh? Maybe while we're out we can do a little recon and see if we can come up with any possible location for this lab thing."

"You mean, 'let's give Cole some space while he deals with everything,' Bianca said. Sure, count me in," and Leo nodded in agreement.

Bran gave me an affectionate tousle of my hair. "I always knew you were a spitfire," he smiled before heading into the hallway.

"Yeah," Bianca said. "You stood up to a demon. With both hands tied behind your back. You are fucking *awesome*. Even if you are a pain in the ass," she added with a wink as she and Leo followed Bran out.

"OK, we gotta get you some more fluids," Lester said, grabbing Marcus's arm. "And maybe some of Bran's clothes will fit you. You can't just be naked all the time."

"I'm not complaining," Alexander said.

"Nobody cares what you think," Lester retorted, dragging Marcus out of the room.

"Hey! I care!" Marcus cried as he disappeared from view.

I barely registered all the activity that was happening around me. I stood and stared, Cuan still wrapping me protectively from behind, my mind a whirl.

"Nephilim...?" I repeated.

I felt Cuan squeeze me tighter. I leaned into the embrace; it felt like the only thing holding me up.

"How... how is this possible?" I stammered.

"Somebody went to great lengths to hide you," Az said. "Angels don't often have sex with humans anymore. And even when they do, heterosexual partners are... less common than humans might expect," he added. "Even those rare times, they usually use prophylactics to prevent offspring, since Nephilim have become so reviled among humanity thanks to Abrahamic religious texts."

"Reviled?" I asked.

"Angels that mated with humans were labeled the 'Grigori', the fallen watchers," Alexander said. "Biblically, the Nephilim were considered abominations by God and were wiped out."

"Which is of course nonsense," Az said. "Humans were the ones who persecuted the Nephilim, not the Divine. Their reasoning was that angels were made, not born, so they shouldn't have offspring."

"But doesn't that same religion think that Adam and Eve were made?" Cuan asked.

"Yeah. Humans. Go figure," Cedric grunted.

"I had heard that angels who do have offspring often hide them, but I haven't heard of a Nephilim being born on Earth in several centuries. It never even occurred to me that you might be such a being. Of course, Nephilim aren't generally at the forefront of my mind, since there's no chance of my sexual partners becoming impregnated."

"Because you are barren?" Cedric asked.

"No, because they're men, asshole," Az replied.

Cuan blinked. "Did... did Cedric just throw shade?" he asked.

"It was a legitimate question," Cedric shrugged.

"Wait a minute," I said, a chilling possibility occurring to me. "We're not related, are we?"

"Don't be ridiculous," Az said. "Angels do not share familial or genetic relationships like earthly life-forms do. We each came into existence at the behest of the Divine, independently; we're no more closely related to one another than two random humans of different lineages on the Earth."

I breathed a sigh of relief.

"And *why* are you so worried about being related to him?" Alexander asked.

"Probably because we had an astonishingly amazing, acrobatic, positively Dionysian threesome last night," Az responded blithely. "Is that what you wanted to hear?"

"Fucking hell," Alexander gaped.

"Fucking heaven," Cuan clarified.

"*Regardless*," Az continued pointedly, "for me to not be able to recognize angelic heritage in someone... that is an extraordinary degree of camouflage."

"What if..." Cuan ventured, "what if someone had sealed him away?"

"You mean like... hiding his Nephilim side?" Alexander asked. "Is that possible?"

"Perhaps," Az said thoughtfully. "Only certain angels would be able to accomplish such a thing. Though... that would explain what happened since."

"Like..." I said thoughtfully, "like how I reacted in the basement?"

"You have a very strong will, Cole," Az said. "Assuming that our postulate about the seal is correct, then when faced with the demonic ritual, rather than just giving in to blind panic, your spirit fought back. Metaphorically, anyway, you cracked the seal placed on you, allowing enough of your angelic power to manifest to repel the demon."

"That makes sense," Cedric nodded. "The shock of forcing the seal open would have physiological side effects."

"Like amnesia," I realized.

"Exactly," Az said. "And in that case, you'd barely be able to wield a fraction of your powers."

"The incorporeality," Cuan said.

"That must be it," Az nodded. "It would explain why the transition is so difficult."

"And why I only understand the Tongue of Souls during my shift back?" I asked.

"Yes, exactly," Az said. "If your transitions are only possible because you've weakened the seal, then the confusion after you return to your normal state must be you inhabiting the angelic aspect of your being behind the seal. But even then, you didn't show any sign of angelfire or any angelic energy I could recognize. And... last night, I should definitely have felt something."

"Oh, I'm sure you felt *something*," I said.

"Well, of course," Az smirked, "but you know what I mean."

Alexander was positively pouting. We ignored him.

"The seal must be extremely potent," Az continued. "Furthermore, your angelic skillset has something to do with spiritual existence."

Alexander blinked thoughtfully. "What about the angel of the unseen?" he ventured.

"Tamiel?" Az asked. "Unlikely. He did have offspring in the past, but he hasn't exactly held humans in high regard since they labeled him 'fallen' and persecuted his children. He doesn't sleep with human women anymore. Plus I don't think Tamiel would be able to create such a powerful seal."

"It would have to be someone capable of ensuring utmost secrecy," Cuan mused.

"That must be it," Az realized. "Raziel. Keeper of Secrets. Your nature is consistent with that, after all: you generally go unnoticed unless you draw attention to yourself or someone is specifically looking for you. Hidden in plain sight: that's Raziel through and through. Keeping you hidden from everyone; keeping the *real* you hidden even from yourself."

"And Cole's memories?" Cuan asked.

"Cole basically pried the seal open in that video, and let some of his Nephilim powers manifest. But a damaged seal works both ways, and things can move in either direction. In all the trauma of the event, your memories must have gotten locked behind the seal. On some level, you might have even subconsciously forced them there to preserve your own sanity: there's no way you would have been able to process what happened without losing your mind, not before learning all you've learned in the past several weeks."

"So... my own memories are sealed away, along with, what, half of my being?" I asked.

"I believe so, yes," Az said. "But now we know what we're looking for. And just as you remain hidden until someone looks for you, it is likely that, now what we know what to seek, we should be able to find your seal, and perhaps remove it."

Cedric nodded gruffly. "Well then, let us get started, shall we? Cole, come into the basement; I will get that seal undone."

"Stay the fuck away from me," I warned.

Cedric gave an exasperated sigh. "I will not shoot at you, OK? Now come." He stepped toward me. I stepped away, and Cuan moved protectively in front of me.

"I will rip out your kidneys and *feed them to you*," Cuan growled.

"OK, fine," Cedric relented. "Well, then, what do you propose?"

"I will help him," Az said. "Just like with other training, back at the hotel. It is quiet and familiar, and we'll have an easier time if you are able to relax."

"Oh, sure, *'relax'*," Alexander said, making exaggerated finger quotes for emphasis. "I don't think that's what they intended when they coined the phrase 'touched by an angel'."

"Well, actually..." Az began.

"Oh, *come on!*" Alexander cried.

"Yeah, I did that, too," I said.

"All over him," Cuan nodded.

"Okay, now you guys are just fucking with me," Alexander groused.

"No, they're fucking with *me*," Az said. "That's kind of the whole point."

Alexander frowned darkly and said nothing.

"If you are quite finished being sophomoric," Cedric interjected, "perhaps you can get to work on that seal? Otherwise, perhaps it would be more efficient for me to bring you to the basement to address it myself."

"The only thing you'll be addressing is the organ donor list after I make pâté out of your liver," Cuan warned.

"Speaking of that basement, though," I wondered, "if I'm half-angel, how was I able to get into the room you were keeping Leo in? Wasn't it designed to keep angels out?"

"Not exactly," Cedric said. "The ward does not specifically ward against angels. Rather, it is designed to allow for those possessing humanity to pass, provided, that is, that the humanity is tinged with the extraordinary. To pass requires a mixture of human blood and something... supernatural."

"And you meet these requirements?" I asked. "What are you, anyway?"

Cedric paused for a moment, then reached up and slowly removed his sunglasses. Behind the lenses, his irises glowed a fiery red.

"I am half-demon," Cedric explained.

We all gaped. Except for Az, that is: he just blinked.

"Holy fucking shit," Alexander gasped, reaching for Candela.

"Oh, put your little glowstick away, for Christ's sake," Cedric replied in exasperation. "Do you really think after all this that I am going to attack you?"

"Honestly, I'm never quite sure," Alexander responded, releasing his grip on the hilt of his sword.

"Huh," Cedric said. "Actually, that pleases me," he admitted.

I looked at Cuan, who was still staring. "Cuan, did you know about this?" I asked.

"Um, I knew his eyes glowed," he said. "He never explained why, though." He looked over at Cedric. "So, now's your chance," he added coolly. "Care to tell us how the offspring of a demon and a human comes to lead the Midnight Hunters?"

Cedric took a deep, slow breath. "It is not a pleasant story," he said.

"I don't imagine it would be," Cuan responded.

"And you in particular may not like it," Cedric added, turning to Alexander.

"And why not?" Alexander asked.

"Because my father was Order of Light," Cedric replied. "He, like so many others, started with a desire to protect his faith, but somewhere along the line that became an obsession with power."

"Well, that sounds familiar," I mumbled.

"He was a researcher, first and foremost," Cedric continued. "Knowledge was his drug. He became a passionate scholar of demons. He learned everything he could about them. Knowledge, as they say, is power."

Cedric grew silent for a moment. His eyes wavered as he took a deep breath, then continued.

"His theory was that the best way to conquer demons was to dominate them, to utterly show mankind's superiority over the infernal. To this end, he spent countless years researching spells and symbols of summoning, warding, and control. Eventually, he uncovered the Greater Key of Solomon—not the watered-down, toothless variation you see in occult bookstores, but the actual tome used by the actual king. Of course, deciphering it took ages, as a significant portion of it—the parts that have not made it into trade paperbacks—is written in the Tongue of Souls. He eventually mastered it, transcribing it meanwhile into English, and annotating it as thoroughly as he could. Once he finished, he decided to put his work into practice, successfully summoning and containing a demon. I do not know what his initial plan was, but it was probably to either ransom the demon, which is folly; to drain it of its power and wield it himself; or to force it to defend the church. Whatever the plan, his ultimate desire was to express dominance. But what he did not expect was for the demon he summoned to be in the form of a voluptuous, virile woman. And so, my father chose to express his dominance in the way that straight men have been asserting it for millennia."

"Fucking hell..." Alexander gasped, horrified.

"Quite literally, in this case," Cedric sighed. "It seems probable that he performed that unspeakable act in the presence of other members of the Order, because they clearly knew of it. Of course, what none of them expected was for the demon to become impregnated. That then led to a different problem. While this particular branch of the Order apparently had no qualms about summoning demons into their sanctuary, nor about perpetrating sexual violence against helpless, bound females, they asserted immediately that if the demon had become pregnant then she should be forced to carry the child to term. She begged, pleaded not to have to bear the seed of her oppressor, but the Order was unmoved by the pleas of a demon, and so kept her, bound in secret, for the entirety of the gestation period. And thus, my mother gave birth to me while bound in spirit chains and a containment ring in a church basement. It was unforgivable: she should never have been forced to carry the child of her assailant against her will in such a way."

"But... if she hadn't been made to have her child, you would never have been born," Alexander said.

"Yes, he would have," Az interjected. "A soul that is ready to incarnate will incarnate. If not from her, then he would have been born from another. Your reasoning—any reasoning—should never supersede a woman's autonomy over her own body."

Cedric's face was dark. "In the days before my birth, that branch of the Order suddenly found itself completely bereft of divine protection. They assumed that it was because they had allowed my father to summon a demon."

Az scoffed. "That, instead of the actual, unforgivable act perpetrated against a woman whom they then forced into captivity beneath the sanctuary to birth her child. This is why humans are terrible."

Cedric nodded. "They never considered that, because they believed all those actions were righteous. So of course they decided on a simple remedy: as soon as I was born, they would slaughter both me and my mother, thus ridding the space of demonic presence."

"If they were going to kill you immediately, why have you be born in the first place?" I asked.

"Fucking religious logic," Alexander spat. "All that matters is that they not perform an abortion."

"Exactly," Cedric said. "And so as soon as I was born, one Order member was instructed to carry me away and kill me while the others set upon my mother."

For once, I had no snappy observation. This was just horrific.

"Thankfully, perhaps, the woman who carried me away decided that infanticide would yet compound the Order's offense. She left the Order of Light and raised me in hiding, teaching me everything she knew about survival. She hid in plain sight, working at an orphanage while raising me at a home she kept secret. Unfortunately, that branch of the Order was not about to suffer a traitor whom they thought had ensured they would incur the wrath of God. My father hunted her down personally. Shortly after my ninth birthday, he found her and killed her when she was at the orphanage, along with an unrelated eight-year-old he had just assumed was me."

"What the fuck..." Alexander gasped.

"Of course, that did not restore the divine protection that the Order believed it had lost, and as such the Order believed it had not yet placated the wrath of God. My father knew that he was next. By the time he had resolved to flee, the Order had already begun to confiscate his belongings. He had feared this would happen, and so never kept his entire manuscript of the Key of Solomon in one place. The Order found one half, however, so he took the other half and fled. About four years later, the Order eventually succeeded in hunting him down, but when they found him, he was already dead. They assumed he had taken his own life, but the second half of the manuscript was never found. By this time, the wider Order of Light had gotten wind of what had transpired and intervened directly, disbanding that entire branch of the Order and putting regional leadership in the hands of another family." He pointed to Alexander. "Yours."

Alexander said nothing.

"Clearly, the half of the Greater Key of Solomon that dealt with binding and controlling entities remained in the Order's hands," Cedric continued. "The half that concerned itself with summoning demons must have eventually made its way to that professor. And Cole here has had the dubious honor of experiencing both first-hand."

"Yaaaay," I muttered, raising my hands in a sarcastic gesture. "Seriously, though, Solomon can burn in hell."

"If that were a thing, he would be," Az replied.

"Wait, there's no HELL?" Alexander asked, aghast.

"It depends on your meaning," Az explained. "Is there a realm of demons? Yes. But if you mean a place where humans burn in constant and unending suffering just because they didn't immerse themselves in holy water and drink Jesus juice, or because they engaged in consensual buttsex, then no; that's just asinine. What kind of brutal, fascist God would do such a thing? Besides, eternally damming up souls in a fiery underworld would cause the wheel of life to grind to a halt and completely destroy the cycle of death and rebirth. No, I'm with the Buddhists; being reborn on Earth is punishment enough."

"But... heaven," Alexander protested weakly.

"Do you mean an eternity in the presence of self-righteous fundamentalist bigots who believe in smothering genuine love and subjugating anyone who thinks differently from them? Five minutes in a place like that and you'd be begging for your hell." He shook his head. "No, but there is something awaiting the souls that have finished their cycle of rebirth on Earth, and it's very nice, but I'm not going to tell you what it is."

"Selfish," I muttered playfully.

"More like 'human methods of communication and comprehension are insufficient to even begin to express it, much less conceptualize it'," Az said with a smug grin.

"So, hold on," Cuan said, turning back to Cedric. "After all that, after all the Order did to you, why create the Midnight

Hunters? I mean, you've always told me that the Hunters protect humans from those supernatural things that threaten them. If humanity was so horrible to you, why protect it?"

"Because," Cedric responded, "I also saw the best of humanity. The woman who saved my life, the work she did at that orphanage... all she wanted was to make life better for those children who had nothing. And it was obvious to me that the church she had come from, the sanctimonious Order of Light, these institutions who claim to be serving the public and working in the interests of humanity, are really just out for their own gain. So I decided to actually work to protect the people that these institutions were casting aside. And at the same time, The Hunters' Home could be a sanctuary for those who needed it."

"Like Leo?" I challenged.

Cedric gave a deep, long sigh, but it was one of regret, not exasperation. "I thought it a necessary sacrifice," he said. "I thought they all were necessary choices. I thought training that was merciless but effective was better than training that produced mediocre results. I thought that Cuan's loyalty was best assured by keeping him from growing too self-confident. I thought that it was worth keeping Leo in the basement if it meant keeping Bianca in her powers and in my house. I thought the number of lives that the Midnight Hunters would save meant that it was worth all those little sacrifices. They were... calculated decisions. But calculated decisions are not always the right ones." He looked to me, to Cuan. "I do not expect forgiveness, nor do I ask for it. And when I tell you that I believed my methods to be a kindness when compared to all that I witnessed in my youth, I do not say it as an excuse or a justification. I made my choices. These are the consequences. But..." he took a deep breath. "For what it is worth, I am sorry for causing you pain. And I owe Bianca and Leo that apology as well."

Cuan was quiet for a moment. Now it was my turn to give him a reassuring arm.

"...Thank you," he said at last. "I... I can't say more than that. Not and mean it, anyway; not now at least. But... thank you."

"For what it is worth," Cedric said slowly, "You have become a strong, confident young man. You and Cole are very well-suited for one another. You make each other better. I am proud of you, Cuan."

Cuan said nothing, but a tear rolled down his cheek. He simply nodded, and squeezed my hand tightly.

Alexander frowned. "Well, look at that," he said, a touch of bitterness in his voice. "That's more than I ever got from my father. Or your father, I mean," he said, turning to Cuan.

"That piece of shit is not my father," Cuan spat. Then he gestured to Cedric. "*This* is my father. He's a fucking mess; he screwed up more than I can possibly express; he is literally hellspawn and I don't like him very much at the moment; but he raised me and I love him."

Cedric's face registered genuine shock. One single, hot ember of a tear formed in the corner of his eye.

"I'm still moving out, though," Cuan added.

Cedric choked out a laugh. An actual, genuine laugh. Then he nodded.

I looked from Cuan to Cedric, then to Az.

"Hey," I said quietly. "If we unlock the seal on me, is it likely that there'll be, like, a burst of angelfire or something?"

"Now that you mention it, yes; that is likely," Az nodded.

"Well, then... maybe we shouldn't do it in your hotel room," I said. "Maybe it would be better if we did it in the basement here, after all." I turned to Cedric. "But you're just observing; do you understand?"

"So, you are saying that you do not want to risk a fire in the hotel, but it is fine if The Hunters' Home burns down?" Cedric asked, grumpy expression back on his face.

"Yes, that's exactly right," I responded.

Cedric actually smirked. "Very well then," he said.

The Hunters' basement looked none the worse for wear, considering the altercation it had recently seen. The door to Cedric's 'office' was once again closed, though the one on the wall bisecting the basement was open. The room beyond was arrayed with weights, exercise equipment, and a few unpleas-ant-looking pointy things that made me wonder just what Cedric's training of Cuan and the others had entailed. We remained in the emptier room, Cedric reclining against the wall, Alexander leaning on a pillar, and Cuan squatting on a mat near me.

"So," Az said, staring intently at me. "If your power has truly been sealed, then it's a very strong seal indeed. And well hidden. I've come to know you—intimately—and yet I did not detect it. However, now that we know what to look for, and we have an idea of how you might have weakened it... there are two things you'll need to do. One is routine by now, but the other will be less pleasant."

"And... what are they?" I asked.

"First, I'll want you to fade, then return. But, if you can, remain in that in-between state in which you comprehend only the Tongue of Souls."

"That's unpleasant enough already," I said. "What's the second?"

"Focus, as vividly as you can, on the memory from the library basement. I want you to recall what you were feeling there, to the greatest extent possible."

Cuan frowned at this, but I nodded. "I get it," I said. "We're going for the same approach that we did to get me to master incorporeality."

I concentrated, letting the now-familiar sensation of the

world feeling a bit less solid wash over me. Slowly, I imagined it all melting away, and presently everything began to leave an afterimage in my vision.

"OK, I'm incorporeal," I said.

"Very good," Az responded patiently. "Now, come back, but linger, if possible, in the state where you speak the Tongue of Souls."

"OK," I nodded. I turned to Cuan, who was looking at me with concern. "Don't worry," I said to him with a smile; "I know how to come back if I need to."

I focused on the solidity of the world, letting it slide back into place beneath my feet. The afterimages folded in on one another until they became a disorienting fog.

"I'm solid again," I said with a nod. Alexander said something that I couldn't understand, and I knew that I was speaking the Tongue of Souls.

"So I see," Az responded in words I could comprehend, and Alexander and Cedric looked at him sharply in surprise.

"This state is so disorienting," I admitted. "I always feel a kind of vertigo when I'm like this."

"That's likely because this is a state you weren't meant to experience," Az said, voice clear and resonant through the fog. "Something about this transition puts you the most in touch with your angelic side. Which means that this is also when it will be the easiest to find whatever's blocking you."

"How so?"

"Think of it like a spiritual scavenger hunt," Az responded. "If Raziel is indeed the one who put the seal on you, then I should be able to identify his energy. But you'll need to push against the seal to make it salient. Which is why I want you to remember, as vividly as possible, the experience of the library that you just saw on the video." Az stood in front of me, hands extended, palms out toward my body, but not touching me. He closed his eyes.

"*Remember*," he instructed.

It wasn't hard to go back to that space in my mind, even though I wasn't particularly keen to. It was a state of white-hot terror, of utter panic. I remembered what it felt like to be tied to the chair, to feel the heat assaulting my skin, the terror of the demon reaching out to me. It was a feeling of horror, of utter helplessness.

Except that it wasn't.

There was something else there, too: defiance. There was a refusal to give up and die like that. A desire to fight back, or to escape, to do *something*. That motivation, that indignation... that was, I felt, where those flames had come from. I focused on it now.

Fortitude. Strength. Defiance.

"Got it," I heard Az say. He exhaled slowly, deeply, a long, drawn-out breath. And as he breathed, I became aware of the magical seal on me.

I couldn't sense it with my eyes, but I could still *see* it, somehow, inside of me, laying across a part of my soul. It was bright and round, a disk of light, covered in intricate lines and symbols and glowing softly. It was beautiful. But it had to go.

"I cannot remove the seal on you," Az said. "You need to remove it yourself."

For an instant I wanted to shout 'How!?', but then I realized that I didn't need to ask. It wasn't simply a matter of overpowering it, of breaking it down: it was a matter of not allowing it to have any power over *me*. I didn't need to push through it, rail against it, throw myself at it. I just needed to release it. In my mind's eye, I reached my hands up to the shining circle over my soul. Carefully but firmly, I gripped one edge. And then, just as though it were a bandage, I simply... peeled it off.

It was like a levee being opened. I felt energy flooding my body, hot and quick. At the same time, the past 21 years of forgotten memories rushed into my mind. The sensation was overwhelming: not painful exactly, but a feeling of being so full that my being was about to burst at the seams.

I cried out as my vision went white. Just as it seemed like I was about to split apart, I felt Cuan wrap his arms tightly around me.

"I'm here," he whispered in my ear, holding me. He was, I felt, metaphorically and literally keeping me together.

Alexander cried out in some kind of alarm, and I realized that the two of us were wreathed in white flames, spinning out from my body. His concern was unwarranted, however: whatever the angelfire was, Cuan remained unharmed. The flames left our bodies, our clothes, even the basement furnishings intact and undamaged, and I realized that these were no normal flames: they only consumed if I willed them to consume.

There was a second rush as the unsealed energy seemed to find purchase in my body, like a battery clicking into place. I felt, rather than saw, all the excess energy my soul was generating focus into my shoulder blades, and it burst forth in two plumes of bright flame, like wings arching from my back.

"Holy fucking shit," Alexander gasped.

"Well met, Nephilim," Az said with satisfaction.

I felt a palm on my cheek as Cuan took my face in his hands. I stared into his eyes, white flames reflected in his golden irises, as he looked at me in a combination of intimacy and wonder.

"You are beautiful, Cole," he said, and then he kissed me.

It was a kiss unlike any other I had ever known, as though finally, fully, I was able to give him the entirety of myself, fully present without a part of myself tucked away out of even my own reach. In that moment I knew what Az had meant when he told us that our love ran deeper than either of us realized. We were—and had been for some time—one.

At long last, Cuan released the kiss. He gazed back into my eyes.

"How do you feel?" he asked.

"Complete," I replied, and I meant more than just having the seal broken.

He smiled that gorgeous, lovable half-smile of his, dimple forming in his cheek, and nodded.

Slowly, he helped me unsteadily rise to my feet.

"This is... overwhelming," I said to Az. "And not just because of the angelfire. My memories..." I paused, trying to let the whirling in my brain settle. It wouldn't. "They're all back."

"Wait," Alexander gasped. "Everything?"

"Everything," I nodded. "All 21 years. It's too much—my brain can't make sense of it all."

"Little by little, it will sort itself out," Az said. "There's nothing to impede it now."

Cedric smiled. "I am glad," he said. "At long last, the promise I made to help you regain your memories is fulfilled. Not that I really had anything to do with it, but still."

"I wouldn't have met Az if I hadn't joined the Hunters," I said with a shrug.

"And I wouldn't have been able to assist Leo if you hadn't been here," Az said to me. "Like the workings of the Tao, the Divine moves to take the messes that humanity makes and put them to a purpose."

"Lemonade out of lemons, huh?" Alexander shrugged.

"Something like that," Az nodded.

The plumes on my back had long dissipated, and finally it began to feel as though my body had reached a new equilibrium. It was strange, but it felt... right. I opened my palm, and with a flick of my will, a small white ball of flame flickered to life in my hand. Everyone stared at it.

"Whoa," Cuan said.

"So… I guess I have some new abilities to figure out?" I mused.

"You do indeed," Az said. "Every Nephilim is different. They'll come to you in time. I can help, but for the most part you'll have to grow accustomed to them on your own. But you should feel more… unified, now. And your transitioning between physical and spiritual states should be much easier. Furthermore…" he paused. When he spoke again, his voice was resonant.

"You should be able to understand this easily, now," he added in the Tongue of Souls.

I smiled. "Indeed," I responded in the same language.

Cuan blinked. Then grinned. "You won't need me in order to get back anymore, huh?" he said.

"I'll always need you," I smiled. "But yeah, I don't think I'll be so helpless after going incorporeal anymore."

"You were never helpless," Cuan noted.

"Um, guys?"

The voice was Marcus's. He was at the top of the stairs, clad now in a black button-down and black jeans. I turned and looked at him, and felt a new sense of familiarity. We had dated. It hadn't been for long, but it was tumultuous and passionate. I had dragged him back to my apartment and given him the blowjob of his life after our first date. He was a grower. He liked sex, a lot. But by our third date it was clear that he had a drug problem, and he liked being high even more than he liked getting head. I remembered being in his apartment once. He'd had a nude selfie of Alexander by his bedside table. It was clear that he cared about me, and I hadn't felt any ill will toward him, but he was too fucked up then for any kind of a healthy relationship, with me or with his ex. Looking at him now, my emotional reaction was one of affability, not resentment.

"Guys?" he said again. "You… might want to come up here."

The urgency in his tone had us on the ground floor in an instant. Marcus had been eating a cup of lemon Greek yogurt when he'd come to get us; a metal spoon was still resting on the half-empty cup on the table. He didn't return to it now, instead looking out the small kitchen window in alarm.

I didn't have to look out the window to know that something was up: the din from outside was deafening. I peeked out around Marcus, but all I could see were crows. Crows filling the tree in the back yard, crows all along the fence, crows covering the power lines. I hurried down the front hallway and peered out the porch window. Every perchable surface in sight was occupied by crows, and more circled overhead, looking for a place to land. In the center of it all was Bran, accompanied by Bianca and Leo.

"Alfred Hitchcock, eat your heart out," I said to myself. I felt Cuan approaching behind me and turned to see him and Cedric, sunglasses back on his face, walking toward the door.

"Um, what's going on?" Alexander asked from the kitchen.

"Should we be worried?" I asked.

Cedric shook his head. "Everything is fine," he replied.

Cuan nodded. "Bran's just holding an assembly."

"A what?" I asked.

Cedric stepped past me and opened the door. The crowd of birds froze, looking uneasily toward the porch.

"It's all right," Bran said, and the birds calmed somewhat, though they continued to watch us warily. Those closest to The Hunters' Home backed away, and a few flew to join those circling above looking for a place to land.

I stepped into the yard, looking around at the flock in wonder.

"What's the good word, Bran?" Cuan asked as we walked down the lawn toward him.

Bran turned toward us. A crow was perched on his shoulder; another balanced stubbornly atop his head.

"Apparently there's been a lot of movement in the city," Bran explained. "With the number of incidents downtown climbing—"

"—By which he means the number of times we've been attacked near the university and the city has tried to explain it away," Bianca clarified.

"Yes," Bran nodded, "with those quote 'incidents' increasing, the city has had an easier time convincing people to evacuate. Plus, property damage caused by the so-called pipe explosions—"

"—ogre attacks," Bianca noted.

"—has made a number of homes unsafe," Bran said, brow twitching in irritation.

"We know all that," Cedric stated.

"The thing we didn't know is what the plans were for all the people who didn't have a place to evacuate *to*," Bran noted.

"But now we do, I assume?" Cedric asked.

"That's correct," Bran said. "Somehow the news media have been gagged or kept in the dark over this, ostensibly as a means to protect everyone's privacy, according to this fellow who overheard a conversation recently," Bran added, gesturing to the bird perched atop his head. "But according to this girl here," he indicated the bird on his shoulder, "the nice woman who leaves scraps for her on her apartment balcony was made to leave on a bus two days ago, carrying a bunch of bags. She followed her until the bus arrived at the university stadium across the river, which is where she and a bunch of other people were unloaded."

"The stadium?" Alexander asked. "But the university is closed."

"Exactly," Bianca said. "That makes it a perfect location for a shelter, no?"

"Wait," I said. "These crows told you that? You understand them?"

"Yes indeed," Bran nodded. "You didn't think I was just a pretty face, did you?"

"Not *just* a pretty face, no," I said.

"Yeah, pretty everything," Alexander said under his breath.

"Cruu-uuush," Marcus teased in a sing-song voice, and Alexander elbowed him good-naturedly in the ribs.

"A number of the others here have seen similar things, in the last two days," Bran added. "There's been a lot of movement toward the stadium during the recent evacuations."

"Wait," Cuan said. "Isn't the stadium domed?"

Bran nodded gravely. "It is indeed."

"So then the Stage Two plan that we saw in the dossier..." I gasped.

"Is the interior of the stadium. That's my guess," Bran nodded.

"This is bad," Cedric said gravely. "We'll need to work fast."

"I'll head out for some reconnaissance," Bran said.

"Good," Cedric agreed. "Be careful."

Bran gave a terse nod, and then turned on his heel and leapt out of sight, a whirlwind of crows rising up around him in a deafening rush. Seconds later, the street was empty except for us and a few drifting black feathers.

"Lester's been working on that serum to reverse the ogreification process," Marcus said.

"Is that even a word?" Alexander asked.

"Shut up," Marcus responded with a playful nudge.

"Good," Cedric nodded. "Go tell him we need it immediately."

Marcus nodded and disappeared back inside the house, Alexander on his heels.

"Bianca. Leo." Cedric looked at them gravely. They looked coldly back at him. "Could I... speak with you in the kitchen for a moment?"

The pair hesitated.

"You'll be glad you did," Cuan said gently to them.

Bianca and Leo looked at him, then at each other, then gave a terse nod and followed Cedric back into the house.

"What'll we do?" I asked, turning to Cuan.

"I wish there were time for Az to help you understand more about your powers," Cuan said wistfully. "Are you sure you're OK, what with your memories coming back and all?"

"I've no idea," I said honestly, "but I do feel more like myself than I have in a long time."

"I am pleased to hear that," Az said. He had been standing silently since we all first stepped outside. "I unfortunately need to go back to my hotel to check on a few things. There is one thing in that video that remains worrisome to me."

"One thing?" I asked.

"Well, one thing in particular," Az responded. "When that blast of energy occurred, and your powers became semi-awakened, what happened to the demon?"

I paused. "I hadn't thought of that," I said.

Cuan looked at me. "If the demon is still out there... could it have something to do with this whole ogre program?"

"That would explain why they've involved Professor Norton," I nodded. "And it would explain why the professor feels personally invested in stopping the whole thing."

"True," Cuan said. "He doesn't sound like the type of person to be doing it out of the goodness of his heart."

"What," I asked sarcastically, "you think he's a bad teacher just because he wanted to use his pupil as a blood sacrifice?"

Cuan snorted. "I bet that's how my bio professor got tenure."

I turned to Az. The talk of blood made me think of something. "Hey," I said. "Now that the seal is removed... is my blood going to behave differently? The doctors described it as kind of... inert, before."

"Ah," Az said. "That's a good question. Yes, now that the

angelic part of your Nephilim essence has been unsealed and has dispersed throughout your body, your blood will carry a lot more spiritual power. It will still be impossible to introduce anything foreign into your blood, but it will now also carry a lot more vital energy."

"Hold up," Cuan said, pausing for a moment. "Is... is that going to be true of, like, *all* his bodily fluids? I mean, is his semen going to—"

"Have a similar effect to mine?" Az responded. "Almost certainly. Well, I'm off," he said, and with a flash of black light disappeared down the street.

Cuan turned to me with a wide-eyed expression, a blend of awe and mischief. "So, Cole," he said, "could you perhaps help me sort through some stuff up in my room for a bit? And if you happened to, you know, cum in my mouth while we're up there, I wouldn't complain."

I grinned at him. "Now *that* is a plan I can get behind," I said. "Or in front of, as the case may be."

Just then the door to the porch flew open, and Alexander poked his head out. "Guys?" he called, "Lester needs your help."

"Dammit," I muttered. "Rain check?" I said to Cuan.

"You'd better believe it," he said. "And there had better be a lot of rain. Down my throat."

"Not that I'm complaining," I said with a grin as we headed to the door, "but when did you get so horny?"

"What can I say?" he smiled. "You bring out the best in me. Besides, you can't expect me to learn that my sexgod boyfriend has developed literal *magic cum* and not want to guzzle it down while giving him a massive orgasm, can you?"

"Is this what you're like when you're not being beaten down by the rest of the Hunters?" I asked. "Because I must say, I approve."

"My Love," he said to me, giving me a peck on the cheek as we headed upstairs, "you ain't seen *nothing* yet."

XV

SPRING AND FALL

As we entered the makeshift medical room upstairs, Lester turned to us and handed us a blood pressure cuff with a digital monitor and what looked like a diabetes self-testing kit with its little pinprick needle.

"Good, you're here," he said. I need your help; in order to properly calibrate this formula I need several vital sign readings from Marcus taken at the exact same time, and I can't do them all myself with the equipment I have."

I blinked. I was less concerned with what Lester was saying and more focused on Marcus, who was on the hospital bed on all fours, again completely naked, ample ass pointed toward the doorway, looking at us over his shoulder. His asshole puckered slightly as we looked at him.

"What is this?" I asked.

"I've been trying to take his temperature, get his blood pressure, and measure his red blood cell count, all at the exact same time," Alexander said, walking to the edge of the bed where a long thermometer was waiting, attached by a wire to a computer where Lester was monitoring all the incoming data, plus Marcus's pulse. "It isn't going well."

"And Marcus looks like something out of a gay porn fetish film because...?" I asked.

"Because," Alexander swallowed, "we have to be as accurate as possible, and the most accurate way to take his temperature is... rectally."

"Well, that explains the precum," I replied blithely. Indeed, Marcus was semihard (he was still a grower), and a thin strand of clear liquid was dripping from the tip of his cock onto the bed.

"Oh, good *GOD*, Marcus!" Alexander cried in exasperation.

"What?" Marcus exclaimed defensively. "You can't expect me to sit here while you're sticking things in my ass and *not* be turned on! Plus, it feels good!"

"I told you were putting it in too far," Lester admonished.

"Sorry," Alexander said sulkily, "I don't exactly have a lot of experience with this."

"With thermometers, you mean," Marcus said. "This reminds me of back when we were dating and you bought me that big fat vibrating double sided dildo for Christm—"

"*Shut up,*" Alexander hissed.

After Cuan and I finished laughing, we prepared to get the simultaneous readings that we needed from Marcus.

"You know," I said to Marcus as I stood in front of him, steadying the blood pressure monitor as the cuff squeezed his arm, "I remember you."

"I should hope so," Marcus responded.

"No, I mean from before," I clarified. "I remember when we were dating, before I lost my memory."

"Oh, great," Marcus said. "So you remember me being a dick."

"I remember you having a nice dick," I said. "Although," I added, tilting my head down, "I don't need memory to see that now."

Marcus chuckled. "Thanks," he said.

"But really, I'm kind of shocked that you seem more together *after* going through a series of monstrous body-modifying experiments than you were before. You even *look* healthier."

"Silver linings, I guess," Marcus grinned. "Though it's probably more of a testament to how close I'd come to OD'ing a couple of times back before Alexander took me off to rehab. Don't get me wrong, I could have done without the whole being-turned-into-a-monster thing, but I really owe Alexander for looking out for—Aw, *fuck*," he gasped suddenly as Alexander pushed the thermometer into his ass a little too far. Marcus's cock jumped, spilling another string of precum onto the table.

"Sorry," Alexander said.

"Don't apologize," Marcus responded, sticking his ass out even more. "just wiggle it around a bit, will you?"

"Oh, for fuck's sake," Alexander groaned, pulling the thermometer backward.

Once the readings were taken, Marcus swung his body around into a sitting position on the edge of the table, and Lester tinkered with a few numbers on the screen as several vials plugged into the edge of his machine bubbled and mixed. Why everything had needed to be taken at the exact same time I had no idea, but Lester insisted that it was necessary to properly calibrate the proportions in the antidote formula he was using.

"OK," Lester nodded. "Now's the hard part."

"That wasn't the hard part?" Alexander asked.

"I dunno, it got *me* pretty hard," Marcus said.

Lester shook his head. "That was the scientific part. Next is the more spiritual, energy part."

"And what's that?" Cuan asked. "Do we need to infuse the serum or something?"

"No," Lester said. "We need a medium to suspend it in. Water."

"What's so difficult about that?" Alexander asked.

"Do we need purified water or something?" I asked.

"Sort of," Lester nodded. "The serum is to reverse or prevent an unnatural transformation and restore someone to a natural state. For that, we need water as close to its natural state as possible."

"But isn't all water natural?" Marcus asked.

"Scientifically, yes," Lester said, "but spiritually, no. We need water that has undergone as little processing as possible."

"But... I assume the serum is for injecting?" Cuan asked. "Doesn't the water need to be purified and sterilized for that?"

"Yes," Lester nodded, "but unless any of you have the means to magically purify water—"

"We could bless it," Alexander said.

"Order of Light holy water? Are you out of your mind?" Lester recoiled. "As soon as it touches the solution it's supposed to counteract, it'd burst into flame. You'd kill everyone you were trying to save."

"Ok, so not that, then," Alexander nodded. Then he turned to me. "Can you do something, Cole?"

"I have no idea," I said.

"Well, we don't have time to experiment," Lester said. "Essentially, since we have to process the water to make it suitable for injection, we need to start with what is as close to natural spring water as possible, otherwise the water will be left with too little potency to allow for a sufficiently rapid recovery."

"So... we need to go buy Poland Springs?" Alexander asked.

"No; bottled water is already processed too much," Lester responded. "We need a natural spring."

"Where are we going to find something like that?" Cuan asked.

"Hold up," I said, "I think we do have access to exactly such a spring."

"What?" Alexander asked. "Where can we get natural spring water?"

"We fucked under a cascade of it," I pointed out.

Alexander's eyes widened. "Holy shit; that's right!" he cried. "The estate!"

"Estate?" Marcus asked.

"It was owned by two former Order of Light members. My parents," he said as realization hit. "That's... that's my estate, by rights."

"Can you get in?" Marcus asked.

"Yeah, to the grounds anyway; I have a key," Alexander nodded. "We can go right away."

"Then here," Lester said, holding out four large beakers, each with a rubber stopper, each gilded with what looked like gold leaf. "Get as much as you can; that way we'll have plenty to work with."

We nodded and each took one of the beakers.

"Guess it's time for a little excursion, huh?" Marcus said as he pulled back on the clothes Lester had borrowed from Bran's room.

As we descended the stairs back to the lobby, I could hear Bianca from the kitchen. I guessed that she was still talking to Cedric.

"...Wow," she said, her voice a bit more serious than I was used to hearing it. "I... really didn't expect to hear that from you. It doesn't make things OK, but... it still means a lot."

"I still think you're a dick," came Leo's voice.

"Understandable," Cedric responded.

Bianca appeared in the hallway. "Oh," she said at the sight of us. "Heading out somewhere?"

"We need to go to Alexander's parents' estate," I said. "It's a bus ride away."

"Count me in," Leo said with a nod. "I'd rather spend as little time here as possible."

With Bianca and Leo in tow, we headed out toward the bus stop. As we walked, Cuan hung back near me.

"So... your memories are back?" he asked. "Are you doing ok with that?"

I shrugged. "I don't know," I admitted. "I'm trying to make sense of stuff. It's weird, because I've been living this past month without them, so it feels almost like... two different lives colliding, in a way. I mean, there's the memory of the past 21 years, where I grew up, was a normal kid, kind of unremarkable, lonely, did well in school, came here for college, did my studies... I didn't have many friends, particularly not any who stuck around. I came out in high school, hooked up with... a good number of guys, but was always still kind of unremarkable, lonely. And then there's the past month, where I've discovered that there's magic in the world, all this supernatural stuff. I've discovered that I'm the child of an angel, for Christ's sake. Yeah, I've been betrayed, locked in a box, shot at; I've tangled with phantoms and ogres and corrupt police; but I also have you, which supersedes everything else. Those past 21 years... they feel like a whole other life. There's no going back. And I wouldn't want to, anyway."

Cuan took my hand, held it tightly. "Do you remember your family?" he asked.

"Oh, yeah, my family," I said, recalling. "My fucking uncle and aunt. My mom died shortly after I was born. Cancer, they said. She had been kind of well off, and it wasn't sudden, so she'd had time to set up a trust for me. My aunt and uncle became my legal guardians, and with me came a fabulous cash prize. They got all the benefits of a meaty trust fund. Thing is... it came with a time limit. The trust was for them to care for me, so they only had it until I turned 18 and graduated high school; then it would revert to me—unless, that is, I went to college, in which case it lasted four years longer until I got my undergraduate degree. The closer it got to reverting to me, the more lavish their spending became. I don't think they ever really saw me as anything more than a cash cow. They saw to my needs well enough, but otherwise they basically just left me alone, occasionally choking out mechanical 'I love you's when they thought it appropriate. It's pretty obvious to me that their goal is to use as much trust fund money as they can before they lose control of the fund. I'll be surprised if I get anything, really."

"Those fuckers," Cuan growled.

"They would travel all the time and just leave me at boarding school or a camp or, later, just at home," I said. "The number of scout camps and shit they shipped me off to... I've blown so many boy scouts; I should have a merit badge."

"I'll make you one," Cuan said. "A nice embroidered dripping cock."

"I'll wear it proudly," I grinned, but my grin soon faded. "They're off on some trip right now, you know."

"Oh?"

"They left almost two months ago on some super-deluxe three-month around-the-world tour cruise," I said. "They won't be back until December sometime. When they're gone, they just cut themselves off from everything. They don't even check phone messages or e-mails."

"That explains why nobody came looking for you," Cuan said.

"Yup," I nodded. "With the university closed, everyone at college must expect that I went home with my family. 'Cept my family up and fucked off and left me."

"Your aunt and uncle can go to hell," Cuan said.

"Except Az said there is no hell like that, remember?"

"Oh, I'm sure we can rectify that," he said with a dark grin, cracking his knuckles. "Say the word and I'll show them hell on earth."

"They're not worth the trouble," I said, waving my hand dismissively. "Though, I do appreciate the sentiment. But whatever. They kept me from dying. They gave me clarinet lessons and an apartment in the city. They were never negligent or abusive or anything, just indifferent. So whatever; I just feel indifferent right back."

Cuan smiled that half-smile of his, with his little dimple showing. "You're too kind for your own good sometimes."

"Look who's talking," I said, squeezing his hand.

We rounded the corner in front of the bus stop. Where a tall black woman was waiting for us.

"Julia?" Bianca said, transparently enthusiastic. "What are you doing here?"

"Alexander texted me," she replied. "He told me about the folder you guys found and the whole Stage Two thing. I figured your trip to the estate and back for some spring water would be a good opportunity for me to get caught up."

"Where's Thomas?" Leo asked.

"The Church," Julia replied. "Rebecca called him and told him that Jacob and Levi had gone out, so he went over to pick up as much stuff as possible from his room while they're gone. Oh, and I might be having him raid the equipment supply room as well," she added with a grin.

The bus ride to the estate was uneventful. I was a little surprised that the buses were running at all, but it seemed to be part of the city's insistence that most everything was business as usual. It left me wondering whether the department of transportation was in on the whole ogre conspiracy. On the one hand, the abandoned subways had been used as labs, but on the other, the police seemed to be pretty good about keeping the program a secret from departments they didn't think needed to be involved.

We got off the bus a ways outside of downtown, and it was a short walk down a block to the large estate. Polished metal chains ran alongside the perimeter of the property, supported by brackets bolted into the fence, and I recognized them this time as spirit chains, able to constrain humans and other entities at a fundamental spiritual level. Alexander had mentioned on our previous visit to the estate that some of the chains seemed to have been missing; that must have been where Jacob sourced the chains that he used to constrain me at the church.

"So," Alexander was explaining to Marcus as we rounded the front of the estate, "the property is secured with a kind of magical lock. The only way to open it is with the key."

"And, so... why is it open, then?" Marcus asked.

We all stared at the estate gate. Marcus was not wrong: the gate hung open, chains lain across the ground instead of in the central lock.

"Didn't you say that this place can't be opened without the key?" Bianca asked.

"That's right," Julia said gravely. "But Alexander's isn't the only key."

Alexander blanched. "Father's here," he said. "Of course. That's why he and Levi aren't at the church right now."

"He must be getting desperate," Julia said. "With his branch of the Order of Light falling apart, and his claim to the property in jeopardy, he's probably tearing the place apart looking for the warding rituals your biological parents supposedly created."

"He's definitely desperate," Alexander said, "or at least feels like he has nothing to lose—he'd never fail to lock the gate behind him otherwise."

"So... what are we going to do, then?" Leo asked.

"My father has always been obsessed with the house; I doubt he even knows there's a waterfall on the property," Alexander observed. "Julia managed to sneak me one of the two keys to the estate a while back, but there's only one key to the building, and Father never leaves it off of his person. That's where he'll be focused again. Cole, you know where the spring is; take Cuan and Marcus and fill up these beakers." He handed his glass container over to me.

"And what are you going to do?" Cuan asked.

"I'm going to take back my house," Alexander declared.

"Not by yourself, you're not," Julia announced.

"Oh, this'll be a fucking *great* time," Bianca grinned, cracking her knuckles. "I wanna give those fuckers a piece of my mind. And a punch in the face."

"I don't want things to get violent if we can help it," Alexander warned.

"Well, I sure as hell do," Bianca said.

"These guys sound like complete assholes," Leo nodded. "I'd be happy to have a piece of them."

"No," Alexander shook his head. "I appreciate the sentiment; I really do, but these are the top two people in our local Order of Light. They *specialize* in slaying supernatural creatures. And sure, you may have had a stomach full of angel blood and it may have fundamentally altered your nature, but you're still a vampire, and that makes you a target. Drinking blood is diametrically opposed to everything the church stands for."

"You do realize that one of the key practices of your religion involves drinking the blood of Christ once a week, right?" Leo asked sardonically.

"He's got us there, Alexander," Julia said.

"Um... OK, that's a good point, and well made," Alexander admitted. "Nonetheless, I need you and Bianca to scout the perimeter of the property; make sure that they haven't split up or anything. It wouldn't do to be confronting my father and have Levi show up out of nowhere brandishing his hammer. Also, if they drove here and parked on the property, it'd be good to know where they are. Key the car or let the air out of their tires or something if it'll make you feel better," he added.

Bianca shrugged. "Eh, property destruction will do, I suppose," she nodded.

"Good," Alexander said. "So, are we all set? Send a text if you come across anything unusual; otherwise, Cole, let us know once you guys have the water, and if we haven't run into Father or Levi, we'll get out of here."

I nodded, and the group of us headed off down the dirt driveway while Bianca and Leo began to follow the fence off to the right. Shortly after we got to the bend in the road, Cuan, Marcus, and I split off from Alexander and Julia, and I led them through the trees toward the clearing.

"So... you fucked in this spring, right?" Cuan asked quietly as we walked. "You told me it had falling water or something, but... how did that work? Wasn't it cramped?"

"Believe me," I said; "when you see it, you'll get it."

We walked a little farther before the clearing came into glorious view. It was filled with emerald grass, making a little shaded spot over on the left side of the clearing, while the right part consisted of a tall rock outcropping hooded with trees. Near the top, a cascade of water emerged from the rock, pouring down in a gentle waterfall to a pool about a foot deep below.

Cuan took one look at the sight in front of him and nodded. "Yup, I get it," he said. "I would absolutely have sex here."

"Ditto that," Marcus agreed. "I kind of want to get naked and get in there right now."

"Not with a crazed zealot on the grounds," I said.

"What do you have to worry about?" Marcus asked. "Isn't your power, like, not getting noticed?"

I shot Marcus a look. "Fill up your beaker," I said.

"You're no fun," Marcus replied, but he did as I asked. I had expected him to scoop up some water from the pool, but instead Marcus pulled off the shoes and socks he'd borrowed and rolled up his trousers, then waded into the water.

"We have to get this stuff as close to spring-fresh as possible, right?" he said. "I'm guessing that means water pouring out of the rock would be better than water from the pool."

It was a remarkably intelligent insight. Marcus held the beaker under the waterfall until it was filled, then replaced the rubber stopper. He waded back toward the edge of the pool. "This water's even warm," he said wistfully, then handed the beaker out toward me. "Here; trade you for an empty one."

Cuan and I took turns handing him beakers, and soon we had four full glass containers of spring water.

"This place is amazing," Cuan mused as he looked around.

"Seriously," Marcus nodded, brushing the water off of his feet with his hands as best he could before pulling his socks back on. "How the hell did you convince Alexander to have sex out here, anyway?"

"Actually, it was his idea," I replied.

Marcus stopped and stared at me. "Get the fuck outta town."

"I'm serious," I said as I pulled out my phone and sent Alexander a quick 'Got the Water' text. "He brought me out here, and he had condoms and lube and everything."

"I really can't imagine that," Marcus said. "Stuck up, tightly wound Alexander, wanting to have sex outdoors, in the open?" He shook his head. "I can't see it. Alexander usually has such a massive stick up his ass that it's impossible to get a cock in edgewise."

"He was like a different person out here," I replied. "Confident, forward, comfortable in his own skin. I think with the way the gates worked, this was a place he could come on days when he knew his father wasn't around and never worry about somebody discovering him. It was Alexander without fear of judgment. He even used to come here and work out naked, you know."

Marcus paused. "Holy fuck that is so hot," he said.

Cuan nodded appreciatively. "I get it," he said.

"The problem was his tendency to lock away that side of him with the rest of the estate," I mused.

Marcus nodded as he finished tying his shoes. "What he did to you is really fucked up," he said. "I don't think I'd even be able to speak to him again if I were in your shoes. But, I dunno, he seems like maybe he's a bit better lately? Maybe it's just because I was, you know, busy being committed and then experimented on and then unconscious the whole time this happened, but the difference between the Alexander I knew a few weeks ago and the Alexander now is remarkable."

"Yeah, well, finding out his father lied to him his whole life probably had an effect on him," Cuan said.

I looked back down at my phone. "He's not replying," I said. "Considering how clear he was with his planning, something must be up."

"It's been like, what, two minutes?" Marcus asked. "Don't panic just yet; give the guy some time."

Just then, gunshots rang out from the direction of the house.

"Okay, now panic," Marcus nodded as we raced toward the noise.

"Hold up," I said as we reached the edge of the clearing. "We don't know how thick the brush is. I'm sure Cuan'd have no trouble racing through here, but we're all carrying glass beakers of water; we can't afford to risk breaking them."

Cuan nodded. "I'll take yours," he said, as I handed mine to him, leaving Marcus with the other two, "but let's go back through the way we came, just to be safe—at least we know there's a path there."

We moved as quickly as we could while still being careful. As soon as we were back on the main road we could hear shouting from the direction of the house. We broke into a careful run.

"So, what, you're just going to lock me out?" came Alexander's voice.

"That's exactly right," came Jacob's.

At the same time, I could hear Julia. "You *shot at me*, you fucking son of a bitch!"

"Don't you speak to my father that way," Levi roared. "You want a bullet in the head? He should put a bullet in your brain!"

God, I hated Levi.

"It's my house by rights," Alexander was insisting.

"Nothing is yours by rights," Jacob responded. "Everything you think is yours belongs to the church. I'll take Candela back, too, if you don't mind."

"The fuck you will!"

By now, we were close enough to see them. The house was gloriously large, an impressive white Victorian-style mansion that had stoically weathered two decades of neglect. Its paint was peeling; some of the wood on the porch had begun to rot, but overall it remained as stately as ever. A rusty brown pickup was parked in the dirt driveway. At the top of the house's massive porch were Julia and Alexander; clearly Alexander had been trying to open the front door when Jacob and Levi, who must have been outside of the house, perhaps in the back, had come around and fired a shot on sight. Levi held Perdition in a pair of gauntleted hands. The four were yelling at one another, but Jacob and Levi's backs were to us, so at least we had been able to approach thus far without drawing attention to ourselves.

"You have no right to this house," Alexander declared. "You've only been able to continue coming here because you've hidden my parentage away. My parents declared that the property should go to their child. You know what the will stipulated."

"The only will I care about is the will of God," Jacob said.

He raised what looked like a semiautomatic weapon in his hand. "You heathens have no right to set foot on this land."

"Holy shit," Marcus gasped.

Jacob levelled his weapon at the porch, but as soon as he did so, the trees to the side of the house exploded in a swarm of black, misty bats.

Jacob threw his arms over his head against the onslaught and began to retreat backward in our direction, still not looking our way.

"Two keys are on a cord on his arm," Cuan said to me quickly as the scene at the house descended into chaos. I could see them when he raised the gun."

"OK; you and Marcus take cover in the brush," I instructed.

"I can help," Cuan said.

"Facing an automatic weapon with a glass beaker in each hand?" I asked.

"Good point," Cuan nodded.

"Trust me;" I said. "I've got this."

Cuan and Marcus ducked into the undergrowth just as Levi managed to pull something up from his belt and toss it in the direction the bats were coming from. I saw it glisten in the light for an instant, a tiny silver ball flying through the air.

A flashsphere.

I'd seen the effect those can have up close before, having used one against a phantom. Even from afar, it would be blinding. I knew to shut my eyes.

Through my closed eyelids I saw the bright flash of pure light that accompanied the 'foomp' of the flashsphere bursting. I opened my eyes again in time to see the black bats evaporating as they spiraled away, leaving a heavy black mist.

"Fuck; I can't see!" I heard Leo's voice from somewhere, and realized that he must not have known what the little silver sphere would do. At least he was just temporarily blinded, however, and not something worse—I remember Alexander mentioning the effect that flashspheres could have on vampires.

The dark mist separated Jacob and Levi from the porch like a thick wall. It was impossible to make out the house through it, but the vague outline of the brown pickup was still visible. Jacob pointed the semiautomatic at the truck and opened fire.

There was an explosion as the bullets penetrated the fuel tank and the entire truck went up like a fireball. I could hear Julia and Alexander shout in alarm, but the truck was too far from the porch to actually endanger them and the house: it was nothing more than a diversion tactic, albeit an effective one. Jacob and Levi turned and ran down the long driveway, making for the bend in the road.

I stood in the driveway, waiting. It was clear that they hadn't even noticed me; they didn't even glance at me as they approached. That was what I was counting on.

A million possibilities raced through my mind—I could ambush them, attack them, maybe even knock them out. But the fact of the matter was that Jacob was carrying a semiautomatic, and I didn't want to risk them retaliating against me or anyone else. No: what was more important was getting those keys.

And for that, all I needed was to reach out my hand.

I had once chance, and I knew it. I readied myself as they approached, focusing on my body, on my identity, my sense of self, on everything I was wearing, everything in my pockets— everything that separated 'me' from 'everything else'. If Jacob so much as raised his weapon, I was prepared to shift right out from solidity. That said, I was intent on delaying that shift if possible.

As Jacob approached, I could see them: two keys dangling from a leather cord hooked over his elbow. They looked like something he would normally wear around his neck; from what I could figure, he had already been holding them in preparation for opening the door to the house when he saw Alexander and Julia on the porch, and in the ensuing altercation he hadn't the opportunity to slip them back over his head.

All the better for me.

Those keys weren't Jacob's; they were Alexander's. But for the next few minutes, I told myself, those keys belonged to me.

Fortunately, the keys were on Jacob's outside arm, not the one next to Levi. As he ran past, I stepped toward him and snatched my hand out. The instant my fist closed around the pair of jangling keys, I let the world slip away, letting my body and everything that I identified with myself at that moment fade into incorporeality. The keys came with me, their leather cord sliding right through them as Jacob ran past and he and Levi rounded the corner.

The instant they were out of my sight, I let the world slide back into place. There was no vertigo this time, no sense of disorientation. Just solidity.

Immediately, noiselessly, Cuan was at my side.

"Did you do what I think you just did?" he asked.

I grinned, holding out a pair of keys in one hand as I pulled my phone out of my pocket with the other.

"That was incredible," Cuan said with a smile.

"We're not out of the woods yet," I said, hurriedly tapping out a text message. "We need to make sure they don't notice their keys are missing until it's too late for them to do anything about it."

"What do you have in mind?" Cuan asked.

"First, a distraction," I said, hitting Send, then holding out my phone so Cuan could see my message to Bianca: 'If you have any bats left in you, send them around the corner.'

"Smart," Cuan nodded as I put the phone away.

"Second..." I examined the pair of keys in my hand. They were large, old-style keys, but thankfully they were not identical: one was engraved with 'HOUSE', the other with 'GATE'.

The house key I slipped into my pocket, then I held the gate key to Cuan. "Give me those beakers and take this. You're the fastest, quietest one here. Get to the front of the estate, but stay in the cover of the trees until they leave the property. Then turn this in the lock on the inside of the gate. And please, be safe."

Cuan nodded, exchanging beakers for key, and vanished back into the woods. A moment later, I heard a rush from near the property.

Bianca overdelivered: she did more than just conjure up a misty swarm of bats. This was a giant, single, monstrous black behemoth of a bat, and it came careening down the driveway, leaving an uncanny screech in its wake.

It was spectacular.

I stepped neatly to the side as it tore past me and made a hard left around the corner. If anything was going to chase those two off the property, that would. A second later I heard distant panicked sounds, then several rounds of gunfire. I feared for a moment for Cuan's safety, but I knew he could take care of himself.

There was brief quiet for about half a minute, and then I heard the reassuring sounds of metal chains clanking as the gate slid back into place. A moment later, the feeling of the air itself shifted, and the estate just felt more... secure.

Silence.

It was a few seconds before Cuan reappeared, sauntering confidently around the corner, tossing the key in his palm.

"Well, that's that," he said to me, beaming his bright half-smile, even showing some teeth. "Amazing ward, that gate. It just shut out the world."

I felt my body relax at the sight of him. "I was worried when I heard the gunfire," I admitted as he gave me a quick peck and I traded one of the glass beakers for the gate key.

"You needn't have been concerned," Cuan said. "Jacob emptied all his ammo into that phantom bat. And then, you should have seen their faces when they were across the street outside the property and the gate started closing!" he added with a laugh. "God, it felt good to stick it to those bastards."

Marcus emerged from the woods as we turned back towards the house. He was shaking slightly, but still held two glass beakers securely in his hands.

"Why does Alexander's father have a fucking semiautomatic?" he stammered as I put a reassuring arm around his shoulder.

"Because he's a stinking pile of shit," Cuan growled as we headed toward the house.

Bianca and Leo were perched on the porch. Alexander and Julia, meanwhile, were standing near the flaming wreckage of the pickup truck, chanting in Latin and tracing intricate shimmering patterns in the air. Whatever they were doing worked, because as we approached the flames died to nothing.

"Well, that was an absolute shitshow," Alexander said. He turned to Cuan as we approached. "Did Father just try to lock us in?" he asked. "Does he not realize that anyone can open the gate from the inside?"

"That wasn't Jacob," Cuan grinned. "It was me."

"Huh?" Alexander asked.

"Anyone want a housekey?" I smiled, holding up the two keys I had lifted from Jacob.

Alexander's eyes fell on the keys and his jaw dropped. "Holy shit," he said. "How did you..."

"Never underestimate the wallflower," I said, my smile broadening.

"I can't believe those two actually blew up their own truck," Julia said, examining the wreckage in the driveway.

"Wait, this was *their* truck?" I asked, shocked.

"They must have hoped the fire would spread to the house," Bianca said from the porch.

"He's out of his fucking mind. They both are," Alexander

said. "I mean, I knew Father *had* guns, but I'd never seen him use them before."

"Well, the enemy was always supernatural before," Julia said. "Now, the enemy is us."

"He's completely off the deep end," Alexander said, turning to us. "I tried to tell him about the stadium, about how the people of the city were in danger. He was all like 'It's not the church's problem.' And then when I pointed out that there were probably parishioners who had been forced to evacuate and were caught up in the thing, he got livid and said that that was *my* fault, because the parishioners would have been able to seek sanctuary in the church if I hadn't brought upon the building's destruction by ruining his plan to keep Cole captive and then leading ogres to their doorstep."

"That is a pretty messed up understanding of the chain of events," I said.

"Speaking of the stadium... is that the spring water?" Leo asked, pointing toward the beakers we had. I nodded in response as Marcus held one out for Leo to carry.

"Good," Bianca said. "Then we can get the fuck out of here."

"But if those crazies blew up their own car, they're gonna need to get home a different way," Leo observed. "What if we run into them out there?"

"Well, they can't take the bus," Julia said, "not while carrying a giant hammer and a semiautomatic weapon out in the open like that. They're going to have to try not to be seen."

"Assuming they're acting with any rationality, that is," Cuan noted. "They could be up to anything. They were pretty steamed when they saw the gates closing. They could even be lurking outside, ready to jump us as soon as we leave."

"Well, at least they're locked out of the estate now," I said.

Alexander looked up at the house. "The estate," he said. "I've been coming here for years, never knowing that I was actually meant to inherit it. I've never even set foot inside the house. I... I know we're on a schedule, but... we're here now; we have a key. I'd really like to see the interior."

"We have about fifteen minutes," Bianca said.

"What are you talking about?" I asked.

"I texted Bran," she said, holding up her phone. "He and fuckface are coming to pick us up."

"Wait, they have cars?" I asked.

"Who's fuckface?" Julia asked.

"Cedric," I explained.

"Ah. Right," she nodded.

Alexander stood in front of the building's tall front door, staring at it as though he could see inside by will alone.

I stepped up next to him, holding out the key.

"It's all yours," I said.

Slowly, Alexander took the key from me. He turned it over in his hand, studying it.

"It's warm," he said. Then he turned back to the door. He took a deep breath, slid the key into the lock, and turned.

There was a click as the tumblers turned in the lock, and suddenly we felt a rush of energy as what felt like an invisible shell melted away from the house.

The house looked no different than it did before, but before it had somehow felt... impenetrable, as though I wouldn't have even been able to fade through its walls. Now, however, it felt welcoming.

Alexander pushed open the door. Immediately, the smell of dust assailed my nostrils. Unsurprising, as the house had stood largely empty for over two decades. It had not, however, been left alone. The signs of Jacob's search for whatever spell or arti-fact he had imagined Alexander's parents kept hidden was evident from the moment we stepped into the foyer: furniture had been dragged along the floor, sometimes overturned, rug corners were flipped up, a writing desk in the front room was opened and its contents spread over the floor.

"Your parents really could have used some decorating advice," Bianca said dryly as she stepped inside the house.

"Shut up," Alexander responded.

"God, he really did a number on this place, huh?" Julia said as she started to look around.

"No respect at all for the property or its contents," Alexander muttered.

There was a click, and the electric overhead lights begrudgingly crawled to life. I looked around in surprise, and saw Marcus standing by a switch.

"Sorry," he said, "I just flipped the switch without thinking."

"How is there power?" I asked.

"Oh, that's right," Julia recalled. "Rebecca said something to me about this; she said that Jacob had this place put back on the grid after Alexander left. He was worried he was running out of time, and thought that maybe there was an electric lock or something."

"Don't electric locks disengage when the power is out?" Leo asked.

"Not all of them," Cuan said. "Some only unlock when the power is on."

Marcus was already in another room. "There's running water, too," he called.

We followed him into the kitchen, which was less of a mess than the foyer and living room, though it had still clearly been searched through.

"Not surprising," Julia said. "I think this place uses well water."

"Ah, from the spring," Marcus nodded. "That makes sense."

"Apparently it has a good filtration system, too," Julia added, "so it should be potable."

The mess of the house got worse as we went upstairs. Drawers were pulled open in bedrooms; cabinets were emptied in the bathrooms. At the end of a hall we reached a large library. If there had been any organizational structure, it was long since forgotten. Books were shoved in shelves seemingly at random, probably having been yanked out and rifled through. Others were discarded on the floor. What was the most jarring of all, however, was the smell.

"Ugh," Marcus grunted, wrinkling his nose. "Something stinks."

Cuan and Leo were both suddenly on high alert. "That's not just any stench," Cuan said.

"No," Leo shook his head in agreement. "That's blood."

"Blood?" Alexander asked in alarm.

"It's coming from... there," Cuan said, pointing toward one bookshelf at the far end of the room.

We cautiously inched toward the shelf. Upon closer inspection, it was slightly uneven with the rest of the wall. I put my hand on the edge and pulled. Whatever mechanism or complicated puzzle had been keeping it shut had long since been disengaged, as it now swung easily open on a hinge.

"Fucking hell," Alexander gasped as we beheld the space inside.

It was a square chamber, about a hundred square feet, patterned with sigils and signs on the walls and floor. These were almost impossible to make out now, however, because the entire room was covered in splattered blood. They were all different shades of red; some looked several years old.

Marcus retched, recoiling back into the library.

"Jesus, Alexander," I said as I beheld the grisly scene; "what, did your parents buy this place from the Manson family?"

"Oh, God, Cole; have some taste," Alexander frowned.

"More like a coven that all went on their periods at the same time," Bianca interjected.

"Augh, Bianca! Bad!" Julia admonished.

Alexander peered at the back wall of the dark room. "Does that look like... the outline of a door to you?" he asked.

"You're right," I observed.

"Something's written here," Leo said, squinting at the wall. "It's not easy to make out, but…"

"You can see that?" Alexander asked.

"Of course, can't you?"

"Yeah," Cuan and Bianca nodded, while Julia and Alexander shook their heads.

"It's in ball pen," Leo observed. "I think someone was trying to decipher all the symbols on the walls. It's older than the blood spatter, though."

"What the hell happened here?" Alexander asked.

"A lot of this is animal blood," Cuan observed, looking around.

"Right," Leo nodded. "But some is human, too. And that," he added, turning over his shoulder and pointing, "that, that, and that… are all from the same person."

"Hold on, I recognize that scent," Cuan sniffed. "It smells like… Jacob."

"Father was murdering people in this room?" Alexander asked, aghast.

"No, I mean… the blood smells like Jacob," Cuan clarified. "I think it's his."

"But… why?" Julia asked.

"This is a really complicated cipher," Leo said, "but I think whoever wrote all this on the wall solved it. I think they distilled it down. 'Blood is the Key', it says here."

"Well, that explains the paint job," I said.

Alexander nodded. "This must have been as close as he came. He probably tore the rest of the house apart trying to solve that cipher."

"And then when he did, he started trying to spill blood all over the room to get in," Julia nodded.

"Nothing worked, though," Bianca said.

"Of course it didn't," I realized. "It didn't work because he was being too literal."

"What do you mean?" Cuan asked.

"Think about it. Everything you've told me about your parents and this estate, Alexander, was that they kept it safe, separate from the Order of Light. It was a place just for them. Their family. Their *blood*." I looked at Alexander. "Father Jacob was so determined to keep everything in this place for himself that he didn't realize the key was right under his nose this whole time. Your parents willed this estate to their kin. They wanted you to have it. It's you, Alexander. You're the key."

"Me," Alexander said as my words sunk in. "I'm the key." He turned slowly toward the far wall. Leo stood aside as he approached. Slowly, carefully, hesitantly, he placed his hand on the bloodied wall in the center of the faint outline of the door. As soon as his palm was flat against the surface, there was a burst of light from behind it, and the room was immediately awash in white light that cascaded across the walls, ceiling, and floor. It was bright, clear, cleansing; in its wake the spattered blood dissolved into nothingness, as did the cryptic scrawlings below it, leaving the room clear and spotless.

"Holy shit," Bianca uttered in awe.

Marcus poked his head around the corner. "Um, did something just... oh."

He stared, wide-eyed, as the wall in front of Alexander slid aside. Beyond was a shallow cabinet, in which sat a number of white boxes, all of different sizes and lengths. Between them all, on a small stand, was an envelope. Alexander lifted the envelope and pulled out its contents: a letter and what looked like a quartz pendant. He unfolded the letter and began to read aloud:

"'Our dearest child—if you are reading this, then it means that some ill fate has befallen us. Given our calling and our chosen path, such danger is often imminent. Hopefully, however, we have been able to enjoy many years together, building many wonderful memories.'" He choked up, and Marcus stepped forward and wrapped an arm around his shoulder. "'Whatever the circumstances, however,'" Alexander continued, "'know that you are loved. It is the Order's duty to care for you in our absence, but we have recently come to feel that it would be in our best interest to hold many of our family's keepsakes safe, and to allow you to use them as you see fit.'"

"Smart thinking," Bianca nodded.

"'Some of the items here you may not be ready to hold, so we have placed seals upon them that you, or others in whom you trust, will be able to release when you are ready. This pendant is an heirloom, one for you to wear until you know whom you wish to share it with. The smallest of these boxes contains a large crystal. Place it in the center of the room, hold it, and it will bond to you. Any who touch it when you also touch it will be recognized and granted passage; able to come and go from this place even when it is warded against others as long as the crystal remains in place. As for the other boxes, not all of their contents will suit you. You may find that some are better suited to those you associate with: your friends, your loved ones. You are our blood, our family, but now is your time to build the family you choose. We love you, our beloved child.'" He finished reading and looked up, a tear running down his cheek.

Julia looked on in awe. "How did they keep all this a secret from the Order?" She wondered.

"They must have realized that the Order of Light didn't always act as the bastion of goodness it claimed to be," I said.

Alexander fastened the pendant around his neck, then looked thoughtfully at the boxes, running his hands over the surface of each one. Finally he laid his hands on the smallest box.

"This one feels warm," he said, pulling it down. He set it on the floor and opened it. Inside, indeed, was a large crystal.

Alexander set the crystal in the center of the room, then placed his palms on it. Slowly, it glowed to life, humming slightly.

"Marcus, come here," he said. Marcus obeyed, handing me the glass beaker he carried long enough to set both hands on the other side of the crystal. For a moment, the crystal's light flashed blue, then it returned to its usual white.

One by one, Alexander had each of us place our hands on the crystal in turn.

"Are you sure about this?" Bianca asked when it was her turn at the crystal.

Alexander nodded. "You all helped me claim my home," he said. "You should all have a right to seek refuge here whenever you need it."

Once we all finished, we left the room and descended back down the staircase to the lobby.

"We should probably get going, huh?" Leo said.

"Yeah," Bianca nodded. "I have like three texts from Bran saying he's here."

"Why didn't you say anything?" Alexander asked.

"Sorry, I didn't want to spoil your whole crystal gesture," she responded.

"Right then," I nodded. "We have our water. We have Alexander's house back. Let's go to that stadium and kick some ass."

As we headed to the door, however, Marcus hung back in the lobby, an uncertain expression on his face.

"What is it?" Alexander asked, turning to him.

"Um... maybe you should go ahead without me," he said.

"What?" Alexander asked incredulously. "Why?"

"You're all prepared for this sort of thing," Marcus said. "You're out there facing down monsters and crazed, trigger happy priests like it's nothing. But that's... that's not me. At least, not right now. I could barely walk a day ago."

"You were pretty willing to leap into the fray when you were all big and blue," Bianca said.

"Yeah, but was I really, though?" Marcus asked. Remembering that day in front of the church when we'd discovered him, I realized he was right. Even as an ogre, Marcus hadn't wanted to throw himself into combat. Perhaps it was because he had recognized Alexander and me. But perhaps it was also because fighting wasn't him.

"What do you suggest, then?" Alexander asked gently.

"Let me hang back here," Marcus responded. "The place needs to be tidied up anyway; I can start on that. There's electricity and running water, so I'll be fine."

"Don't you need food?" Leo asked.

"Not hungry," Marcus responded. "Lester said it might be a few days before I felt the need to intake food. I should be good for the night. Maybe I can even have a few rooms feeling almost livable by the time you're back."

Alexander stepped quietly toward Marcus, then reached into his pocket and pulled out his cellphone and the pair of keys I'd lifted from Jacob.

"Here, take these," he said. "Keep the house safe. We'll use the other key to lock the gate behind us. You can reach us with that phone."

"Don't need the phone," Marcus said, taking the keys and putting them in his pocket, then pulling out a little flip phone. "Lester gave me a burner."

"He did the same for me, way back when," I nodded. We all exchanged numbers with Marcus, then Marcus handed his glass vial to Alexander. We said farewells and walked toward the door.

"One more thing," Marcus called. We turned around.

"Yeah?" Alexander asked.

"Be safe," Marcus said, walking to meet Alexander. "And

give 'em hell." Then he reached around Alexander's neck and pulled him into a kiss.

Cuan grinned at my side, giving my free hand a squeeze as Alexander started in surprise, then kissed Marcus back. They stood like that for a minute or so, kissing, until Bianca's phone chirped insistently.

"Um, I hate to break up the tongue party," she said, waving the phone impatiently, "but we have rides waiting."

"Yeah. Yeah, right," Marcus said, pulling back. "Go. Go on then; save the world. Or just the city. Whatever."

Marcus locked the door behind us as we left, and we felt the whole house return to its previous secure state. This time, however, it didn't feel forbidding, and I knew that, thanks to that crystal, I was always welcome inside.

Alexander grinned like a schoolboy all the way to the car.

XVI

TEAM PLAYERS

THE TRIP BACK TO THE HUNTERS' Home was uneventful. Nobody particularly wanted to ride with Cedric, but ultimately Bianca won out, and so Bianca, Leo, and Julia packed into Bran's black sports car while Alexander, Cuan, and I rode in Cedric's sedan.

"Where is Marcus?" Cedric had asked as we piled in.

"He's staying here," Alexander said.

"Ah," Cedric said, peering at the estate through the windshield. "What is this place, anyway? I feel a very strong energy."

"It's an estate," Alexander responded. "Well, I guess it's my estate, now."

"Hm," responded Cedric, regarding him with approval. "Well done."

Back at The Hunters' Home, we all exited the pair of cars and headed toward the house, Julia included.

"And... why are you here?" Cedric asked, turning to her.

"Bianca told me about Stage Two," she said. "If you're planning an assault on a stadium-turned-lab, then count me in."

"A member of Jacob's Order of Light who actually wants to

be proactive?" Cedric remarked, looking slightly impressed. "Wonders never cease."

"Don't lump me in with that asshole," Julia said darkly.

"OK," Cedric nodded. "I like you."

Julia gave a small smile and a quick nod and then pulled out her phone and started tapping away.

"You are not giving people our address, are you?" Cedric asked suspiciously.

"No; I'm texting Thomas to get Gratia ready for me."

At the sound of the name, Leo perked up. "Thomas is coming?" he asked.

"I'm sure you'd like him to," Bianca said flatly.

"Yeah, all over his face," I said quietly, and Cuan snickered.

Bran walked out into the middle of the street and flicked something up into the air. I realized that it was a small gold-colored marble, its metallic surface glinting in the light.

I had seen one of those before.

"That's... that's like what Cedric gave me back when I first met the Hunters, to signal for Cuan," I recalled as Bran caught the marble on its descent and returned it to his pocket.

"It wasn't to signal Cuan," Bran pointed out. A moment later there was a rustle in the air, and a large black crow alighted on Bran's shoulder.

"Oh," I said, remembering. That same bird, or at least one who looked remarkably like it, had been at my window investigating the golden marble I'd set there shortly before Cuan appeared. I felt like the crow on Bran's shoulder recognized me, too, as it gave me a kind of 'harumph' of a greeting before bending its beak toward Bran and cooing something softly in his ear. Bran whispered back, and the bird replied in turn. This conspiratorial exchange seemed poised to continue for several minutes, so I turned and went into the house to deliver the spring water.

Lester was delighted with the water, though somewhat disappointed to learn that Marcus was remaining on the estate.

"He was good company," he said as he emptied one of the beakers into what looked like a mad-scientist chemistry set out of a bad B-movie.

"Company, as in..." Alexander asked, trailing off with an expectant expression.

"As in it was nice to have another person around," Lester responded, with some irritation.

"For..." Alexander added.

"For conversation, for hearing someone breathing besides me," Lester cried in exasperation. "I'm sorry to disappoint you, but my interest in Marcus's body was limited to the scientific."

"Oh," Alexander replied. He didn't seem entirely convinced.

"Jeez," I said, "if you're this jealous of Lester, God help whoever gives Marcus a colonoscopy."

Alexander gave me an irritated look that shifted into an expression of mild concern, probably as he considered the possibility that some doctor would actually eventually be giving Marcus a colonoscopy.

"Anyway, here," Lester said after a minute or so, taking a small vial out of the end of the machine and handing it to me. "From what I can figure from the schematics, the laboratory equipment that the city is using to incubate ogres works on a fluid delivery system that accepts additional formulae through a modular intake much in the way that intravenous systems in hospitals do. I'll explain further once we're downstairs and everyone is gathered in the kitchen."

It didn't take long for Lester to finish purifying the spring water and using it as a base to suspend his serum. With six vials in hand, he led us down to the kitchen, where Cedric and Julia were already talking seriously with one another. Bianca was perched in her usual chair, and Leo stood at her side.

"With you and Thomas, we should have enough people to cover most of the stadium," Cedric was saying.

"We've got one more," came Bran from behind us. He walked into the kitchen, Az following behind him.

"Az?" I asked.

"I just texted you and asked if you'd finished whatever your preparations were," Cuan said to him.

"I did, and now I'm here," Az nodded.

"Most people also reply to text messages," Cuan added, and Az gave a noncommittal shrug. "Not that I'm complaining that you're here, mind you," Cuan noted.

Our objective was straightforward: we needed to get into the stadium and introduce the serum that Lester developed into the system, which would, in theory at least, reverse the ogre transformation process that the evacuees would be undergoing.

"The problem, however, is that the system works in branches," Lester explained, pointing at the blueprint. "It's a radial-spoke system, wherein the central processing unit that manages serum administration is at the center, and serum is distributed radially through six separate main channels, which then branch further as they move to the edges of the system. In other words, if you're going to have the serum reach everyone, then it needs to be introduced to the system as centrally as possible. From there, four vials of serum should be sufficient to penetrate the entire system."

"That few?" Alexander asked.

Lester nodded. "This serum works through a catalytic reaction that breaks down the transformation process, and is effective even at relatively low doses, particularly thanks to the purity of the water you procured. If you can't get it in the central system, you could theoretically inject a vial into each of the six branches, but... that's a lot more legwork, and there's no room for error in that case."

Planning our approach was difficult, as the dossier we'd obtained gave no information about how the stadium would be staffed or secured. However, Cedric pointed out that the stadium was unlikely to be patrolled in an organized manner: given the secrecy of the program and the haste of the relocation, guards like the police were likely to be on alert but not following a rigidly-defined plan. Bran added that recon showed that guards were more concentrated on the street and near parking lots, but that there was likely to be ad-hoc internal security deployed thanks to hastily-installed security cameras similar to those patched in to the abandoned subway. As a result, the best course of action was likely a diversion tactic, designed to draw out as much security as possible so that others could approach the central lab.

"Cole attracts the least attention, obviously, so he should be the one to carry the serum," Alexander pointed out.

Cedric nodded. "Exactly."

"You OK with that?" Cuan asked, turning to me.

"You can count on me," I said. "I'm just not sure how I'll carry all of this."

"I have a solution for that," Lester announced, producing a small apothecary's satchel. It was a leather pouch about the size of a paperback book, which hung over my shoulder and had neat little loops of leather stitched on the front and back of the inside to hold the vials secure and keep them from hitting against one another.

"Cuan and Cole's task will be to infiltrate the stadium once we have drawn away as much attention as possible," Cedric stated.

"I will accompany them," Az said. "If there's the possibility of a demon at large and involved, it's unlikely that it will show itself outside the complex. The closer they get to the main lab, the greater their chance of running afoul of something of that nature."

"Good point," Cedric nodded.

"Alexander should come with us, too," Cuan suggested. "He's very handy at taking out cameras."

"Right," I nodded, remembering how skillfully he disabled the cameras with conjured beams of light when we first explored the abandoned subways under the city.

"Fine," Cedric allowed. "Bran will cover your approach; he will also be able to let you know when we have created a sufficient diversion."

"Can't you just text us?" I asked.

"Who knows how well cell service will work near the stadium?" Cedric responded. "A concrete building full of all kinds of computing might provide a lot of interference."

"Plus, that's also assuming that the city hasn't installed some kind of cell scrambling technology," Alexander realized. "Think about it: this isn't like the program to get the homeless and addicts. These are people with connections and means; they'd be likely to try to reach someone as soon as they thought something was up."

"Good insight," Cedric nodded, impressed. "OK then: you four will infiltrate, and Bran will cover you. That leaves the rest of us."

Cedric would launch the main assault with Bianca and Leo —this would be less an attempt at breaching and more focused on making as big a spectacle of themselves as possible.

"As if Bianca needs any encouragement," I said.

"Oh, at least I can get noticed," Bianca retorted. "What would you do? Throw glitter and sic doggo on them while holding a sign saying 'Please see me'?"

"First of all, do *not* underestimate my glitter game," I said. "Second of all, Cuan is a person, so fuck you. Third of all, I go unseen because I *want* to."

"Oh, please," Bianca said. "You could prance down the street naked and people wouldn't give you a second glance."

"Oh, yes they would," Alexander and Cuan said in unison.

"Still better than if *you* did that," I retorted. "As soon as you took your clothes off, people would flee screaming."

"Bitch, my body is *fine*," Bianca growled. "Nobody's going to run after seeing this," she gestured to herself.

"Maybe not, but they'd still be fleeing from the stench of fish and baking bread," I replied.

"I will *kill you*," Bianca threatened, leaping onto the table.

"OK, part of me doesn't like this game where you insult my little sister," Leo chimed in, "but part of me also just wants to eat popcorn and watch how this plays out."

"Cole, is this really how you talk to women?" Julia admonished.

"Not women," I said. "Just Bianca."

"Still, though," she said. "Misogynist gay is very last century. I mean, really. There's nothing wrong with Bianca's body."

"Thank you," Bianca said with some degree of smugness, climbing back off the table. "And might I say, Julia, I would *definitely* pay attention if you were walking down the street naked. A lot of attention."

"Child, I'm a decade older than you," Julia responded.

"Good," Bianca nodded. "Then you'll know what you're doing. I like a person with experience."

"I do not have experience robbing the cradle," Julia said.

"There are a lot of things you could do to my cradle," Bianca replied.

"OK, now I know I don't like this game," Leo said.

"Gotta give you credit for that fish line, though," Bianca said to me with a begrudging smirk. "Bitch," she added.

"If you are quite finished," Cedric said with impatience, pointing back to the schematic of the stadium.

The plan turned out to have an additional component: between Cedric's group's approach on the main entrance and Cuan's and my infiltration from the rear, Julia and Thomas would lead a smaller assault on the side entrance. This, too, was not intended to actually breach the stadium, but rather to look like an attempted infiltration. That way, if there were suspicion that Cedric's approach was a diversion, Julia and Thomas would be assumed to be the group that attention was supposed to be diverted from. Once Julia and Thomas were spotted, they were to employ Gratia and Prominence in making a spectacle of themselves, as well. If all went well, there would be almost no chance that there would still be guards expecting the real infiltration party. Lester, as usual, would be hanging back to handle his nebulous 'cleanup'. All told, it was a clever plan, I had to admit.

"One thing, though," Bran said. "We need to start heading over there now. On foot."

"What do you mean, on foot?" Cedric asked.

"We can't drive. The police are running checkpoints on the roads." Bran explained. "If we drive, we won't make it anywhere near there."

"Shit," Cedric said. "All right; dinner is delayed, then. We move."

The streets were dark, but after the fire at the University the police were on high alert, so we traveled in our small assigned groups to keep from attracting too much attention. Our group was one of five, but Az and Alexander hung back a good distance behind us, which helped the illusion that we weren't all together. Cedric and the others had already split off: the stadium was a good ways away but we all needed to be approaching it from different directions, so it made sense to put some distance between us.

Cuan, Bran, and I were following a route that took us near the university, but on a path that skirted the campus, just outside the area that had been forcibly evacuated. Cuan walked alongside me, matching my stride. Before we'd left, he'd dashed up to his old room and swapped out his Wushu pants for his tight compression pants, noting that it was much easier to be stealthy in tight-fitting fabric. He'd had to be extra careful when following Jacob on the estate not to let his Wushu pants rustle and make noise or get them caught on any twigs, so changing would give him one less thing to worry about. I wasn't complaining: the compression pants hugged the muscles of his legs and ass, accentuating his musculature with every step. Bran seemed to notice, too, as he kept glancing down at Cuan's legs as we moved.

"You know, Bran," I said as we walked, "this is the first time I've really spent any time with you in the field."

"Yeah, well, we tend to work in different spheres, I guess," Bran said with a shrug. "I'm more of the information-gathering type, while you have this uncanny knack for getting caught in the middle of things."

"Is that your ability?" I asked. "You can talk to the crows?"

"Among other things," Bran said. "But yeah, it's the information gathering that's probably the most useful for the Hunters."

"You like being a Midnight Hunter, huh?" I asked. "I mean... Cedric doesn't seem to bother you much. You've seemed to take Leo's being stuck in the basement more or less in stride."

"I'm pretty appalled by that, actually," Bran said. "But I've known Cedric a long time. I wasn't raised by him like Cuan was; I came to know him when I was older. Maybe that's why, but I've always kind of known he wasn't perfect. Never thought he'd hold someone captive like that, but... I don't know if I'm going to up and leave over it. Cedric's done a lot of shitty things to people, but he's always been good to me. Maybe it's because he's not afraid of me leaving that he hasn't tried to keep me beholden to him somehow. I dunno how I should take that, but there you are."

"How did you come to meet Cedric, anyway?" Cuan asked. "You've never told me."

"I didn't realize you wanted to know," Bran said.

"You and I used to hook up. A lot," Cuan responded. "Of course I'd be interested in knowing more about you."

"You and I treat hookups very differently," Bran said with a smirk. Then he sighed. "It has to do with my family and how I was born. And my raven affinity, I guess," he said.

"Raven affinity?" I asked.

Bran nodded. "I was born in Ireland. My parents were studying abroad there at the time; they were huge into New Age magic and witchcraft. They weren't Wiccan or anything; they were just really into supernatural magic and the old religion. They joined a kind of enthusiast's group. Well, someone in the group *was* actually Wiccan, and one day they broke oath and shared a ritual script with the group involving the Unseelie."

"The dark fae?" Cuan asked.

Bran nodded again. "So my parents were super excited. And they combined it with some other stuff they had found out about the Morrigan. And then one night they snuck out to the Loughcrew cairns, and got inside one that was partially open and performed the little ritual they'd created. All I know is that it went really... well? And they were so enthusiastic about it that they had sex right there in the cairns, and conceived me."

"Damn," I said. "They must have been really into the occult."

"'Were' being the operative word," Bran said gravely. "When they returned to the States, they apparently decided they were 'over' that 'phase'"—he made liberal use of finger quotes for emphasis—"and they started going to my mothers' parents' super conservative church. Long story short, when I was around 6, I told them once after playing outside that I'd been talking to the crows, and they completely flipped out. They shipped me off to a kind of conversion camp, where the staff did all kinds of horrible stuff. So I knew pretty well not to talk to them about the crows any more."

"Jeez, did they know Alexander's family?" I responded.

"Then when I was older, they saw me kissing a boy, and they freaked out even more. They said it was their fault; that I was cursed because of their sins. That's when they told me the story of my conception. They confessed the whole thing in a crazed prayer session during a church service, and suddenly people were grabbing me, trying to exorcise demons from me, trying to purify me before the Lord. Somebody decided the solution was to re-baptize me by immersing me in holy water, and they filled a giant font and held me down in it." Bran shuddered as he spoke, reliving the memory. "They would have drowned me. I panicked and fought for a bit before I realized the best thing to do was go limp. When they flipped out and let go of me, and when I heard the screaming from above the water, I leapt out of the font and ran."

"It's no wonder that Az is so bitter about religious zealots, when they pull shit like this," Cuan commented. "And… it explains your hatred of the church."

"Your parents sound like terrible people," I said.

"They're not terrible people," Bran responded. "They just found the wrong place to seek guidance. It wasn't too long after that that the crows brought me news of Cedric. So I sought him out. I reconnected with my parents later. They never apologized for anything that went down at the church, but I figure it's because they don't want to ever think about it. I did see a book on their shelf about loving their gay son, so I guess that's something. I still see them once in a while, but we're not close. And of course I never told them anything else I discovered about my powers."

"So there's more than talking to crows, then?" I asked.

Bran nodded. "Cuan's seen most of it at some point or another. I'll just say, there's a reason I'm in the field so much—I can definitely hold my own."

Cuan nodded thoughtfully. "I never knew you'd been

through all that," he said. "No wonder the stuff Cedric's done doesn't seem so bad to you. By comparison, it's nothing."

"Still doesn't make it OK, though," Bran said. "But at least I saw something in Cedric that I've never seen from those religious zealots: remorse. Cedric does some fucked-up stuff when he thinks it's right, but he's also able to admit when he's made a mistake, or at least eventually acknowledge that he could have done something differently."

We were walking by the edge of the university now. There was more yellow tape around now; more streets roped off.

"Wait," Cuan whispered suddenly and sharply, his whole body taut and alert.

"What is it?" I whispered back.

"Smell that?" he asked.

"You know we don't," Bran responded impatiently.

"I smell ogres. Several distinct scents."

"What are ogres doing out here?" I asked. "We're nowhere near the stadium."

Behind us, Alexander and Az noticed us stop moving, and paused, stepping aside out of the lamplight.

"The police have mostly moved to the stadium," Bran whispered. "With that, combined with the labs here being destroyed, maybe there are a few stray ogres who have gone unaccounted for."

"Or maybe they're being put to use to pick up stragglers who haven't evacuated," Cuan noted. "If this is the night that Stage Two is supposed to go into effect, the city might be trying to make a clean sweep of the area."

Up above us, somewhere off to our right, a crow called, three times, short and loud.

"An alarm call," Bran said. "Someone's headed this way. Come on."

We ducked under some yellow tape down a side street as I

hastily shot off a text to Alexander warning him of what was going on.

A few seconds later, I received a reply: "understood. az and i heading different way. meet u outside stadium. b careful."

The road here was dark; the lamplights had either had their power cut or were shattered. The street and buildings, too, looked to be in much worse condition than they had been before. I struggled to make out buildings and shapes in the darkness, but I was sure that Cuan could see well enough for all three of us.

We slipped down another alley. A crow called an alarm from behind us, and Cuan perked up a moment later.

"Footsteps," he whispered. "Heavy ones."

I heard them now, too. They were close. We hurried down the alley in the opposite direction. One ogre, even two ogres, we could probably handle no problem, but we didn't know how many were out and about. Even more importantly, we didn't want to draw attention to ourselves—we were supposed to be the stealthy group, and compromising that, even this far from the stadium, could jeopardize our entire operation.

At the other end of the alley we came to a wider street. One streetlight flickered, barely intact, probably pulling the last bit of electricity from a backup battery. In its light I could see a wrecked storefront. I recognized it.

"That's the café we ate at with Professor Norton," I whispered.

"Damn, you're right," Cuan whispered. "What the hell happened?"

"The ogres might be running rampant," Bran said. "Or they're searching for something—"

Bran was interrupted as Cuan held his hand up sharply.

"Do you hear more ogres?" I whispered.

"No," Cuan replied. "Something else." He sniffed the air. "Close, too."

Carefully, he stepped through the blasted wall of the front of the café, and I followed close behind. Here, in the flickering light from the street, I could see broken glass and pastries scattered across the floor.

Now I could hear it too: rapid, ragged breaths, coming from behind the counter. Slowly, carefully, Cuan crept forward, while Bran kept a lookout. As Cuan rounded the edge of the corner I heard a sharp, terrified whimper, and I peeked my head around after him.

There, cowering behind the counter, was the big-eared, freckled pastry boy of twenty or so years who had been working the counter on our last visit. He looked up at us, eyes wide with terror, his whole body shaking.

"Hey, are you OK?" Cuan whispered softly.

The young man kept shaking. He opened his mouth, but all that came out was a squeak, and he shut it again in terror, as though the sound he'd made was going to be the death of him.

"It's all right," I whispered, and his eyes focused on me. "You're safe. Do you remember us?"

He stared at us for a moment, eyes struggling to make out our features in the darkness, and then to recall them. Finally he nodded.

"What happened?" Cuan asked.

"Everyone was supposed to evacuate," The boy said at last. "We were told it was just a precaution, but the police were rushing everyone out. After we left, I realized I'd forgotten to empty the register, so I snuck back in. And then... and then..."

Cuan placed a reassuring hand on his arm. "You're OK," he said calmly.

"You don't understand," the pastry boy said, his green eyes still wide with fear. "There was this... thing. It was big and red; it came barreling through the building. It had this big metal ball instead of an arm, and it fired it right through the window. I could hear some people screaming outside, but I ducked behind the counter. I didn't see anything else. But there's something out there. I can still hear it."

Cuan nodded gravely. "You're right; there are things out there," he said. "We're going to deal with that though, OK? We'll make sure that people can't still get hurt."

The pastry boy stared at us. "Who are you?" he asked.

"Once we called ourselves the Midnight Hunters," Cuan said, "But we don't really anymore. But we make sure that people can't get hurt by creatures like that."

The pastry boy was silent for a moment. "Well, you're not doing a great job," he said.

"There's been a... boom," Cuan said.

"It's not safe here," I said.

"No shit," the pastry boy replied.

I reached my hand out to him. He hesitated for a moment, then took it, and I pulled him to his feet.

"What's your name?" I asked.

"Peter," he replied.

"I'm Cole," I said. "This is Cuan. Now listen closely. We need to go deal with these things, but you need to get to safety. I know one place that is definitely safe, but you need to be brave to get there, OK?"

Peter swallowed hard, but then nodded.

"Give me your phone," I said, and Peter complied, unlocking the device and handing it to me. I pulled out my own phone and brought up the list of contacts. Lester wouldn't be at the Hunter's Home now, so I couldn't send him there, as there would be nobody to let him in. But there was another option. I brought up Marcus's number and punched it into the contacts list in Peter's phone, adding my own while I was at it. Then I brought up the map and pinned a location.

"There's an estate here," I said, handing the phone back to Peter. "We have a friend there who will help you. His name's Marcus. Do you have a car?"

Peter shook his head.

"OK," I said, "then you'll need to take the bus." I rattled off bus directions, and Peter nodded, jotting down a few notes in his phone as I spoke. "The buses are still running from the outskirts of downtown," I added, "but you have to get there fast."

"I... I don't think I can do that," Peter said.

"You can," Cuan said.

"But... those things might still be out there."

"You'll be fine," Bran said from the light in the street. "I've brought you a guide." On Bran's shoulder sat a crow, fidgeting as it looked around.

"A bird?" Peter asked.

"You'll have to trust us," I said. "The bird will make sure you don't run into any of those things, OK?"

Peter stared at us in wonder, but then nodded.

"Call Marcus when you get to the front of the estate and he'll let you in. Tell him I sent you. And text me when you get there."

Peter nodded.

"Go," Bran said, and the crow lifted off from his arm and flew down onto the pavement, turning to watch Peter expectantly.

"You'll be fine," Cuan said reassuringly. "You can do this."

Peter gave us one more long look, then turned and ran into the night, the crow leading his way. As soon as he was out of sight I shot a text off to Marcus to tell him to expect a guy with red hair and freckles named Peter who needed help. Hopefully Marcus would understand that this was a person in genuine need of refuge and not some booty call being sent for his pleasure, but I had to trust that Marcus would recognize the distinction.

"Well, there's our first good deed of the evening," Bran said. "And that crow also told me that the ogres were moving away from this area, so we might be good now. But we've lost a little time. We have to keep moving."

Cuan and I nodded, and we returned to the darkened streets.

We crossed the campus without further incident. When we reached the river separating the main body of the university from the area where the stadium was located, there were more signs of activity. Here, on the bridges spanning the river, the police had set up checkpoints, carefully checking each car before allowing them to pass.

"They're probably using the pretense of looking for suspects, or for explosives or accelerants or something," Bran said. "The fire at the university must make for a convenient excuse."

"They're diverting the traffic, too," Cuan pointed out. Sure enough, the backup of cars wasn't just a result of the vehicles being checked, it was also due to the number of cars being turned around and sent back the way they came. While they had probably only been letting evacuees through for a while, now only patrol cars and other official city vehicles were being granted passage.

While the roads were heavily guarded, the footbridges over the river thankfully were not. Again, the city's solution to hastily enacting Stage Two with probably fewer resources than planned was to simply cordon off several of the footbridges, and further discourage people from using them by cutting the lights. All it did, however, was give us a convenient means of crossing the river.

"According to the birds' recon, there are two footbridges about a hundred meters apart over there," Bran said.

"Right," Cuan nodded. "They're part of the university's cross-country course, and they're also convenient for spectators watching rowing competitions."

"Apparently, there's only one officer covering both of them," Bran said. "That means that the officer has to patrol."

"That's the moving spot of light I see, then," Cuan said, and I looked at him in fascination. Whatever it was he could see, I couldn't make out for the life of me.

"You can see something?" Bran asked. "Perfect. Is the officer walking between the bridges on one bank, or actually crossing them?"

"Crossing, I think," Cuan said. "The spot of light is moving toward the opposite bank now."

"OK," Bran said. "So when the officer is coming toward this side of the river on one bridge, we want to be crossing in the opposite direction on the other."

We found a spot of cover that afforded the best view of the bridges that we could get, but that was still close enough that we could reach either bridge at a run as soon as Cuan noticed an opportunity to move. It wasn't long before our chance came.

"Ok, officer coming this way on the right bridge," Cuan whispered, and we bolted out of our cover toward the bridge on the left.

While we were hastening across, I could see the spot of light Cuan mentioned, which had to be an officer's flashlight, sweeping the ground as it reached the bank of the river we had just started from. After we ducked under the tape on the other end, we had a more or less clear run toward a wooded area to the south of the Stadium, which was the point from which we were to stage our approach.

We hurried through the trees, and suddenly I heard Az's voice ahead of us.

"You made it."

"We did," Cuan responded.

"Yeah," I said quietly. "Alexander here with you?"

"Yup," Alexander said, and I could just make him out between the trees.

We peered through the trees at the stadium, which was a few hundred yards away. We didn't have the benefit of additional cover between here and there; it was mostly an open field. We'd have to make our break for it at just the right time.

It seemed, however, that Cedric and the others must have already started their assault on the front. The stadium was alive with activity—even from this distance we could hear crashing and echoing shouts.

Bran looked up toward the treetops. "Report time, guys," he called softly. There was a rustle as a number of crows took flight.

"Now we wait," Az said, flexing his fingers impatiently.

We had only been waiting a minute, however, before a crow flew back and landed on Bran's shoulder, cooing something softly into his ear.

"What?" Bran asked in alarm.

Just then, many things happened at once. A klaxon sounded from the stadium, ripping through the air like a knife. At the same time, a large metal shutter on the side of the stadium ripped apart and no less than seven ogres—two with metal spheres for hands—spilled out into the field before us, looking around in anger. Cuan's and Alexander's and my phones all chimed, one with a message from Cedric; one from Julia, and one from Bianca. Their contents were nearly identical, and all echoed what Bran urgently said to us as his crow took back off into the night.

"Somebody else is already here. Go now!"

We burst from the trees at a run and made a beeline for the torn shutter leading into the stadium. As soon as we emerged from the trees, all seven ogres looked sharply in our direction. With a roar, they ran at us, while the two with spiked balls for hands levelled them at us.

Az dashed ahead of us like a streak of black light, darting between the rushing ogres, and suddenly he was in the air above one of the metal-ball-wielding-ogres, Quietus in hand. The ogre lurched back, alarmed, aiming its arms upward and firing its spiked balls wildly up into the air. Az darted around them and cut downward, inflicting a shallow slash in the ogre's shoulder that nonetheless hissed and smoked painfully as the ogre roared.

Alexander, meanwhile, chanted something rapidly in Latin, and a beam of light shot forward a ways before forming into a large sphere in front of one of the ogres. The ogre swatted at it with its hand and the sphere exploded in bright sparks of light in front of its face, causing it to stagger backward in confused rage.

Cuan leapt forward, his body a blur as the second of the metal sphere ogres fired wildly at him, chains crisscrossing the field as they flew. Cuan's foot found purchase on the shoulder of one of the rushing ogres and he launched off of it, catapulting himself into the air. The sky was split with a deafening, echoing howl that for a moment drowned out even the wailing klaxons as Cuan's body was subsumed in light, and when he came down he was covered in gray fur, sporting a wild red mane and long, canine muzzle. He barked as his claws slashed into the arm of one ogre, then he bounded off the ground at another.

Bran and I continued running as the two metal balls Az's ogre had fired fell into the field shortly in front of another rushing assailant, chains cascading behind them. The chains fell in the ogre's path and it immediately got itself tangled in them, crashing to the ground as the ogre who had fired the balls roared in confusion, trying in vain to retract its metal spheres.

"You guys go," Bran shouted. "I can take things from here."

"But, Bran—" I began to protest, but Bran leapt into the air, spinning his body around and throwing his hands out in front of him. As he did, a vortex of black feathers spun out from his fingertips, flying forward like darts as they peppered the two ogres nearest to us.

"Believe me, I got this," Bran grinned, landing on one knee.

"But there's still like four of them coming at us," I said.

"Good," Bran said, his grin widening. "Finally, a fair fight."

He stood, straightening his arms out at his sides. As he did so, the sky above us, already darkened with heavy clouds, became inky black. Then I heard the rustling, and realized that the blackness wasn't more clouds—it was crows.

They descended like screeching hail, dive-bombing the ogres in a relentless torrent of avian fury. As each crow approached the bottom of its dive, it seemed to become more energy than bird; a streak of black cutting through the air before swooping back upward and reforming into a feathered creature.

"OK, you got this," I admitted with a nod. "Be careful," I added before running between the pack of panicked ogres, making for the torn shutter alongside Alexander, Az, and my wolfen-shaped boyfriend.

As we approached, there was an electrical pop from some-where, and the piercing klaxon sound suddenly died into a dull but persistent background wail.

We ducked through the shutter into what was, as far as I could tell, originally a ticketing area and a stalls for vendors beneath the stands.

Now, it was bedlam.

The space was set up like a lab, with a number of large tanks in place. Most of these had been smashed—the ogres had clearly emerged from inside them. How or why they had gotten free, I had no idea, but several were still rampaging through the lab space, overwhelming the three officers trying to subdue them. Two of the officers were emptying pistol rounds into one that was tearing up a piece of lab equipment, while the third was tasing another ogre, successfully bringing that one to its knees. Before he could finish, however, another ogre picked him up by the leg and tossed him towards the wall. In a flash, Cuan was there, catching him, but the officer was already unconscious.

One of the two officers firing handguns looked our way and shouted for us to freeze, but a moment later a flying piece of what looked like a desk bowled him and his partner over, knocking them out cold.

Alexander drew Candela as one of the remaining ogres rushed him, and I quickly tried to get the lay the room. This was either some sort of examination room or a staging area, but what was clear was that the ogres here had essentially completed their transformation process, though they couldn't be the human subjects planned for Stage Two. Indeed, each of the vats that had held them seemed to be more-or-less self-contained units—perhaps this was more of a security area gone wrong? Makeshift walls had been erected to cut the area off from the rest of the space under the stands, though several doors in the walls were standing open.

Before I could think any further, however, the wall to our right burst open and an ogre flew through, propelled by a blast of blue flame. The creature crashed into another ogre and both slumped to the ground, unconscious.

The gout of flame cleared, and through the broken wall I could see a slender woman holding a tall, gleaming staff.

"Rebecca?" Alexander gaped. "What are you doing here?"

Rebecca looked into the room in surprise. "Alexander? Is that you?" She asked.

Alexander nodded. "We're here to stop the city's ogre program," he said.

"So are we," Rebecca said. "Thomas told me about the plan to storm the stadium. After he left, Paul and I resolved to confront Father Jacob and Levi after they got back from wher-ever they'd been and convince them we needed to take action.

When they arrived, however, they were really agitated for some reason, and then they told Paul and me to get our equipment and make for the stadium. I guess they already knew." There was a roar behind her and Rebecca whirled around, waving her staff in front of her as a sheet of white light burst forth from where she stood.

"So... Father actually listened to me," Alexander said to himself, half in shock.

Cuan and Az were just finishing subduing the last ogre in the room, and headed in my direction. At the same time, there was another electronic popping sound, and the klaxon finally fell completely silent.

"We need to get into the center part of the stadium," I said quietly. Cuan, still in wolf shape, nodded.

We stepped through the smashed wall into what was a much more wide open space beneath the stadium stands. Here the fighting continued; Rebecca was at one end with us while I could see Julia and Thomas holding off a group of ogres a few yards away.

"What is the Order's plan of action?" Az asked Rebecca as her wall of light burst into an array of bright beams much as Alexander's had in The Hunters' Home basement.

"Father Jacob and Levi are making for a deeper part of the stadium, where the people are being kept," Rebecca said. "They said they'll find a security card on a guard and get inside, and then they're going to make sure no more ogres are produced."

Rebecca said it innocently enough, but considering what I knew of Jacob and Levi, their objective had an ominous ring to it.

We *definitely* needed to get into the center of the stadium.

"They won't be safe," Az said. "We suspect there's a demon at large."

Rebecca blanched. "They went through there," she said,

pointing to a door leading to the stadium stands, which was now secured with a makeshift security swipe lock.

There was a crash from behind us, and two more ogres burst into the room we'd just been in. Rebecca whirled on them. "I'll cover you," she added, raising her staff.

We ran for the security door. Between it and us were three ogres, and Alexander, Az, and Cuan leapt into the fray. Alexander ducked and swiped, Candela flashing in his hands as he fought with a focus I'd never seen before. Az and Cuan, meanwhile, were blurs in the air, cutting and slashing, and soon the ogres they were fighting buckled before them.

I looked across the room as we ran and saw Thomas crack Prominence in the air, the chain erupting in an arc of flame before him, causing the ogres near him to stagger backward. Julia, meanwhile, thrust Gratia downward into one's shoulder, and it erupted in light.

Just as we reached the security door, we heard a gate bang open behind us, and turned to see a group of cops storm into the room, weapons drawn.

"Freeze, everyone," they shouted, and I knew the room was about to be filled with bullets.

Not a second had passed, however, before a high glass partition above them shattered inward, raining down a shower of broken glass. In their wake came an ogre's ball and chain, swinging down from some unseen place above; riding the massive metal sphere was Bianca.

"I CAME IN LIKE A WRE-CKING BALL," she belted at the top of her lungs, successfully drawing the attention of all the cops and ogres in the room. From behind her, a swarm of mist burst forth, slamming into one of the cops' chests and solidifying just long enough for me to make out Leo's form before the cop careened across the room and the mist rebounded off of him into another officer. The remaining officers aimed at him but were immediately assailed by a cloud of shrieking black

bats that poured forth from around Bianca as she did a neat somersault off of the wrecking ball and planted the heel of her boot in an ogre's face, flashing Julia a wicked smirk as she did so.

They had the situation well under control.

I turned my attention back to the door. It took only a moment's concentration now for me to be able to slide right through its solid form as though it were no more substantial than a bank of fog. The room beyond was, currently, an empty concrete corridor. I turned back toward the door, spying a release handle, and let the world solidify around me as I slammed my fist on it. The door lurched open, and Az, Alexander, and Cuan joined me in the corridor before the door slid shut again, leaving us in relative peace.

Cuan took a deep breath. I could tell he was debating about whether to stay in his werewolf form or not. It took a lot out of him, I knew, but it was even more taxing to shift back and forth. For the time, he seemed to decide to stay as he was.

There was a crash from somewhere far down the corridor.

Alexander turned to me. "Let's go."

I nodded, and we raced into the belly of the stadium.

Eventually we reached a second door. This one had been bashed in. On either side of it were two police officers, slumped over. I couldn't tell if they were dead or just unconscious. I don't think I wanted to know.

We stepped through the smashed door and into what was clearly part of the lab structure. This must have been the stadium proper, but now it was partitioned in various ways with makeshift walls. Large vats were set up in rows throughout the chamber. Suspended inside them were people of all ages, shapes, and sizes, all naked, all hooked into tubes and wires. Some of them had already begun the transformation process. It was... grotesque.

Lab technicians and police officers lay sprawled about on

the ground, along with a few ogres. Apart from the beeping of machinery recording vital signs, the place was eerily silent.

We took a few steps in and then suddenly heard a sharp gunshot from somewhere off to our right. It was followed by three or four more, and then the sound of clicking. We rushed in that direction.

As we rounded the vats, we heard voices. "That's why you shouldn't fire more than necessary; now you've run out of ammo."

"Don't tell me how to conduct myself."

I recognized those voices. We all did. As we rounded the row of vats, we came face-to-face with their owners, standing over the fallen body of a lab technician.

Jacob and Levi.

XVII

THE FALL OF THE HOUSE OF JACOB

"Father," Alexander said in horror, "did you just... kill that person?"

My stomach turned. I had faced down a lot of things in the past few weeks, but until now I had not—to my knowledge, at least—been faced with a dead body, least of all someone who had just been murdered. Next to me, Cuan growled menacingly.

"I am doing God's work," Jacob announced imperiously. "Everyone here is complicit in deceiving those in the vats here, and now they are lost to us. I am going to set it right by doing what must be done."

I didn't like the sound of that.

"Father, what are you planning?" Alexander asked.

"I shall free these poor souls from their torment," Jacob declared. "It is as simple as that."

"Your words *sound* right, but somehow I'm not reassured," Alexander said.

"Well, this doesn't concern you, anyway," Jacob declared, fishing out an ID card from the body of the fallen technician.

"The hell it doesn't," Alexander glared.

Jacob ignored him, turning to Levi. "I'm going to need twenty, maybe thirty minutes," he said. "Keep them occupied until then. Or, if you wish, make sure they can never follow me at all."

"You're not going anywhere!" Alexander shouted, and he, Az, and Cuan all leapt forward. At the same time, however, Jacob threw his hand out, and five or six little silver spheres flew toward us.

"Shit! Father!" Levi shouted, clapping his gauntleted hands over his face.

One flashsphere exploding was bad enough. Six was blinding, even through closed eyelids. Cuan and Alexander had leapt out of the way of the stunning blast, but the light nonetheless left them staggering. Az lunged through the blast undeterred, but stopped a second later when Jacob hurled his empty handgun into a computer monitor, which shattered and burst into flames. In a few seconds, the fire would spread, potentially engulfing several vats that the monitor was hooked into. Like any self-respecting angel, Az chose protecting innocent lives over that of punishing an enemy. He darted to the machine and, with a quick slash, severed the wires connecting the monitor to the vats and to the power supply. The fires winked out, but by the time Az turned around, Jacob was gone.

Levi, however, was not. He lowered the gauntlets from in front of his face and, muttering curses, hefted Perdition. The heavy, long-handled hammer began to spit black smoke menacingly.

Cuan growled again.

"Stand down, brother," Alexander warned.

"Like hell I will," Levi snarled.

"And you think you're going to take us all on?" Alexander asked.

"Three against one?" Levi said. "Easy."

"Four," I corrected.

Levi's eyes focused on me and his features twisted into a look of fury. In the moment of distraction, Cuan lunged at him, but Levi swung the hammer wide and Cuan just managed to catch a pipe leading to a vat and swing his body around it before the hammer hit him.

"That's right," Levi growled. "One hit from this hammer and you, the unworthy, shall be reduced to ash."

"You have a very skewed perception of worthiness," Az said blithely.

"You think we're unworthy to be touched by your hammer?" I challenged. "OK, then, Thor, come at me."

"Do not equate me with a pagan idol," Levi shouted.

"Right," I said, "Thor is waaaay too good for you."

"Enough!" Levi roared, slamming the hammer into the concrete floor. Cracks spread out toward us as black spikes burst up from within. I leapt to one side. The spikes remained, smoking and angry, clear across the floor. Walls of spikes rose up behind Cuan and Az, cutting them off from their planned pursuit of Jacob.

"You can't hold us off," Alexander said. "There are too many of us."

"You forget," Levi snarled, "that I am not some sniveling amateur like you are." He straightened up imperiously. "I am second-in-command of the Church of the Holy Guardian's division of the Order of Light. I am eldest of the sons of Jacob. I am pious. I am righteous. I am a *hand of God*." He thrust a gauntleted hand out in front of him, and declared in a booming voice, "*Lucis hasta!*"

Silence.

Nothing happened.

Levi's eyebrow twitched. He thrust his hand again. "*Ignes Dei!*"

Still nothing.

"*Sanctus iudicium!*"

Silence.

"*Plena tibi excrementum bovis*," Alexander said with a smirk. "Where's all the holy fury?"

"Clearly, you all are too far fallen to even be worthy of it," Levi glowered, his eyebrow twitching again. "You are so far gone that heaven refuses to even touch you."

"I assure you that isn't the case," I said smugly.

"And why have you suddenly gone about wearing those heavy gauntlets?" Alexander asked, pointing to the metal encasing Levi's fists. "Didn't you once make a huge deal about the importance of communing directly with our weapons, nothing between hand and hammer, so that we could be infused with the power of the spirit?"

"I will not be lectured by the likes of you," Levi spat. He extended his fist again. "*Rugiet caelorum*," he shouted.

Still nothing.

"I can't keep looking at that stupid gauntlet," Alexander said, spreading his fingertips in front of him. "*Lucis gladii.*"

Beams of light shot from his fingertips, cutting through the air at right angles before slicing along the outline of Levi's arm. A second later, scraps of metal rained down from his bare hand.

"There. Much better," Alexander said with satisfaction.

With a roar, Levi lifted up Perdition in the one hand still gauntleted and lunged at Alexander. In a flash, Cuan was between them, and his sudden appearance threw Levi off balance. Levi swung his hammer around him, trying to strike Cuan, but Cuan leapt neatly over him and the momentum of the hammer proved too much for Levi to maintain his single-handed grip. His shoulder wrenched behind him and he released the hammer with a grunt. As he landed, Cuan slashed sharply at Levi's gauntlet, and a moment later it, too, fell to the ground in pieces.

Levi rounded on us, snarling, but he didn't move.

"What's the problem?" Alexander taunted. "Now without those gaudy gauntlets, you can commune with Perdition properly."

"No, he can't," Az declared. Quietus winked out of existence in a flash of black light as he stepped calmly to the center of the room. "This man is no longer a threat to us."

"The hell I'm not!" Levi roared.

"Impotent words from a fallen warrior," Az said serenely. "We can relax."

Cuan let out a deep breath, and his body was subsumed in light for a moment before he was back to his normal self again. "Phew," he panted, resting a hand on my shoulder for support. "Good; I need a break. Staying shifted that long really takes it out of me, especially on a day like today when there's no moon out."

"You'll regret that," Levi said. "I still have Perdition."

"A lot of good it will do you," Az replied. "You can bluff all you want, but it means nothing. You can't hold that hammer anymore. Not without those gauntlets, anyway."

"And how do you presume to know anything about the tools of heaven?" Levi asked.

"Because," Az said, "I was there when they were created."

"You're lying," Levi responded.

Az simply smirked, and his suit coat and dress shirt were subsumed in black light. I wondered for a moment if this had been part of the 'preparations' he said he was undertaking: preparing a wardrobe that was easier to shed in case he needed his wings. Sure enough, a moment later, the shirt and suit coat were gone, now replaced with a silver breastplate mounted on a black leather harness. From his exposed back stood two tall, proud wings of white feathers.

"I am not lying," Az declared, voice resonant, "for I am Azrael, Angel of Death."

Levi's eyes widened in true awe for a moment—but just for

a moment. A second later he blinked back to an expression of defiance, but now his eyebrow was twitching rapidly.

"I don't believe you," he said.

"You know it's true," Azrael replied. "Just as you know you have not been able to wield that hammer with any effectiveness for some time. The love of the divine is unconditional, but wielding the powers of heaven as their representative is not. You may have been worthy of them once. And even after you faltered, they likely stayed with you for a time, giving you the benefit of the doubt, hoping you would see the error of your ways. But then you tried to imprison and enslave someone to use as a shield for your self-righteous sanctuary of oppression. You tried to kill your own brother, on multiple occasions. You have taken I don't know how many lives here at this stadium. And still you persist in thinking you are doing the work of the Divine?" Azrael scoffed. "You are so blinded by your own hatred and the hatred taught to you by your father that you have no idea what love actually means. You sit in that stone edifice entreating the heavens to hear your plea and answer your call. Well, I'm here, and I have an answer for you. You are not righteous."

Levi roared and lifted Perdition in both hands. At his touch, the hammer glowed black.

"I will not be lectured on religion by some pretty boy who consorts with sodomites. You call yourself an angel? Your actions tell me everything I need to know about you."

"Actions do speak volumes," Az replied calmly. "Yours, for instance, even now make it clear that you are no longer worthy to wield that hammer. Though perhaps I was wrong: I said you may have been worthy of it once. Now I wonder if you ever truly were."

"Don't you presume to tell me what is righteous and what is not," Levi growled. Wisps of smoke were beginning to seep out where his bare hands were touching the shaft of the hammer.

"I'll bet you even opened your legs to Alexander and let him penetrate your shame."

"No, just the other two," Az said serenely, gesturing to Cuan and me. "And there's nothing shameful about it. It's probably the most holy act I've performed during this particular earthly visit."

"Liar!" Levi roared. His whole body was beginning to give off faint plumes of smoke. "False prophet! I shall strike you down where you stand!" He stepped forward menacingly, eyes flashing. "Angel of Death?" he scoffed. "That is a great misnomer. Death is the greatest evil. But you have no power over me. Christ conquered Death."

"No, he hasn't yet," Az said blithely, "though I wouldn't mind if he did. I imagine he's very good, if he had twelve men following him everywhere."

"I smite thee!" Levi roared. He made to run forward, but his leg buckled on the second step, and he fell to his knees. The smoke rising from his body was turning black now.

"Levi, let go of Perdition!" Alexander cried. "It's killing you!"

"No..." Levi panted, his voice strained. "The righteous need not fear Perdition, for it shall not harm them." He gripped the shaft even more tightly, black smoke billowing from between his fingers, rising off of his skin like steam.

"That is correct," Az said. "But there is no fooling these holy artifacts. They see straight into the soul. They may forgive a transgression or two in the hopes that the person they've bonded to will mend their ways, but they know when someone remorselessly clings to hate."

"I... shall not die... by your hand..." Levi panted. He struggled to his feet, then staggered and fell back to his knees. The head of the heavy hammer crashed to the floor, Levi powerless to continue lifting it, but he kept his grip on it nonetheless. "I... shall not... suffer the punishment... of Death..."

"Death is not a punishment," Az said, his voice still

perfectly calm. "It is simply part of the cycle. No, you shall receive not Death, but Perdition. And you, who has dealt out Perdition on countless occasions, know exactly what that entails."

Levi's eyes flashed briefly with fear, but this, too, was lost to defiance and rage.

"Perdition sunders the soul," Azrael continued. "You will no longer experience the cycle of life. Mercifully Perdition has only visited this fate on those among your victims whom it sensed were so consumed with hatred, so lost to love, that they would blight the cycle rather than enrich it. Now, it perceives that same blight in you. Perhaps the shreds of your soul will find new existence in new forms, bound to other lost existences and able to find renewed purpose and a new chance at life. But those existences will not be yours."

"I... will... not... be... judged... by... a... sodom...ite..." Levi growled.

"OK, You really need to let go of this whole 'Sodom and Gomorrah is about gay sex and gay sex is evil' thing," Azrael said, the irritation in his expression and voice breaking his previously serene, unflappable facade. "Let me make something perfectly clear: Sex, where all parties involved are consenting and happy and there is no power being abused, is the single most holy act anyone can engage in. It literally perpetuates the cycle of life. And not just straight sex, mind you; all sex is a generative, holy act." It was a rant I'd heard before, but I was nonetheless glad to hear it again, for Alexander's sake as much as anyone's. "And considering how much certain elements of humanity have tried to beat down and stamp out homosexuality," Az continued, "gay sex, as an affirmation of love and life in the face of death and oppression, is probably among the most holy acts in modern human existence." He ran his hand through his hair in frustration. "Agh, the Green Man can explain this so much better than I can." He shook his head, regaining some of his earlier composure. "But anyway," he continued, "It is not I who is passing judgement, but Perdition. And you are visiting that judgement upon yourself by refusing to let go. Release the hammer, and continue to exist."

"Let go of the hammer, Levi," Alexander pleaded.

"No..." Levi gasped, his voice strained as his face grew increasingly craggy. "I... am... right... eous... .."

"Levi, STOP!" Alexander's voice was a desperate cry now, tears in the corners of his eyes.

Levi turned to stare at him, his eyes two points of light through the smoke.

"Shut... up... you... .. fucking ... ... little... .. fa... .. ." was all he managed before his voice left him.

Levi's eyes darkened and then seemed to burn away, black smoke billowing out from the empty sockets, pouring out from his mouth and his ears and his nose, as his body collapsed, his hands sliding down the shaft of the hammer before his entire being disintegrated into ash, leaving just his clothes and the hammer behind. We all stood for a moment, staring at it, no one saying a word. Then, finally, Az stepped forward, standing before the hammer and the burned remains that lay around it, some of the ash even piled on the head of the hammer itself.

"You arrogant fool," he muttered. "Was it truly worth visiting this fate upon yourself, just to continue believing in your own righteousness and infallibility?" He shut his eyes for a moment, and somehow I knew he was offering a silent prayer.

I felt Cuan take my hand, and we stood solemnly in the presence of death.

"I'm sorry, Alexander," I said quietly, as Alexander walked over and slipped his hand into my free one.

"Don't be," Alexander replied coldly. "This was his own choice. As much as I hate to say it, the world is probably better without my brother in it."

"He was my brother, too," Cuan said with realization. "Not in the same way that he was yours, but still, blood is blood."

"Maybe, but I don't think blood makes a family," I said. "That's something you've got to earn."

"Yeah," Cuan and Alexander said in unison.

Az finished his prayer and opened his eyes. "Well, that's that," he said with surprising lightness, lifting Perdition easily with one hand as though it were a piece of straw instead of a massive metal hammer. He spun it lightly like a baton, scattering the remnants of ash from it as he did so, then set it over his shoulder. He turned to us. "I don't think we should return Perdition to the Order just now, considering its current state; do you agree?"

Alexander nodded. "I don't think anyone in the Order should wield that hammer."

"Well then, I'll put it to use just once, and then I'll put it away for now." Az gripped the hammer tightly and rushed the giant wall of spikes that had erupted from the ground between us and the direction in which Jacob had fled. With a crash, the hammer smashed through the black spikes, which burst into smoke at the impact. With the path clear, Az turned around and smirked, spinning the hammer lightly in his hand again. "It's got a nice heft to it," he said as it dissolved into black light, just as Quietus often did. He turned to us. "Shall we go?"

With that, we ran in search of Jacob.

The halls of the lab were dark, lit only by creepy lights illuminating the transformation vats from below. As we passed row after row of men, women, and even children in various stages of transformation into ogres, I felt more keenly than ever the importance of administering Lester's antidote. Hundreds, maybe even thousands of lives hung in the balance.

Cuan walked at my side, but suddenly he stiffened, and then dove into me, tackling me to the ground. For an instant I wondered what the hell had gotten into him, but less than half a second later I heard a gunshot and a bullet ricocheted off of a pipe next to where I had just been standing.

"Freeze!" came a shout from a door near us. Two middle-aged cops advanced into the room, pale faces obscured by heavy beards and the guns aimed straight at us.

"Aren't you supposed to shout that before you shoot?" Alexander cried.

"Shut up!" one of the cops shouted. "On the ground."

"You will stop," Az said firmly, turning to face the two officers. He spread his wings wide as he spoke, and his whole body seemed to shine.

"What... what in God's name..." one cop gasped, eyes widening. He dropped his gun to the ground and fell to his knees.

"For fuck's sake, get up!" the other cop yelled, but his partner was already fainting dead away. The cop that remained conscious swore again, then aimed at Azrael and fired three rounds.

None of them connected. In a flash of black light Azrael was suddenly hovering directly above the officer, white wings now shimmering with a black aura, Quietus in hand.

"I have had more than enough of humans like you," Azrael spoke, his voice resonant and menacing. "Your partner at least possesses enough piety to yield before a servant of the Divine. You, however, need to be made to stand down more forcibly." The wide-eyed, terrified cop raised his weapon again, but before he could do anything, Azrael lightly nicked the back of his neck with his black-coated blade. The cop grunted and then collapsed to the ground, spasming before lying still. Az alighted next to him, wings again snowy white, Quietus vanishing into black light, and rolled the cop onto his side.

"So you don't choke on your own saliva," He said, his voice again quiet and serene as the officer stared at him in impotent horror. "The paralysis will last three hours or so, but your vital systems should still function. Pray, take this time to reflect on some of your life choices. Or you can just take a nap, I suppose. But you won't be able to do much else."

"Damn," Alexander said as Az walked back to our side. "You are one badass angel, Az."

"No, his ass is quite good, I assure you," I said.

"Thank you," Az said. "I do think it's one of my better features."

"All your features are pretty nice," Cuan said.

"OK, is now really the right time for you all to be flirting?" Alexander asked impatiently.

"It's always the right time for flirting," I said, and Cuan nodded enthusiastically.

Alexander rolled his eyes. "Let's just find Father," he sighed.

It didn't take much longer to find him. He was bent over a computer, stolen keycard jammed into a console. The computer monitor read "Access Denied; console locked," as did three others near it. Jacob had clearly beaten the side of the machine with what was now a broken metal chair, and was prying open a panel on the system.

"What in God's name are you trying to do, Father?" Alexander said to him as we approached.

Jacob glanced over his shoulder, then back at the machine. "So, Levi failed yet again," he grunted. "Unsurprising. I shall have to have a word with him later."

Alexander opened his mouth to say something, but ultimately just shut it.

"You won't want to be here," Jacob continued. "Someone's sure to come checking up on all these unsuccessful attempts at unauthorized access."

"They already did," Az responded. Jacob spared another glance over his shoulder, this time at Az, and did a double-take before turning and giving us his full attention.

"Who in blazes are you?" He demanded. As he spoke, a glass vial fell out of his lap and rolled a few feet across the floor.

"What's that?" Cuan asked. Jacob lunged at the vial, but Cuan was there in a flash, picking it up and peering at it. It had a little golden cross emblazoned on the front and was filled with a greenish liquid inside. "Are you going to inject this into the system?"

"I wanted to add it as centrally as possible," Jacob said, "but this spot will have to do. At least it'll spread throughout this section."

"Is that an antidote?" Alexander asked in surprise.

"No," Cuan said, recoiling, his nostrils flaring. "It's aconitine."

Holy shit.

"Aconitine?" Alexander asked.

Holy fucking shit.

"Monkshood," Cuan clarified. "Wolf's-bane."

Alexander blanched.

"Get this stuff away from me," Cuan said, disgusted, holding it out.

I took the vial and slipped it out of sight into the satchel I carried, and Cuan immediately breathed a sigh of relief. I, however, was more livid than ever as I glared at Jacob. "You miserable, execrable excuse for a human being," I spat darkly. "You're going to poison all these people? That's your plan?"

"They are corrupted, beyond help," Jacob said matter-of-factly. "It's the only way. This is the only salvation that remains for them."

"Bullshit," Alexander said. "We've worked out an antidote for this. The transformation is reversible."

"I find that hard to believe," Jacob said. "But even if it were true, even if you could renew their bodies, you can never cleanse the taint from their souls. Once one has been corrupted by the power of the Beast, there is no redemption."

"You're out of your mind," Az said, his disgust plain. "Where do you come up with these doctrines?"

"The Word of Christ," Jacob declared.

"Nonsense. The insane ramblings of so-called Christians like you would make Christ weep tears of blood."

"And who are you, to lecture me on the will of God?" Jacob asked defiantly.

Azrael straightened, spreading his wings, his light radiant. "I am the Angel of Death," he declared.

Jacob gave no reaction. Finally, he waved his hand toward the vats. "Good. About time you got here. Go put these people out of their misery."

Azrael glared at him. "I am not here for them," he said.

"So you've come for me, then?" Jacob asked. "Fine. Leave these wretches to their fates. If they were true believers then God would never have allowed this to happen to them in the first place. But I am ready, for I have only ever been a faithful servant of the Lord." He stood, spreading his arms wide, tilting his head back. "I await your welcoming embrace."

"You'll get no hugs from me, you fucking sack of shit," Azrael spat, abandoning his show of divine presence as his expression twisted into one of undisguised revulsion. Jacob almost recoiled in shock. "Why is it that you zealots always want the easy way out?" Az asked in frustration. "It's always, 'I'll die for my beliefs, and I'll go straight to heaven as a righteous warrior of Christ.' How convenient," he continued, "that it absolves you from any realistic responsibility for your actions. Well, you're not getting an easy out."

"You dare speak of Christ with that mouth?" Jacob scowled, ripping the ID card out of the console next to him and shoving it into his coat pocket. "You're no angel."

"I assure you, I am," Azrael said. "And if you think that's colorful, you should hear Gabriel sing."

With surprising speed, Jacob threw his hand out of his coat

pocket, and I realized with a start that placing his ID there was just a distraction while he readied a flashsphere. The ball flew straight at Azrael, but the angel caught it in his fist. He didn't even flinch as it detonated in front of his face.

Now Jacob's jaw actually fell. Unflinching poise in the face of holy light, it seemed, was proof enough for him that Azrael was the genuine article.

"So, finally seeing me for what I am, are you?" Azrael said with mild satisfaction. Then he scowled again. "Well, I see you for what you are, too, failed priest. You believe your wards and spells are losing effectiveness because the world is falling into decadence. The reality, however, is that you are the one who has fallen. You have misused the blessings of the heavens, and so they have left you."

"I am a righteous man," Jacob protested.

"Are you?" Azrael challenged. "The word you spread is one of hatred and division, punishing and excluding any who refuse to follow your very specific interpretation of Divine Will, which has already been filtered through so many layers of human translation and appropriation that it has become almost unrecognizable. You preach oppression and judgement. You smother discourse and curiosity. You decry those who express genuine love and acceptance as servants of a devil that you parade around like a show pony when it suits your purposes. And you think yourself a holy man? You are not a holy man," Azrael scowled. "You are a selfish man. A man so convinced of his divine right to power that he will do anything to keep it, all while believing himself infallible. But tell me, Jacob Lucent: Where is the divine blessing you believe you have? How long has it been since you have actually been able to conjure holy light, to bless a holy artifact, or even to properly perform a sacrament?"

Jacob said nothing, his face ashen.

"Father... you..." Alexander looked deeply shaken. "Have

you been unable to even consecrate communion each week? You've been just going through the motions?"

"It's not as uncommon as you may think," Azrael said. "But this man is no mere priest; oh no, he also stands at the head of a powerful branch of holy warriors. When was the last time you have been able to wield a holy weapon? Instead you are reduced to using your remaining supply of flashspheres, of creating Molotov cocktails in casks made for holy water, of asserting your dominance through guns and bullets—the true mark of an impotent man."

"I..." Jacob struggled to reconcile all the angel had pointed out—all the stinging truths—with the imperious self-righteousness that had characterized his life. "All I did," he claimed, "I did for the glory of God."

"The glory of *you*, you mean," Azrael corrected. "And what has it gotten you? Your desire for moral superiority has cost you the very holiness that you sought. Your oldest son was so indoctrinated by your brand of righteous hate that he essentially killed himself for it."

Jacob blanched anew at these last words. "What?"

"Perdition judged Levi," Alexander said softly, a hint of regret in his voice. "Levi refused to let it go, even as it utterly destroyed him. Father, it *obliterated his soul*."

Jacob fought with this realization. It was a damning condemnation of his entire way of life. The choices he made, the teachings he'd passed on, hadn't just torn his parish apart and caused his youngest children to turn their backs on him. His zealotry had also cost him his firstborn son—his favorite son. The truth was undeniable. And yet, Jacob refused to accept it. "Then he died a hero and a martyr," He said at last, straightening, head held high with false pride.

"Yeah, it looked kind of pathetic from where I was standing," Cuan said scornfully. "Not as pathetic as you look right now, mind you, but pretty close."

"You hold your tongue," Jacob spat at Cuan, sudden violence in his voice. "You will not speak to me with that tone. Honor your mother and father, Cain."

The movement was so quick that it was a blur, but Cuan was suddenly at the other end of the room, hand at Jacob's throat. "Don't you dare call yourself my father," he demanded. "You dishonored the memory of my mother by assigning me responsibility for her death. You abandoned me to die because of how I was born. You replaced me with another child whom you saw only as a substitute instead of as a real person. You conspired with your son to poison and kill me simply as a means to an end. And that end was to take the one who has become the single most important person in my life, deprive him of his freedom, his form, and his existence, and lock him away in a box."

Most important person. I stared at Cuan. The words rang true. And, I realized, they went both ways. Looking at him now, strong, poised, powerful, my love for him was almost over-whelming. He was all I wanted, all I ever wanted, now and always. He was standing straight and tall, holding Jacob up by his neck with authority but not violence, neither constricting his airway nor breaking the skin. He was simply taking control. He stood commandingly, muscles in his arms taught, shirt clinging to his back, compression pants molded to his legs and his tight muscular ass, his eyes gleaming and his voice clear and confident and strong.

"You have never in my entire life done a single thing to in any way earn the respect of a father. You treated me as a cast-away, a blemish, and a monster. Well, I am not a monster. My name is *not* Cain. And I am *NOT* your son."

Dear God, he was sexy.

"Cedric is my father. And he is far from perfect, and he has done a lot of things that I will not be able to forgive for a long time, if ever, but he nonetheless treated me better than I suspect you've ever treated any of your children, least of all Alexander here."

He dropped Jacob, who crumpled to the ground, massaging his throat, still looking up at Cuan in defiance.

"So now the man I love and I are leaving you, and we're going with the Angel of Death—who, by the way, is also a *gay sex machine*—and the boy you treated as a replacement, the one whose heart and mind you clouded with your sick sense of righteousness, whom you filled with fear and self-loathing and hate, and we're going to give the people trapped here *real* help. And when all is said and done, we'll bring that boy back to his estate, his home, the place he feels totally himself, the home you tried to steal from him, where a very hot guy is waiting to fuck him so thoroughly, so completely, that he'll never have another doubt in his mind about what real pride and love and acceptance is. Because you know what true pride is? What love is? It's curling up at night with someone who means the world to you and feeling their breath on your skin. It's living your life and your truth, and helping others to do the same instead of asking them to carve off pieces of themselves for your acceptance. It's having your body drenched in hot, sticky cum while you're heaving and moaning with a soul-shaking orgasm and knowing that there is no reason, absolutely none, that you should feel even a whit of shame or guilt or remorse because what you're doing, whether you're in bed with your one true soulmate or with a group of men you trust and who trust you, is the most sacred, life-affirming act you can possibly undertake. And it's making absolutely sure that no shrieking, hateful zealot spitting fire and brimstone from a pulpit can ever, *ever* take that away from you. Because we are love. And you are *nothing*."

He turned and strode away from Jacob. He stopped in front of me, offering that same dimpled half-smile, all affection and confidence and smoldering sex, and extended his hand.

"You coming, Cole?"

I grasped his hand firmly in mine, a breathless grin on my face.

"I think I just did," I replied.

We turned, walking with Alexander and Azrael toward the center of the complex, leaving Jacob behind.

"You should've killed me," Jacob grunted as we left him.

"No, he shouldn't have," came another voice.

We turned, and he was there, standing over Jacob, looking at him such disdain that it bordered on pity.

"Cedric," Cuan said.

"It doesn't matter how hateful your father is, or how little you knew him," Cedric continued, continuing to fix Jacob with his withering stare. "Call it human nature, call it the spirits of our ancestors, call it social conditioning, but humanity has a deep-seated drive to honor our parents. And so patricide, no matter how justified or even necessary, leaves its mark on a person. Believe me: I know."

And suddenly I realized why, when the Order of Light had finally tracked down Cedric's father, they found him already dead in his chambers. It hadn't been suicide. Cedric had beaten them to the punch. It was vengeance. It was deserved. But it came with a price. Cedric would have been barely a teenager when he killed his father in cold blood, likely the first life he'd taken, the first of his midnight hunts. But in doing so, he had also killed his only remaining family. No wonder, then, that when he built The Hunters' Home and surrounded himself with capable and loyal companions, he could never bring himself to see them as family. To him, family brought nothing but pain. And yet, despite his best efforts to the contrary, Cedric was realizing that the family he'd built could have been something more.

"I have not been a good leader," Cedric said. "Hell, I haven't even been a good person. I haven't treated any of the people who put their trust in me with the respect they deserve. That's not something I can make right. I failed them. And yet, somehow, they are all here now, because they all fundamentally believe the core principle on which I founded the Midnight Hunters: People are worth saving. And so, where you were going to chalk up all these captive bodies as lost and dole out indiscriminate death, they are going to save them. And while they do that, you and I are going to take a little trip. The city's going to want a lot of scapegoats once this is all said and done. A lot of people will be losing their jobs, and a lot of people will be going to prison. But I think it's time we handed them one on a silver platter, don't you? Kidnapper, cop-killer, gunman, attempted mass-murderer... I think there's plenty to book you on. You might get some benefit of the doubt because you're white, but then again, the Order of Light has a long reach, and I don't think they're going to want someone like you roaming free, not when two consecutive branches in this area have committed such utterly detestable acts. No," Cedric grinned wickedly, menacingly. "They're going to want to make an example."

We all stared in silence as Cedric roughly yanked Jacob to his feet, wrapped a piece of computer cable around him, and marched him away.

"Go," Cedric called back over his shoulder as he left. "Go save the city. You can do it. I know you can."

"Save the city," I repeated. "Right," I nodded, looking around at the poor people suspended in vats all around us. "We need to save these people."

"Let's go," Azrael said.

"Are you all right, Alexander?" Cuan asked as we turned and hurried toward the center of the structure.

Alexander nodded. "People deserve saving," he said. His voice was icy cold as he added, "But that man deserves whatever he gets."

The silence only seemed to get heavier as we approached the center of the stadium. Perhaps that was what made the sudden shouts all the more piercing.

Two were men arguing.

The third was a girl screaming.

We broke into a run.

XVIII

CLEANING HOUSE

WE RAN across the makeshift lab with its hastily-built partitions as we made for the screaming ahead of us. This had to be near the center of the stadium proper, now almost completely unrecognizable as a one-time sports arena. Chambers, sheet metal, and particle-board walls separated row after row of vats bubbling and processing captive human beings who were about to be transformed into hulking, disfigured ogres.

As we got closer, the voices became clearer. One, a male voice, was shouting furiously.

"What the fuck are you thinking, Dennis?" The voice cried. "You had me drive out into... what, a fucked up Lovecraftian bio lab, all to pick up your daughter?"

Daughter. That explained the shrieking girl.

"You're my driver; it's your job," the other male voice responded.

We rounded a row of vats and came to a bank of computers. In front of them, a hulking man stood stoically, arms crossed over his chest, his back to us.

Cuan made to run forward but Azrael shot his hand out, placing his palm on Cuan's chest, staying him.

"Don't," Azrael said. "That's not a man."

The shouting voices, still out of view, continued.

"My job is to convey the mayor to the office and to public events, not drive into some fucking war zone at his whim because he wants his child picked up from fucking Franken-stein, Incorporated," the driver was shouting. "Why the hell is she here, anyway?"

"Because," responded the voice that I now recognized as belonging to Mayor Dennis Grafton, "I did all this for her!" He sounded wild, out of his mind on a level that would put even Father Jacob to shame. "We have to protect the children!"

"And so this is your answer?" the unseen driver responded over the child's continued wails. "You created a human processing plant for your daughter? For the *children*? And what about all the children who've wound up in these vats?"

"A necessary sacrifice," the mayor cried. "It's never possible to help everyone. What matters is my own daughter, not those other children."

"Says the mayor of the fucking city," the driver shouted. "You're out of your fucking mind."

"Shut up and do your job!" The mayor ordered. "It's not safe for my child here now, so get her out of here. Drive her to safety."

"And how do you suppose I do that?" The driver responded. "Security almost shot me on sight on my way in here. The place is crawling with I-don't-know-whats. And now this fucking monster of a bodyguard here won't let me leave.

"Just tell him to stand down," the mayor said. "Stand down," he said, raising his voice.

The hulking figure did not move.

"I said *stand down*," the mayor ordered.

"No one leaves until the work is done," the figure said, voice hollow and unearthly.

"Shit," the mayor spat.

"There, you see?" the driver responded. "So we're fucking stuck here. But when this is over, you'd better believe I'm not keeping my mouth shut."

"You're an accessory at this point," the mayor said.

"So what? You're building a mutant army, all for the sake of a little girl you parade around and exploit like a fucking show poodle so the people coo and aww and ignore everything you're doing behind the scenes. Well, you know who's behind the scenes? Me. And I have *everything* on you. You're going down, Mr. Mayor, even if it means I go down too."

"Well, in that case, why don't you go down now?" The mayor said, and the air was pierced by a gunshot. The girl's screams intensified into abject horror.

"Shit! Fuck!" the driver cried.

There was a click. "Dammit," the mayor said. Then there was a beep and the sound of a door sliding open. "Make yourself useful while you're keeping everyone from leaving and finish him off, will you?" The mayor called as there was the sound of a door sliding shut.

The hulking figure still did not move.

"God dammit!" The driver cursed. "Run," he instructed, presumably to the girl. "Run!" The girl kept screaming. "Dammit, come on," the driver insisted, and the sounds got further away.

"We have to help them," Cuan whispered.

Az nodded, but he didn't move his hand.

That same moment, without turning around, the hulking figure spoke again.

"I see you," it declared. "Come out."

Alexander made to move, but before we did anything, Professor Norton emerged from between a bank of computers.

"I was waiting until everyone else was gone," he said.

"And you think it's safe now to make your move?" The hulking man said, turning to face him. His square frame was clad in brown pants and a blue pinstriped shirt with a navy tie, and sported slicked brown hair. That wasn't what caught my attention, however. What demanded my attention was his glowing red irises. At the sight of them, I felt a chill of recognition course through me. Azrael was right: This was not a man. It was a demon—the demon who had tried to collect my soul.

"You haven't harmed me yet," the professor said. "You're here because I brought you here. You're no threat to me."

"You think so?" the demon scoffed. "Perhaps I haven't harmed you because you've been useful to me."

"In securing this program space in the bio labs? In advising the designers of the Stadium? You really think I've been helping you? You think I want this program?"

"And yet," the demon said, "You've designed this facility with care. It's slapdash, sure, but you haven't built in any weaknesses, any backends that you could have used to shut the whole operation down."

"I take pride in my work," Professor Norton said with a hint of haughtiness. "Besides, I didn't want to risk tipping my hand. But I've just been biding my time. I can afford it. You haven't been able to touch me since the moment I brought you here."

"You had protection back when I arrived," the demon growled. "More so than you even realized, by some unhappy accident. But now you have nothing. You wanted to be the one to discover angels were real? You think there aren't many who've already met divine beings on earth?"

"None who have been able to prove their findings."

"Perhaps they didn't think it necessary," the demon replied. "Their faith was enough. But not so for you. And you would prove them with, what, a blurry video of a demon feasting on a human sacrifice? You think that would be your proof?" The man gave a derisive laugh. "Fine, then. You called, and I answered. But the offering you gave me was not acceptable."

"That boy was a failure to the end," Professor Norton grumbled.

"No; he is a success. More than you realize," the demon replied. "But that is irrelevant. What matters now is that I have not received my due. And so I am collecting. With interest that accrues by the day."

"From the people of the city?" Professor Norton challenged. "What have they done to deserve anything?"

"Hah!" the demon scoffed. "What had that boy you offered me done to deserve being a sacrifice? The same as those here: nothing. But I shall have what is owed me."

"So this is your plan, then? Convince the whole city to create some human processing plant and build a monster army to help you reap your sacrifice?" He scoffed. "It's a little convoluted, don't you think? But if this is the method you devised to collect lives, then it ends now." Professor Norton said. "You will not collect. I forbid it."

"Forbid?" The demon asked, an expression of both surprise and amusement on its face. "You are in no position to forbid me anything. Nor are you necessary to this operation any longer. Be wary of what you do next, lest I mete out punishment."

"You will do nothing of the sort," Professor Norton proclaimed. "You have no power over me, for I know your true name. I banish thee," he shouted, pointing his finger imperiously. "Begone, Belphegor."

There was a pause, a long pause where nothing happened. And then the hulking man laughed, a deep, hollow, echoing sound.

"Very amusing," the demon grinned, clapping slowly and sarcastically. "How long did it take you to come up with that?"

"That's... not your name?" Professor Norton said.

"Oh, no, it's my name, all right," the demon replied.

"Then you are bound by it, and must obey," Professor Norton declared.

"Is that really how you think it works?" The demon asked, cocking an eyebrow.

"Yes. I know your true name, and it renders you powerless."

"Hah!" the demon roared. "Names are but words. And yes, words have power, but that power is not unlimited. There are names we are given, names we choose for ourselves; they all have meaning, but the idea that there is one true name that is immutable and unchanging and that renders someone completely powerless is nonsense. If a woman is assigned a man's name at birth, and rejects that name in favor of one she feels represents her genuine self, are you going to insist that the name that has died retains any validity at all? Demons and angels have a multitude of names, all known to different people. Even the names of God are such only by mutual agreement between the worshippers and the Divine."

"And what would you know of God, demon?" Professor Norton challenged. "You have hated God since the beginning of time."

"Hah!" the demon cackled. "Not so. We who are manifestations of deceit and hatred, we who are fueled by a failure to love, we are not the primordial entities you wish to make us out to be. No: we are powered by human hatred, human suffering. You made us what we are." He grinned widely, advancing on the Professor, who backpedaled, fear finally beginning to show on his face.

"So, *human,*" the demon drawled, "what form do you imagine for me? You seem like a traditionalist... perhaps big bat wings and red, burning skin?" As he spoke, his eyes glowed redder, and his skin began to smoke. A moment later, his clothing caught fire and burned away, and suddenly there he was, bold red skin and black hair over thick, sinewy muscle. Red and black webbed wings sprouted from his back, and a long, pointed tail swished behind him.

Professor Norton fell backward onto the ground, scrabbling away from him.

"You wished to meet a demon," Belphegor declared. "Well, I am here to grant your wish. And now, having fulfilled your life's goal, it is time for that life to end."

Alexander made a motion to dash forward, but again Azrael stayed him.

"No," he said firmly. "You cannot fight Belphegor. There would be no contest. You would die."

"But... *he* will die," Alexander protested.

"His life was forfeit the moment he summoned that demon," Azrael said. "He tried to barter with Cole's soul, don't forget. But that's not how this works. The professor will die. If this demon does not collect, then I will. And believe me, the demon will go much easier on him than I would."

"Shit, that's dark," Alexander said.

"Lest you forget; I am Death," Azrael said simply.

Professor Norton lay back on the floor, frozen in terror. I felt a twinge of pity, but only a twinge. This man tried to kill me, after all. At least twice. Cuan watched coldly at my side and I knew he was of the same mind as I.

"You cannot harm me," Professor Norton stammered weakly. "I know your true name. You have... no power here."

The demon reached out a long, red claw, and I shuddered, remembering what it was like when that claw was reaching for me. When it touched Professor Norton's chest, however, there was no burst of white angelfire. Instead, the demon reached directly into his chest, right toward his heart. But there was no blood, only smoke pouring out from the Professor's mouth, his nose, his ears, as his whole body shuddered and shook, burning from the inside out. A moment later, his skin cracked and burned away, and there was nothing left of Professor Norton but a pile of ash.

"That's easier on him?" Alexander whispered.

Az stood and said nothing.

The demon stood, admiring his handiwork, then tilted his head left and right, cracking his neck bones in satisfaction. Then, again, without turning around, he spoke, voice deep and hollow.

"Show yourself."

Azrael strode into the center of the room. "Leave this one to me," he said over his shoulder to us. He turned toward the demon, spread his wings, and immediately he began to shine with black and white light.

The demon took one look at Azrael and roared with laughter.

"Do I look funny to you?" Azrael asked.

"No," the demon replied, its maw of sharp teeth seeming to split its head in half as it grinned menacingly. "But I am amused at the irony. That man's greatest wish was to prove the existence of angels, and yet there was one right here in his last moments, watching as I took his life."

"I thought it a suitable end," Azrael replied.

"Handing out judgements now, are we?" the demon asked. "Here I thought you existed only to carry out orders to the letter."

"I have learned I have some leeway in how I carry out my duties," Azrael said.

"Thinking for yourself," the demon said, sounding almost impressed. "It seems humanity is rubbing off on you."

"They are," Azrael smirked. "And I like it."

The demon laughed again, mirthfully rather than derisively this time.

"And so now you're going to tell me you think humanity is worth something," the demon said. "Even after you've seen what those in power have wrought here. Look at the corruption! It's glorious," he added, licking his lips. "Police mad with power; a mayor convinced he needs an army of monsters for his little girl. And a professor so obsessed with the supernatural that he never noticed the divinity right under his nose."

"You don't know the half of it," Azrael said.

"You mean the Nephilim he tried to use as a sacrifice?" the demon asked. "He was something indeed. I had no idea of his heritage until the moment I tried to collect him. That boy is extraordinary."

"You don't need to tell me that," Azrael replied.

"Fine, the demon responded. "But I still mean to collect."

"I will not allow you to hurt these people," Azrael said.

"You mean to stop me?" The demon grinned. "What, you and those two little ones you brought with you?"

Two. So even the demon hadn't noticed me. That was very good.

"You don't need to concern yourself with them," Azrael responded. "I'm the one you need to worry about."

"Is that so? You, alone, are going to strike me down?"

"You know I can," Azrael replied.

"Heh," the demon chuckled. "Very well. But I won't make it easy. Substituting the lives I'm due for a round of combat with you seems like a fair exchange. I haven't had a good challenge in some time. But you'd better make it worth my while."

Azrael grinned, almost with anticipation. "Don't worry," He said. "When it comes to demons, I don't hold back." He held his hands out in front of him, and a long pole of black light connected his fists as though he were holding a staff. Then, one end curved sharply, and when the light faded, Azrael was holding a long, gleaming, wickedly sharp scythe. "I've been waiting for an opportunity to bring this out."

Without another word, the demon rushed him. Azrael spun the scythe so quickly it was just a series of gleaming circles in the air, each arc parrying a lightning-fast jab of the demon's claws. Azrael parried one more strike and then thrust forward with the butt of the scythe, landing a blow on the demon's chest and sending him flying backward. With a flap of his wings, Azrael took to the air.

"I've got this," he called to us. "Go!" he ordered, and then with another flap he was off after the demon, gleaming feathers fluttering in his wake.

We ran in the opposite direction of the combat, which now raged back and forth across the lab space. Just as long as they didn't damage the serum delivery mechanisms, we were good. I still had to deliver the antidote. But, like a series of nesting dolls, it looked like we weren't yet at the very center. The mayor had run through another door, after all. We saw a door ahead of us and sprinted toward it, but this one, too, had a security lock on it.

"Maybe I can open it from the inside," I suggested.

"Hold up," Cuan said, cocking an ear. He turned sharply to his right, and motioned for us to follow him.

It didn't take long for us to find the noise that he had been following. It was a small, frightened whimper at the edge of the makeshift room, behind a row of vats.

The mayor's daughter.

The little blonde girl was huddled in the corner, pink party dress dirty and torn, more terrified than ever. Lying in front of her, as though to protect her, was the driver, a middle-aged man with slicked-back black hair. He had a wound in his chest.

"What happened?" I asked, rushing to him.

"...Shot..." the driver coughed. "In the back..."

"Don't talk," Alexander urged, kneeling in front of him. "Save your strength."

The driver shook his head. "Too late..." he reached into his coat pocket and pulled out an ID card and a set of keys, holding them out in a shaking hand. "Please," he begged.

"Stop talking, let me work," Alexander instructed, pressing his hands to the driver's chest. "The bullet clearly passed through, so if we can close the wound, then..." He began rapidly whispering syllables in Latin.

"Take... the keys," the driver urged.

"Hold on," Alexander said.

"No! Take..." The driver lurched forward, and as he did a trickle of blood spat between Alexander's fingers where they pressed into the wound.

"God dammit," Alexander hissed, "Stop it." But the driver continued to insist.

"For heaven's sake," Cuan growled in exasperation, snatching the keys.

The driver nodded.

"Please. Please... to safety," he gasped. "Drive. The car is... there," he said, pointing to an open door next to a large shutter. "Just... drive through all the security gates. Button... above the visors... opens the shutters." He coughed, blood spattering onto his white shirt.

We looked at the cowering girl behind him.

"We can't just leave her here," I said. "It's not safe."

"And this man will die if we don't save him," Alexander said. "I can help him, but he's too hurt to be moved."

"I can drive the girl out," Cuan said.

"Leave... me," the driver said.

"Shut up," Alexander responded. "I'm not just gonna sit here and let someone die when I can help him. Too many people are already dying here. Besides, you wanna take the mayor down, don't you?"

The driver finally relented, lying back on the ground.

"Take her to the estate," I said, nodding at the girl. "She'll be safe there. We already sent one person there, after all."

"What?" Alexander asked. "Who?"

"The pastry boy from the coffee shop near the university," I said. "At least, I think he's there," I said, pulling out my phone.

It read 'no service' at the top. "He was supposed to send a text, but I don't think anything can get through."

"I'll head straight there," Cuan said.

"You know where it is from here?" Alexander asked.

"My phone does," Cuan said, waving it. "As soon as I'm out of here and have a signal, we can head right there." He knelt in front of the terrified girl, who was still sobbing on the floor. "You're going to be fine, OK? But you need to be brave, and come with us."

"I want my mommy," the girl cried.

"We'll bring you to your mommy tomorrow, all right?" Alexander said.

"That's right," Cuan said. "For now, we're going to take you away from all the scary monsters here."

She blinked at him. "You'll keep me safe?"

"I'm going to take you to a big magic house that no monsters can ever get inside," Cuan said patiently.

The girl nodded, taking his hand, and stood up.

Cuan turned to me. "You be safe, OK?" he said, giving me a kiss.

"I'll be fine," I said. "Just leave this to me. You be careful. I'll see you afterward. As soon as I'm out of here, I'll send you a text." Cuan's eyes lingered on mine, filled with worry. "I'll be fine," I said again. "This is me, after all." I smirked. "They'll never even know I was here."

Cuan nodded, placing a hand on my cheek. He lingered for just a moment, and then he scooped the girl up in his arms and sprinted in the direction of the car.

Alexander watched them leave, then turned to me. "You go. Let me work. This guy has seconds to live if I don't start." He turned his attention back to the man, muttering again in rapid Latin. Just before I turned to go, I thought I saw a faint white glow from beneath his palms.

I hurried back to the door leading to the center of the structure. Azrael whipped past behind me, dodging a lunge from Belphegor. Off in the distance, I heard the echoing of an engine starting and a vehicle peeling out.

I couldn't let myself be consumed with worry for Cuan's safety, or for Azrael's battle, or Alexander and the driver he was trying to save. I knew that elsewhere, the others were likely also still locked in combat with ogres and dirty cops. They were all doing their part. I had to do mine. I breathed in, and breathed out, focusing only on the door in front of me. It was made of heavy, solid metal. But to me, it was just a bank of fog.

I stepped through.

The room beyond was round and dimly lit, probably about thirty feet across. This, now, was definitely the center of the complex. A large tank in the center of the room held a yellow-green liquid that I recognized as the fluid being pumped throughout the facility. This was clearly the central reservoir into which I had to introduce the antidote. Much of the room was obstructed by machines and pipes, but I could hear Mayor Grafton speaking with someone in quiet, intense tones. I could see something flashing on a large monitor at the opposite end of the room and estimated that was where they were.

"How long until this process is finished?" Mayor Grafton was asking. "Things are getting out of hand. We don't have any time."

"The process requires different amounts of time for different people," a female voice responded. "There are a number of factors, such as the size, weight, and metabolism of the subjects, their physical fitness, the—"

"I don't care," the mayor interrupted. "Just make it go faster."

"I can't 'make it go faster'," came the response. "It doesn't work that way."

"Well, why did you invent a formula that's so slow-acting?"

"I didn't invent the formula; I just perfected it."

"Well, it's clearly not perfect if it takes so long!"

"Tell that to whoever you got it from in the first place!"

While they continued arguing with one another, I began looking around the room. There was a large chamber with a frightening-looking ogre suspended in it, which I suspected was a primary test subject. But that wasn't what needed my attention. Somewhere around the large central reservoir would be a modular interface into which I could connect the vials Lester had entrusted me with. He had pointed it out to me on the schematic, but it was challenging to take what I had seen in a line-drawn blueprint and apply it to an actual constructed machine. Finally I saw what looked like the proper interface. There was a safety cover on a hinge which I flipped up, and there was a series of places to connect different external containers. They were all differently-sized, but the smallest looked right for the vials that Lester had given me. A small plate above them read 'inlet: formula adjustments'.

I crouched down in front of the terminal, opened up my pouch, and pulled out the first of the vials and glanced at their contents, a clear liquid that looked just a tiny bit purple in the light. The vial looked just like the ones used when drawing blood for a blood test. According to Lester, I just needed to press the vial into place, stopper and all, and the terminal would take care of the rest. I pushed the antidote into the machine and felt it lock into place, and watched as the contents began to slowly drain into the machine. Painfully slowly.

The mayor and the woman who I assumed was the head scientist continued to argue with one another over how long the transformation process would take.

"It's chaos out there," the mayor said. "I can't just sit around waiting."

"Well, you're going to have to," replied the scientist. "This isn't like the lab in the subway, when we had fewer subjects and could tailor the formula to each specific body. Here, we have to use one batch for everyone. It's an imperfect process."

"I thought you said you perfected the formula."

"The formula and the process are two different things," the scientist retorted.

Good. Keep arguing. As long as they were arguing, I knew they were distracted.

The first vial finished emptying. I snatched it out and replaced it with a second, which began to drain. Four doses would do it, Lester had said. Three to go.

This vial had only been in a few seconds before I heard a beeping from the direction of the giant monitor.

"What is it? What's happening?" the mayor demanded.

"According to this, the computer has detected a modification to the formula," the scientist said. "I don't understand how that's possible. It must be a malfunction in the sensor unit."

That's right, I thought; blame it on a malfunction. Please.

"How can someone change the formula?" the mayor asked.

"According to this, it's happening at the central reservoir, but that's right here. We're the only ones in here; it's not possible. It must be a mistake."

"How can the formula change in the reservoir?"

"I'm telling you, it's not possible," the scientist replied impatiently. "Someone would have to be here in the room, using one of the terminals directly connected to the vat itself. But there's nobody here; the door hasn't opened."

The second vial finished emptying. Quickly, I pulled it out and plugged in another. Two to go.

"Show me the terminals," the mayor said.

Fuck.

"Fine," the woman groaned in exasperation, and I heard the sound of metal dragging across the floor as she pushed her chair back and stood up.

Double fuck.

I looked over at the vial. It was still half-full. I couldn't pull it out now, but I also couldn't leave it unattended and risk it being removed by someone else. I crouched down and waited.

Don't see me, I silently begged.

"See? There's nothing here," came a voice near the vat.

"Is that the only terminal?" the mayor asked.

"No, there are four." The voices moved. "There's another here, see?"

Footsteps around the edge of the tank. A woman in a white lab coat with a tight red ponytail and dark-rimmed glasses came into view, followed closely by a man in a navy-blue suit with greying temples.

I froze.

"And there's another here—what the hell?" the scientist asked, looking at the vial emptying into the terminal.

"So someone *is* in here," the mayor said.

"That's not possible," the scientist said sharply, walking toward the machine as quickly as she could.

"I'm telling you, there has to be a person here," the mayor insisted. I didn't move. I didn't even dare breathe. At this close distance, I didn't dare do anything to draw attention to myself. But this wasn't good. If someone was searching for me, after all, then with enough effort they would notice me. The mayor's eyes fixed on the vial in the terminal. Then, they followed it down. They followed the line of the desk behind me, passing over me, but then focused on the vials in my apothecary's satchel. A moment later, his gaze settled on my face.

"Who the hell are you?" The mayor shouted.

The scientist started, turning to the mayor and then whipping back around. As she turned, I grabbed one of her legs and pulled. With a shout, she fell to the ground and I scrabbled away.

My mind raced as I tried to figure out what to do next. Going incorporeal would be an easy immediate answer, but it wouldn't solve the problem of getting the fourth vial of antidote into the reservoir. Besides, Az had warned me against shifting back and forth too often in a short span of time. Granted, that was before I had unsealed my Nephilim powers, but better safe than sorry.

Wait. Nephilim powers.

I had no idea what they were or how they worked. But there was one thing I knew I could do. I opened my palm, and a plume of white flame winked to life in my hand.

"Stay back," I warned, as the mayor gaped at my opened palm. He backpedaled away from me as I advanced on him.

I had to be careful with the angelfire. While I implicitly understood that it only consumed if I willed it to consume, any carelessness on my part could damage the plant before the antidote was administered, or even set the entire structure ablaze. Furthermore, maintaining the flame—especially without allowing it to consume an outside fuel source—required a steady supply of energy and concentration on my part. A little ball of fire was all I wanted to risk at this point. Hopefully its shock and surprise value would be enough to bluff my way through.

The mayor continued to step backward.

"Who... who are you people?" he gaped.

"We've come for you," I said menacingly.

"No," the mayor gasped. "I did this all for my daughter, don't you see? It's the only way to keep her safe."

"You're out of your mind," I said.

"Nobody's going to stop me," the mayor cried. He backed up to the large tank with the massive ogre in suspended animation. He turned around, grabbing a medical cart full of various supplies that sat in front of the tank, and tried to half-roll, half-throw it at me. It skittered a few feet across the floor before toppling, sending empty vials and wicked-looking medical syringes everywhere. Then he reached over and pounded his fist on a big red button on the tank behind the cart. The entire bottom of the tank opened like some kind of grate, and the liquid in the vat drained so quickly it almost seemed to plummet out the bottom. A moment later the glass of the vat lifted vertically, and the creature inside stirred.

I let the angelfire wink out of existence and took a hesitant step back.

"There! Kill!" The mayor ordered in a frantic voice, throwing his hands in my direction.

The ogre immediately leapt out of the vat into the room and charged. I dove aside, letting the world fade out of solidity as I did so. The creature rushed right through me, and past me. On the other side of me was the female scientist in her lab coat, pulling herself up off the floor. She looked up, her expression a combination of rage and fear as the ogre bore down on her.

"No, not me, you stupid—"

Her shout was cut off as the ogre's massive fist slammed into her stomach, sending her flying across the room. There was a sickening crack as she hit a computer terminal, and she slumped to the ground, unconscious. At least, I hoped she was only unconscious. I didn't have the space to worry about a morally bankrupt scientist, however: there was the more immediate issue of a rampaging ogre to address.

I couldn't flee now. Not only had I not finished administering the antidote, but I also couldn't risk leaving the lab with that creature at large; if it damaged the reservoir then everything would be for naught.

I looked around for an idea, and then I saw it: amidst all the contents of the medical cart now strewn upon the floor was a large, old-style medical syringe. An idea formed in the back of my mind. I wasn't sure if it would work, but I had to try.

"Turn around, you useless beast!" The mayor cried. The lumbering ogre looked around, confused.

I let the world solidify back into place and lunged for the

syringe. As I did so, however, I felt a lurch at my neck, and then a snap as my leather satchel's strap broke and I heard it fall to the ground. Confused, I turned around as I grabbed the syringe in my fist and looked behind me.

I had been reckless in my haste: when I transitioned back from incorporeality, my body had been free of any material obstacles, but the leather pouch straps had been encircling a leg of a nearby desk. When I had lunged, the pouch caught on the leg and broke. I hurriedly snatched the pouch as the ogre stomped past in confusion. Thankfully, the vials of antidote had been secured to the sides in little leather loops, and all three unused doses were still intact.

"No, you idiot!" the mayor screamed again as the ogre tried in vain to figure out what he was indicating. "There! On the floor, by the desk!"

I jabbed the syringe through the rubber stopper of one of the vials and drew out a full dose of antidote. I didn't know the exact levels I needed to stop an ogre, and I was likely pulling out too much, but then again, I couldn't afford to take too little, nor could I worry about precision. The ogre stopped in front of me and looked down, its eyes finally focusing on me. At the same moment, I jammed the needle into its leg and squeezed out the entire contents into its body.

The ogre roared, kicking at me, but I ducked aside. It lost its balance and fell to the ground, convulsing and shaking.

"What? No! No!!" The mayor cried, rushing to the ogre and kneeling beside it, shaking its body roughly. "Move, you idiot! Fight!"

I hurried out of the way and pulled myself to my feet. The mayor was paying me no heed now; he was completely consumed with the ogre in front of him.

"Fight, damn you!" he cried, standing and giving the ogre a swift, cruel kick. Then he crouched down and started beating it with his fists.

"What the fuck is wrong with you?" I asked in disgust.

The mayor stopped and turned toward me, eyes focusing back on me.

"You," he growled. "You're going to ruin everything!"

"Ruin what?" I asked, "your psycho plan to weaponize the people of the city?"

"It was perfect," the mayor declared. "I was using people nobody cared about anyway; the homeless, the druggies, all the people who posed a danger to law and order."

"What law and order?" I challenged. "The corrupt police and the even more corrupt government?"

"Shut up!" The mayor roared. "Those people were a danger to the children. To *my* child."

"Even if that were true—which I seriously doubt," I said, "how do you justify this stadium full of displaced citizens, all being subjected to this sick experiment? And how did you get an architect to agree to design it anyway? What kind of urban planning project is this? It makes about as much sense as putting a high school over the Hellmouth."

"The what?" The mayor asked in frustration. Then he shook his head. "No matter. There are those that realized that this project is for the greater good," the mayor said. "The people contained here don't matter, anyway. Their beliefs are a sickness on this country. This precinct overwhelmingly voted against me in the election. We don't need people like that in this city."

"Oh, so you're just going to eliminate all your political opponents? I've heard of vote tampering, but this is a sick extreme."

"I would never tamper with the vote," the mayor said. "People are free to vote. It's just better if they're voting for the right things."

"Like a mutant militia?" I challenged.

"It's to fight crime! Crime was rampant here when I came into office!"

"Well then, why didn't you just pull a Mike Haggar and take to the streets armed with your fists and oversized overalls?" I asked. "If it's good enough for Metro City, it should be good enough for you."

"Where the hell is Metro City?"

"Sorry; that reference must be a little outside your sphere of expertise," I said. "But then, considering the fuck-up job you've done while in office, I assume that sphere is pretty damn small."

"You think you know better?" Mayor Grafton challenged. "What do you know about governing a city?"

"Well I've played a lot of *SimCity*," I said. "And, not to brag, but my cities have almost no crime and operate on a surplus, even with disasters on, and I've beaten every scenario. And by the way, none of the solutions involved creating an army of mutant ogres to release on the populous."

"Excuse me; Sim-what?"

"Really?" I asked. "Ok, see? This is what I mean. You're clearly out of touch with the people. No wonder you treat them like cattle."

"They ARE cattle," the Mayor retorted. "They believe what I tell them to believe."

"For Christ's sake," I shook my head. "What, did you keep your moral compass next to an industrial magnet or something? Seriously, Montgomery Burns runs a less corrupt organization than you."

"Who the fuck is that?" The mayor asked in exasperation.

"Come on, I'm tossing you softballs here," I said. "Is the mayor's office located under a rock? This is why you can't connect with the constituency."

"The people love me!" The mayor retorted. "I'm the most popular mayor the city has ever had!"

"I've just recovered from amnesia, and even I know that's wildly untrue."

"That's it," the mayor growled. "I don't know what you're trying to do here, but it ends now."

"Oh, it's already over," I grinned. "I was just keeping you busy talking while the last of the antidote circulated through the system."

The mayor gave a start, then looked past me at the system console. An empty glass vial stood in the machine, the fourth dose of antidote having finished dispersing into the reservoir.

"I swapped it in while you were distracted watching the ogre convulse," I said. "Don't be too hard on yourself, though— I have a tendency to go unnoticed."

"You smug little fuck," the mayor growled, then rushed at me. He swung at me, but I had already let the world slide out of solidity, and he passed right through me and fell to the ground.

"Sorry, but I'm not feeling all there at the moment," I said. The mayor looked over his shoulder at me in shock, then suddenly spied the empty syringe on the floor where the ogre, whose skin was already turning back to normal, had fallen after I'd injected it. Or, her, I should say, as the ogre now looked more like an adult woman.

The mayor whirled around, looking at the scattered contents of the overturned cart that were now strewn across the floor. He snatched a vial of green liquid and held it up triumphantly.

"There are still vials of the formula left," the mayor growled. "I'll make you pay; just you wait."

"Yeah, you seem to be having some trouble grasping the idea that you just passed right through me," I said. "I think you'll have a hard time doing much of anything."

They mayor wasn't listening. Instead, he shoved the needle into the vial, drawing out a syringe full of the green liquid.

"We'll see how smug you are once I transform into your worst nightmare," the mayor sneered.

"I really don't think it's safe to inject that directly—" I started, but the mayor had already jammed the needle into his own leg, squeezing out the entirety of its contents into his bloodstream.

Almost instantaneously, he fell to the ground, convulsing slightly, then was still. The now-empty vial clattered to the ground next to him. As it rolled toward me, I saw a little golden cross emblazoned on the front.

It hadn't been the transformation formula that the mayor had injected into his bloodstream. It was Jacob's aconitine suspension. At that dose, the mayor's death had been cold and swift.

Monitors all over the complex were already beginning to flash warning screens indicating that the intake formula had been altered. Now it was just a matter of hoping that Lester's antidote would do its job. That, and making sure that the other Hunters and Order of Light members got to safety. And helping the civilians who were trapped in the vats. OK, so there was a lot left to do. But the first step was for me to get out of that room. I turned to the door I'd come in from, and, just as I had done before, stepped through.

XIX

HENOSIS

THE ROOM outside the central lab was largely as I'd left it. Alexander was still bent over the driver, who was breathing smoothly but was now either asleep or unconscious. Not far away, Azrael and Belphegor remained locked in combat, trading blows and parrying one another's strikes while flying around the room.

"It's done," I said as the room solidified around me.

"Cole!" Alexander's voice was filled with relief. "You administered the antidote?"

"Yeah," I said.

"And the mayor?"

"Poisoned himself," I said.

"Ugh," Alexander replied. "I hate to hear that anybody died, but... I'm less sorry to hear that than I probably would normally be."

"Is the driver OK?" I asked.

"Yeah," Alexander said. "But Azrael and the demon had their little scuffle come this way, and the driver fainted when he saw them. But not before he gave me this." Alexander held up another set of keys. "Apparently there's a bus in the parking lot that's also an official vehicle. If we can get to it, we can drive it out of here. We'll have to let the others know we're finished here; then we can leave."

"Are we finished, though?" I asked. "Azrael and the demon are still going at it, but even more importantly, there are about to be countless confused people who need to be released from those vats and given help."

"Isn't that what Lester will handle?" Alexander asked. "He said he'd sweep through for cleanup. What does that mean?"

"I haven't a blessed clue," I said. "I don't know how he does what he does, but there's no denying he's very good at it."

"Well, we should probably clear out so he can get started, then," Alexander said. "I don't think there's much we can do to help Az. He seems to be enjoying himself, anyway."

Alexander had a point there. I could only catch brief glimpses of them as their fight raged across the room, but whenever he stopped moving long enough for me to make out his expression, Azrael was wearing an intense grin. His fight with the demon wasn't exactly a friendly one, but it seemed that it was welcome nonetheless. I noted, however, that while the angel may have been enthusiastic, he was not reckless: in fact, he was carefully controlling the flow of battle to keep the demon away from any of the machinery or pipes that were now pumping the antidote to the edges of the stadium.

"How are we going to get the driver out of here?" I asked. "If we wake him up now, won't he freak out and maybe faint again as soon as he sees Az and the demon?"

I have an idea," Alexander said. "Hand me what's left of that satchel."

I handed him the broken satchel, which I'd been carrying in my hand. Alexander carefully removed the remaining vial and slipped it into his shirt pocket, then tore the satchel into leather strips and tied them around the driver's head like a blindfold. Then, gently, he nudged him awake.

"Hunh?" the driver murmured.

"Hey," Alexander said gently. "We're gonna get out of here. You feeling OK?"

"Unh," the driver grunted. "Dark."

"I've put a blindfold on you; just until we're out of this room," he said. "The mayor tried to shoot you, remember? We're gonna make it look like we're holding you captive until we get out of here, just so nobody tries to do you in," he said, lying effortlessly. His excuse made little to no sense, but the driver nodded anyway. "Your hands are free," Alexander added, "so you can remove it whenever you want, but you'll be safest if you don't do so until I tell you you're out of the room."

"OK," the driver said. "Just... one more... minute..." His head lolled back forward.

Alexander sighed. "Dammit, this is going to be a few minutes," he said looking toward the door. "I want to get out of here and make sure everyone's safe. D'you think Cuan got out OK?"

"I'm sure he did," I said, trying to reassure myself with my own words. "I feel like, if he didn't, I'd know, somehow. Still, I wish we had cell reception."

"And that poor girl," Alexander shook his head. "She must have been terrified."

"And her dad's gone now," I added. "Though she's probably better off."

"He was terrible to her," Alexander said. "Before the election, nobody even knew she existed. Can you imagine, being hidden away for what, five, six years? And then once he was in office, he just leveraged her like some political tool."

"I dunno," I mused. "He seemed completely convinced that he was doing everything for her sake. It was as though he thought she wanted all this."

"Sure didn't look like it from where I was standing,"

Alexander said. "She was terrified, screaming for her mother to take her out of there."

"I think I remember seeing the mother on the news once," I recalled. "She didn't seem like a terribly pleasant woman, either."

"Yeah," Alexander said. "Even after all this time, she still swears up and down that she's never had a kid. Maybe the girl'd be better off with social services or something."

"Really?" I asked. "You'd want to stick her in state care in *this* city?"

"Fair enough," Alexander said as the driver began to stir once more. "Well, hopefully we can get her somewhere safe so she can have some semblance of a normal life."

Azrael darted past in the air near us, Belphegor in pursuit. Azrael suddenly whipped around in midair, slashing at Belphegor with his scythe. The demon shrieked as the blade found his arm, slashing deeply.

"Aha! A palpable hit!" Azrael declared with satisfaction as the demon roared.

"Thank you, Osric," I said. "Now do you mind taking your skirmish elsewhere before you freak out this poor driver again?"

The combatants paid us no mind, still wholly engrossed in their contest.

"God, but they're single-minded," Alexander remarked. "And that's the demon that came up with this whole thing? It's unbelievable. He doesn't seem very big-picture."

"Well, if I've learned anything from all this, it's never to underestimate someone based on first impressions," I said.

"Still, what a mess," Alexander continued. "All because a botched summoning gave a demon the opportunity to run rampant. This is why you don't mess with demons. I'm surprised at how quickly he must have been able to prey upon the mayor's fear for his child's well-being and convince him to put all this into action."

"All *too* quickly," I realized. "Belphegor was summoned the day I lost my memory, right? But... the first ogres showed up only a day or so later."

"The transformation process doesn't take long," Alexander said. "Look at how quickly Marcus went all blue."

"But that was with infrastructure and stuff already in place," I noted. "No, the timing is all wrong. Not only did the mayor have to be convinced, but also the police force, the scientists, and everyone else involved. They may have been able to throw this slapdash lab together in the stadium quickly, but they'd have already had to have the tanks and technology in place. Plus, this is their *third* lab—that we know of. The shelters and rehab programs, the relocation of the homeless from the abandoned subway, these were all well underway by the time that demon was summoned. The impetus for this came from somewhere else."

"Do you think the mayor, or someone else in the city, came up with this on their own, then?" Alexander asked.

"They must have, but they'd have to have some connection to the supernatural: Lester said the transformation had a magical, spiritual component, right? Plus, the ogres were so hell-bent on getting the Key of Solomon, there has to be a demonic component somewhere. That last part could have been Belphegor's influence, but..."

"But what if it wasn't?" Alexander nodded. "It would make sense if there were someone else involved. Dennis Grafton was a complete unknown before he swooped in and took the election. If someone else had appeared around the same time, they could have—"

"Holy shit," I interjected as an icy chill of realization ran down my spine. "The daughter."

"What?" Alexander asked.

"She appeared out of nowhere after the election. Nobody had ever heard of her, even the political opponents who'd been digging up dirt in the final run up to the vote. The girl's supposed mother swears up and down she never had a kid. And the mayor is utterly convinced that everything he's doing is for her sake. I mean, does anybody even know her name?"

Alexander gaped at me. "Holy fucking hell," he said.

A second chill ran through me, this one a bolt of horror. "And she's with Cuan."

"Oh my God," Alexander said. "We gotta get out of here." He turned to the driver and started shaking him urgently. "Wake up, goddammit!" he cried.

"Uhhh, what..?" the driver mumbled.

"Come on," I said. "We need to—" I stopped short as a vision, so vivid that I might as well have been seeing it with my own eyes, appeared in my mind.

Cuan, in werewolf form, tumbled up a large flight of stairs in the estate house. Not down; *up*. His body collided with the wall at a turn in the stairs and slumped to the ground. At the base of the stairs, a wild, wiry creature with gray skin, about five feet in height and wearing the tattered remains of a pink party dress, scrabbled forward. It had no discernable features on its head except for a wide, frothing mouth filled with razor-sharp teeth. Where it once had sported human limbs, it now sported massive bone spikes; one of the hind limbs was punctured through the remains of a child's white shoe.

Something about it looked wrong—more wrong, I mean, than the obvious fact that it was a shambling nightmare—and I realized that it was because it had six limbs instead of four: another pair of spiked appendages, identical to the ones fore and aft, were sticking out from the middle of its abdomen, piercing either side of the ruined dress. The creature switched between running on two legs, four, and three, making its movements erratic and difficult to predict. It rushed up the stairs with alarming speed, leaving little punctures in the staircase as it moved. Just before it reached Cuan, he leapt up, springing off of the wall. He tried to pass over the creature's head, but one of its limbs smacked him sideways, sending him crashing into the top of the staircase.

"Cole!" Azrael called, his scythe a blur as he and Belphegor darted around the room, still locked in combat. "Cuan is—"

"I know," I replied anxiously. "I can see him."

"Wait, you can see him?" Alexander asked in surprise.

"Ah, of course you can," Azrael said, the corner of his lip curving upward into a satisfied smirk. "Because you two are soulforged."

"Soulforged?" Alexander asked as Azrael slashed out at Belphegor and the demon parried backwards.

"It's a kind of soulbond forged not from ceremony, but by desire and sheer force of will, often catalyzed by an intense experience." Az explained as he continued to fight. "My guess is that it was the night with the wolf's-bane and the soul prison. But however it formed, like every such bond, it's unbreakable by any outside force. And Cole has angelic blood, so he can essentially act as a guardian angel. Lucky Cuan now has two."

Az went on, the chatter with Alexander seemingly helping his focus, but I wasn't listening. I was too preoccupied with the image in my mind.

Cuan was in the upstairs hallway, dodging the monster's stabs, trying to land a blow. He ducked under a thrust and swung his leg around, but another of the monster's limbs connected with him sideways, sending him crashing through a door in the hallway, tearing off one of its hinges as it flew open. Cuan did a somersault onto what looked like a giant bed, catapulting himself, spinning in the air like a torpedo, whirling through an opening in the creature's assault and landing behind it. He pivoted, but the creature shifted weight onto a different pair of limbs and swung out with its hind leg, catching

Cuan's furry ankle and sending him to the ground. Cuan rolled out of the way of a downward stab and started scrabbling backwards as the creature jabbed its legs into the walls and rushed towards him, stabbing downward again and again with its two free limbs, keeping Cuan from having an opening. The creature was almost on top of Cuan when one of the monster's legs slammed through another door instead of into the wall, breaking another hinge and causing it to stumble slightly—only slightly—buying Cuan a foot or so. It was only a split second, however, not even enough time for Cuan to get back to his feet. Cuan was fast but the monster was faster, and Cuan was about to run out of hallway. Desperation and confusion overcame me. What could I do? Why could I see this, if it was so far away? If I could do nothing?

Or... could I?

The image was so clear, so vivid in my mind, that I felt like it was happening in front of my face. Was this how Azrael always knew when we were in trouble? Is this how he was always right there, a guardian angel swooping in when danger reared its head?

And at that moment, it all made sense. My powers. How I could pass through solid objects. How easily I was able to go unnoticed by everyone but Cuan, because I was the one person who was always on his mind. How Cuan had felt my presence, like a white flame inside his soul, sustaining him when he had been poisoned by Levi and I was locked away in a box. All my powers, my being, my angelic side, my human side, focused in that moment to a single intent: no amount of distance, no obstacles, would keep me from protecting the person I loved.

"He's in danger!" Azrael shouted. "I can't—" he stopped to dodge as Belphegor's fist stabbed right into the space where his head had been.

"That's fine," I said, voice echoing with newfound confidence. "I can."

In my mind, I saw the image of the demon in the pink party dress bearing down on Cuan, raising a spike to deliver a brutal decisive blow. The image was clear, immediate.

I simply stepped in.

Cuan barked in surprise as I suddenly appeared in front of him, catching the demon's thrust in my fist. My hand was wreathed in furious white flame, just like the edges of my vision.

"Stop harassing my boyfriend," I demanded of the creature as it recoiled in alarm. "How'd you like a little taste of heaven?" And then I rammed my free fist into its stupid toothy mouth.

The creature flew down the corridor, white sparks streaming behind it, and crashed into the wall at the other end of the hallway. I'd thought for sure it'd smash right through, but the house was a sturdy one, and it only left a shallow dent in the wood as it hit it and slid to the ground. It lurched unnaturally, limbs bending over its head as it pulled itself back into standing on its hindmost four limbs, giving its head an angry shake.

"See," I said, "this is why little girls shouldn't play with sharp things. It's dangerous."

The creature roared at me and charged, barreling down the hallway. Cuan was already on his feet, throwing open the door to the library at the end of the hallway and darting inside. Good. What I was planning only worked if there was nobody behind me.

The creature lunged, both forearms fully extended, but just as it reached me, I dropped through the floor. I reached in front of me until I felt a support beam, then imagined it as a horizontal bar, letting its slightly more substantial presence direct the momentum of my insubstantial body as I swung up and around like a gymnast. As soon as I was back in the hallway, I released the bar and let the mass return to my body, delivering a powerful kick to the back of the surprised creature's head, sending it stumbling forward into the library. As soon as its head passed through the door, Cuan landed a powerful kick from just inside the door frame, and the monster staggered away. I'd hoped it would slip on the books and pages strewn across the floor, but its spiked legs just stabbed right through them to the hardwood, and so it kept its footing.

"Come on now," I said as I walked through the door to the library. "It's all fun and games until someone loses an eye. But then again, looks like you've already lost yours."

The creature hissed furiously, wide mouth of teeth spitting angrily on its otherwise featureless gray head.

"So, incorporeality is your game, is it?" the creature croaked. "I know how to handle that." Its spikes started to glow an ominous black.

"Oh, it speaks!" I said. "Well, good; maybe you'll listen to reason. That's a nice dress you have, little one, but I generally prefer it when trick-or-treaters stay *outside* the house. How about you take a piece of candy and be on your way?"

"Do not mock me!" the beast roared, rushing recklessly at me. Cuan and I both jumped out of the way to either side, wary of the new black sheen on its spikes. The creature skidded to a halt and then flipped its body completely over, rounding on us, its head twisting back to face us in a sickening full turn. "You have no idea who I am," the creature snarled.

"Well, enlighten us," I said. "What's your name?"

"You shall not know my name," the creature snarled. "You may call me Vengeance."

"That's a stupid name," I said. "I'm going to call you... Susan."

"My name is not Susan," Susan hissed.

"Well, it is now," I said. "So, Susan, who are you vengeancing today?"

The demon sneered, baring its maw of pointy teeth. "This city once claimed someone important to me," it said. "The so-called holy organization known as the Order of Light used forbidden texts to summon her. I never saw her again, but I have come to learn that she was violated and murdered by this same Order. Normally if a demon is slain they merely are banished to the underworld. That is not what transpired. After being thoroughly victimized, she was *obliterated*. If that is what humanity decrees as good and right, then humanity should not exist at all."

"I heard about that," I said. "That was unforgiveable."

"So if you agree, why stand in the way of Vengeance?" the creature asked.

"Because dismantling a system of oppression is not the same as murdering every member of an oppressive group," I said. "Humanity is culpable for a lot of terrible things, but indiscriminately culling everyone in response is just... wicked."

"I am a demon," the creature hissed. "What do I care of wickedness?"

Well, she got me there.

"I waited," she continued. "I waited years until someone was desperate enough to call on me. A mayor wanting election, wanting to secure power, but lacking direction, looking for something to fight for. In the right place at the right time, he swore to give everything to win, to take one more step toward office. And so, called by him, I came, presenting myself as his little daughter, all the while planting seeds in his mind. A campaign to secure the city. An army to secure the state. And from there, a sweep until the entire nation was his. What need would there be for elections when he had fear and power on his side?"

So that was the plan. I had, until then, still felt a tiny bit of remorse that the mayor had injected aconitine into his blood and killed himself. That remorse was gone now.

"I am what humans made me," the demon continued. "They want evil demons to pin their sins on? Then I shall repay those sins with justice. I collected the Key of Solomon that was used to summon her and I destroyed it to keep it from being used against me. And now I will start with this city that took her from me, and spread a new humanity across the land, one that reflects its inner nature of murder and indiscriminate rampage, until it consumes itself and the world is purged."

"Yeah, as much as I agree with some parts of your assessment, I'm not going to let that happen."

"And why not?" the demon demanded. "What is worth saving?"

"Him, for one," I said, pointing to Cuan beside me. "The love of my life is here, and I won't let him come to harm."

"So your love gets to live on and mine does not?" the demon hissed. "No. Unacceptable. You will all suffer and perish!"

With a roar, she darted at me, spiked appendages shining black, moving so suddenly and so quickly that I had no time to react.

But Cuan did. In a gray flash, he intercepted the demon, kicking her in the side, taking her by surprise and knocking her into a wall of books. The demon caught itself on the shelving, then skittered partway up the wall and lunged back toward Cuan.

This time I was ready. Feeling the angelfire well up within me, I threw my hands out as Cuan dodged under the demon's assault, and a gout of white flame caught the creature, wreathing it in fire as it crashed into the opposite wall, sending books everywhere. The fire did not consume the shelving or the books, but the creature writhed in agony, convulsing on the ground. Finally, it struggled to its pointed feet.

"I will not allow you to harm more people," I declared. "I will not let you leave here."

"Ah," the demon grinned, "but then what? You may be able to detain me, but you cannot banish me with mere angelfire. So, are you just going to battle with me until one of us collapses from exhaustion?" The wicked smile widened. "Very well, then. Face me with all you have!"

The creature lunged at me again and I dodged out of the way, then it turned and leapt at Cuan. I dashed forward again, hands wreathed in flame, but this time the creature was prepared, and one of its limbs swiped out at me. I saw it coming and quickly faded, but when the side of the black-glowing spike met my body, it did not pass through.

Instead, it hit my stomach like a baseball bat.

I felt the wind knock out of me, and Cuan barked in alarm as my body rocketed across the room, flying unhindered through one of the bookshelves. In shock I shifted back into solidity, bracing myself on the ground. I was in a square, white room, skidding to a halt beside a large, white crystal in the center of the floor.

This room. The white room. The room that Alexander's parents had prepared for him.

The crystal on the floor was humming gently in recognition. It knew me, for Alexander had arranged for it to acknowledge me as a resident of the estate. That was why I was able to step to Cuan's side even within the wards of the house, I realized. But there was another hum, a softer, lighter hum. It was coming from the wall opposite the entrance, where a set of shelves held all the different weapons and boons, sealed in white boxes until they were ready to be opened.

One of those boxes was now glowing a soft white. I snatched it down and looked at it. It was maybe three feet long. On the cover, in a lightly embossed script, were three words:

"For the Soulbound."

I lifted the lid, and it opened easily. Inside, in a red velvet casing, were a pair of matching rings, one silver, one gold, each inlaid with diamonds. Most of the box, however, was occupied by a glittering sword, its blade so polished it was almost white. Along the blade were a series of engraved characters that I recognized as the Tongue of Souls, letters that were, to me, now as readable as if they were English:

"Shine with the fire of your conjoined souls."

I gripped the hilt of the sword and felt a surge roll through me. It was more than just energy or power. It was something divine. There was a familiarity to it, the same as I'd felt when I once touched Prominence.

This, too, was a holy weapon. And it was judging our worth.

Our worth: not just mine, but Cuan's, also. I knew that there in the adjoining chamber, even as he was fending off the demon, he was feeling the same surge that I was.

It was just for an instant, and it was over. But the sword accepted our bond, and suddenly it was mine to wield. And in that moment, I knew its name.

"Henosis," I whispered, and the blade, in response to my utterance, erupted in white flame. Energy surged through me, and the plumes of white flame erupted from my back once again, spreading like wings.

I could hear the demon in the room beyond. "It seems you are left alone, now, little dog," it gloated. "There is no one left to save you."

"Think again," I shouted, kicking the broken bookshelf door open. The demon had had its back to me but now it whirled around in shock, with a furious roar. "Mind if I cut in?" I said, slashing out with the fiery blade. The demon leapt backward, dodging the strike, but the moment my swing finished the blade vanished in a pool of white light, reappearing in Cuan's hand at the demon's back. With one giant lunge, he thrust the blade forward, running the creature through.

It shrieked and screamed as its body erupted into white flame. Cuan leapt aside as the demon collapsed to the ground, heaving, blade still piercing its torso. Slowly, starting from the tips of its wicked spikes, it began to burn away, body evaporating into the air like ash on the wind.

"The Nephilim always were full of surprises," the creature coughed. "So now I am banished back to my realm, alone, burdened by the knowledge that nothing remains of the one I love. Nothing but emptiness and regret."

"Not nothing," I said. "Did you know she bore a child?"

The creature paused, mouth agape.

"A child?" it asked.

"That's right," I said. "A child that would have died, had it not been saved by a human who defied the order to kill. A child raised by humans who sought to help those who were not fortunate, to aid those who were oppressed. A child who now lives to learn from the mistakes of the past, both his and others', and who seeks to help the humanity that you so desperately wish to destroy."

The demon fell silent for a moment. Its limbs had completely burned away, and now its torso began as well. "A child," it mused. "A child that lives. I suppose that is some consolation. It may sound odd for me to say, but for that knowledge you have a measure of my gratitude."

"I would be more receptive to that had you not thrown the city into chaos and tried to kill everyone I hold dear," I responded.

"Fair enough," the demon said. "But the sentiment remains nonetheless. And it is further consolation that, while I get to leave this place, you must remain here among the humans."

"Eh," I shrugged, with an affectionate look at Cuan. "They're not all bad."

"Heh. Your angelic heritage has not refined your taste."

"Says the demon in the pink party dress," I smirked. "Bye, Susan."

The corner of the demon's maw curled up into what looked like an expression of amusement before its face finally disintegrated, and the last of its body burned away. Henosis clattered to the ground, the fire around it winking out. I knelt down and picked it up, then, with a thought, willed it vanish into a flash of white light, remaining alongside our souls for Cuan or me to summon when needed.

Cuan. He was leaning against the bookshelves for support, out of breath, ears drooping slightly, nostrils flaring. He finally managed to take a full breath, and, as he slowly released it, his body was suffused with light until he was once again his human self, mussed hair and pale skin, tight vest and compression shorts tightening back around his leaner frame.

"You okay?" I asked, walking to him.

"I am now that you're here," he said, finally catching his breath. "But... *how* are you here?"

I smiled at him. "It's a new application of my powers." I said, leaning toward him. "You're my soulmate. I'll always, *always* be here for you." I kissed him. Deeply, passionately, with all the love and affection of my being, and he kissed me back with all of his. His arms wrapped around me, running up my neck, through my hair, as his musky scent filled my nostrils.

Then, a second later, my phone leapt to life, ejaculating a string of insistent notifications as it flooded with messages, finally catching up from its time spent in the dead zone of the stadium.

There were messages from Bianca and Julia and Cedric and Bran, all explaining that they'd gotten out of the stadium and were safe, and that they knew that the antidote had been administered. There was a message from Lester, that he was moving in for cleanup. He didn't explain how, but he said that he and his lab staff—he had staff?—were stepping in to help people as they were coming out of the transformation vats. Apparently the fire department and paramedics were involved too, somehow, but Lester described this as a good thing. Oh, and also a shit ton of media presence, which was going to make for an interesting few weeks. There was a message that pinged in while I was catching up on the message backlog, from Az, saying that he'd managed to banish the demon he was fighting and could sense that we had done the same. It was congratulatory, but also stated that he needed to return to his hotel room to rest.

Then there was a message from a number that wasn't in my contact list. It read simply, "Reached the estate. Got inside. Feel safe. Thanks."

Peter.

"Peter!" I cried in alarm. "Cuan, what happened to Marcus and Peter? Are they Okay?"

"They're fine," Cuan said. "When I got here, Marcus was taking Peter to another building, a guesthouse or a groundskeeper's shack or something, on the other end of the estate to get him situated there for the night. That was well before Strawberry Shortcake went all Silent Hill. They probably don't even know anything happened."

"Well, Marcus is going to be pretty miffed," I said, looking into the hallway with its busted doors and puncture marks all down the hall. "He'd been spending the day getting the place cleaned up."

At that moment, we heard the front door burst open, and Alexander's voice came shouting up from below.

"Cole! Cuan!"

"We're up here," I called. "Everything's fine."

"Oh, holy shit," came Alexander's voice, slightly louder now as he ascended the stairs.

"What the actual fuck?" came Marcus's voice from behind him. "I spent hours cleaning this place!"

Alexander appeared at the top of the stairs, Candela drawn and at the ready. He looked up and down the hallway in horror.

"What happened to my house?" Alexander asked.

"A very stabby demon happened," I said.

"She's gone now," Cuan added.

"Well thank fuck for that," Alexander sighed with relief. He turned to me. "That was some trick you pulled, stepping into nothingness like that."

"Well, looks like I'm half guardian angel, after all," I nodded.

"I'm guessing that's how you two managed to fight off a demon by yourselves?" Alexander asked.

"Well, with some help from your parents," I said, nodding toward the white room, where the open box still lay on the floor.

Cuan raised his hand and Henosis winked to life in his grip. "Apparently we're the beneficiaries of one of their keepsakes," he said as Alexander and Marcus stared wide-eyed at the shining blade.

"Well, they did say that that stuff was for more than just me," Alexander shrugged as Cuan opened his palm and Henosis evaporated back into light.

"Is Peter ok?" Cuan asked.

"Yeah," Marcus said; "he's fine. Cute guy, too," he added before Alexander elbowed him in the ribs. "Anyway," he added, "he's holed up in the other building at the other end of the estate. Probably barricaded in."

"Is he gonna be OK by himself?" I asked. "He was pretty shaken up."

"He's fine," Marcus said. "I gave him a dose of NyQuil that I picked up at the market down the street. The guy was exhausted; he was fast asleep by the time he hit the sheets."

"Marcus, why did you buy NyQuil?" Alexander asked, face flashing with suspicion.

"Hey, believe in me a little bit, will ya?" Marcus protested. "When you said you were sending someone this way, I figured he'd be a wreck by the time he got here. I wanted to get something to calm him, and that was the most innocuous thing I could think of. Would you rather I bought a case of beer?"

"No, I would not rather you bought alcohol," Alexander allowed. "Fine. Good job, Marcus; I'm proud of you."

Marcus grinned.

"Speaking of people I expected to be here," I said, what about the driver?"

"The driver?" Cuan asked. "Is he OK?"

"I dropped the driver off at The Hunters' Home," Alexander explained. "Bran is going to take a statement with a voice recorder, just to help the driver organize all of his thoughts. Besides, The Hunters' Home has food and fresh linens and all of that. He'll be more comfortable there."

"We have all that stuff, too," Marcus said with a smug grin.

"Wait, what?" Alexander asked in surprise.

"I went out and got us some supplies," Marcus explained. "Nothing big, just food and fresh sheets, but I thought it'd be a help. That's how I knew there was a market on the corner when you said that Peter was coming. I made up the beds in two of the bedrooms here, too. That way, I can have one, and Alexander can—"

"You're sleeping with me," Alexander said, grabbing his arm as Marcus beamed. "But I'm exhausted," he noted, "So don't get any ideas—tonight. I just need to crash." He turned to Cuan and me. "You guys can take the other bed. You're probably too beat to go anywhere."

"I can barely stay standing," I nodded.

Marcus had also bought a set of toothbrushes, toothpaste, toilet paper, and shampoo and the like. I was too exhausted to shower, but I managed to stay conscious long enough to brush my teeth. The doors to the bedrooms had been damaged when the demon whipped down the hall and now they didn't close all the way, so we didn't bother undressing; Cuan and I just collapsed on top of the bed and fell asleep almost instantly in each other's arms.

XX

A NEW DAWN

I AWOKE to the sun dancing across my face, rousing me gently from my sleep. I had slept late—my phone said it was 11:24. I wasn't surprised, though: after the previous night, I could have slept for days.

"Good Morning, sunshine," came Cuan's voice next to mine. He was rolled onto his side, looking down at me with a warm smile. He reached up and ran a hand through my hair.

"Hey, you," I smiled back.

"You were amazing yesterday," he said affectionately. "You saved my life, you know."

"You've saved mine plenty of times," I noted.

"But you just... showed up out of nowhere, putting yourself between me and that thing."

"Just like you did the first time the ogres showed up," I grinned.

His smile widened. "That's because I love you. Even then. From the first time I laid eyes on you."

"That's so corny," I beamed.

"It's true," Cuan said. "At first sight, I knew you were special."

"And you're special, too," I said, putting a hand on his cheek. "You're amazing and strong and kind. And you see me. You've always seen me."

"You're worth noticing, Cole," he said softly. "Always remember that, even when the rest of the world looks straight past you." He bent down and kissed me softly on the lips.

"Now that's a nice way to wake up in the morning," I smiled when he released me.

"I can think of another nice way to wake up in the morning," he grinned, pressing himself slightly into my side.

"Wow, you're not wasting any time today," I said. "We just woke up."

"You just woke up, you mean," Cuan said. "I've been awake for an hour or so. I was just resting here, next to you..."

"...getting riled up, clearly," I smirked, feeling him pressing through the front of his compression pants against my thigh. "You're not usually this forward in the morning."

"Sorry," he said, adorable apologetic expression transitioning seamlessly into a lip bite that brought the dimple out in his cheek. "It's just... I spent a really long time in my wolf form yesterday."

"And you transitioned back and forth a lot, too," I said. "Way more than usual. That must have really taken it out of you. No wonder you slept so late."

"It's not just that," he said. "Remember how I described what it's like being in my wolf form? My sympathetic nervous system takes complete control. I'm all fight or flight. But afterward, there's kind of a rebound effect when my parasympathetic nervous system kicks back in. And fight or flight gives way to—"

"Feed and breed," I realized. "Oh, man. So after being in your wolf form for so ridiculously long yesterday..."

"Now I want it *bad*," Cuan said huskily, body squirming against me. "I've never been this horny in my life. And that includes when you fed me a mouthful of Az's cum." He looked at me uncertainly. "But only if you're okay with it, of course."

"Well, far be it from me to deny my boyfriend raucous sex," I said with a wry grin. "But that's probably not a good idea here." I pointed to the door, which still hung open on a hinge. "No privacy. And all things considered, Alexander might not appreciate it if we start vigorously fucking in his guest bedroom. He's pretty big about privacy and boundaries and the like. So how about we get out of here and go back to our apartment, and then you can fill me with enough cum to frost a cake."

Cuan paused. "Wait, what?"

"Sorry, too vivid of a metaphor?" I asked.

"No, that actually turned me on even more," Cuan said. "But... *'our'* apartment?"

"Yeah, why not?" I said. "I mean, you already have a key, and plus you're moving out of The Hunters' Home, right? So let's not call it 'my' place; I think it's 'our' place. I'm with you for the long haul, after all."

"Ok, now I *really* need to have sex with you." Cuan said.

"Then let's go," I said, pulling him into the hall. "We'll just say a quick goodbye to Alexander. Or, hell, I'll just text him when we're on our way. He'll understand. The last thing he'd want is for someone to walk by an open door in his house and see two people going at it like—"

At that moment, we walked past Alexander's room, the door of which also hung off its hinges. Alexander lay on his back on the bed, completely naked, tanned, muscular body on full display, the fine hairs on his body glinting in the light as his chest heaved. His thick erection stood straight up in the air, and he was stroking it furiously, precum shining on its tip and coating his strong fingers. His head appeared to be hanging over the edge of the bed, but his face was partially obscured by

Marcus's body. Marcus was standing at the bedside, muscular back to us, sweat glinting on his olive skin. His round, bare butt cheeks proudly proclaimed the names 'Alexander' and 'Cole' in elaborate tattooed script, though the words were somewhat hard to make out at the moment given the vigorousness with which Marcus was pumping his hips, apparently fucking Alexander's face.

"Or, perhaps he wouldn't think twice about it," I said.

Marcus turned around sharply, strands of saliva splashing off of his weighty erection as it popped out of Alexander's mouth. He was still a grower, and while the procedures performed on him had cost him a little in terms of his endowment, when erect the loss was minimal. He looked at us in mild surprise, pecs and abs still heaving on his chest, naked save for the quartz pendant that now hung from his neck.

Alexander, his view of us now unobstructed by Marcus's balls, rolled over quickly onto his stomach to cover his erection, the effect however ultimately being that he wound up showing off his round, meaty ass, which stood up from the bed like two large melons, beating out even Marcus's enhanced frame's in terms of size.

"Sorry; we thought you were still sleeping," Alexander said.

"Oh, *fuuuuck*," Cuan whined, staring at them. His compression pants were straining to contain his erection, and the material at his groin was now molded to a perfect outline of his cock and balls, even down to the throbbing vein on the side.

"We gotta get out of here," I said. "We need to have sex. Now."

"Gotcha," Alexander nodded, almost too vigorously, face bright red. "Go," he said, waving his hand in an overexaggerated gesture, "we'll catch up later."

"Or...," Marcus said, his voice a hesitant suggestion, "they don't have to leave at all."

"Won't it be weird if we had sex in the next room?" Cuan asked.

"Well," Marcus continued, "I was thinking more... this room."

"Um..." I paused.

"I dunno," Alexander said.

"Yeah, Alexander and I are still kinda not on perfect terms —" Cuan began.

"And I mean with all that's happened, and Cuan and me being more of an *us* now, and you two being *you*, I'm not sure if I'd be comfortable yet having sex with—" I started.

"No, no, I don't want your cocks anywhere near his ass today," Marcus clarified, waving his hands emphatically, "especially not before I've had my own crack at it with these new muscles. That's *my* ass. Well, I mean, ultimately it's Alexander's say whose—"

"It's your ass," Alexander nodded. "But, you do have a point." He turned to us. "I know us having *sex* is not a good idea right now, but... maybe... there's still... other stuff we can do? You know, to make your sex better? I mean, we wouldn't be here, or together, if it weren't for you helping me see how messed up Father's doctrine was and basically saving Marcus and the city and everyone."

"So..." Marcus continued, taking a step toward us, hard cock dripping a strand of precum onto the floor, "how about you let us show you our gratitude?"

I stopped, looking from Marcus to Alexander, then turned to Cuan.

"Don't ask me," Cuan said. "I'm so horny I can barely see straight. I can imagine all sorts of fun things we could do with Marcus, and maybe even with Alexander eventually, but right now every fiber of my being is screaming to have sex with *you*. If they say they can make that better, I'm game, so long as *I'm* having sex with *you*."

I turned back to them. "So… what do you have in mind?"

"You've both been flat-out since yesterday, haven't you?" Marcus said. "Have you even had time to shower?"

"You need to get out of those clothes." Alexander said. He stepped up to me, muscles of his torso moving lightly as he walked, his hard, tanned cock bobbing with each step, dripping precum as he approached. He stood in front of me, my nostrils filling with his chestnut scent as he fixed me with his blue-green eyes.

"May I?" he asked.

I nodded, and slowly he ran his hands down to my waist and, sliding them up my sides, lifted my shirt off of my head, until I felt the air of the room on my skin.

Marcus nodded in approval. "Yeah, I remember that torso," he smiled, then turned to Cuan. "This one, however, is new to me. Can I—"

"Do it," Cuan breathed, and I could see in his eyes a mixture of ardor and desperation. This was turning him on, but he was so turned on already that he really just wanted to vigorously fuck me, and so he was torn between the desire for foreplay and his swollen balls' urgent need for release.

Marcus opened Cuan's vest and slid it off of his body, exposing his tight abs, his pecs that cradled the silver chain around his neck. Marcus looked the pale, cut muscles of his torso up and down with clear approval. "Holy crap," he breathed. "OK, next," he grinned.

"We'll take care of that," I said as Cuan and I stepped away from them and turned to one another. Their touch was fine and all, but it couldn't compare to the heat and the passion between Cuan and me. And when it came time for the unveiling, well, Cuan's was a package I enjoyed unwrapping myself. I pressed my body against Cuan's, feeling his bare chest against mine, the muscles of his firm pecs on my skin, and kissed him, deeply, passionately. The exhibitionist streak we shared was taking over, and if Alexander and Marcus were going to be present for our sex, we were going to make it something they'd remember.

"God damn, they're hot," I heard Marcus gasp, and then Alexander's grunt as Marcus's fingers wrapped around him. Cuan's hands went to my waist, undoing the button of my trousers, and then he pulled the back of them down over my ass, taking my underwear with it. I flexed my cheeks as I leaned into Cuan and I heard Marcus whimper with approval at the sight. Then I stepped back slightly, allowing Cuan to pull my clothes over my crotch and let them drop to the floor.

My erection stood forth, tall and proud, pink cock head winking as the air kissed it.

"It's been a while since I've seen you like this," Alexander smiled.

"Just as nice as always," Marcus smirked. Then his eyes widened as I peeled off Cuan's compression pants and his erection surged forth.

Cuan was perhaps harder than I'd ever seen him, his shaft stiff and engorged, veins pulsing, his fully exposed cock head a deep purple and oozing precum like a faucet. His balls, large and full to begin with, were even fuller than usual, primed and ready for release.

"Wow. Can you even wait for a shower?" Marcus gasped.

"Maybe if it's quick," Cuan moaned.

"It'll be fine," I said, a mischievous gleam in my eye. "Let's see how long I can keep you edging."

"Oh God," Cuan moaned, but it a moan of anticipation more than anything else.

"Don't worry," Alexander said as he and Marcus took our hands and drew us into the master bath. "You're gonna like this shower."

Cuan and I both stared in amazement when we entered the room. The shower, as they called it, looked more like a giant fountain, a wide, square basin with a set of plumes overhead. It could easily fit the four of us with space left over.

"So, not to be indelicate, Alexander," I said, "but were your parents big on orgies or something?"

"Um, I think they were just replicating the spring outside," Alexander said.

Looking closer, I could see it. The wide basin, the arm of the overhead spray, all vaguely resembled the natural waterfall on the grounds.

"Ok then," I said. "Though, mind you, that doesn't preclude my previous question."

Alexander rolled his eyes good-naturedly as Marcus turned on the water and we stepped in. It was clear and fresh, and I could even faintly smell the same scent as the natural spring water from outside. As Julia had suggested, that must have been the water source for the house. Cuan and I stood facing each other, Marcus behind me and Alexander behind Cuan. As Cuan and I washed one another's chests, Marcus and Alexander rubbed shampoo in our hair, then soaped up our backs, running their hands down our torsos. "Can we keep going?" Marcus whispered as their hands got lower, and Cuan and I nodded, our hands around each other. I felt Marcus's palms knead my ass as Cuan groaned appreciatively under Alexander's hands and pressed his erection into mine.

Back when we'd pulled a soaked Alexander into the shower after the revelation that he wasn't actually Jacob's son, there had been a kind of intimacy, but it wasn't sexual. This however, definitely was. As a pair of couples sharing our physicality, we explored one another's bodies with our hands, feeling every line, every contour. I ran my fingers over the ripple of Cuan's ab, the new robustness of Marcus's pec, the roundness of Alexander's ass, the muscles of each arm and shoulder, the skin of each cheek above and below. I felt a wave of pleasure as Marcus's hand cupped my balls while Alexander's ran down my abdomen to curl his fingers around my shaft, my own hands sliding over Cuan's as we gripped Alexander's thick length, then Marcus's. The scent of the water mixed with our moans as we kissed one another's necks, chests, and shoulders, the warm wetness of their mouths contrasting with the cool wetness of their skin on my lips. My fingers danced over Alexander's nipple and he let out a gasp and a cry, cock jumping in Cuan's hand, Cuan gasping his approval. Finally he turned his face to look at Alexander, their eyes meeting for a long moment. At last, Cuan leaned forward and kissed him.

It was not a romantic kiss—though it was definitely sensual —rather, it was an acknowledgement, a clearing of the air. There was no erasing that Alexander had hurt us, but he had also saved Cuan's life, and had grown to learn from his mistakes, to reject the parts of himself that had been as toxic as the aconitine he had purified from Cuan's veins. Alexander and I would never recapture what had been growing between us back before he'd let his father lock me away in a box, but he had come to accept that. He had Marcus now. He had moved on. The kiss was an acknowledgement of that, an unspoken recognition that Cuan was the one I shared my soul with, and yet also a recognition of the fact that his and Cuan's life experiences were intertwined, as his life as the youngest son of the Lucent family could have—should have—been Cuan's, even as Cuan was grateful that he hadn't had to live it.

Marcus's arms wrapped around me from behind, his erection against my back as he kissed my neck. I turned toward him, and he kissed me, too. His kiss was tinged with a hint of poignancy, a memory of the desire he'd held when we were first dating. But at the same time, it was a kiss of joy, for he and Alexander were together again. They had both grown— Alexander letting go of his fear and self-righteousness, Marcus accepting the need for responsibility and care, and both learning to value themselves and one another. They were in love—they had been for a long time, I figured—but they'd finally grown to where they could hold one another up instead of dragging each other down.

The four of us were connected, now: two distinct couples, but existences that overlapped through shared experiences and amity. Our names had been written on one another's lives as surely as my name was written on Marcus's ass. I reached my hand down to where I knew 'Cole' was tattooed on his thick, meaty butt cheek and kneaded my name in his palm. Marcus half-chuckled, half-moaned in acknowledgement as he smiled into my lips.

Marcus released our kiss and I turned to Cuan, the love of my own life, and he fixed me with his golden eyes as I pulled him toward me, feeling his lips on mine, the full, open passion between us that nobody else could possibly match.

There was something else in his kiss, too—overwhelming need. He was bursting at the seams. I grinned slightly as I pulled back from his kiss. Marcus and Alexander had moved aside to hold one another, hands tracing each other's skin as they watched us. I leaned back, cock still pressed against Cuan's, and moved my hands up his firm chest.

I'd promised to keep him edging: it was time to deliver. I flicked my fingers over his nipples, lightly at first, then more vigorously. Cuan gasped and squirmed with surprise and unbridled arousal, his cock throbbing where it was pressed between us. His fingers ran down my back, over the curve of my buttocks, until they began to tease between my cheeks. I felt a finger slide inside me and moaned approval at the push of pleasure through my insides as I intensified my focus on his chest. His eyes were locked on mine, his golden irises shining as water cascaded off of his red hair and over his face, and he pushed further inside me to massage my prostate. I gasped, feeling a stream of precum escape me as I frotted against him, the red curls above his shaft teasing my own as I slid up and down.

"Fuck, this is hot," Marcus breathed.

"I... I can't... I can't take anymore," Cuan finally begged. "I need it now. *Now*."

I barely had time to finish toweling off before Cuan had me on the edge of Alexander's bed, standing at its side as Marcus had been doing when we first saw him.

"Please," he begged, arms already wrapped around my legs as he held them up, "Please let me fuck you now."

Marcus and Alexander followed us into the room, then climbed onto the bed on either side of me.

"There's something else we can do," Marcus whispered sultrily. "If I remember, your nipples are really sensitive, right?" He leaned forward on the massive bed and gingerly lapped at my chest.

"Oh, God!" I cried as pleasure shot through my body like lightning.

"You want more?" Alexander asked from the other side of me.

"Yes," I panted, "More."

They each lay down, heads toward Cuan and feet toward the top of the bed, lips right level with my chest. They closed their mouths over my nipples and began to suck, lap, and dance their tongues over me.

I writhed as the sensation cascaded through me, tingling and powerful, my legs shaking in Cuan's grip. Behind my head, Alexander and Marcus moved their hands to one another's cocks and began to stroke each other as they continued their ministrations on me. I looked up at Cuan who was watching me, his expression filled with desire.

Now it was my turn to beg.

"Cuan, please...! Inside me!" I moaned. Cuan broke into an excited half-smile, dimple forming in his cheek, and I felt his urgent erection finally pushing between my cheeks. There was nothing but a flood of pleasure as he pressed inside, my body shuddering as it swallowed his length, tightening around him as he pressed against my prostate.

"Fuuuck," I cried as I heard Alexander and Marcus stroke one another faster. Their heads were tilted up slightly, and I realized they were watching Cuan penetrate me as they sucked my chest, and that knowledge turned me on even more.

Cuan began to pump, quickly and powerfully, my own erection flapping up and then slapping against my torso, spattering Marcus and Alexander with precum as my balls bobbed up and down below me. I couldn't stroke myself as Alexander and Marcus were lying over my arms, but I didn't know if I'd be able to anyway—I could barely see straight.

Each of Cuan's thrusts was like a massive wave crashing through my body, carrying with it an overpowering crest of pleasure that surged from him through me, past my extremities, propelled on by the added ministrations of Marcus and Alexander on my chest.

As Cuan fucked me, his eyes focused on my erection, which had grown even stiffer and now wasn't flapping back and forth but rather straining upward, constant and firm. All at once, without abating his own rhythm, he bent at the waist like a hinge and took my length in his mouth. Fully.

Damn, but he was flexible.

The sight and the feeling of Cuan's hot, wet mouth on my length sent me barreling toward the edge. Alexander and Marcus moaned their surprise and appreciation at Cuan's prowess and began stroking each other ever more quickly.

My nostrils filled with the combined scents of musk and chestnut and spice and sweat and sweet saliva, and the room was a symphony of moans and grunts and licks and the suction of sex. All the waves of pleasure cascading through me roiled into a giant tsunami, and I felt my balls tighten against Cuan's chin as the crest grew closer... closer...

And then, all at once, I burst, body bucking as I fired into

Cuan's mouth with such force that I spurted out the corners of his lips, white and hot and creamy. At the same instant Cuan groaned and exploded into my ass, flooding me. He growled and whined into my cock as his whole body vibrated with the intensity of his orgasm, which only increased the stimulation on my prostate and erection. I realized as the climax rocked my body that Cuan had created a sexual feedback loop, each mouthful of my own newly-awakened semen replenishing his libido as fast as his orgasm was expending it, and he pumped me so full of cum that it began to spatter out around his cock and run down the edge of the bed.

The rollicking orgasm continued to cascade through me, and I continued to buck and heave until finally Cuan straightened, releasing my cock with a pop and gasping like a swimmer coming up for air. I continued firing, spattering his torso with white strands of sticky sex.

"Fuck, that's too hot," Marcus cried, rolling off me and scrambling to Alexander. "I need it now."

"Bring it," Alexander exclaimed, wrapping his arms around him as Marcus rolled on top of him, quartz pendant dangling from his neck, and began to pound into his ass.

Cuan pulled out, a warm, thick dribble of cum flowing out of me after him, and then pulled me to my feet and kissed me passionately, my mouth filling with the taste of my own seed, which was suddenly potent and intense and delicious.

We were both still rock hard.

"That's some cum you have there, my Nephilim," Cuan whispered into my ear with a grin. "I'm rutting even harder than before."

"Me too," I said, my own fully exposed cock head pressing into his side. "Guess I have some angelic stamina, after all."

"C'mon," he said gently, tugging on my hand. I turned for a moment toward Marcus and Alexander. Alexander was groaning in ecstasy, legs splayed in the air as Marcus's tattooed ass jackhammered up and down over him. They were completely lost in one another.

I turned with a grin to Cuan and followed him out of the room as he pulled me over to the bedroom we had slept in.

"That was ridiculously hot and sexy and fun and all—" he began as he lay on the bed, drawing me on top of him.

"—But there's something special about just being together with you," I nodded with a smile as I lay over him, pressing my body to his, feeling the stickiness between us as I kissed him deeply. Daring, adventurous, playful sex was all well and good. Better than good, in fact. But the sensuous closeness of being alone with Cuan, of feeling the entire world melt away until we were just two souls conjoined, *that* was heavenly.

I released his kiss and pulled back, looking into his glittering golden eyes.

"I love you, Cuan," I said.

"And I love you," he smiled back, that dimple of his appearing again. "Now, let's make the world turn."

I nodded with a grin, then paused for a moment.

"Cuan?" I asked. He looked at me with a question on his face. "Can I cum inside you?"

He smiled again.

"You wanna top me?" he asked.

I nodded. "I mean, you've got such a great ass," I said.

His smile widened. "It's been awhile," he said. "It's gonna be tight."

"Just how I like it," I said.

Thankfully, my cock was so soaked with saliva and cum and precum that it couldn't have possibly been more lubricated. He propped his head up on some pillows and then lifted his legs as I hovered over him, the tip of my cock teasing the cheeks of his muscular ass.

"Are you ready?" I asked gently.

He nodded. "I'm all yours," he said.

Slowly, I tilted my hips forward, feeling my length part him. He half-groaned, half-sighed with pleasure as I eased in, his insides holding me tightly, the tingle of stimulation coursing through me, followed by a wave of sensuous passion. Finally, I felt the resistance of his prostate as my balls kissed the cheeks of his ass.

"I'm all the way in," I whispered.

"It feels amazing," he smiled back.

"Yeah," I nodded. "It does."

I kissed him lovingly as I began to move. This was, I realized, the reason he'd propped his head up on the pillows: because of the difference in our heights, this let us kiss at the same time as I made love to him.

He sighed into my mouth as each slow, sweeping thrust swept through us like a gust of pleasure, our conjoined bodies mirroring our conjoined souls. Gradually our pace increased, the gust becoming a gale.

From the other room we heard a pair of long, drawn-out groans as Alexander and Marcus finally climaxed, and we broke into childish laughter for a moment before we continued our sensuous rhythm. In the distance I was aware of the sound of the shower starting up again, and then even that faded away as the world was carried away on the wind, the gust of pleasure again growing into a gale, sweeping ever higher, ever wider.

Cuan's eyes were on mine, his irises shining, his mouth slightly open, his breath mingling with my own. He was my everything. And I was his.

I moved faster and faster, and the gale became a tempest, and then, suddenly, our bodies tightened and the storm broke. He cried out as a blast of white spattered across our chests, and I felt him tighten around my length; at the same instant, I gasped aloud as I poured forth my essence into him.

The orgasm continued, long and intense and wet, Cuan's irises glinting white along with the corners of my own vision.

We were a hurricane, at once a wild, sweeping vortex of passion, and a calm, still eye, where nothing existed outside of one another and the love we shared. We came, again and again, filling him with hot passion, filling the space between us with rich, sticky, sweet cum, until finally the hurricane died down, and the world returned around us as I slid out of Cuan and leaned into his waiting embrace.

Eventually we had to get back up, and returned to the massive shower just as Marcus and Alexander were leaving it. They looked at us in wonder.

"You came THAT much?" Marcus exclaimed, looking at our soaked bodies. "How are you not dead?"

"Magic," I replied smugly. "Mind if we use the shower?"

"Sure," Alexander said. "We haven't yet put any shampoo in the bathroom connected to your room."

"Wait," I said, blinking. "*Our* room?"

Our room. Alexander explained his idea as Cuan and I showered. We had left the Order of the Light and the Midnight Hunters, so why not band together in an organization of our own? We'd have our own room, and once the doors were fixed, we'd even have privacy. It was a compelling idea, and the estate did make a perfectly good headquarters.

But we did, however, already have our own apartment. So Cuan and I decided to take Marcus and Alexander up on their idea, but with the estate as more of a second home for us, a place to stay when we were planning or working on assignments or socializing.

And we do 'socialize' frequently. We share meals often, and that glorious shower, and even our beds and sometimes bodily fluids. We do set clear boundaries, though: Alexander and Marcus are good people at heart, and damn hot, but there's still some baggage to be careful of.

Not so with Az, who visited us in our apartment a few days later now that his tasks were complete. For him, sex with us is a way of enjoying Cuan's and my love for each other and letting us explore our soulforged bond in new ways. That particular visit was exciting and intense—with two angelic beings to feed him divine semen, Cuan came so much that I was surprised he didn't dehydrate—and the next morning Az bid us a fond farewell before returning to the heavens. True to his word, however, he's never gone for long; every time some task or another calls him to Earth, we always make time to spend a while together. He retains his standing hotel room, which becomes our third home when he's in town. Az says it gives him something to look forward to, as now he gets to balance the grim work of delivering death with an activity that affirms life. Cuan and I love him dearly—not in the same way we love one another, mind you, but still, love is love.

At around the same time as Az's visit to our apartment, Bianca and Leo showed up at the estate. Bianca remained set on leaving the Midnight Hunters and, after hearing what we were planning, wanted to join us. There was a lot of work left to do on the estate house, but we prioritized getting a third and fourth bedroom shaped up, and now they're also living comfortably in the big white home.

Part of the reason we could get rooms ready so quickly was Peter. As it turns out, he's pretty handy, and he was also working to get a degree in horticulture, so—what with the café he worked at and the apartment he'd lived in both in ruins—Alexander asked him to stay on as the estate's groundskeeper, offering to let him live in the separate building he'd stayed in that first night. He was happy to accept. With him living on the estate, we couldn't very well keep him in the dark about who we were or what we did, but surprisingly he took everything in stride, saying that once he'd seen an ogre rampaging through the café, there wasn't a lot left to surprise him. We'll see, however: I'm sure at some point he'll inevitably stumble across Marcus and Alexander or Cuan and me having boisterous sex under the spring's waterfall, but I guess that's a bridge we'll cross when we come to it.

With Cuan and Bianca both moved out, The Hunters' Home started to feel a bit empty. To our surprise, Cedric, in acknowledgement of his past mistakes, turned leadership of the Midnight Hunters over to Bran, though he still counts as a member. They're hoping to grow their numbers again in the future—with Bran at the helm, hopefully that will be a smoother process than it was for Bianca, Cuan, and me. We worry a little bit about how well Cedric will do at actually respecting Bran's leadership when the chips are down, but he seems to be making a genuine effort of it. Considering how tight Bianca and Bran are and that Marcus credits Lester with saving his life, we enjoy a close relationship with the Midnight Hunters. That relationship has now extended beyond the supernatural realm, too, as Alexander recently started a job in Lester's lab.

Lester, meanwhile, is always full of surprises: he outdid himself in terms of Stadium cleanup. I'm not sure how he managed it, but every person in the those vats wound up safe and sound. There was intervention at the state level, with Lester somehow calling in multiple cities' fire departments and hospital staff (just who was this guy before he joined the Hunters?) and the governor stepping in to oversee some things once media coverage picked up. There were a few casualties among ogres and scientists and the police at the stadium, however—and the police's involvement in particular was a major cause for alarm.

There are a lot of things that can be spun and covered up, but a police-run human processing plant is a pretty hard one to manage. We never read a hint of the supernatural side of things in the news—if anyone had heard about it, they probably wouldn't have believed in it anyway. In light of everything that happened, the police department had its funding slashed while it was heavily restructured with a focus on transparency, and the city pledged to create new public programs to restore and rebuild the destroyed parts of the city and to provide affordable housing for the people who were displaced.

The university, too, came under scrutiny, though it did eventually restructure and promise to reopen its doors. I'll be finishing my degree there—now in the Queer Studies department—and Cuan will be earning his Masters right alongside me.

While the university seems to be getting its act together with surprising speed, I am dubious as to how successful or long-lasting the city's public initiatives will be. For the moment, at least, things seem to be moving in a positive direction locally. The farther outside the city we get, however, the less the whole ogre initiative was seen as a genuine tragedy and the more it was positioned as political farce. Victims of the ogre program were dismissed as 'crisis actors' by certain news outlets, with the entire tragedy spun as an elaborate conspiracy to dismantle the police and wage war on Christianity.

That latter accusation arose during Father Jacob's trial. His attempt to kill a bunch of officers and murder everyone held captive did get plenty of press, just as Cedric said it would. Jacob was defiant to the end, convinced that the Order would somehow swoop in and save him, but they wanted nothing to do with him after hearing what he'd done. He's now rotting away in a cell somewhere. Rumor has it that the Order has arranged for him to get no visitors. Not that any of us would.

With his deeds as head of the Church of the Holy Guardian laid bare, the Order was quick to swoop in to find a replacement. Considering his and Levi's track record, appointing another Lucent was out of the question, not that there were many of them left willing to take the helm. The Order had to make a strong statement, something to demonstrate that this time, things would be different. Paul, ever the negotiator, found an ingenious solution.

And so, after a great deal of discussion (and some gratifying begging from leadership), Julia Orli returned to the Order of Light, not only as head of the local order but as pastor of the church. A number of people left the congregation in protest when a Black woman donned the priest's robes and officiated a service, but Julia's response was straightforward and direct.

"Fuck 'em," she said with a grin, "I'm just getting started."

Indeed she was, and she began enacting some sweeping changes to make the church more welcoming and diverse, including encouraging people to ask challenging questions and to incorporate other religious beliefs into their spiritual lives. She's also much more of her badass self, and can frequently be found around the parish sporting her wickedly awesome leather pants and thigh-high boots.

Thomas returned as well, and immediately started decorating the church in pride flags. He also started stocking the halls with sex-positive literature and challenging common stigma about sexual activity. Az is very proud.

We don't know precisely why Thomas is suddenly so gung-ho about sex, though we're sure part of it has to do with finally feeling freed from under his father's thumb. He also looks at Leo in much the same way that Bianca looks at Julia, so that may be a factor in there somewhere. Whenever Thomas and Leo are in the same room, they flirt shamelessly with one another, and we're sure it's just a matter of time before they hook up. I mentioned to Cuan that Leo might finally be able to enjoy that whip of his, but Cuan just groaned.

"That's my brother, you know," he said.

"Well, good that I didn't sleep with that one, then," I said.

"But you would have when you thought he was Alexander's brother?" Cuan asked, raising an eyebrow.

I just shrugged and grinned.

Ultimately, though, while Thomas, Paul, and Rebecca have had an impact, the real credit for turning the church around falls to Julia. She has not only steered her church in a new direction, but also has gone back to upholding the Order of Light's oath to protect everyone, no matter where they are or what creed they believe, rather than staying holed up in the church's walls. Like Gratia, she's the bright spearhead lighting the church's path to a brighter, more positive future.

And as part of that path, one of Julia's first acts as pastor of the Church of the Holy Guardian was to perform our wedding. It was a small affair, just the Order, the Hunters, those at the Estate, and Az, all of them beaming with pride as Cuan and I said our vows and exchanged rings—his silver, mine gold, both inlaid with diamonds. In the end, we decided to hyphenate our last names, joining them together like we'd joined our souls. While Ingolf-Hamilton may have rolled off the tongue a little more easily than Hamilton-Ingolf, Cuan won me over with his argument for the latter option: the martial artist in him thought it would be very symbolic to have our initials spell out CHI: the energy of life.

Deciding on our joint surname wasn't the only new naming challenge we faced, however: now that those of us at the estate had decided to form a new organization, we needed something to call ourselves. It was an interesting discussion:

"Let's go with something hopeful," Cuan suggested.

"I like that," Marcus said. "How about… 'the Instruments of Hope?'

"What are we, a religious pop group?" Bianca said. "Veto."

"Ok, well, what about the Night Guard?" Leo asked.

"Well, first, ew," Marcus said. "Second, that sounds like we should be running around with flashlights in a museum while all the exhibits come alive."

"Besides, it's too dark," Alexander said. "What about something brighter, like… like the Warriors of Light?"

"This isn't *Final Fantasy*," I said.

"What's *Final Fantasy*?" Alexander asked, looking around in confusion. "Is that, like, a band?"

"Oh, no, sweetie, no," Marcus said, pressing a finger to Alexander's lips. "Just, shh."

"Well, we're kind of a combination of the Midnight Hunters and the Order of Light," Cuan observed. "Maybe something in-between, like how we're both light and darkness, and how we don't see things in black or white?"

"Oh!" Bianca shouted. "Like, Fifty Shades of—"

"*Veto*," the rest of us shouted in unison.

"Maybe something between day and night?" Peter asked from the corner of the room.

We all started at the sound of his voice. "Damn, you're sneakier than Cole," Leo said.

"Oh, but I like that idea," Alexander said. "Maybe we call ourselves something like... Twilight?"

"I will *cut you*," Leo growled.

"Veto!" Bianca shouted. "I veto Alexander."

"You can't veto me, it's my fucking house," Alexander cried. He turned to Marcus. "Why are they so mad?"

"You poor, sheltered boy," Marcus said. "Don't worry, tomorrow I'll introduce you to some movies, and you can understand why they're so angry and also drool over Taylor Lautner."

"Eh," Leo said, "If you want some Hollywood werewolf to drool over, you'd be better off with Colton Haynes."

"Oh, fuuuck yes," Bianca groaned in appreciation.

Leo turned to her in irritation. "Sister, must you ruin everything I enjoy?"

"Um, excuse me," Peter said, "but weren't you trying to come up with a name?"

"Right," Cuan said. "Something hopeful, something that's between day and night, light and dark..."

"Oh!" I exclaimed. "I've got it!"

So now, at the entrance to our estate, our home of people who were once rejected and hidden away, told to fear themselves and others, there is a plaque proudly proclaiming our new beginning, our identity, and our pride.

For we are:

The Wings of Dawn.

THE END

ABOUT THE AUTHOR

Cort Channon loves stories: collecting them, creating them, and sharing them. He is a historian, theologian, and sociologist, but above all, a writer. A world traveler who hates the actual process of traveling, he has lived on three different continents and speaks multiple languages—some of them even well. He has worked as a game designer, researcher, illustrator, and author, but throughout it all, he strives to infuse his work with spiritual consciousness, social awareness, and sex-positivity. That, or he just really likes writing cute guys having lots of hot sex. Cort currently resides in the Pacific Northwest with his beloved spouse, Casey, and their two cats.

ALSO BY CORT CHANNON

Light and Midnight:

Book I: Midnight Hunters

Book II: Wings of Dawn